"Linda Goodnight's sweet story,
In the Spirit of…Christmas joyfully portrays
the true spirit of the holiday season."
—*RT Book Reviews*

"This unique story has an uplifting and
healing conclusion."
—*RT Book Reviews* on *A Very Special Delivery*

"Linda Goodnight does her protagonists
justice with her sensitive writing in
A Season for Grace."
—*RT Book Reviews*

"From its sad, touching beginning to an
equally moving conclusion, *A Touch of Grace*
will keep you riveted."
—*RT Book Reviews*

LINDA GOODNIGHT
In the Spirit of...Christmas

A Very Special Delivery

Steeple
Hill®

Published by Steeple Hill Books™

STEEPLE HILL BOOKS

Steeple Hill®

Recycling programs for this product may not exist in your area.

ISBN-13: 978-0-373-65133-7

IN THE SPIRIT OF...CHRISTMAS AND
A VERY SPECIAL DELIVERY

IN THE SPIRIT OF...CHRISTMAS
Copyright © 2005 by Linda Goodnight

A VERY SPECIAL DELIVERY
Copyright © 2006 by Linda Goodnight

CONTENTS

Books by Linda Goodnight

Steeple Hill Love Inspired

In the Spirit of...Christmas
A Very Special Delivery
*A Season for Grace
*A Touch of Grace
*The Heart of Grace
Missionary Daddy
A Time to Heal
Home to Crossroads Ranch
The Baby Bond
**Finding Her Way Home

*The Brothers' Bond
**Redemption River

LINDA GOODNIGHT

Winner of the RITA® Award for excellence in inspirational fiction, Linda Goodnight has also won the Booksellers' Best, ACFW Book of the Year, and a Reviewers' Choice Award from *RT Book Reviews*. Linda has appeared on the Christian bestseller list and her romance novels have been translated into more than a dozen languages. Active in orphan ministry, this former nurse and teacher enjoys writing fiction that carries a message of hope and light in a sometimes dark world. She and her husband, Gene, live in Oklahoma. Readers can write to her at linda@lindagoodnight.com, or c/o Steeple Hill Books, 233 Broadway, Suite 1001, New York, NY 10279.

IN THE SPIRIT OF...
CHRISTMAS

You will go out in joy and be led forth in
peace, the mountains and hills will burst into
song before you, and all the trees of
the field will clap their hands.

—*Isaiah* 55:12

Dedicated with love to my aunts and uncle: Bonnie, Pat, Carmalita and Robert. I'll never forget how you stood, a wall of family, supporting me at my first book signing and at every signing since. You're the best!

Chapter One

Leaning over the steering wheel of his blue-and-gray Silverado, Jesse Slater squinted toward the distant farmhouse and waited. Just before daybreak the lights had come on inside, pats of butter against the dark frame of green shutters. Still he waited, wanting to be certain the woman was up and dressed before he made his move. She had an eventful day ahead of her, though she didn't know it.

Aware suddenly of the encroaching autumn chill, he pulled on his jacket and tucked the covers around the child sleeping on the seat beside him, something he'd done a dozen times throughout the night. Sleeping in a pickup truck in the woods might be peaceful, but it lacked a certain homey comfort. None of that mattered this morning, for no matter how soul-weary he might be, he was finally back home. *Home*—a funny word after all these years of rambling. Even though he'd lived here only six years after his mother had inherited the farm, they were formative years in the life of a boy. These remote mountains of southeastern Oklahoma had been the only real home he'd ever known.

Peace. The other reason he'd come here. He remembered the peace of lazy childhood days wading in the creek or fishing the ponds, of rambling the forests to watch deer and squirrel and on a really lucky day to spot a bald eagle soaring wild and regal overhead.

He wanted to absorb this peace, hold it and share it with Jade. Neither of them had experienced anything resembling tranquility for a long time.

The old frame house, picturesque in its setting in the pine-drenched foothills of Oklahoma's Kiamichi Mountains, was as it had always been—surrounded by green pastures and a dappling of scattered outbuildings. Somewhere a rooster heralded the sun and the sound sent a quiver of memory into Jesse's consciousness.

But his memory, good as it was, hadn't done justice to the spectacular display of beauty. Reds, golds and oranges flamed from the hills rising around the little farm like a fortress, and the earthy scent of pines and fresh air hovered beneath a blue sky.

"Daddy?"

Jesse turned his attention to the child whose sleepy green eyes and tangled black hair said she'd had a rough night too.

It was a sorry excuse of a father whose child slept in a pickup truck. And he was even sorrier that she didn't find it unusual. His stomach knotted in that familiar mix of pain and joy that was Jade, his six-year-old daughter.

"Hey, Butterbean. You're awake."

Reaching two thin arms in his direction, she stretched like a kitten and yawned widely. "I'm hungry."

Jesse welcomed the warm little body against his, hugging close his only reason to keep trying.

"Okay, darlin'. Breakfast coming right up." With one eye on the farmhouse, Jesse climbed out of the truck and went around to the back. From a red-and-white ice chest he took a small carton of milk and carefully poured the contents into a miniature box of cereal.

Returning to the cab, he handed the little box to Jade, consoling his conscience with the thought that cereal was good for her. He didn't know much about that kind of thing, but the box listed a slew of vitamins, and any idiot, no matter how inept, knew a kid needs milk.

When she'd eaten all she wanted, he downed the remaining milk, then dug out a comb and wet wipes for their morning ablutions. Living out of his truck had become second nature for him during fifteen years on the rodeo circuit, but in the two years since Erin had died, he'd discovered that roaming from town to town was no life for a little girl. She'd been in and out of so many schools only her natural aptitude for learning kept her abreast of other children her age. At least, he assumed she was up to speed academically. Nobody had told him different, and he knew for a fact she was smart as a tack.

But she needed stability. She deserved a home. And he meant for her to have one. He lifted his eyes to the farmhouse. This one.

A door slammed, resounding like a gunshot in the vast open country. A blond woman came out on the long wooden porch. Of medium height, she wore jeans and boots and a red plaid flannel jacket that flapped open in the morning air as she strode toward one of the outbuildings with lithe, relaxed steps. No hurry. Unaware she was being watched from the woods a hundred yards away.

So that was her. That was Lindsey Mitchell, the modern-day pioneer woman who chose to live alone and raise Christmas trees on Winding Stair Mountain.

Well, not completely alone. His gaze drifted to a monstrous German shepherd trotting along beside her. The animal gave him pause. He glanced over at Jade who was dutifully brushing her teeth beside the truck. She hadn't seen the shepherd, but when she did there would be trouble. Jade was terrified of dogs. And for good reason.

Running a comb through his unruly hair, he breathed a weary sigh. Dog or not, he had to have this job. Not just any job, but *this* one.

When his daughter had finished and climbed back into the cab, he cranked the engine. The noise seemed obscenely loud against the quiet noises of a country morning.

"Time to say hello." He winked at the child, extracting an easy grin, and his heart took a dip. This little girl was his sunshine. And no matter how rough their days together had been, she was a trooper, never complaining as she took in the world through solemn, too-old eyes. His baby girl had learned to accept whatever curves life threw her because it had thrown so many.

Putting the truck into gear he drove up the long driveway. Red and gold leaves swirled beneath his tires, making him wonder how long it had been since anyone had driven down this lane.

The woman heard the motor and turned, shading her eyes with one hand. The people in the nearby town of Winding Stair had warned him that she generally greeted strangers with a shotgun at her side. Not to worry, though, they'd said. Lindsey was a sweetheart, a Christian woman who wouldn't hurt a flea unless she had to. But she wasn't fool enough to live alone without knowing how to fire a rifle.

He saw no sign of a weapon, though it mattered little. A rifle wouldn't protect her against the kind of danger he presented. Still, he'd rather Jade not be frightened by a gun. The dog would be bad enough.

He glanced to where the child lay curled in the seat once again, long dark eyelashes sweeping her smooth cheeks. Guilt tugged at him. He'd been a lousy husband and now he was a lousy father.

As he drew closer to the house, the woman tilted her head, watching. Her hair, gleaming gold in the sun, lifted on a breeze and blew back from her shoulders so that she reminded him of one of those shampoo commercials—though he doubted any Hollywood type ever looked this earthy or so at home in the country setting. The dog stood sentry at her side, ears erect, expression watchful.

Bucking over some chug holes that needed filling, Jesse pulled the pickup to a stop next to the woman and rolled down the window.

"Morning," he offered.

Resting one hand atop the shepherd's head, Lindsey Mitchell didn't approach the truck, but remained several feet away. Beneath the country-style clothes she looked slim and delicate, though he'd bet a rodeo entry fee she was stronger than her appearance suggested.

Her expression, while friendly, remained wary. "Are you lost?"

He blinked. Lost? Yes, he was lost. He'd been lost for as long as he could remember. Since the Christmas his mother had died and his step-daddy had decided he didn't need a fourteen-year-old kid around anymore.

"No, ma'am. Not if you're Lindsey Mitchell."

A pair of amber-colored eyes in a gentle face registered surprise. "I am. And who are you?"

"Jesse Slater." He could see the name held no meaning for her, and for that he was grateful. Time enough to spring that little surprise on her. "Calvin Perrymore sent me out here. Said you were looking for someone to help out on your tree farm."

He'd hardly been able to believe his luck when

he'd inquired about work at the local diner last night and an old farmer had mentioned Lindsey Mitchell. He hadn't been lucky in a long time, but nothing would suit his plan better than to work on the very farm he'd come looking for. Never mind that Lindsey Mitchell raised Christmas trees and he abhorred any mention of the holiday. Work was work. Especially here on the land he intended to possess.

"You know anything about Christmas-tree farming?"

"I know about trees. And I know farming. Shouldn't be too hard to put the two together."

Amusement lit her eyes and lifted the corners of her mouth. "Don't forget the Christmas part."

As if he could ever forget the day that had changed the direction of his life—not once, but twice.

Fortunately, he was spared a response when Jade raised up in the seat and leaned against his chest. She smelled of sleep and milk and cereal. "Where are we, Daddy?"

The sight of the child brought Lindsey Mitchell closer to the truck.

"You're at the Christmas-tree farm." She offered a smile that changed her whole face.

Though she probably wasn't much younger than his own thirty-two, in the early-morning light her skin glowed as fresh as a teenager's. Lindsey Mitchell was not a beautiful woman in the Hollywood sense, but she had a clean, wholesome, uncomplicated quality that drew him.

Something turned over inside his chest. Indigestion, he hoped. No woman's face had stirred him since Erin's death. Nothing stirred him much, to tell the truth, except the beautiful little girl whose body heat warmed his side just as her presence warmed the awful chill in his soul.

"A Christmas-tree farm. For real?" Jade's eyes widened in interest, but she looked to him for approval. "Is it okay if we're here, Daddy?"

The familiar twinge of guilt pinched him. Jade knew how her daddy felt about Christmas. "Sure, Butterbean. It's okay."

In fact, he was anxious to be here, to find out about the farm and about how Lindsey Mitchell had come to possess it.

"Can I get out and look?"

Before he had the opportunity to remember just why Jade shouldn't get out of the truck, Lindsey Mitchell answered for him. "Of course you can. That's what this place is all about."

Jade scooted across the seat to the passenger-side door so fast Jesse had no time to think. She opened the door, jumped down and bounded around the pickup. Her scream ripped the morning peace like a five-alarm fire.

With a sharp sense of responsibility and a healthy dose of anxiety, Jesse shot out of the truck and ran to her, yanking her shaking body up into his arms. "Hush, Jade. It's okay. The dog won't hurt you."

"Oh, my goodness." Lindsey Mitchell was all

sympathy and compassion. "I am so very sorry. I didn't know Sushi would frighten her like that."

"It's my fault. I'd forgotten about the dog. Jade is terrified of them."

"Sushi would never hurt anyone."

"We were told the same thing by the owner of the rottweiler that mauled her when she was four." Jade's sobs grew louder at the reminder.

"How horrible. Was she badly hurt?"

"Yes," he said tersely, wanting to drop the subject while he calmed Jade. The child clung to his neck, sobbing and trembling enough to break his heart.

"Why don't you bring her inside. I'll leave Sushi out here for now."

Grateful, Jesse followed the woman across the long front porch and into the farmhouse. Once inside the living room, she motioned with one hand.

"Sit down. Please. Do you think a drink of water or maybe a cool cloth on her forehead would help?"

"Yes to both." He sank onto a large brown couch that had seen better days, but someone's artistic hand had crocheted a blue-and-yellow afghan as a cover to brighten the faded upholstery. Jade plastered her face against his chest, her tears spotting his chambray shirt a dark blue.

Lindsey returned almost immediately, placed the water glass on a wooden coffee table and, going down on one knee in front of the couch, took the liberty of smoothing the damp cloth over Jade's tear-soaked face. The woman was impossibly near. The clean scent of her hair and skin blended with the sweaty heat of his daughter's tears. He swallowed hard, forcing back the unwelcome rush of yearning for the world to be normal again. Life was not normal, would never be normal, and he could not be distracted by Lindsey Mitchell's kind nature and sweet face.

"Shh," Lindsey whispered to Jade, her warm, smoky voice raising gooseflesh on his arms. "It's okay, sugar. The dog is gone. You're okay."

The sweet motherly actions set off another torrent of reactions inside Jesse. Resentment. Delight. Anger. Gratitude. And finally relief because his child began to settle down as her sobs dwindled to quivering hiccups.

"There now." Adding to Jesse's relief, Lindsey handed him the cloth and stood, moving back a pace or two. She motioned toward the water glass. "Would you like a drink?"

Jade, her cheek still pressed hard against Jesse's chest, shook her head in refusal.

"She'll be all right now," Jesse said, pushing a few stray strands of damp hair away from the child's face. "Won't you, Butterbean?"

Like the trooper she was, Jade sat up, sniffed a couple of times for good measure, and nodded. "I need a tissue."

"Tissue coming right up." Red plaid jacket flapping open, Lindsey whipped across the room to an end table and returned with the tissue. "How about some juice instead of that water?"

Jade's green eyes looked to Jesse for permission. He nodded. "If it wouldn't be too much trouble."

"No trouble at all." Lindsey started toward a country-kitchen area opening off one end of the living room. At the doorway, she turned. "How about you? Coffee?"

The woman behaved as if he were a guest instead of a total stranger looking for work. The notion made him uncomfortable as all get out, especially considering why he was here. He didn't want her to be nice. He couldn't afford to like her.

Fortunately, he'd never developed a taste for coffee, not even the fancy kind that Erin enjoyed. "No thanks."

"I have some Cokes if you'd rather."

He sighed in defeat. He'd give a ten-dollar bill this morning for a sharp jolt of cold carbonated caffeine.

"A Coke sounds good." He shifted Jade onto the couch. Her hair was a mess and he realized he'd been in such a hurry to get here this morning, he hadn't even noticed. Normally, a headband was the best he could do, but today he'd even forgotten that. So much for first impressions. Using his fingers, he smoothed the dark locks as much as possible. Jade aimed a wobbly grin at him and shrugged. She'd grown accustomed to his awkward attempts to make her look like a little girl.

He glanced toward the kitchen, saw that Lindsey's back was turned. With one hand holding his daughter's, he took the few moments when Lindsey wasn't in sight to let his gaze drift around the house. It had changed—either that or his perception was different. Eighteen years was a long time.

The wood floors, polished to a rich, honeyed glow, looked the same. And the house still bore the warm, inviting feel of a country farmhouse. But now, the rooms seemed lighter, brighter. Where he remembered a certain dreariness brought on by his mother's illness, someone—Lindsey Mitchell, he supposed—had drenched the rooms in light and color—warm colors of polished oak and yellow-flowered curtains.

The house looked simple, uncluttered and sparkling clean—a lot like Lindsey Mitchell herself.

"Here we go." Lindsey's smoky voice yanked him around. He hoped she hadn't noticed his intense interest. No point in raising her suspicions. He had no intention of letting her know the real reason he was here until he had the proof in his hands.

"Yum, Juicy Juice." Jade came alive at the sight of a cartoon-decorated box of apple juice. "Thank you."

Lindsey favored her with another of those smiles that set Jesse's stomach churning. "I have some gummy fruits in there too if you'd like some—the kind with smiley faces."

Jade paused in the process of stabbing the straw into the top of her juice carton. "Do you have a little girl?"

Jesse was wondering the same thing, though the townspeople claimed she lived alone up here. Why would a single woman keep kid foods on hand?

If he hadn't been watching her closely to hear the

answer to Jade's questions, he'd have missed the cloud that passed briefly over Lindsey's face. But he had seen it and wondered.

"No." She handed him a drippy can of Coke wrapped in a paper towel. "No little girls of my own, but I teach a Sunday-school class, and the kids like to come out here pretty often."

Great. A Sunday-school teacher. Just what he didn't need—a Bible-thumping church lady who raised Christmas trees.

"What do they come to your house for?" Jade asked with interest. "Do you gots toys?"

"Better than toys." Lindsey eased down into a big brown easy chair, set her coffee cup on an end table and leaned toward Jade. Her shoulder-length hair swept forward across her full mouth. She hooked it behind one ear. "We play games, have picnics or hayrides, go hiking. Lots of fun activities. And," she smiled, pausing for effect, "I have Christmas trees year-round."

Christmas trees. Jesse suppressed a shiver of dread. Could he really work among the constant reminders of all he'd lost?

Jade smoothly sidestepped a discussion of the trees, though he saw the wariness leap into her eyes. "I used to go to Sunday school."

"Maybe you can go with me some time. We have great fun and learn about Jesus."

Jesse noticed some things he'd missed before. A Bible lay open on an end table near the television, and a plain silver cross hung on one wall flanked by a decorative candle on each side. Stifling an inner sigh, he swallowed a hefty swig of cola and felt the fire burn all the way down his throat. He could work for a card-carrying Christian. He had to. Jade deserved this one last chance.

"We don't go anymore since Mama died."

Jesse grew uncomfortably warm as Lindsey turned her eyes on him. Was she judging him? Finding him unfit as a father because he didn't want his child growing up with false hopes about a God who'd let you down when you needed him most?

He tried to shrug it off. No way he wanted to offend this woman and blow the chance of working here. As much as he hated making excuses, he had to. "We've moved a lot lately."

"Are you planning to be in Winding Stair long?"

"Permanently," he said. And he hoped that was true. He hadn't stayed in one spot since leaving this mountain as a scared and angry teenager. Even during his marriage, he'd roamed like a wild maverick following the rodeo or traveling with an electric-line crew, while Erin remained in Enid to raise Jade. "But first I need a job."

"Okay. Let's talk about that. I know everyone within twenty miles of Winding Stair, but I don't know you. Tell me about yourself."

He sat back, trying to hide his expression behind another long, burning pull of the soda. He hadn't expected her to ask that. He thought she might ask for references or about his experience, but not about him specifically. And given the situation, the less she knew the better.

"Not much to tell. I'm a widower with a little girl to support. I'm dependable. I'll work hard and do a good job." He stopped short of saying she wouldn't regret hiring him. Eventually, she would.

Lindsey studied him with a serene expression and a slight curve of a full lower lip. He wondered if she was always so calm.

"Where are you from?"

"Enid mostly," he answered, naming the small town west of Oklahoma City that had been more Erin's home than his.

"I went to a rodeo there once when I was in college."

"Yeah?" He'd made plenty of rodeos there himself.

With a nod, she folded her arms. "What did you do in Enid? I know they don't raise trees in those parts."

He allowed a smile at that one. The opening to the Great Plains, the land around Enid was as flat as a piece of toast.

"Worked lineman crews most of the time and some occasional rodeo. But I've done a little of everything."

"Lineman? As in electricity?"

"Yes, ma'am. I've helped string half the power lines between Texas and Arkansas."

His answer seemed to please her, though he had no idea what electricity had to do with raising Christmas trees.

"How soon could you begin working?"

"Today."

She blinked and sat back, taking her coffee with her. "Don't you even want to know what the job will entail?"

"I need work, Miss Mitchell. I can do about anything and I'm not picky."

"People are generally surprised to discover that growing Christmas trees takes a lot of hard work and know-how. I have the know-how, but I want to expand. To do that I need help. Good, dependable help."

"You'll have that with me. I don't mind long hours, hard work or getting dirty."

"The pay isn't great." She named a sum barely above minimum wage. He wanted to react but didn't. He'd made do on less. Neither the job nor the money was the important issue here.

"The hours are long. And I can be a slave driver."

Jesse couldn't hold back a grin. Somehow he couldn't imagine Lindsey as much of a slave driver. "Are you offering me the job or trying to scare me off?"

She laughed and the sound sent a shiver of warmth into the cold recesses of Jesse's heart. "Maybe both. I don't want to hire someone today and have him gone next week."

"I'm not going anywhere. Jade's already been in two schools this year, and it's only October."

Her eyes rested on Jade as she thought that one over. One foot tapping to a silent tune while she munched gummy faces, his daughter paid little attention to the adults.

"I have about twenty acres of trees now but plan to expand by at least another ten by next year. Would you like to have a look at the tree lot?"

"Not now." Not at all, ever, but he knew that was out of the question. Once he took possession the Christmas trees would disappear. "Just tell me what I'll be doing."

For the next five minutes, she discussed pruning and replanting, spraying and cutting, bagging and shipping. All of which he could do. No problem. He'd just pretend they were ordinary trees.

"I'll need character references before I make a final decision."

Jesse reached in his jacket pocket and pulled out a folded paper. He'd been prepared for that question. "Any of these people will tell you that I'm not a serial killer."

"Well, that's a relief, I'd hate to have to shoot you."

He must have looked as startled as he felt because she laughed. "That was a joke. A bad one, I'll admit, but I can shoot and I do have a gun."

Was she warning him to tread lightly? "Interesting hobby for a woman."

"The rifle was my granddad's. He had quite a collection."

"Is he the one who taught you to shoot?"

"Mostly. But don't worry about safety." She glanced at his adorable little girl with the missing front tooth. "I have a double-locked gun safe to protect the kids who come out here. Owning a firearm is a huge responsibility that I don't take lightly."

Rising from the overstuffed armchair, she took the sheet of references from his outstretched fingers. The clean scent of soap mixed with the subtle remnants of coffee drifted around her. The combination reminded him way too much of Erin.

"I'll give some of these folks a call and let you know something this afternoon. Will that be all right?"

"Sure."

"I'll need your telephone number. Where can I reach you?"

Jesse rubbed a hand over the back of his neck. "Hmm. That could be a problem. No phone yet."

"Where are you living? Maybe I know someone close by and could have them bring you a message."

"That's another problem. No house yet either."

She paused, a tiny frown appearing between a pair of naturally arched eyebrows. Funny that he'd notice a thing like a woman's eyebrows. "You don't have a place to live?"

Jade, who'd been as quiet as a mouse, happily sipping her juice and munching green and purple smiley faces, suddenly decided to enter the conversation. "We live in Daddy's truck."

Great. Now he'd probably be reported to child welfare.

But if Lindsey considered him a poor parent, she didn't let on in front of Jade. "That must be an adventure. Like camping out."

"Daddy says we're getting a house of our own pretty soon."

Jesse was glad he hadn't told the child that he'd been talking about *this* house.

Lindsey's eyes flickered from Jade to him. "Have you found anything yet?"

Oh, yes. He'd found exactly the right place.

"Not yet. First a job, then Jade and I have a date with the school principal. While she's in school I'll find a place to stay."

"Rental property is scarce around here, but you might check at the Caboose. It's an old railroad car turned into a diner on the north end of town across from the Dollar Store. Ask for Debbie. If there is any place for rent in the area, she'll know about it."

"Thanks." He stood, took Jade's empty juice carton and looked around for a trash can.

"I'll take that." Lindsey stretched out a palm, accepting the carton. No long fancy nails on those hands, but the short-clipped nails were as clean as a Sunday morning.

"Come on, Jade. Time to roll." Jade hopped off the couch, tugging at the too-short tail of her T-shirt. The kid was growing faster than he could buy clothes.

Stuffing the last of the gummy fruits into her mouth, she handed the empty wrapper to Lindsey with a shy thank-you smile, then slipped her warm little fingers into his.

"How about if I give you a call later this afternoon," Jesse asked. "After you've had a chance to check those references?"

"That will work." She followed him to the door.

Jade tugged at him, reaching upward. "Carry me, Daddy."

He followed the direction of her suddenly nervous gaze. From the front porch the affronted German shepherd peered in through the storm door, tail thumping hopefully against the wooden planks.

Jesse swept his daughter into his arms and out the door, leaving behind a dog that terrified his daughter, a house he coveted and a woman who disturbed him a little too much with her kindness.

He had a very strong feeling that he'd just compounded his already considerable problems.

Chapter Two

Uncertainty crowding her thoughts, Lindsey pushed the storm door open with one hand to let the dog inside though her attention remained on the man. He sauntered with a loose-limbed gait across the sunlit yard, his little girl tossed easily over one strong shoulder like a blanket.

Jesse Slater. The name sounded familiar somehow, but she was certain they'd never met. Even for someone as cautious of the opposite sex as she was, the man's dark good looks would be hard to forget. Mysterious silver-blue eyes with sadness hovering at the crinkled corners, dark cropped hair above a face that somehow looked even more attractive because he hadn't yet shaved this morning, and a trim athletic physique dressed in faded jeans and denim jacket over a Western shirt. Oh, yes, he was a handsome one all right. But looks did not impress Lindsey. Not anymore.

Still, she couldn't get the questions out of her head. Why would a man with no job and a child to raise come to the small rural town of Winding Stair? It would be different if he had relatives here, but he'd mentioned none. Something about him didn't quite ring true, but she was loath to turn him away. After all, if the Christmas Tree Farm was to survive, she needed help—immediately. And Jesse Slater needed a job. And she'd bet this broad-shouldered man was a hard worker.

The child, Jade, hair hanging down her father's back like black fringe, looked up and saw that Sushi was now inside, then wiggled against her father to be let down. She slid down the side of his body then skipped toward the late-model pickup.

At the driver's-side door, Jesse boosted the little girl into the cab and slid inside behind her. Then for the first time he looked up and saw Lindsey standing inside the storm door, watching his departure. He lifted a hand in farewell, though no smile accompanied the gesture. Lindsey, who smiled—and laughed—a lot, wondered if the darkly solemn Jesse had experienced much joy in his life.

The pickup roared to life, then backed out and disappeared down the long dirt drive, swirling leaves and dust into the morning air.

Lindsey, who preferred to think the best of others, tried to shrug off the nagging disquiet. After months of seeking help, she should be thankful, not suspicious, to have a strong, healthy man apply for the job.

But the fact that she'd almost given up hope that anyone would be willing to work for the small salary she could afford to pay was part of what raised her suspicions.

She wrestled with her conscience. After all, the poor man had lost his wife and was raising a small daughter alone. Couldn't that account for his air of mysterious sadness? Couldn't he be seeking the solitude of the mountains and the quiet serenity of a small town to help him heal? Even though she knew from experience that only time and the Lord could ease the burden of losing someone you love, the beautiful surroundings were a comfort. She knew that from experience too.

Stepping back from the doorway, she stroked one hand across Sushi's thick fur. "What do you think, girl?"

But she knew the answer to that. Sushi was a very fine judge of character and she hadn't even barked at the stranger. Nor had she protested when the man had come inside the house while she was relegated to the front porch.

Looking down at the sheet of paper still clutched in one hand, Lindsey studied the names and numbers, then started for the telephone.

"If his references check out, I have to hire him. We need help too badly to send him away just because he's too good-looking."

Later that afternoon, Lindsey was kneeling in the tree lot, elbow-deep in Virginia pine trimmings, when

Sushi suddenly leaped to her feet and yipped once in the direction of the house.

A car door slammed.

Pushing back her wind-blown hair with a forearm, Lindsey stood, shears in hand and strained her eyes toward the house. A blue Silverado once more sat in her driveway and Jesse Slater strode toward her front door.

Quickly, she laid aside the shears and scrambled out of the rows of pine trees.

Hadn't the man said he'd call for her decision? What was he doing out here again? Her misgivings rushed to the fore.

"Hello," she called, once she'd managed to breech the small rise bordering the tree lot. The house was only about fifty yards from the trees, and Sushi trotted on ahead.

Jesse spun on his boot heel, caught sight of her and lifted a hand in greeting.

"No wonder you didn't answer your phone," he said when she'd come within speaking distance.

With chagrin, Lindsey realized that it had happened again. While working in the trees, she frequently lost track of time, forgot to eat, forgot about everything except talking to the Lord and caring for the trees. Maybe that's why she loved the tree farm so much and why she'd been so reluctant to take on a hired hand. While among the trees, she carried on a running conversation with God, feeling closer to Him there than she did anywhere— even in church.

"I'm sorry. I didn't realize it was so late." Holding her dirty hands out to her sides, she said, "Why don't you come on in while I wash up? Then we can talk."

Jesse, who'd managed to shave somewhere since she'd seen him last, hesitated. "I hate to ask this, but would you mind putting the dog up again? My daughter is with me."

Lindsey pivoted toward the truck, aware for the first time that a small, worried face pressed against the driver's-side window. "I don't mind, but that is something else we need to discuss. If you're going to work for me, we have to find a way for Jade and Sushi to get along."

A ghost of a grin lit the man's face. "Does that mean none of my references revealed my sinister past?"

"Something like that." In fact, his references had been glowing. One woman had gone beyond character references though, and had told Lindsey about Jesse's wife, about the tragic accident that had made him a widower, and about his raw and terrible grief. Her sympathy had driven her to pray for the man and his little girl—and to decide to hire him.

"If you'll carry Jade inside again, I'll hold Sushi and leave her outside while we talk."

Jesse did as she asked, galloping across the lawn with the child on his back, her dark hair streaming out behind like a pony's tail. Dog forgotten in the fun, Jade's giggle filled the quiet countryside.

"Would you like some tea? Or a Coke?" Lindsey asked once the child and man were seated inside on the old brown sofa. "I've been in the trees so long I'm parched as well as dirty."

"A Coke sounds great, although we don't intend to continue imposing on your hospitality this way."

"Why not?"

He blinked at her, confused, then gave a short laugh. "I don't know. Doesn't seem polite, I suppose."

She started into the kitchen, then stopped and turned around. "If you're going to work for me, we can't stand on ceremony. You'll get hungry and thirsty, so you have to be able to come up here or into the office down at the tree patch and help yourself."

"So I have the job." With Jade glued to his pants leg, he followed Lindsey into the kitchen, moving with a kind of easy, athletic grace.

Lindsey stopped at the sink to scrub her hands. The smell of lemon dishwashing liquid mingled with the pungent pine scent emanating from her skin and clothes. It was a good thing she loved the smell of Christmas because it permeated every area of her life. Even when she dressed up for church and wore perfume, the scent lingered.

"If you want it. The hours are long. The work is not grueling, but it is physical labor. You can choose your days off, but between now and Christmas, things start hopping."

An odd look of apprehension passed over Jesse's face. He leaned against the counter running along-side the sink. "What do you mean, *hopping?*"

"Jesse, this is a Christmas tree farm. Though I'm

mostly a choose-and-cut operation, I also harvest and transport a certain number of trees to area city lots, grocery stores, etc., about mid-November." She dried her hands on the yellow dishtowel hanging over the oven rail.

"Do you do that yourself or have someone truck them?" He followed her to the refrigerator where she handed him two colas. He popped the lids and gave one to Jade, then took a long pull on the other, his silver eyes watching her over the rim.

"Right now I'm delivering them myself, but long-range I want a large enough clientele to ship them all over the country." Her shoulders sagged. "But that takes advertising and advertising takes money— which I do not have at present." Taking a cola for herself, she waved a hand. "But I'm getting off topic here. Let's go sit down and discuss your job. Jade," she said, glancing down toward the child, "I have some crayons and a coloring book around here somewhere if you'd like to color while your dad and I talk."

The child's eyes lit up, so Lindsey gathered the materials she kept stashed in a kitchen drawer and spread them on the table.

The child eyed the table doubtfully and clung tighter to her father's leg. She pointed toward the living room, not ten feet away. "Can I go in there with you and Daddy?"

The poor little lamb was a nervous wreck without her daddy.

"Of course, you can." Lindsey swept up the

crayons and book and proceeded into the living room, settling Jade at the coffee table.

All the while, she was aware of the handsome stranger's eyes on her. His references were excellent. She could trust him. She *did* trust him. She even felt a certain comfort in his presence, but something about him still bothered her.

Was it because he was too good-looking? She had been susceptible to good looks once before and gotten her heart broken.

No. That had happened a long time ago and, with the Lord's help, she had put that pain behind her.

Hadn't she?

The sharp tang of Coke burned Jesse's throat as he watched the play of interesting emotions across Lindsey's face. She was not a woman who hid her feelings particularly well. If he was to pull this off, he would have to win her confidence. And right now, from the looks of her, she was worried about hiring him.

"I'm a hard worker, Miss Mitchell. I'll do a good job."

"Lindsey, please. There can't be that much difference in our ages."

"Okay. And I'm Jesse. And this lovely creature is Jade." He poked a gentle finger at Jade's tummy.

His little girl beamed at him as though he'd given her a golden crown and, as usual, his heart turned over when she smiled. That one missing front tooth never failed to charm him. "Daddy's silly sometimes."

"I guess I'll have to learn to put up with that if he's going to work out here. What about you? What are we going to do about you and my dog?"

"I don't like dogs. They're mean." When Jade drew back against the couch, green eyes wide, Jesse sighed.

What in the world was he going to do about this stand-off between dog lover and dog hater? He'd give anything to see Jade get over her terrible fear of dogs, but the trauma ran so deep, he wondered if she ever would. In fact, since Erin's death, her fear had worsened, and other fears had taken root as well. She didn't want him out of her sight, she was terrified of the dark, and her nightmares grew in intensity.

He took a sip of cola, thinking. "Could we just play it by ear for a while and see how things go? Jade will be in school most of the time anyway."

"I work long, sometimes irregular hours, especially this time of year."

"I don't mind that." The more hours he worked the more money he'd make. And the more time he'd have to question Lindsey and check out the farm.

"Then I have a suggestion. The school bus runs right by my driveway. Why not have Jade catch the bus here in the morning and come back here after school?"

Jesse breathed an inward sigh of relief. He'd hoped she'd say that. Otherwise he would have to take off work twice a day to chauffeur his child to and from school.

"That would be a big help."

"Yes, but coming here will also put her in contact with Sushi morning and night."

"Hmm. I see your point." Pinching his bottom lip between finger and thumb, he considered, but came away empty. "Any ideas?"

"Yes, but fears like that don't disappear overnight. We'll need some time for Jade to acclimate and to realize that Sushi is one of the good guys." She smiled one of those sunshine smiles that made him feel as though anything was possible—even Jade accepting the dog.

"In the meantime, while Jade is here, Sushi can remain outdoors or in one of the bedrooms with the door closed. When we're working in the field, sometimes she hangs out in the office anyway. She won't like being left out, but it will only be until Jade feels more comfortable with her around."

There she went again, tossing kindness around like party confetti. He had to stop setting himself up this way. Liking Lindsey Mitchell could not be part of the deal. "I'm sorry about this. Sorry to be so much trouble."

"Don't worry about it. Jade's fear isn't your fault, and she certainly can't help it." She shot a wink toward Jade who looked up, green eyes wide and solemn. "Not yet, anyway."

The child was poised over a drawing of the Sermon on the Mount, red crayon at the ready. Jesse swallowed hard.

"Daddy, I want to see the Christmas trees."

The knot tightened in Jesse's chest. Pictures of Jesus. Christmas trees. What was next? "How about tomorrow?"

Jade didn't fuss, but disappointment clouded her angelic face. She resumed coloring, trading the red crayon for a purple one.

"Come on, Jesse." Lindsey rose from the armchair. "You may as well see where you'll be spending most of your time. While we're down there, I'll show you the little office where I keep the equipment and explain my plans for this Christmas season."

He'd have to do it sooner or later. Feeling as if he were being led to the gallows, Jesse swigged down the remainder of his Coke and stood.

"Where are the Christmas trees?" Gripping Jesse's hand, Jade took in rows and rows of evergreens, swiveling her head from side to side plainly searching for something more traditionally Christmas.

She might be disappointed, but Jesse inhaled in relief, feeling the pungent pine-scented coolness in his nostrils. They were just trees. Plain ordinary pine trees, no more Christmassy than the thousands of evergreens lining the woods and roads everywhere in this part of Oklahoma. The only differences were the neat rows and carefully tended conical shapes of a specific variety. Nothing to get all worked up over.

"Where are the decorations? And the presents?" Jade was as bewildered as she was disappointed.

Kneeling in the rich dirt, Lindsey clasped one of

Jade's small hands in hers. "Listen, sweetie, don't fret. Right now, the lot doesn't look like anything but green pine trees, but just you wait another month. See that little building over there?"

After turning to look, Jade nodded. "Are the Christmas trees in there?"

Lindsey laughed, that warm, smoky sound that made Jesse's stomach clench. "Not yet. But the decorations are in there. Lights, and Santas, and angels. Even a nativity set and a sleigh."

"Yeah?" Jade asked in wonder.

"Yeah. And with your daddy to help me this year, we'll set out all of the decorations, string lights up and down these rows, hook up a sound system to pipe in Christmas carols. Maybe you and I can even decorate one special tree up near the entrance where cars pull in. Then every night and day we'll have a Christmas party. People will come to choose a tree and we'll give them wagon rides from the parking area through the tree lot."

The woman fairly glowed with excitement and the effect was rubbing off on Jade. Pulling away from her dad for the first time, she clapped her hands and spun in a circle.

"Let's do it now."

"Whoa, Butterbean, not so fast." He laid a quieting hand on her shoulder. "Lindsey already told you that part comes later." The later the better as far as he was concerned.

"But soon, though, sweetie." Lindsey couldn't

seem to bear seeing Jade disappointed. She motioned toward an open field where a large brown horse grazed on the last of the green grass. "See that horse down there? He loves to pull a wagon, does it all the time for hayrides—but at Christmas he gives visitors rides from the parking area through the tree lot."

"What's his name?"

"Puddin'. Don't you think he looks like chocolate pudding?"

Jade giggled. "No. He's big."

"Big, but very gentle. He likes kids, especially little girls with green eyes."

"I have green eyes."

Lindsey bent low, peering into Jade's face. "Well, how about that? You sure do. You'll be his favorite."

Jesse watched in amazement as Lindsey completely captivated his usually quiet daughter. If he wasn't very careful, he'd fall under her spell of genuine decency too. Given his mission, he'd better step easy. Common sense said he should discourage Jade from this fast-forming friendship, but she'd had so little fun lately, he didn't have the heart to say a word.

"Can I go see the Christmas in your building?"

"Sure you can." Popping up, Lindsey dusted her knees and looked at Jesse. His reluctance must have shown because she said, "If we can convince your daddy there are no monsters in there."

Mentally shaking himself, Jesse forced a smile he didn't feel. Santas and angels and horse-drawn wagons. Great. Just great. He wanted no part of any of it. But he wanted this job. And he wanted this farm. To get them both he'd have to struggle through a couple of months of having Christmas shoved down his throat at every turn. It was more than he'd bargained for, but he'd have to do it.

Somehow.

Chapter Three

Delighted to see Jade so excited and to find a fellow Christmas lover, Lindsey clasped her small hand and started toward the storage building. Jesse's voice stopped her.

"You two go ahead. I'll get busy here in the trees."

Lindsey turned back. A crisp October breeze had picked up earlier in the afternoon, but the autumn sun made the wind as warm as a puppy's breath. "Work can wait until tomorrow."

"You have plenty of trimmings here to get rid of. I'll start loading them in the wheelbarrow."

If reluctance needed a pictorial representation, Jesse Slater had the job. Hands fisted at his side, the muscles along his jawbone flexed repeatedly. Lindsey's medical training flashed through her head. Fight or flight—the adrenaline rush that comes when a man is threatened. But why did Jesse Slater feel threatened? And by what? She was the woman alone, hiring a virtual stranger to spend every day in her company. And she didn't feel the least bit threatened.

"Don't you want to see all my Christmas goodies?"

His expression was somewhere between a grimace and a forced smile. "Some other time."

He turned abruptly away and began gathering trimmed pine branches, tossing them into the wheelbarrow. Lindsey stood for a moment, observing the strong flex of muscle beneath the denim jacket. His movements were jerky, as though he controlled some deep emotion hammering to get loose.

Regardless of his good looks and his easy manner, something was sorely missing in his life. Whether he realized it or not, Jesse was a lost and lonely soul in need of God's love.

Ever since coming to live on her grandparents' farm at the age of fifteen, Lindsey had brought home strays, both animal and human. She'd been a stray herself, healed by the love and faith she'd found here in the mountains. But there was something other than loneliness in Jesse. Something puzzling. Maybe even dangerous.

Then why didn't she send him packing?

"Could we go now?" A tug from Jade pulled her attention away from the man and back to the child.

"Sure, sweetie. Want to race?"

The storage and office buildings, which looked more like old-time outhouses than business buildings, were less than fifty feet from the field. Lindsey gave the child a galloping head start, her short, pink-capri-clad legs churning the grass and leaves. When enough distance separated them, Lindsey thundered after her, staying just far enough behind to enjoy the squeals and giggles.

When Lindsey and Jade returned sometime later, Jesse had shed his jacket and rolled back his shirt-sleeves. The work felt good, cleansing somehow, and he wanted to stay right here until nightfall.

"That was fun, Daddy." Jade pranced toward him with a strand of shiny silver garland thrown around her neck like a boa. "Lindsey let me bring this to decorate a tree."

"Little early for that isn't it?" He tried not to react, tried to pretend the sight of anything Christmassy didn't send a spear right through his heart. But visions of gaily-wrapped gifts spilled out around a crushed blue car still haunted him.

Lindsey shrugged. "It's never too early for Christmas. Looks like you've been busy."

He'd filled and emptied the wheelbarrow several times, clearing all the rows she'd trimmed today.

"Impressed?"

She rested her hands on her hipbones and smiled. "As a matter of fact, I am."

"Good." Yanking off his gloves, he resisted returning the smile. "What's next?"

"Nothing for now. It will be dark soon."

She was right. Already the sun bled onto the trees

atop the mountain. Darkness would fall like a rock, hard and fast. He'd run away once into the woods behind the farm and darkness had caught him unaware. He'd spent that night curled beneath a tree, praying for help that never came.

"Guess Jade and I should be heading home then."

Knocking the dust off his gloves, he stuffed them into a back pocket, letting the cloth fingers dangle against his jeans.

"Did you find a house to rent today?"

"Your friend Debbie hooked me up. Sent me to the mobile-home park on the edge of town."

She picked up his jacket, swatted the pine needles away and handed him the faded denim. "Is it a nice place?"

He repressed a bitter laugh and tossed the jacket over one shoulder. Anything was nice after living in your truck. When Jade had seen the tiny space, she'd been ecstatic.

"The trailer will do until something better comes along." He couldn't tell her that the something better was the farm she called home.

By mutual consent they fell in step and left the tree lot, Jade scampering along between them, deliberately crunching as many leaves as possible.

Before they reached his truck, Lindsey said, "I have extra linens, dishes and such if you could use them."

Don't be so nice. Don't make me like you.

He opened the door and boosted Jade into the cab. "We're all right for now."

"But you will let me know if you discover something you need, won't you?"

Grabbing the door frame, he swung himself into the driver's seat.

"Sure." Not in a hundred years. What he needed was somewhere in the courthouse in Winding Stair and she didn't need to know a thing about it—yet. He'd planned to start his investigation today, but finding a place to live had eaten up all his time. Soon though. Very soon he would have the farm he'd coveted for the past eighteen years.

Lindsey wiped the sticky smear of Jade's maple syrup off the table, trying her best not to laugh at the father-and-daughter exchange going on in her kitchen. In the week since she'd hired Jesse Slater, he and Jade had become a comfortable part of her morning routine. As many times as she'd offered, Jesse refused to take his meals with her, but he hadn't objected when she'd taken to preparing breakfast for his little girl.

Now, as she cleaned away the last of Jade's pancakes, Jesse sat on the edge of a chair with his daughter perched between his knees. Every morning he made an endearingly clumsy attempt to fix the child's beautiful raven hair. And every day Lindsey itched to do it for him. But she said nothing. Jade was, after all, Jesse's child. Just like all the other children she loved and nurtured, Jade was not hers. Never hers.

Normally, he smoothed her hair with the brush, shoved a headband in place, and that was that. This morning, however, Jesse had reached his limit when Jade announced she wanted to wear a ponytail like her new best friend, Lacy. Lindsey suppressed a smile. From the expression on his face, Jesse considered the task right next to having his fingernails ripped out with fencing pliers.

A pink scrunchie gritted between his teeth, he battled the long hair into one hand, holding it in a stranglehold. He'd once let slip that he'd ridden saddle broncs on the rodeo circuit and, Lindsey thought with a hidden smile, that he must have done so with this same intense determination.

Finally, with an audible exhale, he dropped back against the chair. "There. All done."

"Jess…" Lindsey started, then hushed. As much as she longed to see the little girl gussied up like the princess she could be, she wouldn't interfere.

Jade touched a hand tentatively to her head. The lopsided ponytail resided just behind her left ear. A long strand of unbound hair tumbled over the opposite shoulder and the top of her head had enough bumps and waves to qualify as an amusement-park ride.

"Daddy, I don't think Lacy wears her ponytail like this."

Lindsey couldn't hold back the laughter bubbling up inside her. Dropping the dishtowel over the back of a chair, she covered her face and giggled.

Jesse heaved an exasperated moan and rolled his silver eyes. "What? You don't appreciate my talent?"

Lindsey could barely get her breath. "It isn't that— It's just, just—" She took one look at the child's hair and started up again.

Jesse had never joked with her before, didn't smile much either, but this time a reluctant half smile tugged at one corner of his mouth and kicked up, setting off laugh crinkles around his eyes. "If I were a hairdresser in LA, this would be all the rage."

"If you were a hairdresser in LA, I'd stay in Oklahoma."

"All right, boss lady, if you think you can do better—" He bowed toward Jade, extending his arm with a flourish. "She's all yours."

"I thought you'd never ask. I have been itching to get my hands on that gorgeous hair." She grabbed the hairbrush and guided the grinning child back into the chair, then stood behind her. As she'd suspected, the dark hair drifted through her fingers like thick silk. In minutes she had the ponytail slicked neatly into place.

"Impressive," Jesse admitted, standing with his head tilted and both hands fisted on his hips.

"I love playing hairdresser."

"No kidding?" His gaze filtered over her usual flannel and denim. "You don't seem the type."

"I think I should be insulted." She smoothed her hand down Jade's silky ponytail. "Just because I dress simply and get my hands dirty for a living doesn't mean I'm not a girl, Jesse."

He held up both hands in surrender. "Hey, no offense meant. You are definitely a girl. Just not frilly like some."

Like your wife? she wondered. Was she frilly? Is that the type you prefer?

As soon as the thoughts bounded through her head, Lindsey caught them, shocked to even think such things. Once she'd dreamed of marrying a wonderful man and having a houseful of children, but after her fiancé's betrayal, trusting a man with her heart wasn't easy. Add to that the remote, sparsely populated area where she'd chosen to live, and she'd practically given up hope of ever marrying. Besides, she had a farm to run. She didn't want to be interested in Jesse romantically. He was her hired hand and nothing more.

She turned her attention to Jade, handing the child a mirror. "There, sweetie. See what you think."

Jade touched her hair again. Then a smile bright enough to light a room stretched across her pretty face. "I'm perfect!"

Both adults laughed.

Jade flopped her head from side to side, sending the ponytail into a dance. "How did you make me so pretty?"

"My Sunday-school girls come out for dress-up parties sometimes. We do hair and makeup and wear fancy play clothes. It's fun."

"Can I come sometime?"

"Sure. If it's okay with your dad. In fact, tonight

is kid's night at church if you'd like to come and meet some of my Sunday-school students."

"Daddy?" Jade asked hopefully, her eyebrows knitted together in an expression of worry that made no sense given the harmless request.

Some odd emotion flickered over Jesse, but his response was light and easy. He pecked the end of her nose with one finger. "Not this time, Butterbean. You and I have to work on those addition facts."

The child's happiness faded, but she didn't argue. Head down, ponytail forgotten, she trudged to the couch and slid a pink backpack onto her shoulders. Her posture was so resigned, so forlorn that Lindsey could hardly bear it.

"Hey, sweetie, don't worry. My Sunday-school class comes out here pretty often. Maybe you can come another time."

The child gave a ragged sigh. "Okay." She hugged her father's knees. "Bye, Daddy."

He went down in front of her, drawing her against his chest.

Lindsey's throat clogged with emotion. The man was a wonderful dad, the kind of father she'd always dreamed of having for her own children someday. But someday had never come.

"I'll get the dog," she said, going to the door in front of Jade as she had every morning this week. She brought Sushi inside, watching through the glass storm door as the little girl headed to the bus stop, a small splash of pink and white against the flaming autumn morning. In the distance, Lindsey heard the grinding gears of the school bus.

As a teenager she'd ridden that bus to high school and home again, and in the years since she'd watched it come and go year after year carrying other people's children. But this morning she watched a child make the journey down her driveway to the bus stop, and, for the first time, felt a bittersweet ache in her throat because that child was not her own.

By noon the damp October morning had given way to blue skies and the kind of clouds Jade called marshmallows. A bit of breeze swirled down from the north, promising a frost soon, but Jesse wasn't the least bit cool. As he sat on the top step, leaning backward onto the front porch, he enjoyed what had become his usual lunch, a Coke and a ham sandwich, and pondered how one little woman had ever done all this work by herself.

Besides the routine weeding and spraying, he'd helped her clear several acres of land in preparation for planting another thousand or so trees next week. And from her description of November's chores, October was a vacation.

He had to admit, however reluctantly, that he admired Lindsey Mitchell. She never complained, never expected him to do anything she wasn't willing to do herself. As a result he worked twice as hard trying to lift some of the load off her slim shoulders, and her gratitude for every little thing he did only made him want to do more.

She was a disconcerting woman.

Twisting to the left so he could see her, he said, "Mind if I ask you a question?"

Wearing the red flannel and denim that seemed so much a part of her, Lindsey sat in an old-fashioned wooden porch swing sipping her cola. A partially eaten ham sandwich rested at her side. Sushi lay in front of her, exercising mammoth restraint as she eyed the sandwich longingly.

"Ask away." With dainty movements, Lindsey tore off a piece of ham and tossed it to the dog.

"What would entice a pretty young woman to live out here all alone and become a Christmas-tree farmer?"

The corners of her eyes crinkled in amusement as she wiped her fingers on her jeans. Jesse's stomach did that clenching thing again.

"I didn't exactly plan to be a Christmas-tree farmer. It just happened. Or maybe the Lord led me in this direction." One hand gripping the chain support, she tapped a foot against the porch and set the swing in motion. "My parents are in the military so we moved around a lot. When I was fourteen—" she paused to allow a wry grin. "Let's just say I was not an easy teenager."

Surprised, Jesse swiveled all the way around, bringing one boot up to the top step. Lindsey was always so serene, so at peace. "I can't see you causing anyone any trouble."

"Believe me, I did. Dad and Mom finally sent me

here to live with my grandparents. They thought stability, the same school, the country atmosphere and my grandparents' influence would be good for me. They were right."

"So you didn't grow up here?" Now he was very interested.

Lindsey shook her head, honey-colored hair bouncing against her shoulders, catching bits of light that spun it into gold. Odd that he would notice such a thing.

"Actually none of my family is originally from around here. My grandparents bought this farm after they retired. Gramps began the Christmas Tree Farm as a hobby because he loved Christmas and enjoyed sharing it with others."

Jesse decided to steer the conversation toward her grandparents and their purchase of the farm, feeling somewhat better to know Lindsey had not been involved in what had happened eighteen years ago.

"How long did your grandparents own this place?"

"Hmm." Her forehead wrinkled in thought. "I'm not sure. They'd probably been here three or four years when I came. I've lived here nearly fifteen years."

Jesse did the math in his head. The time frame fit perfectly. He rotated the Coke can between his palms then tapped it against his upraised knee. So her grandfather had been the one.

"Did you have any idea who your grandfather bought this place from?" As soon as he asked, Jesse wanted his words back. The question was too suspicious, too far off the conversation, but if Lindsey noticed she said nothing.

"I haven't a clue. All I know is after Granny passed away, Gramps put the farm and everything on it into my name. By then, I wanted to live here forever, so other than bringing me to a faith in Jesus, this was the greatest gift they could have given me."

The too-familiar tug of guilt irritated Jesse. He had no reason to feel bad for her. She'd enjoyed the benefit of living here for years while he'd wandered around like a lost sheep. Only during his too-short time with Erin had he ever found any of the peace that hovered over Lindsey like a sweet perfume. And he was counting on this farm to help him find that feeling again.

"So you became a tree farmer like your grandfather."

Stretching backward, Lindsey ran both hands through the top of her hair, lifted the sides, and let them drift back down again. Jesse found the motion as natural and appealing as the woman herself.

"I tried other things. Went to college. Became a lab tech. Then Sean and I—" She paused, and two spots of color stained her cheekbones. "Let's just say something happened in my personal life. So, when Gramps passed away three years ago, I couldn't bring myself to let the tree farm go. After that first year of doing all the things he'd taught me and of watching families bond as they chose that perfect Christmas tree, I understood that this was where my heart is."

Though curious about the man she'd mentioned, Jesse decided to leave the subject alone. Knowing about her love life would only make his task more difficult. "So you gave up your job to dedicate all your time to the farm."

"I still take an occasional shift at the hospital and fill in for vacations in the summer to keep my skills sharp or to put a little extra money in the bank. But this is my life. This is what I love. And unless economics drive me out of business, I'll raise Christmas trees right here on Gramps' farm forever."

Though she couldn't possibly know his thoughts, to Jesse the announcement seemed like a challenge. Averting his eyes, he ripped off a piece of sandwich and tossed the bit of bread and ham to the dog.

Sushi thumped her tail in thanks.

"You spoil her more than I do."

"Yeah." He pointed his soda can toward the north. "We have visitors."

A flock of geese carved a lopsided V against the sky, honking loudly enough to rival a rush-hour traffic jam.

"They're headed to my pond."

"And then to a vacation in Florida."

Lindsey laughed and drew her knees up under her chin. "Watching them makes me feel lazy."

"What's on for this afternoon now that we've cleared that new plot of land?"

"Tomorrow we'll need to go over to Mena and pick up the saplings I've ordered. So this afternoon I thought we'd get ready for the wienie roast."

"Who's having a wienie roast?"

"I am. Well, my church actually, but since I have such a great place for it, complete with a horse to give wagon rides, I host the party out here every fall. I hope you and Jade will come."

"I wouldn't want to impose." In truth, the idea of hanging out with a bunch of church people made him sweat. He'd played that scene before, for all the good it had done him in the end.

"Trust me, after you drag brush for the campfire, whittle a mountain of roasting sticks and set up tables, chairs and hay bales, you will have earned a special place at this function."

"I don't know, Lindsey. I'm not sure I would fit in."

Dropping her feet to the porch floor, Lindsey leaned forward, face earnest, hair swinging forward, as she reached out to touch his arm.

"Please, Jesse. Jade would have so much fun. And having a little fun now and then wouldn't hurt you either."

He was beginning to weaken. A wienie roast was not the same as going to church. And Jade would love roasting marshmallows over a campfire. More than that, it was high time he got moving on his mission.

Lindsey's words echoed his thoughts. "Winding Stair is full of good people. The party would be a great opportunity for you to get acquainted with some of them."

She was right about that. He needed to get friendly

with the townsfolk. But not for the reasons she had in mind. He gulped the rest of his cola, taking the burn all the way to his stomach.

Somebody in this town had to know what had happened eighteen years ago. The more people trusted him, the sooner he could have his answers—and the sooner he and Jade could take possession of this farm.

Likely no one would remember him. Les Finch had not been a friendly man, and they'd kept to themselves up here in the mountains. As a boy, Jesse had been a quiet loner, preferring the woods to school activities. And his name was different from his mom and stepdad. His secret was, he believed, safe from the unsuspecting folk of Winding Stair.

He didn't like playing the bad guy, but right was right. This was his home...and he intended to claim it.

Chapter Four

"Think this will be enough?"

At Jesse's question, Lindsey dumped an armload of firewood into a huge oval depression in the ground. Dusting bark and leaves from the front of her jacket, she evaluated the stack of roasting sticks Jesse had piled next to a long folding table.

"How many do you have there? Fifty, maybe?"

He hitched one shoulder, distant and preoccupied as if whittling enough roasting sticks was the last thing on his mind. "Close."

"That should do it." She knelt beside the campfire pit and began to arrange the wood. "Some of the older boys like to make their own—especially when they have a girlfriend to impress."

"It's a man thing." Jesse tossed the last stick onto the pile and snapped shut a pocketknife, which he then shimmied into his front jeans' pocket. "I think we're about set. What time will the guests arrive?"

"Sevenish. Some will meet at the church and bring the bus. Others will drift in at will throughout the evening." Leaning back on her heels, she gazed up at him. The look on his face said he wanted to be a thousand miles away by then. "It'll be fun, Jesse."

Jade, who resided less than five feet from her daddy at all times, sat on a bale of hay munching an apple with childish contentment. One tennis-shoed foot was curled beneath her while the other beat a steady rhythm against the tight rectangle of baled grass.

"I never went to a wienie roast before," she said.

She'd been ecstatic, hopping and dancing around her father like a puppy when he'd told her of the plans. Lindsey wished Jesse showed half that much enthusiasm.

"You'll like it. We'll play games and take a ride in the wagon and roast marshmallows." Playfully bumping the child's hip with her own, Lindsey sat down next to her. "You'll need your coat. The temperature gets pretty cool after the sun goes down."

Jesse propped a booted foot on the end of the bale next to Jade. He rubbed at his bottom lip, pensive. "We better head home and get cleaned up."

Jade frowned at one palm and then the other. Apple juice glistened on her fingers. "I'm clean."

Jesse shot Lindsey a wry glance. "Well, I'm not." Scooping his daughter up into strong arms, he rubbed her nose with his. "And we'll stop by the store for some marshmallows."

The gap-toothed smile appeared. "Okay!"

He tossed Jade over his shoulder the way Lindsey had seen him do a dozen times. After a thoughtful pause, he said, "I guess we'll see ya at seven then."

Watching the enigmatic man and his child cross the yard, Lindsey experienced an uncomfortable sense of loss and loneliness. Given the number of times she'd asked him or Jade to church functions, she'd been pleasantly surprised when Jesse had agreed to come to the party. He'd been more than clear on a number of occasions that spiritual issues were on his no-call list.

Still, she had a funny feeling about Jesse's decision to join tonight's festivities. He'd been almost grim all afternoon while they'd made the preparations, as if the party was a nasty medicine to take instead of a pleasure to be enjoyed.

Going to release a resentful Sushi from her office confinement, Lindsey heard the roar of Jesse's pickup truck fading into the distance and wondered if he would return at all.

By seven-thirty, friends of every age milled around the clearing along the back side of Lindsey's farm, but there was no sign of Jesse and Jade. Disappointment settled over Lindsey like morning fog on a pond as she watched the driveway for the familiar silver-and-blue truck. The party would have been good for father and daughter. That's why her disappointment was so keen, not because she missed their company, although she was too honest to deny that fact completely. Still, she had plenty of other friends around, and the party, as always, was off to a roaring start.

Beneath a full and perfect hunter's moon, the scent of hickory smoke and roasting hotdogs circled over a crackling campfire. The night air, cool and crisp, meant jackets and hooded sweatshirts, many of which lay scattered about on hay bales or on the short browning grass as their owners worked up a sweat in various games.

A rambunctious group of teenagers and young adults played a game of volleyball at the nets she and Jesse had strung up. Smaller children played tag by lantern light or crawled over the wagonload of hay parked at an angle on the north end of the clearing. Most of the adults chatted and laughed together around the food table and a huge cattle tank filled with iced-down soda pop and bottled water.

"Where's that hired hand of yours, Lindsey?" Pastor Cliff Wilson, standing with a meaty arm draped over the shoulder of his diminutive wife, was only a few years older than Lindsey. She still had difficulty believing that this gentle giant had once spent more time in the county jail for drinking and disturbing the peace than he did in church. Just looking at him reminded Lindsey and everyone else of the amazing redemptive power of Jesus' love. "I thought we'd get to meet him tonight."

"I did, too, Cliff," she said. "But it looks like he backed out on coming. Jade will be so disappointed." So was she. Jade needed the interaction, and though Jesse held himself aloof, he needed to mingle with people who loved and served God.

"Jade?" Cliff's wife, Karen, spoke up. "What a pretty name. Is that his little girl?"

Karen and Cliff had yet to conceive and every child held special interest for the pastor's wife.

"Yes. She's adorable. A little shy at first, so if they do come, give her some time to warm up." Lindsey took a handful of potato chips from a bag on one of the long folding tables and nibbled the salt from one. "Aren't you two going to eat a hotdog?"

Karen laughed and hugged her husband's thick shoulder. "Cliff's already had three."

The pastor rubbed his belly. "Just getting started."

Downing a sizeable portion of cola, the minister slid two franks onto the point of a stick and poked it into the flames. "One for me, and one for my lady friend here."

Lindsey smiled, admiring the open affection between the pastor and his wife.

"Come on, Lindsey." Debbie Castor, the waitress at the Caboose Diner and one of Lindsey's closest friends, had joined the volleyball game. "We need someone who can spike the ball. Tom's team is waxing us."

Tom was Debbie's husband, and they loved competing against each other in good-natured rivalries.

"Okay. One game. I still haven't had my hotdog yet." To shake off her disappointment at Jesse's absence, Lindsey trotted to the makeshift court. She was in good shape from the physical aspect of her job and was generally a good athlete, but tonight her mind wasn't on the game. Up to now, Jesse had always kept his word, and she experienced a strange unease that something was amiss.

When Tom's team easily defeated Debbie's, she stood with hands on her knees catching her breath. "Sorry, guys. I wasn't much help tonight. I must be losing my touch."

"Maybe after you eat you'll regain your former glorious form, and we'll play another game."

With a laugh, she said, "No deal, Tom. You just want to beat us again."

"Right on, sister." Tom teased, bringing his arms forward to flex like a body builder. Balding and bespectacled, the fireman fooled everyone with his small stature and mischievous nature. Only those who knew him understood how strong and athletic he really was.

Still grinning, Lindsey fell in step beside Debbie and headed back to the campfire. "Have you eaten yet?"

"Half a bag of Oreos," Debbie admitted. "All I want lately is chocolate." Leaning closer she whispered, "I think I'm pregnant again."

Lindsey's squeal was silenced by Debbie's, "Shh. I don't want Karen to hear until I'm sure. I wouldn't want to hurt her."

"Ah, Deb. She's not like that. Karen will be happy for you."

"But to see someone like me have an unplanned pregnancy when she can't even have an intentional one must be difficult for her."

Lindsey knew the pain of wanting, but never having children, and yet her joy for her friends was genuine.

"Does Tom know yet?"

Debbie nodded, her orange pumpkin earrings dancing in the firelight. "He's still a little shell-shocked, I'm afraid. Finances are so tight already with the three we have, but he'll come around."

"You and Tom are such great parents. This baby will be the darling of the bunch, you wait and see. God always knows what He's doing."

"You're right, I know, but it's still a shock." Looking around, she spotted Tom across the way. "I think I'll go over and let the daddy-to-be pamper me awhile."

Lindsey watched her friend snag another cookie as she sashayed around to the opposite side of the campfire where her husband waited. A twinge of envy pinched at her as she gazed at the group gathered on her farm. They were mostly couples and families, people who shared their lives with someone else. Even the teenagers paired up or hung together in mixed groups going through the age-old ritual of finding a partner.

Lindsey loved these people, liked attending functions with them, but times such as these made her more aware than ever of how alone she was.

To shake off the unusual sense of melancholy, Lindsey found a roasting stick and went in search of a frankfurter to roast. She had too much to be thankful for to feel sorry for herself. She'd chosen to live in this remote place away from her family where there were few unattached men her age. If the Lord intended for her to have a mate, He'd send one her way.

An unexpected voice intruded on her thoughts.

"Could you spare two of those for a couple of fashionably late strangers?"

A pair of solemn silver eyes, aglow in the flickering firelight, met hers.

Her heart gave a strange and altogether inappropriate lurch of pleasure.

Jesse was here.

Jesse stared into Lindsey's delighted eyes and wished he was anywhere but here. From the minute he'd left the farm, he had struggled with a rising desire not to return. Except for his promise to Jade, he wouldn't have. He no more belonged with Lindsey and her holy church friends than he belonged in Buckingham Palace with the queen.

Jade gripped his leg, eyes wide as she watched children running in wild circles outside the perimeter of the firelight.

"You didn't think we were coming, did you?" he said to Lindsey.

She handed him a roasting stick, eyebrows lifted

in an unspoken question. "I was beginning to wonder if something had happened."

The open-ended statement gave him the opportunity to explain, but he let the moment pass. His life was his business. Lindsey's gentle way of pulling him in, including him, was already giving him enough trouble.

"We brought marshmallows." Jade's announcement filled the gap in conversation. She thrust the bag toward Lindsey.

"Cool. Let's eat a hotdog first and then we'll dig into these." Lindsey placed the bag on the table and took a wiener from a pack. "Do you want to roast your own?"

Jade pulled back, shaking her head. "Uh-uh. The fire might burn me."

"How about if I help you?" Lindsey slid the hotdog onto the stick and held it out

Jesse could feel the tension in his child's small fingers. Her anxiety over every new experience worried him. He squatted down in front of her. "It's okay. Lindsey won't let you get hurt."

Indecision laced with worry played over his daughter's face. Lindsey, with her innate kindness, saw the dilemma. Jade wanted the fun of roasting the hotdog, but couldn't bring herself to trust anyone other than him. Jesse hid a sigh.

"This hotdog will taste better if Daddy cooks it. Isn't that right, sugar?" Lindsey said, handing him the loaded stick. "I'll grab another."

Squatting beside Lindsey with Jade balanced

between his knees, Jesse thrust the franks into the flames. Jade rested a tentative hand just behind his.

More than anything Jesse longed to see Jade as confident and fearless as other six-year-olds. Deep inside, he was convinced that regaining his inheritance, giving her a stable home environment and surrounding her with familiar people and places would solve Jade's problem. Tonight he hoped to take another step in that direction.

Letting his gaze drift around the campfire, Jesse studied the unfamiliar faces. Somebody here must have known Lindsey's grandparents and probably even his stepfather. Some self-righteous churchgoer standing out there in the half darkness sucking down a hotdog might have even been involved in the shady deal that had left him a homeless orphan.

"Everyone here is anxious to meet you," Lindsey said, her voice as smoky and warm as the hickory fire.

Given the train of his thoughts, Jesse shifted uncomfortably. "Checking out the new guy to make sure you're safe with me?"

The remark came out harsher, more defensive than he'd planned.

Serene brown eyes probing, Lindsey said, "Don't take offense, Jesse. This is a small town. They only want to get acquainted, to be neighborly."

He blamed the fire and not his pinch of guilt for the sudden warmth in his face. She was too kind and he wished he'd followed his gut instinct and stayed at the cramped little trailer.

"Here you go, Butterbean." Taking the hotdog from the flames, he went to the table for buns and mustard. Lindsey and Jade followed.

One of the biggest men he'd ever seen handed him a paper plate. "You must be Jesse."

Lindsey made the introductions. "This is my pastor, Cliff Wilson."

Jesse's surprise must have shown because the clergyman bellowed a cheerful laugh. "If you were out killing preachers, you'd pass me right up, wouldn't you?"

Cliff looked more like a pro wrestler than a preacher. A blond lumberjack of a man in casual work clothes and tennis shoes with blue eyes as gentle and guileless as a child's and a face filled with laughter.

"Good to meet you, sir," Jesse said stiffly, not sure how to react to the unorthodox minister.

"Everyone calls me Pastor Cliff or just plain Cliff." The preacher offered a beefy hand which Jesse shook. "You from around this area?"

"Enid." Giving his stock answer, Jesse concentrated on squirting mustard onto Jade's hotdog. No way he'd tell any of them the truth—that he'd roamed this very land as a youth.

"Lindsey says you're heaven-sent, a real help to her."

"I'm glad for the work." He handed the hotdog to Jade, along with a napkin. "Lindsey's a fair boss."

By now at least a half dozen other men had sidled

up to the table for introductions and food refills.
Jesse felt like a bug under a magnifying glass, but if
he allowed his prickly feelings to show, people might
get suspicious. He needed their trust, though he
didn't want to consider how he'd eventually use that
trust against one of their own.

"A fair boss? Now that's a good 'un." A short,
round older man in a camouflage jacket offered the
joking comment. "That girl works herself into the
ground just like her grandpa did. I figure she expects
the same from her hired help."

Jesse stilled, attention riveted. This fellow knew
Lindsey's grandparents and was old enough to have
been around Winding Stair for some time. He just
might know the details Jesse needed to begin searching the courthouse records.

"Now Clarence." Eyes twinkling a becoming gold
in the flickering light, Lindsey pointed a potato chip
at the speaker. "You stop that before you scare off the
only steady worker I've ever had."

"Ah, he knows I'm only kidding." Clarence aimed
a grin toward Jesse. "Don't you, son?" Before Jesse
could respond, the man stuck out his hand. "Name's
Clarence Stone. I live back up the mountain a ways.
If you ever need anything, give me a holler."

A chuckle came from the man in a cowboy hat
standing next to Clarence. His black mustache
quivered on the corners. "That's right, Jesse. Give
Clarence a holler. He'll come down and talk your
ears off while you do all the work."

Clarence didn't seem the least bit offended. He grinned widely.

"This here wise guy is Mick Thompson," he said with affection. "Mick has a ranch east of town, though if it wasn't for that sweet little wife of his, he'd have gone under a long time ago."

Mick laughed, teeth white in his dark face. "I have to agree with you there, Clarence, even if Clare is your daughter. I wouldn't be much without her."

Jesse's mind registered the relationship along with the fact that Mick owned a ranch. Now that was something Jesse understood.

"You raise horses on that ranch of yours?" he asked, making casual conversation while hoping to turn the conversation back to Lindsey's grandparents.

"Sure do. You know horses?" Mick sipped at his plastic cup.

"I've done a little rodeo. Bronc-riding mostly."

"No kidding?" Mick's eyebrows lifted in interest. "Ever break any colts?"

"Used to do a lot of that sort of work." Before Erin died. But he wouldn't share that with Mick.

"Would you like to do it again?"

"I wouldn't mind it." He missed working with rough stock, and breaking horses on the side would put some much-needed extra money in his pocket.

"Don't be trying to hire him away from Lindsey, Mick," the jovial Clarence put in. "She'll shoot you. And I'll be left to support your wife and kids."

"You'd shoot me yourself if you thought Clare and

the kids would move back up in those woods with you and Loraine."

Both men chuckled, and despite himself, Jesse enjoyed their good-natured ribbing.

Lindsey, having drifted off in conversation with a red-haired woman, missed the teasing remark. Without her present, Jesse wanted to turn the conversation back to her grandfather, but wasn't sure how to go about it without causing suspicion.

"Tell you what, Jesse," Mick said, stroking his mustache with thumb and forefinger. "When you have some time, give me a call. I have a couple of young geldings that need breaking, and I can't do it anymore. Bad back."

Were all the people of Winding Stair this trusting that they'd offer a man a job without ever seeing him work?

"How do you know I can handle the job?"

Mick's mustache quirked. "Figure you'd say so if you didn't think you could."

"I can."

"See?" Mick clapped him on the back and clasped his hand in a brief squeeze. "My number's in the book. And I pay the going rate."

"Appreciate the offer, but I doubt I can get loose from here until after the holidays."

The familiar sense of dread crawled through his belly. He'd much rather be tossed in the dirt by a bucking horse than spend one minute in Lindsey's tree lot. He'd counted on the old adage that familiarity breeds indifference. So far, that hadn't proven true. If anything, he dreaded the coming weeks more than ever.

Mick sipped at his soda before saying, "After Christmas is fine with me. Those colts aren't going anywhere. Meantime, if you need help hauling these trees, let me know. I got a flatbed settin' over there in my barn rustin'."

"He sure does," Clarence teased. "And it would do him good to put in a full day's work for a change."

An unbidden warmth crept through Jesse. Offers of help from friends didn't come too often, but this off-hand generosity of strangers was downright unsettling.

"Jade, Jade." Two little girls about Jade's age came running up and interrupted the conversation. One on each side, they grabbed her hands and pulled. "Come play tag."

She looked to Jesse for approval. "Can I, Daddy?"

"Don't you want to finish your hotdog?"

"I'm full." She handed him the last bite of the squeezed and flattened sandwich.

He downed the remains and wiped the mustard off her face. "Go on and play."

She grabbed his hand and tugged. "Come with me."

Jesse shook his head, standing his ground for once. "I haven't finished my own hotdog. I'll be here when you get back. Promise."

After a moment of uncertainty, the desire to play with her friends won out.

Jesse's heart gladdened to see his little girl race

away with the other children for once instead of clinging to his leg like a barnacle.

Biting into his smoky hotdog, Jesse watched and listened, hoping for an opportunity to casually probe for information. His attention strayed to the gregarious preacher.

Pastor Cliff seemed to be everywhere, laughing, joking and making sure everyone had a great time. The teenagers flocked around him as though he was some football star, begging him to join their games, occasionally pelting him with a marshmallow to gain his attention. Punctuating the air with a few too many "praise the Lords" for Jesse's comfort, the preacher nonetheless came across like a regular guy. He'd even overheard Cliff promise to help repair someone's leaky roof next week. The big man sure wasn't like any minister Jesse had ever encountered.

"When are we taking that wagon ride, Lindsey?" Cliff bellowed, indicating a small boy perched on his shoulders. "Nathaniel says he's ready when you are."

"Do you kids want the tractor or the horse to pull us?" Lindsey called back.

"The horse. The horse," came a chorus of replies from all but the preacher.

Jesse knew the big, powerful horse stood nearby inside a fenced lot, his oversized head hanging over the rails, waiting his opportunity. The animal liked people and was gentle as a baby.

"How about you, Cliff? What's your preference?" A man called, his face wreathed in mischief.

The oversized preacher waved his upraised hands in mock terror. "Now, Tom, you know I don't mess with any creature that's bigger than me."

"Which wouldn't be too many, Cliff," came the teasing answer.

Everyone laughed, including Cliff, though the joke was on him. Grudgingly, Jesse admired that. The minister he'd known would have seen the joke as an offense to his lofty position.

"You're out-voted, preacher," Lindsey called, starting toward the gate. "I'll get Puddin'."

Shoving his hands into the pockets of his jean jacket, Jesse fell into step beside her. Though mingling with the church crowd provided opportunities to gather information, he needed some distance. He hadn't expected their friendliness, the ease with which they accepted him, and most of all, he'd not expected them to be such everyday, normal people. Lindsey's church family, as she called them, was fast destroying his long-held view of Christians as either stiff and distant or pushy and judgmental.

"Need any help?" he asked.

She withdrew a small flashlight from inside her jacket, aimed the beam toward the gate, and whistled softly. "I put his harness on earlier. All I need to do is hook the traces to the wagon."

Jesse stepped into the light and raised the latch. In seconds the big horse lumbered up to nuzzle at his owner while she snapped a lead rope onto his halter. Together they led him toward the waiting wagon.

"He's a nice animal." Jesse ran a hand over the smooth, warm horseflesh, enjoying the feel again after too much time away from the rodeo. "What breed is he?"

"Percheron mostly." She smiled at the horse with affection. "Although I'm not sure he's a full-blood since I have no papers on him, but he has the sweet temperament and muscular body the breed is known for. And he loves to work."

"Percheron." Jesse rolled the word over in his head. He knew enough about horses to know the name, but that was about it. "Different from the quarter horses I'm used to."

"Certainly different from the wild broncs. Puddin' doesn't have a buck anywhere in him." One on each side of the massive horse, they headed back toward the heat and light of the bonfire. "Every kid within a ten-mile radius has ridden him, walked under him, crawled over him, and he doesn't mind at all." She turned toward him, her face shadowed and pale in the bright moonlight. "What about you? Do you still have horses?"

He shook his head. "No. After Erin died, I—" He stopped, not wanting to revisit the horrible devastation when he'd sold everything and hit the road, trying to run from the pain and guilt. He'd told Lindsey more about his past than he'd ever intended to, but talking about Erin was taboo. "I'd better find Jade."

He stalked off toward the circle of squealing children, aware that he'd been abrupt with Lindsey and trying not to let that bother him. He'd intentionally sought her company, and now he was walking away.

Ruefully, he shook his head. What a guy.

In the distance he spotted Jade, her long hair flying out behind her as she ran, laughing. With a hitch beneath his rib cage, he watched his daughter, grateful for the rare display of playful abandon. Letting the shadows absorb him, he stood along the perimeter of children, hoping this place would ultimately heal them both.

"Hey, Jesse." A hand bigger than Puddin's hoof landed on his shoulder. The preacher. "Great party, huh?"

"Yeah." Though he didn't belong here, he had to admit the party was a success. Just seeing Jade carefree was worth a few hours discomfort on his part.

"Lindsey's a great gal."

Jesse followed the minister's gaze to where Lindsey, surrounded by too many youthful helpers, attached the patient horse to the wagon. Silently, he agreed with Cliff's assertion. Lindsey *was* a good woman. Her decency was giving his conscience fits. "You known her long?"

"A few years. Ever since coming here to minister." Cliff nodded at the rowdy crowd around the fire. "Most of these folks have known her and each other much longer, but God really blessed me when he sent me to Winding Stair. I feel as if Lindsey and all the others out there are my family now."

Clarence approached, this time accompanied by

a small, gray-haired woman with rosy cheeks who carried a plate of homemade cookies. "That's the way it's supposed to be, ain't it, preacher?"

Cliff reached for the cookies. "Yep."

"How about you, Jesse?" Clarence motioned toward the plate.

Out of courtesy Jesse accepted the dessert, taking a bite. He liked the mildly sweet flavor of the old-fashioned cookie. "These are good."

"Course they are," Clarence said. "Loraine makes the best oatmeal cookies in the county. And if you don't believe me, just ask her."

"Oh, Clarence, you old goof." The smiling little woman flapped a hand at him. "Jesse, don't pay any mind to my husband. This isn't my recipe and he knows it. Lindsey's grandma gave it to me. Now that woman could cook."

Blood quickening, Jesse saw the opportunity and took it. "You knew Lindsey's grandparents?"

"Sure did. Better folks never walked the earth, as far as I'm concerned." She paused long enough to dole out more cookies to passers-by. Jesse kept his mouth shut, waiting for her to go on, blood humming with the hope that he was about to learn something.

"Betty Jean—that was her grandma—could do about anything domestic. A country version of Martha Stewart, I guess you'd say." She chuckled softly at her own joke. "And she wasn't stingy about it either. Would share a jar of pickles or a recipe without batting an eye. A fine neighbor, she was. A real fine neighbor."

She looked a little sad and Jesse shifted uncomfortably. He needed to keep Loraine and Clarence talking but he didn't want to think of the Mitchells as decent folks. There was nothing decent about stealing from an orphan.

Keeping his tone casual, Jesse said, "Lindsey's a good cook too."

"Betty Jean would have made sure of that." Loraine thrust the nearly empty plate toward him. "Another cookie?"

"Might as well take one, Jesse," Clarence put in with a chortle. "She ain't happy unless she's feeding someone."

Jesse hid a smile. It was hard not to like Loraine and Clarence Stone. "Thanks."

He accepted the cookie, mind searching for a way to gain more information. He'd suffered through an hour of stilted conversation to get this far. He wasn't about to let this chance slip away.

"What about Lindsey's grandpa? I guess he's the one who taught her to use that rifle…."

"Yep," Clarence said. "That was Charlie, all right. Me and him used to hunt and fish together, and he liked to brag about Lindsey's shooting. Called her his little Annie Oakley."

Jesse's stomach leaped.

Charlie.

His patience had paid off. At last, he had someone to blame along with his stepfather. Lindsey's grandfather, the man who'd stolen this eighty-acre farm from a teenage boy, was named Charlie Mitchell.

In the shadowy distance, snatches of conversation and laughter floated on the night air. One particular laugh—a throaty, warm sound that sent shivers down his spine—stood out from the rest.

Lindsey.

He wanted to put his hands over his ears, to block out the sound. He'd finally discovered some information, and nobody, no matter how sweet and kind, was going to stop him from using it.

Chapter Five

Lindsey draped her jacket over the back of a kitchen chair and went to the sink. She'd had a long afternoon without Jesse there to help, but she couldn't complain. In the weeks he'd worked on the farm, this was the first time he'd asked for time off. So she had spent the afternoon marking the trees they'd soon cut and bale for delivery.

Ever since the night of the cookout, she'd noticed a shift in him. He worked harder than ever on the farm, putting in long hours and cutting himself no slack. But he seemed to be bothered by something—not that there was anything new about that—but this was a subtle mulling as though he had something heavy on his mind.

With a sigh, Lindsey acknowledged how much she'd come to depend upon the mysterious Jesse. She needed him, and regardless of his inner demons, she liked him. He was a good man with a heavy burden. If only she could find a way to help him past that burden—whatever it was.

Two or three times today she'd turned to ask Jesse's advice about something before remembering he was gone. Funny how she'd never needed anyone before other than Sushi and the Lord, but Jesse had changed all that. And she wasn't sure becoming dependent on her hired hand was such a good idea.

Turning the water tap, she filled a glass and drank deeply, thirsty even though the early November weather was cloudy and cool with the promise of rain hanging like a gray veil over the land. In the back of her mind, she faintly registered a rumbling in the distance but paid little mind. After washing and drying her hands, she headed to the refrigerator.

She had one hand on last night's chicken and rice when the screaming began.

An adrenaline rush more powerful than an electric shock propelled her into action. Faster than she thought possible, Lindsey bounded into the bedroom, unlocked the gun case, removed her rifle and rushed out into the yard, loading the weapon as she moved. An occasional mountain lion roamed these hills.

Peering in the direction of the screams, Lindsey stopped…and lowered the gun.

Jade stood halfway down the gravel driveway, frozen in fear, screaming her head off. Directly in front of her, Sushi lay on her back, feet in the air, groveling for all she was worth.

With a feeling somewhere between relief and exasperation, Lindsey stashed the rifle on the porch and loped down the driveway.

What was Jade doing here? Where was Jesse? And when would the child realize that Sushi was her friend?

"Sushi, come," she called. The German shepherd leaped to her feet, shook off the dust and leaves and trotted to Lindsey's side. Pointing to a spot several yards away from the terrified child, she commanded, "Stay."

The dog obeyed, plopping her bottom onto the dirt, tongue lolling, while she watched Jade with worried eyes.

Jade's screaming subsided, but the harsh sobs continued as Lindsey went down on her knees and took the little girl into her arms. She had a dozen questions, but now was not the time to ask them. Soon enough she could discover why Jesse had not picked up Jade at school as he'd planned.

"Jade, listen to me." Pushing the tangled hair, damp with tears, back from Jade's face she said gently, "Stop crying and listen. We need to talk like big girls."

Jade gave several shuddering sobs, scrubbing at her eyes with her fingertips. "The dog was going to get me."

"That's what we have to talk about. Sushi will not hurt you. Look at her. She's sitting down there begging for you to like her, but she won't even come near you unless I tell her to."

"She ran at me. I saw her teeth."

"She was smiling at you. You're part of her family now and she was excited to see you. That's how she behaves when I come home from someplace, too."

"It is?" Wary and unconvinced, Jade glanced from Lindsey to Sushi and back again.

"Sure. Every time you come home, she whines to be let out so she can play with you. It makes her very sad that you don't like her."

Jade's expression said she was thinking that over, but still she clung tightly to Lindsey.

"Where's my daddy?"

"I'm not sure, sweetie. He was supposed to pick you up at school."

The little girl's small shoulders slumped. "He's probably dead." And she burst out crying again.

"No, Jade, no." Please God, let me be right. Don't let anything else happen to this child. The loss of her mother had completely destroyed her sense of safety. "Your daddy is running late and didn't get back in time. He'll be here soon, and while we wait, you and I can have a dress-up tea party."

Lindsey could see she scored some points with the idea so she pressed the advantage. "Sushi wants to come, too. She even has some dress-up clothes."

Jade found that amusing. A hesitant smile teetered around her mouth. "Really?"

"Absolutely. All my Sunday-school kids invite Sushi to their tea parties because she's such a nice dog, so she has a hat, a boa and a fancy vest to wear."

"She might bite me."

"No." Lindsey said firmly. "She will not." Sliding Jade to the ground, she took the child's hand. "Come on. I'll show you."

Sushi waited right where she'd been told to stay, eagerly thumping her tail at the first sign of movement in her direction.

Jade pulled back. "Uh-uh."

Lindsey sighed, but relented and swept the little girl into her arms. "Okay, then. I have another idea."

She carried Jade to the house. A bewildered Sushi remained in the driveway as commanded.

"Stand here inside the house where you can see Sushi and me through the glass door." Lindsey took a piece of leftover chicken from the fridge. She'd planned to have the meat for supper, but helping Jade begin the process of overcoming this phobia was far more important. "Watch what a good girl Sushi is and how she loves to play, but she always minds me when I tell her to do something. Okay?"

Nodding and wide-eyed, Jade stood inside the door, her face pressed to the glass while Lindsey stepped onto the porch and called the dog. When Sushi arrived, skidding to a stop at her owner's command, Lindsey spent several minutes putting the animal through all her obedience commands. Extremely well disciplined, Sushi even resisted the piece of baked chicken, though Lindsey knew the meat was her favorite treat.

Then she played with Sushi, petting her, tossing sticks that the dog retrieved, scratching her belly.

Finally, Lindsey lay down on the porch to show her total trust of the dog. Sushi responded by plopping her big head onto Lindsey's chest with a delighted sigh that made Jade laugh.

Sitting up, Lindsey rotated toward Jade. "See what a good girl she is?"

"Uh-huh."

"Would you like to pet her?"

"Uh-uh." But Lindsey could see that, for once, she wanted to.

Confident they'd made progress, Lindsey relented. "Maybe next time?"

Leaving Sushi on the porch, Lindsey dusted her clothes and came inside. She peeked at the yellow teapot clock hanging over the cook stove. Jade had been here at least thirty minutes and still no sign of Jesse. Refusing to worry, she internalized a little prayer, and turned her attention to occupying Jade. The little girl didn't need to fret about her daddy even if Lindsey was.

"I'm starved."

"Me, too."

Using her best imitation of an English lady, Lindsey said, "Shall we prepare tea and dine?"

Jade giggled. "Can we dress up too? And you can be the princess and I'll be the queen?"

"Lovely idea, my queen. Right this way, please." Nose in the air as befit royalty, she led the way to the huge plastic storage bin in her bedroom closet where she kept a variety of thrift-shop and novelty-store play clothes. Jade, getting into the spirit of the game, followed suit. She fell upon the container, carefully lifting out one garment after another, exclaiming over each one as if the clothes came from Rodeo Drive.

In no time, she'd chosen outfits for both of them and they traipsed on plastic high heels, boas trailing, into the kitchen to prepare the Oklahoma version of high tea.

"Let's make fancy sandwiches first. Later, we'll do cookies."

"Do you have Christmas cookie cutters?" Jade shoved at her sun hat, repositioning the monstrosity on her head. Bedecked with more flowers than Monet had ever painted, the hat tied with a wide scarf under the child's chin. Lindsey thought she looked adorable.

"A bunch of them. We can use them on the sandwiches if you want to."

"Cool. Do you gots sprinkles too?"

"Oh, yeah. I have tons of sprinkles. All colors. But let's not put those on the sandwiches."

Jade giggled. "For the cookies, silly. I want to make Daddy a big red cookie." Her face fell. "I wish my daddy would come. I'll bet he's getting hungry."

"He'll be here soon," Lindsey said with more confidence than she felt as she spread the sandwich fixings on the table. "Tell you what. Let's say a little prayer asking Jesus to take care of him and bring him safely home."

She hardly noticed that she'd referred to her own house as home for Jesse and Jade. Semantics didn't matter right now.

"Okay." To Lindsey's surprise, Jade closed her eyes and folded her little hands beneath her chin. Even though Jesse shied away at the mention of God, someone had taught this child to pray.

Closing her own eyes, Lindsey said a short but heartfelt prayer.

"Amen."

Jade's shoulders relaxed. "Jesus will take care of Daddy, won't He?"

"Yes, He will. And He'll take care of you too." She smeared mayo on a slice of bread, handing it to Jade to layer on the meat and cheese. "Did you know you have a guardian angel who is always with you?"

Shaking her head, Jade licked the mayo off one finger.

"Well, you do. Everybody does. But God has very special guardian angels that take care of children. Jesus loves you so much He tells your very own angel to keep watch over you day and night."

"Even when I'm asleep?"

"Yes." She chose an angel from the pile of cookie cutters. "That's why you don't need to be afraid of anything—ever. Your angel is always here, looking after you."

Jade took the metal angel, studied it, and then pressed the shape into a sandwich. "Does Daddy have a guarding angel?"

Lindsey smiled at the mispronunciation. "He sure does."

"Can I save this angel sandwich for my daddy?"

"Of course you can. We'll make enough of everything so he can eat, too, when he gets here."

That seemed to satisfy Jade, and Lindsey wished she were as easily comforted. Where was Jesse? Leaving Jade alone was so uncharacteristic of him. Had something happened? In the weeks of their acquaintance she'd grown fond of him, fonder than was comfortable, and the thought of something happening to him was unspeakable.

Agitated and filled with self-recriminations, Jesse stormed across Lindsey's yard, hoping with everything in him that Jade was here. He couldn't believe he'd gotten so busy, so deeply enmeshed in the stacks of court records that the time had slipped away and he'd forgotten to pick Jade up from school until she was long gone. What kind of lousy father was he anyway?

Sushi bounded out to meet him, a good sign. His spirits lifted somewhat, though he'd feel better if the German shepherd bit him. He deserved to be punished. For all his searching, he hadn't found a bit of useful information; not one single reference to any transaction between Charles Mitchell and Les Finch.

The day as gray as his mood, Jesse mounted the porch—and heard singing. A husky adult voice that sent an unexpected shiver of pleasure dancing along his nerve endings blended sweetly with a higher, childish melody.

Relief flooded him. Jade was here. Pausing at the open door, he could see the two through the glass.

They were in the kitchen at the table, their backs turned, singing "Mary Had a Little Lamb" while they worked at something.

He squinted, leaning closer. What kind of get-ups were they wearing?

With an inner smile, he waited until they finished their song before pecking lightly on the door. Two heads swiveled in his direction.

"Daddy!" Jade dropped something onto the table and clambered off her chair. She ran toward him, nearly tripping over a long, white dress that looked suspiciously like a well-used wedding gown. Taking a moment to hike the yards of wrinkled satin and lace into one hand, she stumbled onward, lime-green high heels clunking against the wooden floor.

Mood elevating with every step his baby took, Jesse opened the door and stepped inside the living room.

"My, don't you look beautiful," he said.

But Jade was having none of his compliments. She got right to the point. "The teacher made me ride the bus 'cause you didn't come."

"I'm sorry I was late, Butterbean. Your teacher did the right thing sending you to Lindsey where you would be safe and happy."

"Where were you? I got scared. I thought you were dead like Mommy."

A searing pain cut off Jesse's windpipe. Of course, she'd think that. That's why he always made a point of being exactly where she expected—to allay her well-founded fears.

Lindsey appeared in the living room. "Your daddy is here now, Jade, and he's just fine."

"Jesus took care of him the way you said."

A serene smile lit Lindsey's eyes. "Yes, He did."

Jesse didn't know what was going on with their talk of Jesus and decided not to ask. He looked to Lindsey, grateful for her care of Jade, but not wanting to tell her where he'd been. Wearing a hat with peacock feathers sticking out the top, and a rather bedraggled fake fur stole over someone's old red prom dress, she looked ridiculously cute. If he hadn't felt so guilty, he would have laughed.

"I'm sorry for putting you out this way."

"Jade is no problem. But we were a little concerned about you."

Exactly what he didn't need—Lindsey's concern, although he knew it was there, felt it day in and day out as she carefully avoided subjects she'd discovered were painful or taboo. Always, that gentle aura of peace and inner joy reached out to him.

"I had some personal business to handle which took much longer than I'd planned. Somehow the time got away from me, and by the time I rushed over to the school…" He lifted his hands and let them fall.

"Well, you're here now." Lindsey smiled that sweet, tranquil smile that changed her face to a thing of beauty. Jesse tried, but failed, to resist the pleasure that one motion gave him.

And then she made things worse by asking, "Are you hungry?"

An unbidden rush of warmth filled him from the inside out. Coming to this house and this woman was starting to feel far too natural and way too good.

"Come on, Daddy. Come see. We're making a tea party, and I'm the queen." Skirts sweeping the floor, Jade led the way into the kitchen and lifted an odd-shaped bit of bread from the table, thrusting it at him. "I made this guarding angel for you."

"Tea, huh? And an angel sandwich." He took the offering, examining the small figure with all due seriousness. "Sounds delicious. Anything I can do to help?"

Lindsey nodded toward a plate of fresh fruit. "You could slice up the apples if you'd like."

"Lindsey." Jade's plaintiff protest drew both adults' attention. She eyed her father skeptically. "He can't come to the tea party without dress-up clothes."

An ornery gleam flashed in Lindsey's brown eyes. "She's right, Dad. Tea requires formal attire."

Before he could object on purely masculine grounds, Jade rushed off, returning with a purple boa, a tarnished tiara, and a yellow-and-black satin cape. "Here, Daddy, you can be king."

Lindsey laughed at the pained expression on Jesse's face and in return, received his fiercest glare of wry humor.

"I'll get you for this," he muttered under his breath as Jade dressed him, carefully twining the boa around his neck before placing the crown on his head with a triumphant—if somewhat crooked—flourish.

Lindsey wrinkled her nose at him and adjusted her

stole with a haughty toss of her head. "Mess with me, mister, and I'll find you a pair of purple plastic high heels to go with that dashing feather boa."

Jesse surprised himself by tickling her nose with the aforementioned boa. "I'm the king, remember. Off with your head."

She laughed up at him, and he realized how much smaller she was than he, and how feminine she looked in a dress, even a silly outfit like this one. Out of her usual uniform of jeans and flannel, she unsettled him. Lindsey was a pretty woman as well as a nice one.

One more reason he needed to find the answer to his questions and get out of here. He couldn't get attached to a woman he'd eventually have to hurt.

For all his searching today, he'd found no record of this farm or the transaction between his stepfather, Les Finch, and Charles Mitchell. If he didn't find something next time, he'd be forced to ask the clerk for information, a risk he hadn't wanted to take. Asking questions stirred up suspicion. Someone was bound to want to know what he was up to. Sooner or later, word would filter back to Lindsey and he'd be out of a job and out of luck. Discretion made for a slow, but safer, search.

Lindsey whacked his shoulder with her boa. "Are you going to slice that fruit or stand there and stare at my glorious hat?"

Her humor delighted him. "The hat does catch a man's eye."

Lindsey and Jade both giggled at his silliness.

Even he wondered where the lightheartedness came from. He'd had a rotten afternoon, but the warmth of this house and the company of these two females lifted his spirits.

Taking up the stainless-steel knife, he sliced an apple into quarters. "What kind of sandwiches are we making?"

"Baloney and cheese."

"Ah, a gourmet's delight." Placing the apple slices on a plate in as fancy a design as he could manage, he plucked a few grapes and arranged them in the center.

Lindsey clapped a slice of wheat bread on top of the meat and cheese. "And afterwards, we'll make sugar cookies."

"With sprinkles," Jade chimed in, her face a study in concentration as she pushed the metal cutters into the sandwiches.

"Jesse, why don't you arrange the fancy sandwiches on this plate while Jade finishes cutting them. Then we'll be ready to eat."

They were only sandwiches. Bread, baloney, cheese and mayonnaise. He could do this. Looking at his beaming child instead of the Christmas shapes, Jesse made a circle of sandwiches on the platter.

"What about the tea?" Jade asked.

"Oh. The tea!" Lindsey clattered across the floor in her high heels, opened a cabinet and removed a quart fruit jar. "I hope the two of you like spiced tea."

"Hot tea?" Jesse asked doubtfully.

She dumped a healthy amount of the mixture into a blue ceramic teapot. With a twinkle in her eye, she admitted, "Spiced tea tastes a lot like apple cider. Grandma taught me to make it. It's a conglomeration of tea, orange drink mix, lemonade and a bunch of yummy spices."

"Sounds better than hot tea," he admitted, pointing an apple slice at her before popping it into his mouth. "Maybe I can stand it."

Lindsey sailed across the floor and tapped his hand with the spoon. "Even the king has to wait until we all sit down together."

"Meanie." He snatched a grape. At her look of playful outrage, he laughed and snitched another.

She stopped dead, spoon in one hand, silly hat tilted to one side in rapt attention. "Jesse," she said, her smoky voice breathy and soft.

"What? Am I drooling grape juice?"

"You laughed."

He opened his mouth once, closed it and tried again. Sure he laughed. People laughed when they were happy. The realization astonished him. He'd laughed because he was happy. When was the last time he'd felt anything even close to happiness?

"I won't do it again."

"Oh, yes you will." All business and smiles, she shouldered him out of the way. "Go get that little card table in the laundry room and set it up. Jade will put on the table cloth and centerpiece while I finish our tea fixin's."

"Yes, ma'am." He saluted, slung his cape over his face in a super-hero imitation and did as he was told.

By the time the table was ready and they'd sat down to dine on the odd little meal, Jesse had gotten into the swing of the tea party. Wearing a get-up that would make his rodeo buddies howl, knees up to his chin, he reached for one of Jade's raggedy cookie-cutter sandwiches.

"Let's bless the food," Lindsey said, folding her hands in front of her.

A worried expression replaced the glow on Jade's face, and nearly broke Jesse's heart. Seated across from him at the small square table, she looked from Lindsey to him, waiting. Jesse did the only thing he could. He bowed his head, closed his eyes, and listened to Lindsey's simple prayer. When he looked back into his daughter's face, he knew he'd done the right thing. Playing the hypocrite for fifteen seconds hadn't killed him.

Stunned to realize he not only hadn't been bothered by the prayer or the other Christian references, Jesse chewed thoughtfully on the most delicious baloney and cheese sandwich he'd ever tasted and watched Lindsey do the same. He wondered at how time spent with her had changed him, easing the prickly sensation that usually came at the mention of God. Most of all he wondered at how easily Lindsey Mitchell, the lone pioneer woman, had become a part of his and Jade's lives. Considering how dangerous that was for him, he should toss down his Santa sandwich and run. But he knew he wouldn't. Lindsey's gentle female influence was so good for Jade. He tried to be a decent dad, but there were things a little girl needed that a man never even thought of.

"Tea, your highness?" Lindsey said to Jade, holding the pretty teapot over a dainty cup.

"Yes, your princess-ness. Tea, please." Pinky finger pointed up—he didn't know where she'd learned that—Jade lifted the poured tea and sipped carefully. "Delicious. Try it, Daddy."

"That's 'your daddy-ness' to you, queenie." Taking a sip of the surprisingly tasty tea, Jesse relished the sound of his child's giggle.

Yes, Lindsey was good for her. And as disturbing as the thought was, she was good for him, too.

Taking a sandwich from the serving dish, Jade said, "I think Sushi wants this one." She handed the food to Lindsey. "Will you give it to her so she won't be sad?"

Jesse couldn't believe his ears. Jade was worried about upsetting the dog? Capturing Lindsey's glance, he asked a silent question with his eyes.

Brown eyes happy, Lindsey only shrugged and said, "We're gaining ground." Getting up from her chair, she started toward the door. "Come with me, Jade. You can watch from inside."

When Jade followed, Jesse couldn't be left behind. He had to see this with his own eyes—if he could keep his tiara from falling down over them. Sure enough, Jade stood inside the glass door, a tentative smile on her face, while Lindsey stepped out on the porch and fed the dog.

If Jade overcame her fear of dogs, he'd almost believe in miracles.

Lindsey must have noticed his bewildered expression because she laughed.

"Doubting Thomas," she said to him, then leaned toward Jade. "Did you see the way Sushi wagged her tail? That means thank you."

Holding onto her flowered hat, Jade pressed against the glass and whispered to the dog. "You're welcome."

When Sushi licked the door, Jade jumped back, almost stumbling over her skirts, but at least she didn't scream.

"Sushi gave you a kiss, Butterbean," Jesse offered after he'd swallowed the thickness in his throat.

"Uh-huh. I saw her, but I didn't want a doggy kiss. I'm the queen." Resuming her air of royalty, she lifted the tail of her dress and clomped to the kitchen. "Can we make cookies now? It's almost Christmas."

Lindsey, satin skirts rustling, peacock feather flopping, followed behind Jade like a cartoonist's version of a royal lady-in-waiting. "You're right. Christmas will be here before we know it. Guess what your daddy and I are doing tomorrow?"

Jesse had a sneaky feeling he didn't want to know.

The gap in Jade's mouth flashed. "What?"

"We're going to put up the decorations and get the Christmas-tree lot ready for visitors."

"Yay! Can I help? Can I decorate a tree? Can I put

up the angel?" Jade wrapped her arms around Lindsey's red-satin-covered knees and hopped up and down. "Please, please, please."

Jesse's stomach sank into his boots. The day he'd dreaded had come. The Christmas season was upon him.

Chapter Six

"It Came Upon a Midnight Clear" blared from a loudspeaker positioned over the gate that opened into the Christmas-tree lot. The smell of pine mingled with the musty scent of Christmas decorations brought out of storage this morning. Though the temperature was in the high thirties, Jesse stripped away his jean jacket and hung the worn garment on the fence next to Lindsey's red plaid one.

He didn't have to look around to find the jacket's owner. Every cell in his body knew she was near—a sensation he found singularly disconcerting, to be sure. Last night, in the midst of a costumed tea party, some subtle shift in their boss/employee relationship had occurred. And Jesse didn't know if the change was a good thing or a very dangerous one.

From his spot stringing lights on staked poles, he turned to find her just inside the entrance, rubbing dust from a large wooden nativity scene. She'd shared her plans with him for the lot, and though the overwhelming dose of Christmas wasn't his idea of a good time, Lindsey's customers would come for this very atmosphere of holiday cheer.

Shoppers would park outside the gate then ride in the horse-drawn wagon down a lane aglow with Christmas lights and dotted with various lighted holiday ornaments: the nativity, a sleigh with reindeer, angels, snowmen. Jesse couldn't imagine anything she'd forgotten.

Chest tight, whether from watching Lindsey or thinking too much, he turned his concentration to the electrical part of his job. Electricity he knew. Lights he knew. The rest he'd ignore. And as soon as the opportunity arose, he'd kill that music.

"Jesse, could you put more speakers along the drive and down into the lot? I'm not sure we can hear the music all the way."

His shoulders slumped. So much for killing the tunes. After twisting two wires together, he rose from his haunches and asked, "Wouldn't my time be better spent cutting and baling those trees we marked this morning?"

She paused, pushed back her hair with one hand and studied him. When those eyes of hers lasered into him he couldn't do anything but wait until she finished speaking. She had pretty eyes, golden-brown and warm and slightly tilted at the edges like almonds.

"Why do you dislike Christmas?"

He blinked, squeezing hard on the pliers in his fist. "Never said I didn't like Christmas."

"Okay, then," She gave a saucy toss of her head. "Why do you dislike Christmas *decorations?*"

If the subject weren't so problematic, he'd have smiled. Lindsey's way of injecting humor into everything could lift anybody's mood.

Sushi chose that moment to insinuate her furry self against his legs, almost knocking him into the row of linked-together stakes.

Squatting, he took refuge in the dog, scuffing her ears with both hands. "Did I remember to thank you last night?"

"You just changed the subject."

He gave a little shrug. "So I did."

"Okay, I'll let you off the hook—for now." She lifted the hair off her neck, a habit of hers that Jesse liked. The movement was so utterly female. Erin had done that. Jade did it sometimes too.

"What are you thanking me for? Or was that just a ruse you use to avoid answering my question?

He shook his head. "No ruse. I owe you big-time."

"For what?"

She really didn't know?

"About a dozen things. Looking after Jade until I got here. For supper."

"Such as it was." She laughed, letting her hair tumble down. Even without the sunlight, her hair looked shiny and clean.

"I've eaten worse than baloney sandwiches and sugar cookies."

"Don't forget the fruit." She tilted a wise man backwards and washed his ancient face. "Last night was fun, Jesse."

"Yeah." No point in denying the truth. Rising, he gave Sushi one final stroke. "Most of all, I appreciate your patience with Jade about the dog. I know leaving her outside is a pain."

Lindsey captured him with her gaze. "I don't want thanks for that, Jesse. I just want to see Jade confident and unafraid."

Taking up the next strand of lights waiting to be hung, he sighed. "Me, too."

"She'll get there." The wise man satisfactorily cleaned, she left him and the rest of the nativity. Coming up beside Jesse, she took one end of the lights, holding them in place while he secured them to the poles. "She's already less fearful than when she first came."

"I noticed. She didn't even fuss when I put her to bed last night. She said her guarding angel would watch her sleep." He glanced toward her, noticed the curve of her cheek and the tilt of her lips, then quickly looked away. "She talked a lot about that."

"I hope you didn't mind me telling her."

He hitched a shoulder, not wanting to go there. "It's okay. Whatever works."

Lindsey laid a hand on his arm. "The Bible works because it's true, Jesse," she said, her smoky voice soft. "Aren't you comforted knowing your own special angel watches over you?"

The warmth of her fingers spread through his shirt sleeve. He tried to concentrate on twisting plastic fasteners.

"Can't say I've given it much thought."

"Maybe you should." She dropped her hand and went back to straightening the tangle of lights, but her touch stayed with him like a promise made.

Could Lindsey be right? Was there more to this Christian thing than he'd ever realized? Being around her and her church friends, witnessing her steadfast faith and the way she handled the bumps in her life with a certain assurance had him thinking about God with a fresh perspective. As a boy he'd believed, had even accepted Jesus as his savior at church camp when he was twelve. And then life had turned him upside down, and the God of the universe had seemed so far away.

But why would a caring God, a God who assigned each person an angel, take a man's wife and leave a little girl motherless? Why would He allow a vicious drunk to steal a boy's home and toss him out on the streets to fend for himself? Where was God in that?

He didn't know. But more and more lately, he wanted to reconcile Lindsey's God with the one in his head.

"Silent Night" drifted into his awareness. Lindsey moved away, back to the nativity. Other than the flood-lights she'd asked him to rig up, the set looked ready to him. As she adjusted the sheep and fluffed the hay inside the manger, joy practically oozed from her.

Sure she was happy. Why shouldn't she be? Other than losing her elderly grandparents, Lindsey had probably never had a moment's heartache in her life. Loving God and exuding tranquility was easy for her.

Frustrated at his line of depressive thinking, he yanked hard on a tangled cord, and turned his mind to more important matters—his search.

They had trees to haul this week which would give him the time and opportunity to ask questions in town. Yesterday at the courthouse he'd slipped up once, expressing to the clerk his interest in the transaction that gave Lindsey's grandfather ownership of the Christmas Tree Farm. When the woman had looked at him curiously, he'd covered his tracks with vague remarks about Lindsey's plans for expansion. If only he could talk freely with someone like Clarence or Loraine Stone, the couple who claimed to have known Charlie Mitchell so well. Sooner or later, by biding his time and listening, he'd have his opportunity.

After dusting and organizing the main pieces of the nativity, Lindsey went back to the storage shed for the final figure—the eight-foot-tall animated camel who blinked long-lashed eyes and mooed. She tugged and pulled, careful not to damage the heavy object in the journey across the rough field. Stopping to readjust, she saw Jesse leap the fence and trot in her direction.

"Why didn't you say something?"

"I can get it."

With a look of exasperation, he hoisted the camel into his strong arms. "You shouldn't have to. That's why you hired me."

Oddly touched and feeling more like a helpless female than she'd ever felt in her life, Lindsey traipsed along beside him. How could she not admire this man? Every time she turned around, he was lifting work from her shoulders, both literally and figuratively. She'd nev-er seen anyone work so hard for so little pay. And for all his silences and secrets, Jesse had a way of making her feel special.

Lindsey wasn't sure if that was such a good idea, given the spiritual differences between them, but she liked Jesse Slater. And she loved his little girl.

As if he'd heard her thoughts of Jade, Jesse spoke. His voice came from the opposite side of the camel's hump.

"Jade will be excited when she sees all this."

"You don't think she'll be disappointed that we did so much without her?" She'd worried about that all day. After the way Jade had begged to take part, Lindsey didn't want her hurt. But setting up the farm for Christmas took time.

"I explained to her last night that we'd have to do most of the work today. She was okay with it as long as she gets to do something."

A jingle bell came loose from the saddle and Lindsey ducked beneath the camel's neck to retrieve it.

"I promised to save the 'best stuff' until she gets here. She and I are going to put up the wreaths and decorate that tree up front." She pointed toward the entrance, the bell in hand jingling merrily. "And she can flip on the lights as soon as the sun sets. I hope that's enough."

Jesse's silver eyes, lit by an inner smile, slanted toward her. "You're amazing with her, you know it?"

Buoyed by the compliment, Lindsey shook the bell at him and grinned. "I cheat. I use Christmas."

The teasing admission moved the smile from Jesse's eyes to his lips, changing his rugged, bad-boy expression into a breathtaking sight. That solitary action shot a thrill stronger than adrenaline through Lindsey. Someday, she'd break all the way through the ice he'd built around himself and make him smile all the time.

Startled at such thinking, Lindsey rushed ahead to open the gate. Where had that come from? Jesse was her employee and maybe her friend. But that was all he could be.

Heart thudding in consternation, she analyzed the thought. As a Christian, she wanted to see him happy. She wasn't falling for him. Was she? She'd been in love with a man like Jesse before—a devastatingly handsome man filled with secrets. And Sean had betrayed her so completely she'd come home to the farm and promised never to fall for a pretty face again.

Jesse eased the camel into place alongside the rough wooden building that sheltered the baby Jesus and his earthly parents. He'd already positioned bales of hay around the site and spread straw on the ground. Later, he'd rig up the spotlights and the Star of Bethlehem to bring the scene to life.

In minutes, he had the camel bellowing and blinking.

With a grimace, he shut off the mechanism. "Jade will love that monstrosity."

With laughter and a clap of her hands, Lindsey put aside her troubled thoughts. "I thought as much. We'll let her turn it on as soon as she gets home from school."

Jesse dusted his hands down the sides of his jeans, one corner of his mouth quirking ever-so-slightly. "What's next? Singing Santas? Yodeling elves?"

"Nothing quite that fun. We'd better begin cutting and baling. I'd like to haul the first load tomorrow if we have enough ready."

"So soon?"

"The rush begins on Thanksgiving. That's only a week away. Stores and lots like to have their trees ready to sell."

Switching off the last strains of "Silent Night," he gestured in the direction of the trees. "Lead on, boss lady."

Though disappointed to lose the beautiful music, Lindsey hummed Christmas carols as they began the process of cutting the marked and graded trees. Jesse manned the chain saw and as each tree toppled, Lindsey slid a rolling sled-like device beneath the pine and pulled it to the waiting baler.

Accustomed to lifting the heavy trees, Lindsey man-handled each one into the cone-shaped baler to be compressed into a tight bundle and secured with netting.

Saw in one gloved hand, Jesse poked his head around a tree. "Leave those for me to lift and bale."

"We'd never get finished that way. I'm used to the work, Jesse. Stop fretting."

But pleasure raced through her blood when he laid aside the saw long enough to lift the baled tree onto the flatbed truck. She might be accustomed to heavy work, but being treated like a girl was a novel and somewhat pleasant, if misguided, occurrence.

Following him back into the wide row, and lost in thought, Lindsey never saw the danger coming. One minute, she was examining a hole in her glove and the next she heard the crack and whine of falling timber.

"Lindsey, look out!"

She looked, but all she saw was green blocking the gray-blue sky and rapidly closing in on her.

Then all the air whooshed from her lungs as Jesse came flying and knocked her to the ground, taking the brunt of the felled pine across his back and head.

She tasted dust and pine sap. Prickly needles poked over Jesse's shoulders and scratched the side of her face. Her pulse pounded and her knees trembled as if she'd done jumping jacks for the last hour.

One arm flung protectively over her head, his chest lying across her back, Jesse's warm breath puffed against her ear. "Are you okay?"

He sounded scared.

"Fine." She struggled to draw air into her lungs. "You?"

"Yeah." Jesse's heart raced wildly against her shoulder blades. The situation was anything but intimate, and yet Lindsey was aware of him in an entirely new way.

"You're crushing me," she managed.

"Sorry." He shoved the tree to one side before rolling to a sitting position.

Offering a hand, he pulled Lindsey up to sit beside him. Breath coming in rapid puffs, his concerned gaze checked her over.

With a tenderness usually reserved for Jade, he stroked one calloused finger down her cheek. "You have a scratch."

She studied his face, but resisted the urge to touch him. Already her skin tingled from his simple gesture, and her insides were too rattled from the accident to think straight. Her throat felt tight and thick. "So do you."

He flicked one shoulder, tossing off her concern like an unwanted gum wrapper.

"I'll heal." He took a deep breath and blew out a gusty sigh. "Man, that scared me. I can't believe I let that tree get away from me."

"Not your fault. I heard the saw. I knew you were harvesting, but I was...distracted." She wasn't about to tell him that he'd been the distracting element. And now she was more discombobulated than ever. Jesse had put himself in harm's way to protect her.

And she liked the feeling of having a man—of having Jesse—look after her.

Oh, dear. She could be in real trouble here if she didn't watch her step. There was no denying Jesse's attractiveness, but the idea of letting another handsome face turn her head was worrisome. Jesse's secretiveness and his resistance to the Lord bothered her, too. But as a Christian, she wanted to provide a shining example of Christ's love; to share the incomprehensible peace of mind the Lord had given her.

Somewhere there had to be a midway point between being Jesse's friend in Christ and falling for him.

She only wished she knew how to find it.

Chapter Seven

"Are you sure you don't mind?" Jesse asked the moment he and Jade arrived on Thanksgiving Day. "We can still head down to the Caboose and grab a bite to eat."

A sharp wind, the likes of which rip and tear across Oklahoma with the energy of wild, vicious dogs, swept a draught of cold air into the farmhouse.

Though the oven had warmed the place considerably, Lindsey wasn't one to fritter away expensive heating fuel. She plucked at the quilted sleeve of Jesse's coat and pulled him inside.

"And waste this feast I've been cooking all morning? Not a chance, mister. You are stuck with my home cooking. No arguments."

Ducking beneath her daddy's arms, Jade slipped into the house and started shedding her outerwear. She wore a red wool coat Lindsey had never seen before over a plaid jumper, black tights and patent-leather shoes. Lindsey's heart did a funny stutter-step. Jesse had dressed her up for Thanksgiving dinner.

"You guys toss your coats in the bedroom. I need to check on the dressing and sweet potatoes."

Hands on the snaps of his jacket, Jesse stood in the kitchen doorway sniffing the air. "Candied sweet potatoes?"

She nodded. "With marshmallows and brown sugar."

He let out a low groan. "Forget the Caboose. I wouldn't leave now even if you chased me with that shotgun of yours."

Lindsey couldn't hold back the rush of pleasure. She knew she was blushing and quickly bent over the oven door to blame her increased color on the heat.

Asking Jesse and Jade to Thanksgiving dinner made perfect sense. They had no other place to go, and she had no family living close enough to cook for. In fact, she'd been as energetic as that silly bunny for the three days since Jesse had agreed to share the holiday with her.

"So," Jesse said, coming back into the kitchen from putting away his wraps. "What can we do to help?"

The foil-covered turkey was nicely basted and already out of the oven. The dressing and sweet potatoes were almost ready as were the hot rolls. Though she didn't want to admit as much to Jesse, she'd gotten up earlier than normal to bake everything the way her grandmother always had.

"We'll be ready to eat soon." She turned with a smile, wiping her hands on her bib apron. "You could set the table if you'd like."

"Come on, Butterbean," he said to Jade. "The slave driver is putting us to work."

He was in high spirits today, a rare occurrence to Lindsey's way of thinking. And she liked seeing him this way, without the load of care he usually wore like an anvil around his neck.

Jade's dress shoes clicked on the kitchen floor as she helped her daddy spread the white lacy tablecloth and set out three of Granny's best Blue Willow place settings.

After carefully positioning a knife and fork on top of paper napkins, she looked up. A small frown puckered her brow. "Where's Sushi going to eat?"

"Sushi?" Lindsey hesitated, a potholder in one hand. "I put her in the extra bedroom."

"Oh." Turning back to her job, Jade said nothing more about the dog. The adults exchanged glances.

Jesse mouthed, "Don't ask me."

Jade seemed unmindful that she'd raised adult eyebrows with her concern for a dog she supposedly despised. Letting the subject drop, Lindsey returned to the task of getting the food on the table. In her peripheral vision, she caught the red flash of Jade's plaid jumper and gleaming shoes.

"You sure look pretty today," she said.

"Well, thank you, ma'am." Jesse's teasing voice had her spinning toward him. "You look pretty, too."

Jade burst into giggles. "Daddy! She meant me. I'm pretty."

On tiptoes, the little girl twirled in a circle.

Jesse slapped a hand against one cheek in mock embarrassment. "Do you mean to tell me that I don't look pretty?"

Gap-tooth smile bigger than Dallas, Jade fell against him, hugging his legs. "You're always pretty."

Lindsey had to concur, even though she'd never before seen Jesse in anything but work clothes. Seeing him in polished loafers, starched jeans, and a light blue dress shirt that drew attention to his silvery eyes took her breath away.

Considering how decked-out the Slaters were, she was glad she'd taken the time to dress up a bit herself. Though her clothes were still casual, she'd chosen dark brown slacks instead of jeans and a mauve pullover sweater. And she'd put on earrings, something usually reserved for church. They were only small filigree crosses, but wearing them made her feel dressed-up.

With a wry wince of remembrance, she glanced down. If only she'd exchanged her fluffy house shoes for a snazzy pair of slides… Ah, well, she was who she was. As Granny used to say, you can't make a silk purse out of a sow's ear.

Delighted to have guests on Thanksgiving Day, she didn't much care what anyone wore. Just having them here was enough.

After sliding a fragrant pan of yeast rolls from the

oven, she slathered on melted butter, and dumped the rolls into a cloth-covered basket.

Without waiting to be told, Jesse put ice in the glasses and poured sweet tea from the pitcher Lindsey had already prepared.

"What's next?" he asked, coming to stand beside her at the counter. He brought with him the scent of a morning shower and a manly cologne that reminded Lindsey of an ocean breeze at sunrise.

She, on the other hand, probably smelled like turkey and dressing with a lingering touch of pine.

"I think we're about ready." She handed a bowl of cranberry sauce to Jade. "If you'll put this beside the butter, your daddy and I will bring the hot stuff."

Jade took the bowl in both her small palms, carefully transferring the dish to the table. Jesse and Lindsey followed with the rest and settled into their places.

The trio sat in a triangle with Jesse taking the head of the table and the two ladies on either side of him. Lindsey, out of long habit, stretched out a hand to each of them.

Jade reacted instantly, placing her fingers atop Lindsey's. After a brief, but noticeable interval, Jesse did the same, and then joined his other hand to his daughter's.

The moment Jesse's hand touched hers, Lindsey recognized her error. She hoped with all her might that the Lord would forgive her, because she was having a hard time concentrating on the prayer with Jesse's rough, masculine skin pressing against hers.

Somehow she mumbled her way through, re-membering to thank God for her many blessings during the past year, including the blessing of Jesse and Jade.

Jesse tensed at the mention of his name. At the closing "amen," he cleared his throat and shifted un-comfortably. Jade, on the other hand, beamed like the ray of sunshine she was.

"Guess what?" she offered, with the usual scat-tered thought processes of a six-year-old. "I have a loose tooth."

"Let's see." Lindsey leaned forward, pretending great interest as Jade wiggled a loosening incisor. "Maybe it will fall out while you're eating today."

Jade's eyes widened in horror. "What if I swallow it?"

The poor little child was afraid of everything.

"Well, if you do," Jesse said, helping himself to the sweet potato casserole, "it won't hurt you."

"But I can't swallow it. I have to show it to my teacher so she can put my name on the tooth chart."

Doing her best to suppress a laugh, Lindsey placed a hot roll on her plate and passed the basket to Jesse. His eyes twinkled with his own amused reaction. Swallowing the tooth wasn't the problem. Jade was afraid of being left out, a perfectly healthy, normal worry for a first-grader.

"I don't think you'll swallow the tooth, Jade, but if you do, the teacher will still put your name on the chart."

Green eyes blinked doubtfully. "How will she know?"

"She can look at the new empty place in your mouth."

The little girl's face lit up. She wiggled the tooth again. "Maybe it will come out today."

"We have corn on the cob. That's been known to do the trick."

"Okay." Jade reached eagerly for the corn Lindsey offered. "Eat one, Daddy."

Jesse quirked an eyebrow in teasing doubt. "I don't know, Butterbean. Your old dad can't afford to lose any of his teeth."

"Oh, Daddy." She pushed the platter of steaming corn in his direction. "It's good."

"Okay, then. I just hope you don't have to go home with a toothless daddy."

Jade grinned around a huge bite of corn as her daddy filled his plate.

"This all looks terrific, Lindsey." Jesse added a hearty helping of turkey and dressing. "You've worked hard."

"Cooking was fun. I haven't had a real Thanksgiving dinner since Gramps died."

He spread butter on the golden corn, his surprised attention focused on Lindsey. "Why not? Don't you usually visit your family for holidays?"

"Some holidays, but not this one. I can't. Thanksgiving begins my peak season, and lots of families want their tree the weekend after Thanksgiving."

"Then your family should come here."

"Oh," she gestured vaguely, then scooped up a bite of green bean casserole. "They're all pretty busy with their own lives. Kim, my sister, is expecting a baby early next year. She's in Colorado near her husband's family so naturally, they have their holidays there."

Chewing the creamy casserole, Lindsey had to admit the food tasted incredible. Could she credit the home cooking? Or the company?

Jesse absently handed Jade a napkin. With a sweet smile filled with yellow corn, she swiped at her buttery face.

Having a child—and a man—at her dinner table gave Lindsey an unexpected sense of fulfillment.

"What about your parents?" Jesse asked, coming right back to the conversation.

"Like Kim, they want me to come to them. Right now they're in Korea, so that wasn't possible this year."

"You wouldn't leave the trees anyway."

"I might sometime if I could find the right person to run the place for a couple of days."

He chewed thoughtfully, swallowed and took a drink of tea before saying, "I would have done it this year if you'd said something."

Lindsey's insides filled, not with the sumptuous Thanksgiving meal, but with the pleasure of knowing Jesse meant exactly what he'd said. She mulled over the statement as she watched him eat with hearty male abandon.

"I never would have considered asking you."

Fork in hand, he stiffened. His silver eyes frosted over. "You don't trust me to do a good job?"

"Of course, I trust you." Almost too much, given how little she knew about him. "I only meant that leaving you to do all the work while I vacationed would be a huge imposition."

His tense jaw relaxed. "Oh."

He studied the rapidly disappearing food on his plate, some thought process that Lindsey couldn't read running amok inside his head.

A vague unease put a damper on Lindsey's celebratory mood. Why had Jesse reacted so oddly?

She bit into the tart cranberry-and-sage-flavored dressing, pondering. Had she offended him? Or was the problem deeper than that?

Jade, who'd been busily doing damage to the ear of corn, stopped long enough to take a huge helping of turkey.

"You won't eat that," Jesse said, reaching for the meat.

Jade slid the plate out of his reach. "It's for Sushi. She's hungry and lonely. She might be crying."

Lindsey couldn't believe her ears. Jade worried about the dog without any encouragement from the adults? Was this the break she'd been praying for?

Jesse seemed to recognize the moment, too, for he tossed down his napkin and said, "Can't have Sushi crying." Chunk of dark meat in hand, he pushed back from his chair. "Let's take her this."

Lindsey thrilled when Jade slipped down from her chair to follow her dad. She took his outstretched hand, her own tiny one swallowed up in the protective size of her father's.

Unable to avoid the parallel, Lindsey thought of her heavenly Father, of how His huge, all-powerful hand is always outstretched in protection and care. The comparison brought a lump to her throat. She'd messed up a lot in her life, but the Father had never let her down. Even when she'd sequestered herself here on Winding Stair to hide from the hurts of this world, He'd come along with her, loving her back to joy, giving her this farm in place of the things she'd lost.

Jesse and his daughter took three steps across the sun-drenched kitchen before Jade stopped and turned. She stretched out a hand.

"Come on," she said simply as though Lindsey was an expected presence, a part of her life.

The lump in Lindsey's throat threatened to choke her. How long had she hungered for a child? A family? And now, on this Thanksgiving Day she felt as if she had one—if only for today.

Dabbing at her mouth with a napkin, she rose and joined the pair, asking tentatively, "Would you like Sushi to come out and play?"

"I don't want to play."

Before Lindsey had time to express her disappointment, Jade went on. "But she can come out and sit by you."

At the bedroom door, Lindsey went down in front

of the child. "You are such a big girl. I'm so proud of you for being nice to Sushi. She *is* lonely in there all by herself and she doesn't understand why she's locked up."

Dark hair bouncing, Jade nodded. "I know."

"We'll give her this turkey." She indicated the meat in Jesse's hand. "And then I'll pet her a little before letting her out. She might be excited and jump because she's happy to see us."

Jade reached both arms toward her father. "Hold me up, Daddy."

With a sigh that said he didn't consider this progress, he hoisted his daughter. Lindsey opened the door and commanded, "Sushi, stay."

The German shepherd, already spring-loaded, wilted in disappointment, but she followed her owner's command. Tail swishing madly, ears flicking, she waited while Lindsey stroked and murmured encouragements. Once convinced that Sushi's self-control was intact, she gazed up at Jade.

"She's all ready for that turkey. Hold it by your fingertips and give it to her."

Heart thudding with hope, Lindsey told the dog to sit and be gentle.

Worried green eyes shifting from the dog to Lindsey, Jade gathered her courage. When she looked to Jesse, he winked and gave her an encouraging nudge. "Go ahead."

Taking the poultry, Jade strained forward. Jesse held on tight, face as tense and hopeful as Lindsey's heart.

As if she understood the child's dilemma, Sushi waited patiently, and then daintily took the meat between her front teeth.

Jade's nervous laugh broke the anxious moment. Lindsey hadn't realized she was holding her breath. As casually as she could while rejoicing over this huge step, she turned back to the kitchen. Sushi's toenails tapped the floor as she followed. She pointed to a spot far away from Jade, and the dog collapsed in ecstasy.

To her delight, Jade slithered out of Jesse's arms, unafraid to be on even ground with the animal.

"How about some pecan pie?" Lindsey asked, tilting the pie in their direction.

Jade shook her head. "Can I play with your playhouse?"

She indicated the extra room where Lindsey kept toys and games for her Sunday-school girls.

"Sure. Go ahead."

As Jade skipped off into the other room, Lindsey lifted an eyebrow toward Jesse. "Pie?"

Jesse patted his flat, muscled stomach. "Too full right now. Later maybe?"

"Later sounds better to me, too. I'm sure there are plenty of football games on if you'd like to watch television while I clean the kitchen."

"No deal. You cook. I wash."

Lindsey was shocked at the idea. "You're my guest. You can't wash dishes."

Already rolling up his shirtsleeves, Jesse argued. "Watch me."

"Then I'm helping, too." She tossed him an apron, the least frilly one she owned.

He tied it around his slender middle, and in minutes they had the table cleared and water steaming in the old-fashioned porcelain sink.

As Lindsey stacked the dishes on the counter, Jesse washed them. The sight of his strong dark arms plunged into a sink full of white soapsuds did funny things to her insides.

They were down to the turkey roaster when the crunch of tires on gravel turned their attention to visitors.

"Who could that be?" Lindsey asked, placing a dried plate into the cabinet before pushing back the yellow window curtain. "I don't recognize the vehicle."

Jesse came up beside her. A hum of awareness prickled the skin on Lindsey's arms.

"I'll go out and check." Her breath made tiny clouds on the cool window. "Could be an early customer."

Her prediction proved true, and though she normally didn't open until the day after Thanksgiving, she was too kindhearted to turn them away.

Upon hearing their story, she was glad they'd come.

"Thank you for letting us interrupt your holiday," the woman said as she watched her children traipse happily through the thick green pines. "We thought decorating the tree before their dad shipped out for the Middle East tomorrow would help the kids. They've never had Christmas without him."

Lindsey placed a hand on the woman's arm. "It's us who owe you—and your husband—thanks."

As they went from tree to tree, discussing the perfect shape and size, Lindsey realized that Jesse and Jade had disappeared. In moments, she knew why. Red and green lights, dim in the bright November sun, flicked on all over the lot. Then the gentle strains of "Away in a Manger" filtered from the stereo speakers Jesse had stretched from the gate into the trees.

When he returned, coming up beside Lindsey with Jade in tow, she couldn't hold back her gratitude. "Thank you for thinking of that."

He shrugged off the compliment. "Some people like this stuff."

But you don't. What could have happened to turn Jesse into such a Scrooge? She wanted to ask why again, to press him for information, but now, with a customer present, was not the moment.

The family found the perfect tree and Jesse set to work. In no time, the tree was cut, baled, and carefully secured on top of the family's car. Three exuberant children piled inside the four-door sedan, faces rosy with excitement and cold. The soldier reached for his wallet, but Lindsey held out a hand to stop him.

"No way. The tree is a gift. Enjoy it."

The man argued briefly, but seeing Lindsey's stubborn stance, finally gave in. "This means a lot to my family."

He got inside the car and started the engine.

"Merry Christmas." Lindsey said, leaning down into the open window. "You'll be in my prayers."

With more thanks and calls of Merry Christmas, the family drove away, the Virginia pine waving in the wind.

"That was a real nice thing you did," Jesse said, his arm resting against hers as they watched the car jounce down the driveway.

"I love to give trees to people like that. What a blessing."

"You don't make money giving them away."

"No, but you create joy, and that's worth so much more."

Jade, who'd been listening, rubbed her hand across the needles of a nearby pine and spoke in a wistful voice. "I wish I could have a Christmas tree."

"What a grand idea!" Lindsey clapped her hands. The sound startled several blackbirds into flight. "Let's pick one right now. You and your daddy can decorate it tonight."

Beside her, Jesse stiffened. A warning sounded in Lindsey's head, but she pushed it away, intent upon this latest happy project.

"Come on." She gestured toward the smaller trees. "You can choose your very own tree. Any one you want."

Jade held back, her face a contrast of longing and reluctance.

The warning sound grew louder. "What's wrong, sweetie? Don't you want a tree?"

Small shoulders slumping with the weight, Jade wagged her head, dejected. "Daddy won't let me."

"Sure he will."

But one look at Jesse told her she was wrong.

"Jesse?" With a sinking feeling, she searched his face. What she found there unnerved her.

"Leave it alone, Lindsey," he growled, jaw clenching and unclenching.

"Daddy hates Christmas." Tears shimmered in Jade's green eyes. "Mommy—"

"Jade!" Jesse's tortured voice stopped her from saying more. He stared at his daughter, broken and forlorn.

Jade's eyes grew round and moist. Biting her lower lip, she flung her arms around Jesse's knees.

Expression bereft, Jesse stroked his daughter's hair, holding her close to him.

Heart pounding in consternation, Lindsey prayed for wisdom. Whatever had happened was still hurting Jesse and this precious little girl. And avoiding the issue would not make the pain go away.

She touched him, lightly, tentatively. "Let me help, Jesse. Talk to me. Tell me what's wrong."

"Talking doesn't change anything." His face was as hard as stone, but his eyes begged for release.

She hesitated, not wanting to toss around platitudes, but knowing the real answer to Jesse's need. "I don't know if you want to hear this, but there's nothing too big for the Lord. Jesus will heal all our sorrows if we let him."

"I wish I could believe that. I wish…" With a weary sigh, he lifted Jade into his arms and went to the little bench along the edge of the grove and sat down. With a deep, shivering sigh, he stared over Jade's shoulder into the distance, seeing something there that no one else could.

Unsure how to proceed, but knowing she had to help this man who'd come to mean too much to her, Lindsey settled on the bench beside him and waited, praying hard that God would give her the words.

Something terrible had broken Jesse's heart and her own heart broke from observing his pain.

After an interminable length of silence disrupted only by the whisper of wind through pine boughs, Jade climbed down from her daddy's lap.

Her dark brows knit together. "Daddy?"

"I'm okay, Butterbean." He clearly was not. "Go play. I want to talk to Lindsey."

"About Mommy?"

Jesse dragged a hand over his mouth. "Yeah."

Lindsey saw the child hesitate as though she felt responsible for her father's sorrow. Finally, she drifted away, going to the parked wagon where she sat anxiously watching the adults.

When Jesse finally began to speak, the words came out with a soft ache, choppy and disconnected.

"Erin looked a lot like Jade. Black hair and green eyes. Pale skin. She was a good woman, a Christian like you." He hunched down into his jacket, though the afternoon air wasn't cold. "I tried to be one, too, when she was alive."

So that explained how Jade had learned to pray and why she knew bits and pieces about Jesus. Jesse and his wife had known the Lord, but something had driven him away from his faith.

"Christmas was a very big deal to her. She loved to shop, especially for Jade and me. We didn't have a lot of money." He kicked at a dirt clod, disintegrating the clump into loose soil. "My fault, but Erin made the best of it. We always had a good Christmas because of her. She could make a ten-dollar gift seem worth a million."

Something deep inside told Lindsey to be quiet and let him talk. Letting the pain out was the first step to healing, and the cleansing would give the Lord an opportunity to move in. Granny had taught her that when she'd wanted to curl into a ball and disappear from the pain of Sean's betrayal.

"Two years ago—" He stopped, sat up straight and tilted his head backward, looking into the sky.

"What happened?" she urged gently.

"Christmas Eve. Erin had a few last-minute gifts to buy. One present she'd had in layaway for a while, though I didn't know it at the time. She'd been waiting to have enough money to pick up that one gift." He swallowed hard and scrubbed a hand across his eyes. "Jade and I stayed at the house, watching Christmas cartoons and munching popcorn balls. We were waiting for Erin to get home before we hung the stockings. We never hung them because Erin never came home."

Biting at her lower lip, Lindsey closed her eyes and prayed for guidance.

"Oh, Jesse," she whispered, not knowing what else to say. "I'm so sorry."

He shifted around to look at her. "I'm not telling you this for sympathy."

But sympathy wasn't the only emotion rushing through her veins.

She was starting to care about Jesse. Not only the way a Christian should care about all people, but on a personal level too. Every day she looked forward to the minute the blue-and-silver truck rumbled into her yard, and he swung down from the cab and ambled in that cowboy gait of his up to the front porch. She relished their working side by side. She enjoyed looking into his silvery eyes and listening to the low rumble of his manly voice. She appreciated his strength and his kindness.

She cared, and the admission unsettled her. He was too wounded, too broken, and too much in love with a dead wife for her to chance caring too much. She could be a friend and a shoulder to cry on, but that was all she could let herself be.

Jesse gripped the edge of the bench, needing Lindsey's compassion and afraid of flying apart if he accepted it. Now that he'd begun the awful telling, there was no way he could stop. Like blood from a gaping wound, the words flowed out.

"Three blocks from our house a drunk driver hit her, head-on."

He'd been sitting in his recliner, Jade curled against him watching Rudolph when the sirens had broken the silent night. He'd never forget the fleeting bit of sympathy he'd felt for any poor soul who needed an ambulance on Christmas Eve. Safe and warm in his living room, he had no way of knowing the holiday had chosen him—again—for heartache.

"A neighbor came, pounding on the door and yelling. She'd seen the wreck, knew it was Erin's car. I ran." He didn't know why he'd done that. A perfectly good truck sat in the driveway, but he hadn't even thought of driving to the scene. "Like a fool, I ran those three blocks, thinking I could stop anything bad from happening to my family."

He relived that helpless moment when he'd pushed past policemen, screaming that Erin was his wife. He recalled the feel of their hands on him, trying to stop him, not wanting him to see.

"She was gone." Stomach sick from the memory, he shoved up from the bench, unable to share the rest. Lindsey was perceptive. She'd understand that he'd witnessed a sight no man should have to see. His beautiful wife crushed and mangled, the Christmas gifts she'd given her life for scattered along the highway, a testament to the violence of the impact.

Back turned, he clenched his fists and told the part that haunted him still.

"The present she'd gone after was mine." He'd wanted the fancy Western belt with his named engraved on the back, had hoped she'd order it for him. Now the belt remained in its original box, unused, a reminder that Erin had died because of him.

"Now you know why I feel the way I do about Christmas." He spoke to the rows and rows of evergreens, though he knew Lindsey listened. He could feel her behind him, full of compassion and care. When she laid a consoling hand on his back, he was glad. He needed her touch. "Jade and I both have too many bad memories of Christmas to celebrate anything."

Jesse looked toward the wagon which had already been outfitted for hauling visitors through the grove. Jade had crawled beneath the down quilt and lay softly singing along with the music, waving her hands in the air like a conductor. He'd somehow tuned out the carols until then.

Lindsey's hand soothed him, making small circles on his back. "Don't you want Jade to remember her mother?"

"Of course I do. How could you ask me that?"

"You said Erin loved Christmas and wanted the holiday to be special for you and Jade. Those times with her mother are important to Jade, and Christmas is one of the best memories of all."

Not for him. And not for Jade either.

"I'd never take away her memories of Erin," he said gruffly.

"When you refuse to let her have a Christmas tree, you're telling her child's mind to forget her mother and to forget all those wonderful times with her."

"That's not true," he denied vehemently. "I'm protecting her. I don't want her to relive that terrible night every Christmas."

"Are you talking about Jade? Or yourself?"

He opened his mouth to refute the very idea that he was protecting himself instead of Jade. But words wouldn't come.

"You can't allow your own pain to keep Jade from having a normal childhood." Her warm, throaty voice implored him.

"I'd never do that," he said, but the denial sounded weak. With growing angst, he realized Lindsey could be right. In his self-focused pain, he'd hurt his little girl, denying her the right to remember her mother laughing beneath the tree on Christmas morning, the three of them dancing to "Jingle Bell Rock."

He squeezed his eyes closed as memories washed over him.

"Not intentionally, but don't you realize that she reads everything you do or don't do, interpreting your actions in her childish understanding? She wants to have Christmas, but she worries about you."

A great blue heron winged past, headed to the pond. Out in the pasture, the black horse grazed on an enormous round bale of hay, summer's green grass a memory.

"I don't want her worrying about me."

"You can't stop her. She wants you to be happy. She loves you. God loves you, too, Jesse, and He wants to help you get past this."

"I don't know how." And even if he did, he wondered if "getting past" Erin's death wouldn't somehow be disloyal.

"Erin's death wasn't your fault. Start there."

"I can't help thinking she would be alive if she hadn't gone shopping."

"Those are futile thoughts, Jesse. You would be better served to wonder how you can honor her life."

He turned toward her then. She'd hit upon the very thing he longed for. "I don't know how to do that either."

"You already are in one way. You're raising Jade to be a lovely child. But God has more for you. He wants you to have a life free of guilt and anger. Full of peace."

Jesse felt the tug of that peace emanating from his boss lady. A fierce longing to pray, something he hadn't done in two years, gnawed at him.

"Let's go choose a tree," Lindsey urged, holding out a hand. "For Jade."

He took a breath of clean mountain air and blew it out, his chest heavy and aching. He could do this for his baby. A Christmas tree wasn't that big a deal, was it? He'd worked in the things for a couple of months now without dying.

His eyes drifted over the acres of pines, noting one

major difference. These were bare. If he took a Christmas tree back to the trailer, Jade would want to decorate it.

He turned his attention to the wagon where his brave little trooper no longer sang and conducted. Huddled down into the quilt, her black hair tousled, she lay sleeping.

Last Christmas, the first anniversary of Erin's death, he'd done his best to ignore the holiday altogether. Erin's family, far away in Kentucky had sent gifts, but he'd tossed them in the garbage before Jade had seen them. The few times she'd mentioned presents, he'd reacted so harshly she'd quickly gotten the message that the subject of Christmas was off limits.

But she'd cried, too. And that forgotten memory of her tears tormented him.

Fighting down a rising sense of dread, Jesse took Lindsey's hand. "Let's go wake her."

Lindsey's quiet eyes studied him. "Are you okay with this?"

Though uncertain, he nodded.

They went to the wagon where Jade lay sleeping like an angel, her black hair a dark halo around her face. Sooty lashes curved upon her weather-rosy cheeks. One arm hugged the covers, rising and falling with the rhythm of her silent breath.

"Look at her, Jesse. You have so much to be thankful for. I know people who'd give anything to have a child like Jade." Her voice grew wistful. "Including me."

Her soft-looking lips turned down, one of the rare times he'd seen her unhappy. He didn't like seeing her sad.

"I thought you were perfectly content up here alone." They spoke in hushed tones so as not to startle the sleeping child. But the quiet created an intimacy that made him feel closer to Lindsey than he had to anyone in a long time.

"I'm learning to be content in the Lord, but that doesn't mean I don't think about having a family someday."

Something stirred inside Jesse. Lindsey would make a great mother—and a good wife to the right man. Someday one of those holy churchgoers who'd never committed a sin in his life would marry her.

Already miserable with the forthcoming Christmas tree, he didn't want to think about Lindsey with some other man.

Fighting off the uncomfortable thoughts, he stroked a knuckle down Jade's cheek. "Hey, Butterbean. Wake up. Ready to get that Christmas tree?"

His little girl blinked, her green eyes sleepy and confused, but filled with a hope that seared him. "Really?"

With a nod, he swallowed hard and helped her down from the wagon. As if she expected the offer to be rescinded at any moment, Jade wasted no time. She grabbed each adult by the hand and pulled them toward the grove.

An hour later, laden with lights and tinsel and lacy

white angel ornaments Lindsey had given Jade from a box in her Christmas building, they'd headed back to the trailer. Jade had been ecstatic over the three-foot tree, raising the level of Jesse's guilt as well as his anxiety. All the way into town he'd wondered if he could actually go through with it, if he could spend a month staring at a reminder of all he'd lost.

In the end he'd been a coward, placing the small, shining tree in Jade's bedroom where he wouldn't have to see it. His child had been so thrilled with the thing, she hadn't questioned the reason. He'd nearly broken, though, when she'd crawled exhausted beneath her covers, the sweetest smile on earth lifting her bow mouth. "Is it okay if I say a prayer and thank Jesus for my tree and all my guarding angels?"

"Sure, baby, sure."

Long after she'd fallen asleep, he'd sat in the trailer's tiny living room, staring blindly at the paneled wall.

What had he gotten himself into? Lindsey Mitchell with her sweetness and overwhelming decency was tearing him apart. His frozen heart had begun to thaw. And like blood-flow returning to frost-bitten fingers, the sensation was pure torture.

Chapter Eight

Jesse was tired, bone-weary. A basket of laundry at his feet, he sat on the plastic couch in his mobile home folding clothes. Jade was in her tiny excuse of a bedroom playing with a small dollhouse borrowed from Lindsey.

After the busy Thanksgiving weekend, he'd worked half of last night, and even though the tree farm was jumping this morning, he'd knocked off at noon. He felt bad about leaving Lindsey alone with the customers, but he had business to attend to.

Then he'd spent hours in the courthouse and on the telephone, leaking out bits of himself to strangers in exchange for information about his stepfather. One conversation had given him the name of a backwoods lawyer who'd been around eighteen years ago. A lawyer with a drinking problem who'd been known to do "buddy deals." Trouble was, no one remembered where the man had gone when he'd left Winding Stair years ago.

His stomach growled and he tried to remember if he'd eaten today. Probably not. Lindsey usually forced lunch on him, but he'd left too early for that.

He needed answers worse than he needed food. Day after day in Lindsey's company was starting to scare him. And for all the good she'd done his child, Jade was getting too attached. He had to bring this situation to an end soon.

A sudden knock rattled the entire trailer. Tossing aside a worn towel, he went to answer the door, bristling at the sight of his oversized visitor. Preacher Cliff whatever-his-name-was. No wonder the trailer had shaken under the pounding. So Lindsey had betrayed his confidence and sicced her minister on him. Preparing for an onslaught of unwanted advice, pat answers and sympathy for his loss, he opened the door.

"Hey Jesse, how are you doing?"

Jesse accepted the warm handshake and exchanged greetings. "Come on in."

Not that he really wanted the preacher in his house, but he didn't want to upset Lindsey either.

"No, no. I can't stay. The men are working on the church Christmas display tonight, and Karen threatened not to feed me if I was late to supper." He gave a hearty laugh and tapped his belly. "Can't be starving the skinny little preacher."

In spite of himself, Jesse smiled. It was hard not to like Lindsey's pastor.

"I hate to bother you with this," Cliff went on, "but Lindsey tells me you're a whiz with electrical hookups. Brags to everyone about you. We're having a bit of trouble at the church getting our display to work right, and she thought you might be willing to have a look."

Jesse's first impulse was to say no and slam the door, but the preacher's words soaked through first. Lindsey bragged about him to other people?

In spite of himself he asked, "Any idea what's gone wrong?"

"Aw, I don't know. Clarence and Mick seemed to think the problem is in the breaker box, but we can't fix it."

Jesse squinted in contemplation. "Clarence and Mick will be there?"

"They're at the church right now. That's why I came by to talk to you. They're at their wits' end with this thing."

Clarence Stone was a man who'd been around a while, a man who might know more about the lawyer, Stuart Hardwick. Spending time in his company, even at a church, could be worth the effort. And he'd seen Mick Thompson several times since the cookout weeks ago and liked the guy. He wasn't one of those preachy kind of Christians who didn't know how to get his hands dirty. And their common interest in horses might someday lead to friendship. He'd need a friend when he regained the land that Lindsey now called home.

Ignoring the pinch of regret that grew worse each time he thought of Lindsey's reaction to losing the farm, he looked at his watch. "I'll head over there now, see what I can do."

Cliff clapped Jesse on the shoulder. "Great. I'll meet you in the parking lot."

Jesse knew where Winding Stair Chapel was located and, after collecting Jade and her dolls and making sure his tools were in the truck, drove to the church.

Three other pickups were parked outside the native-rock building. Their owners were scattered around the outside of the church at various projects. They'd set up a life-sized nativity and lined the railed walkway from the parking area to the entrance with luminaries. The two huge evergreens standing sentry on each corner of the lot had been draped with lights, and the outline of an enormous star rose high over the chapel. A man wearing a leather tool belt balanced on the roof, laboring over the star.

The men had gone to a lot of trouble, and from the looks of things, they were far from finished.

He was surprised to find himself here, at a church. Not that he didn't believe in God, but part of him wondered if God believed in him. He'd felt empty for such a long time.

"Man, are we glad to see you," Mick Thompson called as soon as Jesse and Jade exited the pickup. "Help's on the way, boys," he bellowed to the remaining men. "Lindsey's expert is here."

Lindsey's expert? The friendly greeting buoyed

Jesse. As tired as he was, he wanted to help if possible. "I'll do what I can. What's the main trouble?"

Clarence Stone waved his arms at a latticework of electrical circuitry spread over the churchyard. "Everything. We're all hooked up, cords and wires are run, but the angels won't flutter and Baby Jesus won't shine."

Jesse squelched his amusement at the old man's joking manner.

"Show me your electrical setup and where all the breakers are. I have my tester and tool pouch in the truck. Maybe we can find the source of the problem and work from there."

Boots crunching across the gravel drive, Mick motioned toward the lighted building. "My wife is in the Sunday school preparing next week's lesson. Your little girl can play with my kids if she wants to. Clare will keep an eye on her while you're busy."

Jade jumped at the chance and was taken inside by the giant preacher who'd wheeled in behind Jesse. It did Jesse's heart good to see Jade willing to be out of his sight for a few minutes.

"Breaker box is in the church office," Clarence said and led Jesse down the long hall to the back of the church. To Jesse, the older man's presence and eager conversation was a stroke of good luck.

"The tree farm hopping yet?" Clarence asked as Jesse stepped up on a ladder to examine the box that housed the breakers. He unscrewed four screws and removed the face plate.

Jesse nodded, concentration riveted more on

testing the voltage to the breakers than on the conversation. "We've been real busy since Thanksgiving."

Clarence peered upward, leaning an arm against the rock wall below Jesse. "I reckon Lindsey's in her element. Never seen a child love Christmas the way she does. Been that way ever since I knew her."

"How long has that been?" Jesse said the words casually, never taking his eyes off the readings. The breakers had power. The problem was likely in the attic.

"Ever since she moved in with Charlie and Betty Jean. Before that really. I'd see her now and again when she and her folks came to visit."

"Lindsey thought a lot of her Grandma and Grandpa Mitchell." He flipped the main breaker to the off position.

"Mitchell?" Clarence stared up at him, puzzled for a moment. "You mean Baker, not Mitchell. Mitchell was the other side of the family. I never knew them. Now Charlie and me, we was good friends. Hauled hay with each other. Things like that."

As Clarence rattled on about his friendship with Lindsey's grandfather, the light came on inside Jesse's head. The volt meter trembled in his fingers as adrenaline zipped through him. No wonder he'd had such a hard time finding data. He'd been looking under the wrong name.

"I suppose the Bakers have owned that farm for generations." He knew better, but figured tossing the idea out in the open would keep Clarence talking.

"Nah. Charlie bought the place when he retired from the phone company. Let's see..." Clarence squinted at the ceiling, rubbing his chin. "'Bout twenty years ago, I reckon. Before that a man name of Finch owned it, if memory serves. I didn't know him too well. Not a friendly sort. Charlie started the tree farm."

Les Finch. Jesse's gut clenched. No, his stepfather wasn't a friendly sort unless a man had a bottle of whiskey or something else he wanted. And he had never owned the farm, either, but he'd wanted everyone to think he did.

Carefully, he guided the subject away from Les Finch. No use helping Clarence remember the boy who'd lived on that farm with the unfriendly Finch.

"I have an idea what the problem is, but I need to get up in the attic." He looked around, saw the opening and moved the ladder beneath.

Clarence followed along, eager to help and full of chatter, but otherwise basically useless. "Think you can fix it?"

Taking his flashlight from his tool pouch, Jesse shoved the attic door open and poked his head into the dark space above. The problem was right in front of him. "Should have the power up and running in no time."

Clarence clapped his hands. "Lindsey said you would. She sure thinks highly of you, and that means something to us around here. Lindsey's like her grandma. Has a heart of gold and will do about anything for anybody. But she don't trust just everyone. Kinda got a sore spot where that's concerned."

A sore spot? Lindsey? Tilting his face downward at the old farmer, curiosity piqued, he asked, "Why do you say that?"

"Well, I reckon you'll hear it if you stay around here long enough, though I'm not surprised Lindsey didn't tell you herself. Some things are kinda painful to discuss."

Jesse concentrated on repairing a ground wire that had been chewed in half by some varmint, likely a squirrel, but every fiber of his being was tuned in to Clarence.

"Some college fella without a lick of sense or decency broke her heart a few years back. Poor little thing come crying home all tore up and hasn't left that farm for more than a day or two since. Sometimes I think she's hiding out up there so no one can hurt her again."

Jesse wrestled with the need to punch something but used his energy to splice the line and wrap the ends with insulated tape. His blood boiled to think of Lindsey crying over some snot-nosed college boy.

"I've never noticed anything wrong." But that wasn't exactly true. Hadn't he seen the shadows in her eyes when she talked about wanting a child like Jade? "She seems happy enough."

"Naturally. She's got the Lord. I don't know how folks that don't know the Lord get by when hard times come."

Jesse was beginning to wonder that himself.

"I figure she's over the guy by now." At least, he hoped so. He collected his tools, placing each one in his pouch.

"No doubt about that. She's a strong young woman, but the heartache of having her fiancé get some other girl pregnant while she was away making money for the wedding, won't ever leave her. That's why I say trust don't come easy."

Jesse's pliers clattered to the tile below. He clenched his fists as anger, swift and hot, bubbled up in him. What kind of low-life would do such a thing? Gentle, loving Lindsey, who gave and helped and never asked for anything in return, shouldn't have been treated so cruelly. She must have been crushed at such betrayal from the man she loved and trusted.

Clumping down the ladder, he went to the breaker box, insides raging at the injustice. A good woman like Lindsey deserved better.

As he flipped the breaker switch, illuminating the darkening churchyard, the awful truth hit him like a bolt of electricity. Lindsey trusted him, too. And he was going to hurt her almost as much.

Lindsey was happy enough to sing—and so she did—inside the Snack Shack, as she liked to call the small building where she and Jade served hot apple cider and Christmas cookies to their "guests." Gaily bedecked with holiday cheer, the cozy room boasted a long table where customers could warm up and enjoy the music and atmosphere while Jesse baled their chosen tree and Lindsey rang up their sale.

At present, a family of five occupied the room, admiring Lindsey's miniature Christmas village while they munched and waited. They'd had their ride through the grove, all of them singing at the top of their lungs, the children so full of excited energy they kept hopping off the wagon to run along beside. Their unfettered cheer delighted Lindsey and had even brightened Jesse's usually serious countenance.

Jade, catching the good mood, had agreed to let Sushi roam free as long as Jesse was within sight.

Yes, Lindsey's life was full. Not since before Gramps died had the holidays seemed so merry.

The door flew open and Jesse stepped inside, rubbing his gloveless hands together. A swirl of winter wind followed him. The collar of his fleece-lined jacket turned up, framing his handsome face.

An extra jolt of energy shot through Lindsey. More and more lately, Jesse's presence caused that inexplicable reaction. With a simple act like walking into a room, he made her world brighter.

Two nights ago he'd solved a problem with the electricity at the church, and she'd been so proud of him. He was smart and resourceful and the hardest, most honest worker anyone could ask for.

"Daddy!" Jade charged from behind the homemade counter where she'd been doling out gingerbread men. "Want a cookie?"

Lindsey grinned. Jade had forced the sweets on

him every time he'd entered the building. He never stayed long, just grabbed the cookie and ran. Even though he had been busy with a steady stream of customers all night, she suspected that the holiday atmosphere still bothered him.

"I'm stuffed, Butterbean." Absently patting her head, he said to the eagerly waiting family, "Your tree's ready to go. It's a beauty."

After giving the kids a few more cookies and the man a set of tree-care instructions, she, Jade and Jesse escorted the family out into the clear, cold night. Together they stood, Jade between them, watching the car pull away. For a moment, as cries of "Merry Christmas" echoed across through the crisp air, Lindsey had the fleeting thought that this is what it would be like if the three of them were a family bidding goodbye to friends after a fun-filled visit.

A gust of wind, like an icy hand, slapped against her.

Flights of fancy were uncharacteristic of someone as practical as she. And yet, here she stood, in the nippy, pine-scented night, behaving as if Jesse and Jade belonged to her. The need for family had never weighed as heavy nor had the longing been so great.

Wise enough to recognize the symptoms, Lindsey struggled to hold her emotions in check, to fight down the rising ache of need. She loved the dark-haired child clinging to her hand. And she had feelings for Jesse, though she refused to give those feelings a name.

Jesse was good help, and he was great company,

but they were too different. His grief for his late wife, coupled with his ambivalence toward God, were all the roadblocks the Lord needed to put in her way. She had ignored the signs before. She wouldn't let herself be that foolish again.

The evening's pleasure seeped away. Maybe she wasn't meant to have a family. Maybe the Lord intended her to be alone, growing trees for other families to enjoy, and sharing her maternal love with the children from her church. After the foolish mistakes she'd made with Sean, perhaps the Lord didn't trust her to make that kind of decision.

Jesse pulled Jade against him to block the wind and tugged her coat closed, though his mind was on Lindsey. He felt her sudden withdrawal as if she'd turned and walked away. When the customers pulled out of the drive she'd been laughing and happy, but now her shoulders slumped, and she stared into the distance like a lost puppy.

"Are you okay?"

"Tired, I guess." She pulled the hood of her car coat up and snapped the chin strap.

Sure she was tired. Had to be after the long days of hard work they'd been putting in. Though things would settle down after the holidays, this was the busiest time of year for the farm. He knew for a fact she was up every morning with the sun and worked on the books long after he went home. He'd tried to take more of the physical labor on himself, but when he did she added something else to her own chore list. Still, he had a feeling more than exhaustion weighed her down tonight.

"Let's close up. It's nearly ten anyway." They normally locked the gates and cut the lights at ten.

Solemn-faced, she nodded. "I'll unharness Puddin' and get him settled."

As she turned to go, Jesse reached out and caught her elbow. He had the sudden and troublesome yearning to guide her against his chest and ask what was wrong. Not a smart idea, but an enticing one.

"You and Jade take care of things inside," he said. "I'll tend to Puddin' and the outdoor chores."

The wind whipped a lock of hair from beneath her hood and sent it fluttering across her mouth. Tempted to catch the wayward curl, to feel the silky softness against his skin, Jesse shoved his hands into his pockets.

"Come inside and warm up first," she said, tucking the stray hair back in place. "You've been out in this wind all evening."

So had she for the most part, but he didn't argue. A warm drink and a few minutes of rest wouldn't hurt him and it would please her. Funny how pleasing Lindsey seemed important tonight.

Inside the building, Jesse stood amidst the cheery knickknacks breathing in the scents of cinnamon and pine and apples. The room reeked of Lindsey and the things she enjoyed. If he wanted to stop thinking about her—and he did—here among her decorations was not the place to do it.

Normally, the Snack Shack and all the holiday folderol depressed him, but depression plagued him less and less lately. He'd figured he was just too busy and tired to notice, but now he worried that Lindsey and not fatigue had taken the edge off his sorrow.

To avoid that line of thinking, he gazed around the room at the lighted candles, the holly rings, and all the other festive things that Lindsey loved. Looking at them didn't hurt so much anymore.

"You ought to put a little gift shop in here." He didn't know where that had come from.

"I've thought about it, but never had enough help to handle gifts and the trees." Lindsey was behind the counter helping Jade seal leftover cookies into zip-up bags.

"You should consider the idea."

"Too late this year. Maybe next."

Jesse could see the notion, coming from him, pleased her. He had other ideas that would please her, too. Some he'd shared, like the concept of developing a Website for the farm and using the Internet for free marketing. He'd even volunteered to start tinkering with designs after the rush season.

Lifting a glass angel, he turned the ornament in his hands. What was happening to him? Why was he thinking such ridiculous, useless thoughts?

Lindsey didn't need a Web site or advertising or even a gift shop. This time next year she and her Christmas trees would be long gone. That's the way it had to be. Justice would be served. He'd have his home...and his revenge.

The tender, loving expression on the angel's face mocked him. Discomfited, he put the ornament back on the shelf.

Lindsey bustled around the counter, carrying a steaming cup. "Cider?"

Her inner light was back on, and he was glad. Taking the warm mug, he smiled his thanks and waited like a child expecting candy for her to return the smile.

His fingers itched to touch her smooth skin, and this time, before he could change his mind, he cupped her cheek. A question sprang to her eyes—a question he couldn't answer because he didn't understand himself.

Dropping his hand, he avoided her gaze and pretended to sip the warm drink. Ever since Clarence had told him of Lindsey's cheating fiancé, he'd struggled against the need to take her in his arms and promise that no one would ever hurt her that way again. The reaction made no sense at all.

A strange energy pulsed in the space between them and he knew she waited for him to say something, to explain his uncharacteristic behavior. But how could he explain what he didn't understand?

He felt her move away, wanted to call her back, wanted to say...what? That he liked her? That he was attracted to her?

He heard her murmuring to Jade, but his head buzzed so much he couldn't make out the conversation. He sipped the sweet cider, hoping to wash away his deranged thoughts. Attracted? No way. Couldn't happen.

He looked up to find Lindsey gathering his drowsy daughter into her arms. Most nights Jade fell asleep long before closing and Lindsey put her to bed on an air mattress behind the counter. Tonight being Friday, Jade had stayed awake as long as possible, but a few moments of quiet stillness had done her in.

His baby girl snuggled into Lindsey's green flannel, eyes drooping as she relaxed, contented and comfortable. Expression tender, his boss lady brushed a kiss onto Jade's peaceful forehead. They looked so right together, this woman and his child.

Something dangerous moved inside Jesse's chest. A thickness lodged in his throat. Lindsey Mitchell was slowly worming her way into his heart.

A war raged within him. He couldn't fall in love with Lindsey. He couldn't even allow attraction. To do so would betray Erin's memory and interfere with his plans for restitution and revenge. He was within arm's reach of everything he'd dreamed of for years. He and Jade deserved this place. No matter how sweet Lindsey Mitchell might be, he would not be distracted.

Once he'd discovered Lindsey's grandfather's real name, he had easily found the information he needed. Sure enough, Stuart Hardwick, the crooked lawyer, had done the deal. When'd he'd told the court clerk this morning that he'd been searching under the wrong name, she'd curled her lip in reproach. "Coulda told you that if you'd asked."

Now that a clerk knew he was searching Lindsey's farm records, it was only a matter of time before word leaked out and Lindsey knew his intent. He thought about going to the sheriff with what he knew, but a confession from Hardwick would settle matters more quickly. He needed to find Stuart Hardwick first—and fast.

He took one last glance at Lindsey.

He was too close to the truth to let anything—or anyone—stop him now.

Hardening his heart, he went out into the cold night.

Chapter Nine

Waving a paper, Jade barreled down the lane, pink backpack thumping against her purple coat.

"Lindsey. Lindsey! Can you make a costume?"

On her knees, clearing away the remains of a tree stump, Lindsey braced as Jade tumbled against her. Mother love too fierce to deny rose inside her. Jade needed her love and attention, regardless of the sorrow Lindsey would someday suffer when the child was gone. She wasn't foolish enough to think a man of Jesse's talents would always work for minimum wage.

"What kind of costume, sweetie?"

"An angel. An angel." Jade's excitement had her fluttering around waving her arms like wings. "I'm the guarding angel for Jesus."

Every year the elementary school put on a Christmas program. The conclusion of the play was traditionally a nativity scene with the singing of "Silent Night" by the entire audience. Once there had been talk of removing the religious scene from the school, but such an outcry arose that the tradition remained. The town loved it, expected it, and turned out en masse to see the little ones dressed in sparkly, colorful costumes. Jade, with her milky skin and black hair, would be a beautiful angel.

Jesse came around the end of a row where he'd been cutting trees for a grocer who had requested a second load.

"What's all the noise about?" he demanded, his expression teasingly fierce. "I can't even hear my chain saw with you two carrying on this way."

Jade threw her arms around his legs and repeated her request for an angel costume. The fun drained out of Jesse's face.

"Lindsey's too busy with the farm," he said shortly.

Jade's happy expression fell, and Lindsey couldn't bear to see her disappointment.

Jesse had behaved strangely all day, his manner brusque and distant. He'd even refused their usual lunch break of sandwiches in the Snack Shack, saying he'd eat later. But there was no reason for him to dim Jade's happiness.

"Making a costume for Jade would be my pleasure. You know that."

"Don't bother yourself." Jesse spun away and started back into the trees.

"Jesse." She caught up to him, touched his arm.

"I'd love to make the costume for Jade. What's wrong with you today?"

"You're not her mother. Stop trying to be."

Stricken to the core, Lindsey cringed and pressed a shaky hand to her lips. Was that what he thought? That she wanted to take Erin's place?

Jesse shoved both hands over his head. "Look. I shouldn't have said that. I'm sorry. It's just that—" His expression went bleak. He squeezed his eyes closed. "No excuses. I'm sorry."

"Daddy." Jade, whom they'd both momentarily forgotten, slipped between them, tears bright in her green eyes. "It's okay. I don't have to be in the play."

Lindsey thought her heart would break—for the child, for herself and even for the troubled man.

Jesse fell to his knees in front of Jade and gripped her fiercely to him, his face a mask of regret. "Daddy didn't mean it, Butterbean. You can be in the play."

Over her dark head, he gazed at Lindsey desolately. "Make the costume. It would mean a lot to both of us."

Throat thick with unshed tears, Lindsey nodded, confused and hurt. She'd never intended to touch a nerve. She'd only wanted to see the little girl happy.

Pushing Jade away a little, Jesse smoothed her dark hair, leaving both hands cupped around her face. "You'll be the prettiest angel in the program. Lindsey will make sure of that." He raised pleading eyes. "Won't you, Lindsey?"

Like the Oklahoma weather, Jesse had changed

from anger to remorse. Bewildered and reeling from his sharp accusation, Lindsey's stomach churned. But not wanting Jade to suffer any more disappointment, she swallowed her own hurt and agreed. "Jade and I can shop for materials tomorrow after school if that's okay."

She felt tentative with him in a way she never had before. What had brought on this vicious outburst in the first place?

"Whatever you decide is fine. Anything." Rising, he turned Jade toward the Snack Shack. Lindsey knew their conversation wasn't over, but he didn't want the little girl to hear any more. "Better head up there and do your homework. You and Lindsey can talk about the costume later."

With the resilience of childhood, Jade started toward the building, but froze when the German shepherd bolted from the trees to follow.

"Sushi!" Lindsey commanded. "Come." The disappointed dog obeyed, coming to flop in disgust at Lindsey's feet. Jade was making progress, but not enough to be alone in the building with the animal.

As soon as the door closed behind his daughter, Jesse said, "You have been nothing but good to Jade and me. I had no right to snap at you, to say such an awful thing."

"I'm not trying to replace Erin," she said quietly.

"I know. I'm sorry." Absently, he stroked the adoring dog, his body still stiff with tension. "How can I make it up to you?"

"Forget it ever happened." She smiled, perhaps a bit tremulously, although she felt better knowing he hadn't intended to hurt her. "And I'll do the same."

His jaw tightened. Her forgiveness seemed to anger him. "Don't be so nice all the time, Lindsey. When someone treats you like dirt, take up for yourself."

She wanted to disagree. Arguing over small injustices and taking offense served no good that she could see, but Jesse seemed bent on picking a fight. And she refused to play into his bad mood. "I don't understand you today."

"Welcome to the club." He shoved his hands in his pockets and looked up at the gray-blue sky. "I'm a jerk, Lindsey. You should fire me."

She longed to comfort him, though she was the wounded party. Normally, Jesse was easygoing and pleasant company. More than pleasant company, if she admitted the truth. But something was terribly wrong today, and getting her back up wasn't the solution.

"Your job is safe. I can't get along without you."

The Freudian slip resounded in the chilly afternoon air. She not only couldn't get along without him, she didn't want to. He'd become too important.

Resisting the urge to smooth her fingers over the rigid line of his jaw and tell him that, another wayward notion drifted through her mind. Jesse Slater, even in a bad mood, was a better man than her former fiancé would ever be. Her stomach hurt to make the comparison, but the ache cleared when she realized that no matter what torment beat inside

Jesse, he was too honorable to do the kind of things Sean had done. Jesse knew when he was wrong and apologized. Sean never had.

His gaze riveted on the sky, Jesse's quiet voice was filled with repressed emotion. "Do you think God plays favorites?"

Lindsey blinked. Where had that come from? And what did it have to do with sewing an angel costume? "Do you?"

"Sure seems that way."

"Is that what's bothering you today? You think God doesn't care about you as much as he does other people?"

"I've wondered." A muscle twitched along one cheekbone. "But maybe I don't deserve it."

She ran her fingertips over the soft needles of the closest tree, praying for the right words to help her friend. "Jesus loved us—all of us—so much he died for us."

"I've been giving that a lot of thought lately." He studied the ground as if the Oklahoma dirt held the answers to the mysteries of the universe. "But not everyone is as good as you are, Lindsey. Definitely not me."

Lindsey's pulse did a stutter-step.

"I'm not perfect, Jesse," she said. "I've done things I'm not proud of, too."

Picking up her shears, she clipped at a wayward branch, unable to look at Jesse but compelled to share. "I was engaged once."

Snip. Snip. She swallowed, nervous. "And I did things I regret. I trusted the wrong man, telling myself that love made our actions all right." She snipped again, saw the shears tremble. "But that was a mistake. He was a mistake."

Jesse's work-hardened hand closed over hers, gently taking the clippers. "Lindsey."

Her gaze flew to his face.

She wondered if she had disappointed him, but Jesse needed to understand that she had made her share of wrong choices—and yet God loved her.

Fire flashed in Jesse's silvery eyes. "The man," he said, "was a moron."

Sweet relief washed through Lindsey. Jesse wasn't angry *at* her. He was angry *for* her.

"So was I. Then. But God forgave me, and eventually I forgave myself." She reached for the cutters, her fingers grazing his. "He'll do the same for you."

"Yeah. Well…" Jesse let the words drift away.

She knew he'd tried to serve God in the past, but had drifted away when Erin died. Understandable, but so backwards. She'd learned the hard way to run *to* the Lord when trouble struck instead of away from Him.

They stood in silence, contemplative for a bit until Jesse bent to retrieve the chain saw.

"Guess we better get back to work if I'm going to haul that load in the morning."

For all the conversation, trouble still brooded over him like a dark cloud.

"Jesse."

He paused.

"Is there anything else bothering you?" she asked, certain that there was. "Anything I can help with?"

Silver eyes studied her for several long seconds. He took her hand and squeezed it. "I'm grateful to you, Lindsey. No matter what happens. Remember that."

Puzzled by the strange declaration, Lindsey waited for him to say more, but before he could, a truck rumbled through the gate, and the moment was gone. As if relieved by the interruption, Jesse hurried to greet the customer.

She'd seen so much change in Jesse since the day he'd first driven into her yard asking for a job. She'd watched him grow more comfortable with her talk of God. He was easier around the Christmas decorations too, and since telling her of Erin's death, he'd opened up some about his feelings of guilt in that department. And he smiled more too.

But today, regardless of his denial, Jesse battled something deep and worrisome. And given his peculiar behavior, she had a bad feeling that his troubles had something to do with her.

Heat from the farmhouse embraced Jesse as he came through the door. The dog, curled beside the living room furnace, lifted her head, recognized him, and lay down again with a heavy sigh. Jesse stood for a moment in the doorway, taking in the warm, homey comfort of this place. A sense of déjà vu came over him, a subconscious memory of long ago when the world had been right.

The aroma of roast beef tickled his nose and made his hungry stomach growl. The tree patch was quiet, only one buyer since noon, and Lindsey had knocked off early to make Jade's costume and cook supper for them all. After his behavior the other day, he found it hard to refuse her anything.

Jade's giggle blended with Lindsey's rich laugh in a sweet music that had Jesse longing to hear it again and again. They were at the table, happily laboring over some kind of gauzy white material and yards of sparkly gold tinsel.

He'd been wrong to jump on Lindsey about making the costume and even more wrong to accuse of her trying to take Erin's place. No one could do that. But Lindsey's love and motherly care was changing Jade for the better. Only a fool would deny or resent the obvious.

And he'd almost told Lindsey the truth. He'd yearned to admit that her farm was his and that he wanted it back. The torment was eating him alive because, to get what he wanted, he had to break Lindsey's heart. He'd tried praying, as she had suggested, but his prayers bounced off the ceiling and mocked him.

Lindsey spotted him, then, standing in the doorway, watching. Her full mouth lifted. "You look frozen."

He gave a shiver for effect. The temperature had

plummeted into the twenties, unusual for this part of the country. Working outside in the Oklahoma wind proved a challenge.

"I thought you could make that costume in an hour?"

"I can. But I'm teaching Jade."

Stripping off his heavy coat, he came on into the kitchen. "Isn't she too little for sewing?"

"Daddy!" Insulted, Jade jammed a saucy hand onto a hip. "I have to learn sometime. Besides, I'm the tryer-on-er."

Amused, he tilted his head in apology. "I stand corrected."

"We'll have the body of the gown finished in a few minutes. Coffee's on and Cokes are in the fridge. Whichever you want."

No matter how cold the weather, Jesse liked his cola. Going to the refrigerator, he took one, popped the top and turned to watch the womenfolk do their thing.

Patiently, Lindsey held the gauzy fabric beneath the sewing-machine needle, demonstrating how to move the gown without sewing her own fingers. She looked so pretty with her honey hair falling forward, full lips pursed in concentration. He'd been right the first time he'd seen her. Lindsey, beneath her flannel and denim, was very much a woman.

He sipped his cola, wanting to look away, but he couldn't. Watching Lindsey gave him too much pleasure.

When the seam was sewn, Jade took the scissors and proudly clipped the thread.

"There you go, Miss Angel." Lindsey held the white flowing garment against Jade's body. "Perfect fit."

Jade looked doubtful. "Where's the wings?"

"We'll do those after supper. Jesse, if you'll move the machine, we can set the table."

"Anything to hurry the food." He unplugged the old Singer that must have belonged to her grandmother, and hefted it into Lindsey's spare room.

"Tell me your part again," Lindsey was saying as he came back into the kitchen.

"Below the angel's shining light, love was born on Christmas night," Jade recited, slowly and with expression.

"You're going to be the very best speaker." Scooping the remaining materials off the table, Lindsey spoke to Jesse. "Isn't she, Dad?"

"No doubt about it." He hooked an arm around Jade's middle and hoisted her up. Her giggle made him smile. "And the prettiest angel, too."

"Are you going to come watch me?"

The question caught him by surprise. Slowly, he eased her down into a chair. "Well…I don't know, Jade. I'm awfully busy here at the tree farm."

Whipping around, a steaming bowl in one hand, Lindsey refused to let him use that excuse. "We'll be closed that night."

Jade was getting too involved with all this Christmas business. Next thing he knew, she'd be talking about Santa Claus and wanting to hang up stockings.

"I'm not much on Christmas programs. You two can go without me."

Both females looked at him with mild reproach. The room grew deafeningly quiet until only the tick of the furnace was heard.

Finally, Lindsey slapped a loaf of bread onto the table and turned on him. Her golden-brown eyes glowed with a hint of anger. "The program is important to Jade, and you need to be there. You might actually enjoy yourself."

He doubted that, but he didn't want Lindsey upset with him again. He was still battling guilt over the last time.

With a defeated sigh, he followed her to the stove, took the green peas from her and carried the bowl to the table.

"All right, Butterbean," he said, tapping Jade on the nose. "If the tree lot is closed, I'll be there."

"Really, Daddy?" The hope in her eyes did him in.

"Really."

Her beauteous smile lit the room and illuminated his heart.

As he drew his chair up to the table, the familiar gnaw of dread pulled at his stomach. A Christmas program. What had he gotten himself into?

The atmosphere at the Winding Stair Elementary School was one of controlled chaos. After dropping an angelic Jade at her classroom with a gaggle of lambs and ladybugs, Jesse followed Lindsey down the long hall to the auditorium. The noise of a community that knew each other well filled the place with cheer. Everyone they passed spoke to Lindsey and many, recognizing him, stopped to shake his hand and offer greetings.

He hadn't been to a school Christmas program since he was in grade school himself, but the buzz of excitement was the same.

At the door, a teenage girl in a red Santa hat offered him a program and a huge flirtatious smile.

"Hi, Lindsey," she said, though her eyelashes fluttered at him. He ignored her, staring ahead at the milieu of country folks gathered in this one place.

Lindsey greeted the girl warmly, then began the slow process of weaving through the crowd toward the seats. She'd been right. The program was a community event. Everyone was dressed up, the scent of recent showers and cologne a testament to the importance of Winding Stair's Christmas program.

"I think you have an admirer," Lindsey teased when they were seated.

He knew she meant the teenager at the door, but the idea insulted him. "She's a kid."

Lindsey laughed softly. "But she's not blind or stupid."

Surprised, he turned in the squeaky auditorium seat. What had she meant by that? But Lindsey had taken a sudden interest in studying the photocopied program.

"Look here." She pointed. "Jade is on stage for a long time."

"No kidding?" He looked over her shoulder with interest. The sweet scent of jasmine rose up from the vicinity of her elegant neck and tantalized his senses. From the time she'd climbed into his truck, he'd enjoyed the fragrance, but up close this way was even nicer.

She looked pretty tonight, too. He'd never seen her in a real dress and when she'd opened the front door, he'd lost his breath. Surprise, of course, nothing more. In honor of the occasion, she wore red, a smooth, sweater kind of dress that looked pretty with her honey-colored hair.

The lights flickered, a signal he supposed, for the crowd hushed and settled into their seats. The doors on each side of the auditorium closed and the principal stepped out in front of the blue velvet curtain to welcome everyone.

In moments, the curtains swooshed apart, and Jesse waited eagerly for the moment his baby would come on stage.

The program was festive and colorful and full of exuberant good will if not exceptional talent. Most of the children were animals of some sort and each group sang to the accompaniment of a slightly out-of-tune piano.

When two ladybugs bumped heads, entangling their antenna, Jesse laughed along with the rest of the crowd. A teacher scuttled from backstage, parted the antenna and with a smiling shrug, disappeared again. The children seemed unfazed.

Another time, one of the fireflies dropped his flashlight and the batteries came clattering out. To the delight of the audience, the little boy crawled through legs and around various other insects until he'd retrieved all the scattered parts of his illumination.

Despite his hesitancy to come tonight, Jesse was having a good time. None of the awful, tearing agony of loss overtook him as he'd expected. He had to credit Lindsey and his little angel for that.

"There she is," Lindsey whispered and pushed at his shoulder as if he couldn't see for himself the vision moving onto the stage.

Beneath the spotlight, his angel glittered and glowed in the costume Lindsey had so lovingly created. Her halo of tinsel shimmered against the shining raven hair as she bent to hover over the manger. Even from this distance, he could see her squinting into the crowd, looking for him.

In a sweet, bell-like voice, she spoke her lines, and Jesse reacted as if he hadn't heard them a thousand times in the past two weeks.

"Beneath the angel's shining light, love was born on Christmas night."

Tenderness rose in his throat, enough to choke him.

As he watched Jade, angel wings outstretched, join her class in singing "Silent Night," he thought his heart would burst with pride. Such sweetness. Such beauty. And he'd almost missed it.

Erin should have been here, too.

He waited for the familiar pain to come, and was surprised when it didn't.

Jade caught sight of him somehow and her entire face brightened. Had she thought he wouldn't stay?

With a start, he realized how wrong he'd been to let his own loss and pain affect his child's happiness and wellbeing. Huddled in his darkness, he'd let two years of Jade's life pass in a blur while he nursed his wounds and felt sorry for himself.

As the program ended and Jade was swept away in the thundering mass of first-graders, Jesse looked down. At some point during the play, he'd taken hold of Lindsey's hand and pulled it against his thigh. How had that happened? And why didn't he turn her loose now that the play was over? But with her small fingers wrapped in his, he was reluctant to let her go.

"She was wonderful," Lindsey said, eyes aglow as she turned to him.

"The best one of all."

"Of course." And they both laughed, knowing every parent in the room thought the same thing about his or her own child.

And even though she wasn't Jade's parent, Jesse knew Lindsey loved his daughter unreservedly.

Still holding her hand, and bewildered by his own actions, Jesse rose and began the shuffle out of the jammed auditorium and down the hall to the classrooms. There they collected Jade from the rambunctious crowd of first-graders and headed out the exit.

"Excuse me." A man about Jesse's age stopped

them as they started down the concrete steps. A vague sense of recognition stirred in Jesse's memory. "I saw you earlier and couldn't help thinking that I should know you? Did you ever go to school here?"

Jesse stiffened momentarily before forcing his shoulders to relax. No use getting in a panic. Play it cool. "Sorry. I'm a newcomer. Moved here back in October."

The man tilted his head, frowning. "You sure remind me of a kid I went to junior high with. Aw, but that's a long time ago."

"Well, you know what they say," Jesse shrugged, hoping he sounded more casual than he felt. "Everybody looks like someone."

"Ain't that the truth? My wife says I'm starting to resemble my hound dog more and more every day."

They all laughed, and then using the excuse of the cold wind, Jesse led the way to the truck. He'd been expecting that to happen. Sooner or later, someone was bound to recognize him from junior high school. He glanced at Lindsey as she slid into the pickup. Still smiling and fussing over Jade, she hadn't seemed to notice anything amiss.

Cranking the engine, he breathed a sigh of relief. That was a close one.

Chapter Ten

"Ice cream, Daddy. Pleeease." Jade, who'd begged to keep her costume on, bounced in the seat of the Silverado. She was still hyper, wired up from her very first Christmas program. With every bounce, her angel wings batted against Lindsey's shoulder.

Lindsey awaited Jesse's reply, hoping he'd see how much Jade needed a few more minutes of reveling in the moment.

Jesse shook his head as he turned on the defrosters. "Too cold for ice cream."

The three of them had rushed across the schoolyard to the parking lot, eager to escape the cold wind after the brief, but chill-producing delay by the man who'd thought Jesse looked familiar. The truck was running and heat had begun to blow from the vents, but they still shivered.

"Hot fudge will counter the cold," Lindsey suggested, casting a sideways grin at Jesse. "We gotta celebrate."

"You're no help," he said, rolling his silver eyes. "But if you ladies want ice cream, ice cream you shall have. Let's head to the Dairy Cup."

A quiver of satisfaction moved through Lindsey. Jesse had enjoyed tonight, she was certain. But what had really stunned her was when he'd reached over and grasped her hand. For a second, she'd almost forgotten where she was, though she doubted Jesse had meant anything by it. Most likely, he'd reached for her in reaction to Jade's thrilling grand entrance. Still, those moments of her skin touching his while they shared Jade's triumph lingered sweetly in her mind.

As the truck rumbled slowly down Main Street, her legs began to thaw.

"I'll be glad when the weather warms up again," she said.

Jesse's wrist relaxed over the top of the steering wheel. "Supposed to tomorrow, isn't it?"

"Some. But there's a chance of snow too."

"Snow!" Jade exclaimed and started bouncing again. "Can we make a snowman?"

Lindsey patted the child's knee. "Wouldn't be any fun unless we did."

Jesse glanced her way. "I have a load of trees to haul to Mena tomorrow. I hope we don't get snow before that's done."

"If it snows, you can't haul those trees. These mountain roads can be treacherous in snow or ice."

"Might as well get the job done. I have some other business to take care of in Mena, too."

His personal business intrigued her, though she would never pry. Several times he'd taken off an afternoon for "business reasons." And just last Sunday at church someone had mentioned seeing him at the municipal building several times. What kind of business would require so many visits to the courthouse?

"Well, all right, stubborn. I'll just pray the snow holds off."

She managed to distract the wiggling Jade by pointing out the Christmas decorations visible everywhere. They drove past closed businesses gaily decorated with white stenciled greetings and flashing red and green lights. Fiber-optic trees rotated in some display windows, and attached to the light posts were giant candy canes that caught the reflection of car lights and wobbled with each gust of wind.

Winding Stair looked as lovely and quaint as always at Christmas.

"This town is like a step back in time," Jesse said, as though he'd read her mind.

"I love it."

"The place grows on you, that's for sure."

She wasn't certain what he meant by that, but at least he hadn't criticized her beloved town. Small, provincial and backwoods it might be, but Winding Stair took care of its own.

"There are a lot of good people here. Not fancy, but good to the bone."

He stared at her across Jade's head for so long she feared he'd run a stop sign.

"Yeah," he finally said. "There are."

What was that supposed to mean?

Her pulse was still thudding in consternation when they pulled into the graveled drive of the Dairy Cup and got out. From the number of cars around the café, other playgoers had also experienced a sudden need for celebration.

Jade raced to the door, black hair blowing wildly from beneath her tinsel halo. Her wings sparkled and jostled against her back. Lindsey had wanted to replace the wings with a coat, but Jade had pleaded to wear the costume a while longer. They had compromised by sliding the coat onto her arms—backwards.

The small, independently owned Dairy Cup boasted all of five booths and a short counter with three stools. Jesse took the only empty spot, a back booth next to the jukebox. Lindsey slid onto the green vinyl seat across from him while Jade rushed to the jukebox.

"Can we play a song, Daddy?"

Jesse fished in his pocket and handed over a quarter.

"The menu is up there," Lindsey said, pointing to a signboard above the cash register. "Tell me what you want and I'll go up and order for us."

"My treat," Jesse said. "I owe you for making me go to the play tonight."

She smiled, pleased at his admission. "So you really did have a good time?"

"Yeah. A real good time." He folded his hard-working hands on the tabletop. "So what will you have, Miss Mitchell?"

Jade's quarter clunked in the slot. A slow, romantic love song poured out of the machine.

You, Lindsey wanted to say. And the thought shocked her. She looked up at the menu so that Jesse couldn't read the answer in her eyes.

"Chili sounds good."

"I thought you were all for hot fudge."

She flopped her palms out to each side and grinned. "I'm female. I changed my mind."

"Chili sounds good to me too." He turned in the seat toward his daughter. She was twirling in a circle to the music, the glitter on her wings sparkling beneath the fluorescent lights. "Hey, Butterbean, what do you want?"

She twirled right on over to him and plopped onto the vinyl seat. She took his cheeks between her small hands and smooched him. "A hotdog."

"A hotdog! You wanted ice cream."

She shrugged small shoulders. The gossamer wings rose and fell, and then she scooted out of the booth and began twirling again. "A hotdog."

Lindsey pressed a hand to her mouth, suppressing a giggle.

Jesse shook his head, the edges of his mouth quivering. "Women. I'll never understand them."

Pretending exasperation, he rose and went to order. Lindsey watched him. In truth, she couldn't keep her eyes off him. Though the notion was ridiculous, she felt as if they were on a date. All evening, there had been small sparks between them. He'd even looked at her differently when she'd opened the door wearing a dress. Something had happened tonight, some subtle change in their relationship. And she knew without a doubt, this was something she'd better pray about.

The next afternoon, Jesse pulled the long flatbed truck next to the curb on a side street in the town of Mena. Lindsey's prayers must have worked because the snow had held off, although the sky had that shiny white glare that usually meant wintry weather. He was loaded down with trees, but the delivery stop would have to wait. This one couldn't.

A row of nicely appointed residences, all with wide lawns and wreaths on the doors, lined the street. He pulled the small scrap of paper from his jacket and read the number for the hundredth time. Yes, this was the place. According to his information, a retired lawyer lived here. Stuart Hardwick.

Heart racing, he strode to the door and knocked. He'd rehearsed his speech all the way from Winding Stair, but when the door opened, the words stuck in his throat.

An old man, with a bulbous nose and a shock of white hair, squinted at him. "Yes?"

"Mr. Hardwick?"

"I'm Hardwick. Who are you?"

"Jesse Slater." Placing a hand on the wooden door

to keep it from being closed in his face, he said, "May I come in? We need to talk."

"I don't know you, Mr. Slater."

Using his free hand, Jesse fumbled for the copied document, drew it out and flipped it open beneath Hardwick's nose. "You knew my stepfather, Les Finch."

The old man peered at the paper, scratching his chin. "Maybe I did and maybe I didn't. I worked for a lot of folks over the years."

"Could we at least discuss it?"

Hardwick considered for a minute before stepping back. "Too cold to stand in the door. Come on in."

Passing through a small entry, they entered a musty-smelling, overheated living room. The man clicked on a lamp and shuffled to a table littered with glasses and papers.

"Care for a drink, Mr. Slater?" He lifted a half-empty whiskey bottle.

"No thanks." After living with Les Finch, strong drink had never tempted Jesse.

"You won't mind if I do then." After filling a glass to the rim, he sipped, then sat down in a chair and waved for Jesse to do the same.

"Now what's this business of yours? Let me see that paper."

Jesse handed over the form his stepfather had signed, making the sale of Jesse's farm valid.

"Eighteen years ago my mother died, leaving her

parents' farm to me. My stepfather, Les Finch, somehow managed to sell the place, claiming ownership."

"What's that got to do with me?"

"Someone smarter about legal and business affairs than Les had to do the paperwork."

"And you think I'm that man?"

"I know you are."

"Look, son, I'm an old man. Retired now. Eighteen years is a long time." His tone was soothing, compassionate, and Jesse figured he had perfected this tone in years of making deals. "Why don't you just let this thing go?"

"Because I have a little girl, and she deserves the home I never had. That farm belongs to me, and I want it back—for her."

Studying the paper, the lawyer took another sip of whiskey. "This document looks legal enough to me. How are you planning to prove the place is yours?"

"You. I want you to tell the truth. Confess that you helped Les Finch figure a way to forge my mother's name to forms that gave him ownership."

"Whoa now, boy. You're accusing me of a crime."

The old hypocrite. He *had* committed a crime, probably more than one. Anger hotter than the stifling room temperature rose in Jesse.

"What did he pay you, Hardwick?" he asked through clenched teeth. "Part of the profits? A gallon of Kentucky bourbon?"

Jesse regretted his outburst immediately. Stuart

Hardwick's bulbous nose flared in anger while his manner grew cool as the December day.

"I'm afraid I can't help you, Mr. Slater. Now if you will excuse me, it's time for my afternoon nap."

He tossed back the remaining liquor and pushed out of the chair.

Jesse leaped to his feet, unwilling to let the crooked lawyer off the hook. He squeezed his hands tight to keep from grabbing Hardwick by the shirt collar and wringing the truth out of him.

"Listen, old man, Les Finch stole everything I owned, moved me off to an unfamiliar city, and then tossed me out like a stray dog when I was barely fifteen. Scared, alone, heartbroken, hungry. Do you know what that's like?" He slammed his fists together. "That's never going to happen to my little girl. Never."

Hardwick turned away, went to the table and poured another drink. His hand trembled on the glass. "Any man who'd treat a kid so badly isn't worth much."

"No, he's not. He wasn't." The lawyer stood so long with his back turned, leaning on the table with shoulders slumped and the whiskey in front of him, that Jesse softened. "Maybe you didn't know that Finch would abandon me once he had his hands on the sale money. Maybe you would have done things differently if you'd known. Isn't that reason enough to help me now?"

Hardwick slowly shook his head. "I don't know, boy. Like I said, that was a long time ago." He took a deep pull of the liquor, shuddered, and backhanded his mouth. "Tell you what. You write down where you can be contacted. If I remember anything, I'll get in touch."

There was nothing left for Jesse to do short of physical violence, and he wouldn't lower himself to that. Deflated and disheartened, he scribbled his address on the back of the paper and left the house.

By the time he reached the retailer who'd ordered the extra load of pines, he'd regained a splinter of hope. After all, Hardwick hadn't flatly refused to help him. If the old bird had any conscience left at all, maybe he'd still come through.

"Looks like a nice bunch of trees, Mr. Slater," the lot owner said as he inspected the pines piled high on Lindsey's flatbed.

Pride welled up inside Jesse as he slipped on his leather gloves and loosened the tie-down ropes to unload. "Miss Mitchell takes very good care of her lot. All her trees are in perfect condition like this."

"My customers have sure been happy with that first load you brought in. They sold fast." The owner waved his hand toward the Christmas trees remaining on his lot. "These you see out here now came in from out of state, but they're about gone too. Can't be running low on trees with Christmas still more than a week away."

To Jesse's way of thinking, the out-of-state pines weren't half as green and well-shaped as Lindsey's. The man should have bought all his stock from the Christmas Tree Farm.

The lot owner turned toward his office and bellowed, "Jerry, get out here and help get these trees in place."

A man, presumably Jerry, came out, buttoning his coat against the chill, and began moving the trees onto the lot. In minutes, the three had unloaded the truck.

As Jesse shouldered a final baled pine, an idea came to him. "Mr. Bailey, have you ever considered ordering all your trees from us? You can't get trees this fresh anywhere else."

The man stopped, thought a minute, then said, "You're right about that, but I like to offer more variety to my customers. You folks have nice trees, but all of them are Virginias."

"Look out there, Mr. Bailey." Jesse gestured to where the new Virginia pines were being erected alongside the less fresh trees. "Which do you think people will buy? Will they care if it's a Virginia instead of a Scotch, or will they want the freshest, prettiest tree available?"

"Got a point there, Slater. Tell you what." He dug in his pocket for a business card. "I own six lots in this part of the country. You have Miss Mitchell give me a call when the season ends, and we'll talk about it. Maybe we can work out a deal for next year."

Jesse's spirits soared. An exclusive sale to six area dealers would be a huge boost to Lindsey's business. They'd need to clear and plant more acres, but that was no problem. He could do it.

With a firm handshake and a hearty thanks, Jesse leaped into the truck and started back up the winding road toward home. He slapped the steering wheel and whistled "Jingle Bells" as the old truck bounced and chugged up the mountain. Visions of Lindsey's golden eyes, her tawny hair and her pretty smile danced before him sweeter than sugar plums.

Man, he couldn't wait to tell her the news and to feel her smoky laugh wrap around him like a warm hug. She'd be so happy.

And she'd think he was the biggest hero in town.

The cheerful thoughts no sooner filtered through his brain than reality crowded in.

His fingers tightened on the wheel.

For now he had to play the role of Mr. Nice Guy, helping Lindsey's business grow and prosper. For the sake of his child, he had to lie and deceive. He wasn't sure what that made him, but one thing was for sure—he was nobody's hero.

Chapter Eleven

Fat white flakes of snow began falling about an hour before closing time. The last customer, her tree in the back of an SUV, hurried away before the roads became troublesome.

Standing beneath the dark sky, snow swirling around her in the still cold, Lindsey knew they'd have no more business tonight. She stroked a hand over Sushi's pointed ears, smiling when the dog licked at a snowflake.

Jesse's news about a possible exclusive contract had been especially encouraging, given how slow the farm had been for the last several days. Her big days were always on the weekends, but with an employee's wages to pay, she needed cash coming in.

She'd tried not to worry, trying instead to pray and let the Lord handle everything. And the possibility of selling more trees locally was surely an answer to those prayers. The lot owner in Mena had paid cash for this last load, too, and that was doubly good news. She lifted her heart in silent gratitude.

Jesse had been, for him, almost animated when he'd arrived home that afternoon. She'd laughed with joy, restraining the urge to throw her arms around him. Lately, she wanted to do that every time she saw her hired hand.

"Might as well shut down for the night," she said, pulse accelerating as he came toward her. Crossing the short, shadowy distance between them, he looked lean and mysterious and incredibly attractive.

"Where's Jade?" His voice raised goose bumps on her arms.

She rubbed at them and hitched her chin toward the Snack Shack. "Inside."

His boots crunched as he twisted toward the building. "Let's get her and take a ride. Puddin's still harnessed."

"Are you serious?" Although she enjoyed driving families through the trees, she'd never taken a ride for her own personal pleasure. Riding alone had held no attraction. But riding with Jesse...

"Come on. It'll be fun." He paused, then frowned down at her in concern. "Unless you're too tired."

"No. No. Not at all." In fact, energy strong enough to run the Christmas lights suddenly zipped through her. "A ride sounds wonderful."

"You know what they say in this part of the country.

Enjoy the snow fast." He rubbed his gloved hands together and smiled. "It will be gone tomorrow."

Lindsey's stomach went south. If she'd known a wagon ride would make him smile, she'd have suggested one sooner.

"Race ya to the shack," she said, eager to encourage his cheerful mood. "Last one to tell Jade is a rotten egg."

Before Jesse could react, she grabbed the advantage and took off in a hard run.

"Hey!" His boots thudded against the hard ground, and she watched his long shadow rapidly overtaking hers. Catching up in record time, Jesse nabbed her elbow. As if she'd reached the end of a bungee cord, Lindsey plummeted backward, banging into his chest.

He quickly righted her so that she wouldn't fall, and they stood staring at each other, smiling and panting. His strong, workman's hands held her by the upper arms. Bright Christmas lights around the window of the shack blinked off and on, bathing them in alternating shades of red and green.

Sushi leaped around their legs, barking in excitement.

"Cheater," he said, eyes twinkling an odd shade of blue in the rotating light.

He was inches away, his mouth so close and so tempting. She wanted him to kiss her.

The door to the Snack Shack opened behind them, and Jade called out in a worried voice. "Why is Sushi barking?" And then the child noticed the fluffy white flakes. "It's snowing!"

Coatless, she rushed outside and twirled around, grabbing for snowflakes, fear of the dog forgotten in her excitement.

Jesse dropped his hands and stepped away from Lindsey. A vague, but troubling disappointment crept over her. She had no business wanting more from Jesse than friendship. Crossing her arms, she hugged herself against the sudden cold.

"Get back inside and get your coat on," Jesse called, moving menacingly toward Jade.

The child yelped like a stepped-on pup and, giggling, bolted for the warm building. Jesse growled like a bear and gave chase.

Trying to forget that infinitesimal moment when she'd thought Jesse might kiss her, Lindsey followed them inside.

"Yay! Yay! Yay!" Jade cried, hopping and dancing and squealing in the wagon bed. She opened her mouth, trying to catch snowflakes on her tongue.

"Better get under those covers, Butterbean."

To Lindsey, the child's exuberance was a refreshing change from the frightened little girl of months ago. She still feared the dark and anything unfamiliar, but according to Jesse the nightmares had slowly disappeared, and she seemed so much easier in her own skin.

At her daddy's suggestion, though, Jade settled

down and slid beneath the downy covers. She hummed happily.

After a double-check of Puddin's harness, Lindsey came around to step up into the wagon. Jesse appeared at her side, hand on her elbow, and guided her safely onto the bench. She felt both feminine and foolish, considering the number of times she'd boarded alone.

Sushi stood on the ground a few feet away, tail thumping madly, mouth open and smiling, begging to join the fun.

Lindsey twisted around. "Jade, Sushi wants to ride with us."

She let the suggestion hang in the air, waiting for the little girl to make the decision.

Jade levered up to peer over the side at the begging German shepherd who managed to look so pitiful Lindsey was hard-pressed not to laugh.

"Okay." Jade pointed toward the very end of the wagon. "Down there."

Lindsey rejoiced for the progress.

Jesse gave a quick look of gratitude and squeezed her hand.

Once the dog was safely ensconced, Jesse rattled the reins and Puddin' plodded forward. Jingle bells, attached to the sides, tickled the air and blended with Christmas carols still echoing from the sound system.

Jesse didn't complain about the carols anymore. Could he be healing?

Heart full and happy for reasons she hadn't yet considered, Lindsey clapped her hands and began singing at the top of her lungs.

Jesse laughed.

The beautiful, male sound thrilled her so much that she sang all the louder, standing in the wagon to throw her hands into the air.

"You're crazy, woman." And he laughed again.

Jade crawled from beneath her covers to join the rowdiness. Jesse shook his head. "Now you're corrupting my daughter."

Lindsey gave him a playful push. "Oh, come on, Scrooge, sing."

"You don't know what you're asking for." He guided the horse along the perimeter of the trees, turning down a wide alleyway. "For all you know, I can't carry a tune."

"You can't be that bad." When he only grinned, she taunted, "Can you?"

As she'd hoped, Jesse rose to the teasing challenge. In the next moment, all three were belting out a loud and energetic version of "Frosty the Snowman" with Jesse providing the "thumpety, thump, thump" at the appropriate time.

At the end of the song, they all laughed so hard, tears welled in Lindsey's eyes. Jade flopped onto the seat between the adults, pointing out every snowflake that landed on the horse's back, asking questions about angels and Jesus and Christmas. While the briskly refreshing air reddened noses and cheeks, the pleasure of a family feeling warmed Lindsey from the inside out. She loved this little girl as if she'd borne her.

At last, Jade's energy was exhausted, and she drooped against her daddy's side. He stopped the wagon.

"Looks like the princess is tuckered out," he said quietly.

Scooping her into his arms, he carried Jade to the wagon bed and gently placed her beneath the quilts.

Lindsey turned on the seat to watch them, heart overflowing as Jesse adjusted his daughter's covers, snugging them securely under her chin. When he bent to kiss the angel face, Lindsey knew what she'd been trying to deny for so long. She not only loved Jade.

She loved Jade's daddy.

She'd been building to this moment since the day he'd arrived. Over the weeks, he'd not only lightened her workload and given her great new ideas for the farm, he'd filled her with a new sense of purpose and joy.

Closing her eyes at the wonder and beauty of so tremendous an emotion, she felt the wagon give as Jesse returned to his seat.

"Ready to head for home?" He asked, his voice muted.

She turned to look at him and knew the light of love was there for him to see.

Snowflakes tumbled down and the ground resembled a sugar-sprinkled spice cake. Tips of tree branches were flocked white. Indeed, they needed to call it a night.

But she was reluctant to leave this cold cocoon that had been spun around them here in the snowy, lighted grove.

"Whenever you are." The words came out in a whisper.

Shifting on the seat, he said, "You're snow-kissed," and rubbed his thumb across her lower lip.

He stared at her for two beats, then bent his head and brushed his lips over hers. Where her mouth was cold, his was warm and subtle and incredibly tender. So tender, tears sprang to her eyes.

When the kiss ended, their gazes held for the longest time.

"You're a very special lady, Lindsey Mitchell," he said at last and leaned his forehead against hers. His warm breath puffed softly against her skin, raising gooseflesh.

Pulse tripping madly, Lindsey caressed his cheek. "No more special than you—and that little girl back there."

Straightening, he took her hand and pulled her close beside him on the wagon seat. "We were both a mess when we met you. But you've changed us. And I'm grateful."

"I love her." She dare not say she loved him, too, though it was true. She'd never expected to trust enough to love again, but even with his faults and moods, Jesse had proven himself a thousand times over to be an honorable man.

She wanted to ask his feelings for her. He cared, yes, but love? She didn't know.

Lord, she thought, I need your direction. I've waited so long to love someone again. But is Jesse the right one? Or have I been alone too long to see things clearly?

She loved Jesse. There was no doubt in her mind about that, and real love was always from God. But as much as she loved him, Lindsey loved the Lord more. As long as Jesse had spiritual issues to resolve, she would do what she'd done for so long—wait upon the Lord, and pray that He would renew her strength. Because, if Jesse was wrong for her, it would take all the strength she had to get over him.

"Jade loves you too," Jesse replied. He gazed off into the dark woods. "I don't know what to do about that."

"Do?" His statement bewildered her. "Love is a good thing, Jesse, not a problem you have to fix."

"I don't want her to be hurt anymore. Erin—" He shifted in the seat, putting distance between them as if he'd somehow betrayed his dead wife by kissing Lindsey.

Suddenly, the hurtful words of days ago came back to her. "Are you afraid that if Jade cares for me, she'll forget her mother? That I'll replace Erin in Jade's life?"

He shook his head in denial, but Lindsey felt his

withdrawal. Giving her hand a quick squeeze and release, he gathered the reins, shook them, and set the horse plodding forward.

The tinkling bells had lost their cheer.

Jesse had the strongest urge to grab his child, get in his truck and run. Instead, he guided the placid Puddin' out of the Christmas trees toward the barn.

The jingle of harness and the plod of hoofed feet were the only sounds to break the pristine night.

He could never run far enough to forget what had just happened between him and Lindsey.

Lindsey.

"She won't."

Jesse shifted his gaze to the parka-clad woman beside him, mind too scattered to catch the drift of her conversation. "What?"

"Jade will remember Erin. Maybe not specifics, but she'll have memories. Most of all she'll remember the way her mother loved her."

"I hope so."

"She does. We've talked about it."

He blinked in surprise. "You and Jade talked about Erin?"

"She needs to talk about her mother, Jesse, to share her memories, to ask questions."

Discussing Erin had always hurt too much. He'd assumed Jade felt the same.

"What kind of questions could a six-year-old have?"

Lindsey blinked up at him. "Plenty. She asked me

where her mama was now and if dying had hurt. Things like that."

"Oh, God." He squeezed his eyes closed. That his baby would worry about such things cut him to the quick.

"Yes. That's exactly what I told her. Because Erin was a Christian, she was with God now, in his big, wonderful house in Heaven."

"Did that upset her? Talking about her mother's death, I mean."

He'd never considered discussing such a horrible event with a child. And at the time, Jade had barely been four. Surely she couldn't remember that much.

"Just the opposite. She seemed happy, relieved. Her little mind had some things about that day very confused."

Jumping down from the wagon to open the barn door, Jesse frowned. "What kind of things?"

"For some reason, Jade thought she was to blame for her mother's death."

The old wooden door scraped back, clattering against the wall. Snow swirled up from the motion.

"Where would she get such a crazy idea?"

"Who knows? Children don't think like we do. They're egocentric. The world turns because of them. So when something bad happens, it must have been because they were bad."

"That's ridiculous."

"She said you were mad for a long time." She stuck

a gloved hand out and caught a giant snowflake. "I tried to explain the difference between mad and sad."

Climbing back onto the cart, Jesse rattled the reins to send the horse into the barn.

"She was right. I was angry."

"That's normal, isn't it?"

"But I never dreamed Jade would take the blame on herself or think I was mad at her. She's my heart. My reason for going on."

"She's very secure in your love, Jesse. You're a good father." The lights from the barn reflected in her guileless eyes. "We're making a memory book. A Mama and Jade memory book."

Something turned over in Jesse's chest. "What's that?"

"Jade is drawing pictures of all the things she remembers about her mother. And I'm helping her write down other memories." She touched his arm. "She won't forget."

No. Jade wouldn't forget. Not with Lindsey around to gently, lovingly preserve those precious memories.

Wonder expanded inside him.

What kind of woman would nurture a dead woman's memory for the sake of a child? A woman she hadn't even known?

He had the overpowering desire to kiss her again. To hold her and tell her all that was in his heart.

Lindsey Mitchell was something special.

She was sweet and good. And loving.

Indecision warred within him. Feelings, long sublimated, rose to the surface. Falling for Lindsey Mitchell was the worst thing that could happen, for both of them. She deserved better. He cared about her. He cared a lot and didn't want ever to see her hurt. And hurting her would be the ultimate end of their relationship.

Part of him wanted to confess everything here and now and beg her forgiveness. But fear held him back. He'd enjoyed their sweet kiss. He'd seen the tenderness in her eyes, and he didn't want to replace that affection with loathing.

Lindsey valued honesty above everything, and he'd lied to her from the beginning. She'd never forgive him for his deceit.

And what about Erin? Being faithful to her was as important to him as remembering was to Jade. He'd made a promise at her funeral to take care of their little girl. Giving her this farm was the only way he knew how to keep that promise.

Oh man. He was in a mess. For weeks, he'd envied Lindsey's easy way of praying, of turning troubles over to the Lord. More than anything, he wished he could do that now.

He'd known for a while that he wanted to kiss her. But tonight, she'd given him back his joy. He'd laughed and sung like a maniac—and enjoyed every crazy second.

Then when he'd looked around and had seen her surrounded by snowflakes, he'd no longer had the will to resist.

Long years from now when she was gone from this place, he'd recall the cold snow dissolving against her skin as he'd warmed her soft lips with his.

He drew the horse to a stop next to a stall, hopped to the ground and reached up for Lindsey. Swinging her down from the wagon, he stood with his hands on her waist. "I had fun."

"Me too." An ornery glint turned her eyes to gold. She poked a gloved finger into his chest. "And now that I know you can sing…"

He quirked a brow, glad they were still comfortable with one another. "Are you threatening blackmail?"

"Of course."

"A good Christian woman like you. What an example," he said mildly.

She whopped him on the arm and turned away to unharness the horse. Puddin' stood patiently waiting for his warm stall and extra feed.

"You didn't mind my talking to Jade about her mother, did you?"

"No. I'm glad." If he'd been a better father, he would have recognized the need.

"Good."

The barn grew silent. Outside, snow filtered down like feathers from angel wings. Jesse crossed to the feed bin. The rich scent of hay and sweet feed filled the shadowy barn.

"Jesse." Lindsey's hushed tone was serious again, warning him. His hand stilled on the galvanized feed bucket.

"Yeah?" He turned his head, but Lindsey stood with her back to him, her hands making absent circles on the horse's neck.

The bells on the harness jingled. Then another moment of silence passed. Jesse got a sinking feeling in the pit of his stomach.

Lindsey's shoulders rose and fell. The horse blew impatiently.

When she finally spoke, her smoky voice flowed out on a sigh. "I have feelings for you."

Jesse drew in a deep, sorrowful breath of horse-scented air and squeezed his eyes shut. He exhaled slowly, trying to control the riot inside his chest.

"I know," he said quietly. Dread, like a lead weight, pressed down on him. The last thing he needed right now was to get emotionally involved with a woman—especially this one. And yet, he was.

She gave a little self-deprecating laugh that hurt his heart. "Just wanted to get it out in the open. It won't affect our working together."

He'd never thought of Lindsey as anything but strong and capable. But she looked small and vulnerable beside the massive horse, her hair bunched around the neck of her coat in a child-like tangle.

What did he say without hurting her? The truth? That he'd come here under false pretenses. That he planned to take away the farm she worked so hard to hold onto? Did he tell her he felt something, too, but old grievances were too deeply engrained to turn back now?

He shook his head ruefully. No, the truth would hurt her most of all.

Pouring the sweet feed into the trough, he waited for the noise to subside and then said the only thing he could. "Not a problem."

Liar, he thought, his insides rattling like hail on the tin roof of his trailer.

Lindsey's feelings were a major problem.

And so were his own.

Chapter Twelve

Desperation drove Jesse down the curvy mountain road on Sunday morning. Desperation also allowed Jade to attend Sunday school with Lindsey at Winding Stair Chapel. Jesse dare not take Jade where he was going.

The only way to avoid more suffering on the part of everyone involved was to bring the situation to its rightful end. He'd give Stuart Hardwick one more opportunity to come clean and then he'd find his own lawyer and go to the sheriff. The story could break out into the open soon and Lindsey could discover the truth about him.

His chest tightened. Both were bound to happen anyway

He wished he'd never met Lindsey Mitchell.

No. That wasn't true. He wished she didn't live on the property that belonged to him.

He never should have kissed her. The memory of her sweetness stayed with him like the haunting lyrics of a bittersweet song.

Halfway down the mountain, he passed the turn to Clarence Stone's place and slowed the Silverado, bringing the truck to a stop in the middle of the muddy road. A coyote leaped from the field and loped across in front of him. Jesse watched the wild, wily creature disappear.

He had taken a liking to the old farmer and had the strongest urge to drive up and talk to him.

He glanced at the clock on the dashboard.

"The guy's probably in church already," he muttered.

Just the same, he threw the truck into reverse, backed up and made the turn. All the way up the road, he questioned his own reasoning.

A talk with Stuart Hardwick was pressing. So why was he on his way to see a man he hardly knew? To talk? To somehow reassure himself that taking back the farm was the right thing to do?

The idea scared him. Nobody, but nobody was going to talk him out of that farm.

Mud splattered against the side of the truck as the road narrowed and curved sharply upward. In minutes, the lane dead-ended at a small frame house surrounded by a knee-high white fence. Two dogs of questionable heritage leaped from the front porch to loudly herald his arrival.

The front door, gaily decked with a holiday

wreath, opened immediately. Jingle bells swayed merrily with the movement. Loraine Stone's face appeared, then disappeared as Jesse stepped down from the truck and slammed the door.

Clarence shoved the old-fashioned storm door open. "Come in here, boy. Good to see you."

The snow had disappeared almost as quickly as it had come, leaving behind wet, soggy ground.

Jesse picked his way across the spongy yard and carefully wiped his boots on the welcome mat before stepping into the warm living room. The scent of recently fried bacon hung in the air.

"Well, Jesse. What brings you down the mountain this morning?"

He was wondering the same thing himself.

Taking in Clarence's church attire, he shifted uncomfortably. "I guess you're about to leave for church. I don't want to delay you."

"Don't worry about that. Sit down and tell me what's on your mind." Clarence pushed a drowsy cat to one side and joined her in a big flowered easy chair, relaxing as if he had nothing better to do than sit and visit. "A feller doesn't drive back up in here on a muddy day for no reason."

Jesse took the couch opposite him, thinking he should be in Mena by now.

"I don't really know why I stopped by."

One corner of the old man's mouth twitched as if he knew why. The notion irritated Jesse somewhat.

"Anything to do with Lindsey?"

"No." But the denial came too quickly. Leaning his elbows on his thighs, he clarified. "Partly."

Clarence studied him for a minute while scratching the cat behind one ear. His wife appeared in the living room, dressed for church and carrying a shiny black purse.

"You want me to go on, hon?" she asked.

Jesse leaped to his feet. "No, I'll go. We can talk again some other time." Since he had no idea why he'd come here, he might as well leave. And he had no intention of coming back again.

Clarence gestured him down. "You stay put. The Lord has a reason for you showing up on my doorstep on Sunday morning."

The Lord? Not since coming to Winding Stair had Jesse considered that God was interested in anyone's day-to-day activities. But according to Lindsey and her friends, God cared about everything.

Loraine Stone leaned down and pecked her husband on the cheek. "You might take a peek at that roast after a while."

Purse hooked over one elbow and a fabric-covered Bible in her hand, she left, acting neither upset nor surprised that her husband had stayed behind to talk to a virtual stranger. Clarence had once referred to himself as a good listener. Maybe others made this trek up the mountain to seek wisdom from the old guy.

Jesse wanted to laugh. Seeking wisdom sounded a bit too mystical for his comfort.

In minutes, the putter of a car engine sounded and then faded in the distance.

"You want some coffee, son?"

"No, thanks. I really should go. I have some business to attend to in Mena." But he didn't get up.

Clarence rose and got them both a cup of coffee anyway. Setting the mug on the polished coffee table in front of Jesse, he said, "Mind my asking what kind of business a man conducts on Sunday morning?"

As a matter of fact, Jesse did mind. "Personal."

Settling back into the chair, Clarence adjusted the cat before asking the same question again, "Have anything to do with Lindsey?"

"No." Jesse shook his head to clear away the lie. "Yes."

Clarence's grin gleamed in the sunlight that sliced a space between the drapes. "When your mind's made up, you're full of indecision, ain't ya, boy?"

The gentle jab brought a smile. "I have a problem, Clarence. And I don't know what to do about it."

"I don't either. But I know Someone who does."

Jesse knew what was coming. For once, he didn't mind. He was just grateful that Clarence hadn't asked for details about his problem.

"The Lord knows everything." Clarence paused to blow across the top of his coffee and sipped lightly before continuing. "He has the answer to every question and every problem every time."

"You make it sound easy."

"Nothing easy about living right in this crazy world.

But letting God direct your path and trusting that He has everything under control is as easy as pie."

"I don't know how to go about that."

"Just start by talking to Him. He's like any other friend. The more you visit, the closer you get."

"I never thought of God as a friend." Jesse took the coffee from the table and studied the warm mug between his palms, pondering God as an approachable being. That wasn't the way he'd been taught, but he'd observed that kind of attitude in Lindsey.

"Well, he is. Jesus is the best friend you'll ever have. And he's always there to listen to your troubles and to help you work out the answers."

"Is that it? Just pray and the answer will come?"

"Most of the time. But remember that God ain't Santa Claus. He'll give you what you need, and that's not always what you want."

To Jesse the words seemed like a warning. A warning he didn't want to hear.

"But doesn't a man have a right to do what he believes is best?" The heat of the room coupled with his heavy jacket increased the pressure building inside him. He clinked the mug onto the table, shoulders bunching forward in tension. "Shouldn't I fight for what I know is rightfully mine?"

He caught himself and stopped, having almost said too much.

"Rights. We sure hear a lot about people's rights these days." Clarence's voice was conversational as if he hadn't noticed the edge in Jesse's words. "But when I get to thinking about Jesus and what he did for us, I know we've become a self-centered world, too stuck on our own desires. Jesus could have demanded his rights—and gotten them. But he chose to do what was best for others instead of what was easy for himself."

Jesse thought about that, his chest tight with indecision. Clarence had something special in his life just as Lindsey did, but the old man couldn't possibly understand what he'd been through. Clarence had a home and stability and people who cared for him.

A small voice pecked at his conscience. Everyone had heartache. Just because he didn't know about theirs, didn't mean they hadn't suffered too.

"Anything you'd like me to pray with you about, Jesse?"

Jesse declined with a shake of his head. "No, thanks, but I appreciate the offer."

He stood to leave. Clarence pushed the lazy calico cat to one side and followed suit.

"Well, I'll be praying for you anyway. You'll make the right decision. Whatever that may be."

Jesse only hoped Clarence was right, because regardless of all that had been said, they'd solved nothing. Not that he'd expected to, but he'd had hope. He was as confused as he had been before. Only now, he'd wasted thirty minutes of precious time.

There was nothing left for him to do but resume the trip to Mena and try once more to change the mind of a certain crooked lawyer with a drinking problem.

* * *

The stars were bright that night—as bright, Lindsey imagined, as they had been on the first Christmas. The inky sky resembled diamonds on black velvet, sparkling and twinkling with such beauty, she wanted to stand forever here in the cold, hands in her coat, head tilted back to take in the wonder of God's creation.

"The sky does look pretty, doesn't it?" From behind her, Jesse's boots thudded softly against the hard ground.

It was closing time. He had turned off the music for the night and all but the security lights were now dark. Quiet lay over the land like a reverent prayer.

Turning, she smiled up at him. Her pulse bounded, reacting as it always did now that she knew she loved him. Having him here and near was enough, she'd told herself. Loving him was enough.

Jesse hadn't said a word about her admission that she cared for him. And she was grateful. Unless he could return her feelings, anything he might say would only embarrass them both.

At church, she'd prayed especially hard to understand the Lord's leading. Maybe Jesse and Jade had been sent for her to help them find the healing they needed. Maybe she'd been meant to love them back to health and then to let them go. She didn't know.

Pastor Cliff had preached on the scripture, "Trust in the Lord with all your heart and lean not unto your own understanding," and the message had seemed ready-made for her. But following through with the advice wasn't easy.

"I like to think about the days when God created the world. What an awesome thing to know He made all this beauty just for us to enjoy. He must love us so much more than we can ever understand."

"Pretty amazing, all right." Jesse stared into the distance, the line of his face pensive. "I'm going out to feed the horse. Want to come with me?"

Though they'd already taken Puddin' and his wagon to the barn, a belated customer had interrupted them. The horse hadn't been properly groomed or fed.

She shook her head, though the temptation to spend every minute in his company was great. "Jade's finishing up your Christmas present. I told her I'd help her wrap it before you left tonight. She wants it under her tree at home."

She waited for his eyes to frost over and his face to close up the way it always did when Christmas gifts were mentioned. But this time proved different. Though he looked serious, he nodded. "She's getting pretty fired-up about Christmas."

"Have you bought her a present yet?" She knew Jesse had ignored Christmas last year. And Jade remembered all too well.

"No." He jammed his hands into his pockets.

"I could go shopping for you if you'd like."

"I'll do it."

Happiness bubbled up inside her. "You will?"

He shrugged and a grudging grin tugged at his mouth.

Before she could think better of the action, Lindsey threw her arms round his waist and laughed. When she started to pull away, Jesse held on a moment longer before letting her go.

"I'll be back in a few minutes." He started off across the semi-darkened field toward the barn.

"Don't hurry. Jade and I need time to wrap a certain present."

His chuckle echoed back to her on the chilly night breeze.

Suddenly lighthearted, Lindsey rushed inside the Snack Shack. The warm scent of sugar cookies made her stomach growl. She snitched a broken one and took a bite.

"Where's Daddy?" Jade was at the table laboring over the specially designed and decorated candies Lindsey had helped her make. From the looks of them, the finishing touches were almost in place.

"Gone to feed Puddin'."

The child looked up, affronted. "He said I could help him."

"I'm sorry, sweetie. I guess he forgot." Lindsey took some wrapping paper from beneath the counter and laid the roll on the table.

"I can catch up." Jade rushed to the door and shouted into the darkness. "Daddy, wait! I'm coming."

"What about wrapping your daddy's present?"

"You do it. Please, Lindsey. I saved something 'specially for Puddin'." She struggled into her coat, small fingers fumbling with the zipper until Lindsey reached down to help.

Lindsey followed her to the door and watched as she ran across the grass in pursuit of Jesse, pleased that Jade had a treat for the horse she'd once considered too big and scary.

The barn was less than a hundred yards away and Lindsey spotted Jesse's shadowy form beneath the diffused security lights. Satisfied that Jade would overtake her daddy, she turned back inside.

With a heart filled with gladness, she set to work wrapping Jesse's gift. Using candy molds, Lindsey had helped Jade create hearts and angels and various other chocolate delights for her daddy. Tonight Jade had added sprinkles and nuts.

After wrapping each piece in plastic wrap, Lindsey placed the treats into a pretty decorated tin she'd saved from last year. She wrapped the present and placed a big red bow on top, then set about cleaning up the Snack Shack for the night.

She was washing the coffeepot when the door opened and Jesse stepped inside. A small draught of cold air snaked in with him.

Smiling, she opened her mouth to speak, but the words died in her throat.

He was alone.

"Where's Jade?"

He looked around the room as if he expected the

child to jump from beneath the table or from behind a chair. "Isn't she here?"

Slowly, Lindsey replaced the glass carafe and shook her head. "No. She wanted to go with you. I watched her until she was almost caught up. Didn't you see her?"

"Yes, but she came back here. She gave me a piece of apple for the horse. Then she said she was coming back to help you."

Lindsey pressed a hand to her mouth and fought down fear. "Where is she?"

"I don't know," Jesse answered grimly. "But I aim to find out."

He yanked the door open with such force the Shack rattled.

Going into the yard, he cupped his hands around his mouth and bellowed. "Jade!"

Trembling, Lindsey threw on her coat and followed. "I'll check the house."

"I'll head back to the barn."

They took off in a dead run, both returning in minutes without Jade. Lindsey had taken the time to grab her rifle and a pocketful of ammunition. If they had to go into the woods, they'd need it. Jesse eyed the weapon but didn't comment.

Together they searched the other out-buildings and the tree lot, calling Jade's name over and over, but there was no sign of the little girl.

Lindsey had thought she was panic-proof, but anxiety knotted her stomach and the nerves in her neck.

"She's terrified of the dark. Where could she be?"

"We know she was between here and the barn, so let's walk a circle around that area. If we don't find her, we'll widen the circle until we do. She's out here somewhere."

And likely crying her eyes out. The night was cold and dark, except for the stars. And there were wild animals in the woods and mountains behind Lindsey's farm.

Taking flashlights from the Snack Shack, they searched the grounds and then the area around the barn until finally reaching the wooded treeline that led up into the mountain.

"Surely, she wouldn't have gone into the woods alone," Lindsey said.

"Unless she got confused or something scared her and she ran without thinking." Suddenly, he stopped and shone his flashlight all around Lindsey. "Where is Sushi?"

"I don't know. She was outside earlier. I assumed she'd followed you to the barn." As soon as the words were out, she knew what Jesse was thinking. "Sushi wouldn't do anything to scare Jade. She knew Jade was easily frightened."

His jaw clenched, unconvinced. "Then where is she?"

"Maybe she went along with Jade, to protect her."

"Or maybe she chased her into the woods. Maybe she's the reason Jade ran away in the darkness."

"I don't believe that."

"Can you think of any other reason Jade would take off this way?"

She couldn't, but she also wouldn't believe the protective, loving German shepherd was responsible for Jade's disappearance. If anything, Sushi had followed Jade because she loved her and was worried about her. Convincing Jesse of that, however, was another matter.

"We'll find her, Jesse."

His jaw clenched and unclenched in barely controlled anger. "If that dog has hurt her, I'll kill it with my bare hands."

His assumption of the worst angered her. "You'd better be more concerned about the real dangers out there."

"The real danger is the one I know about."

"Sushi is not a danger. She wouldn't harm anyone unless they threatened me. Jade was even beginning to accept her company."

"And maybe that wasn't a good thing. If you hadn't forced the situation, Jade wouldn't have felt she had to accept the dog to please you."

Hurt pierced her like a sharp nail. "That's not true. Jade knew I was trying to help her."

"Yeah? Well, look where that got us." He jerked around and stalked off into the darkness, calling back over his shoulders. "I mean it, Lindsey. That dog is dead if she's harmed my daughter."

Lindsey felt as if he'd slapped her. Did he really believe she'd force Jade to do something that would

ultimately harm her? Did he really believe she'd bring
an animal into Jade's life that would turn on her?

She trembled, not from cold, but from the harsh-
ness of Jesse's accusations. Tears burned inside her
throat. Stiffening her spine, she swallowed and shook
them off. Her own heartache had to take a back seat
to the current crisis. She would cry later. Right now,
a scared little girl waited.

*Take care of her, Lord. And help us find her safe
and sound.*

She hoisted the rifle onto her shoulder, aimed the
flashlight into the cold night…

And started walking.

Chapter Thirteen

Sometime after midnight the wind died, and the temperature hovered in the upper thirties. Above the shadowy forest, the Milky Way smeared the indigo sky and stars danced and twinkled.

So beautiful…and so scary for a little girl alone.

Cold and more worried than he had ever been in his life, Jesse huddled deeper into his fleece jacket and thought about going back to the house to call the police. But Winding Stair was a small town manned by one police officer per shift. By the time the officer rounded up a search party, morning would be here. Surely, he'd find Jade before then.

Stomping on through the woods, twigs and branches snapping beneath his feet, he thought of how terrified Jade must be. Every sound magnified in the silence. For a child who feared the dark and suffered nightmares, the dark woods held unfathomable terrors.

He envisioned her as she'd been in the barn. Though warmly dressed in her coat and heavy jeans, her hood had been down. Would she think to put it up?

Was she cold? Was she crying? Was she hurt?

The torments of not knowing ate at him like hungry wolves.

For the first two hours he'd run on adrenaline. Now he was running on sheer determination.

From in front of him came a scratching, rustling noise.

A dark form loomed, and, with a swift surge of hope, he rushed forward. His boots snagged on twisted, twining tree roots growing above ground. He stumbled but managed to catch himself on the rough bark of an ancient blackjack, jarring his wrists in the process.

A startled possum drew back to hiss a warning, beady red eyes aglow in the flashlight beam. Jesse sagged in disappointment and hoped Jade didn't encounter any nocturnal animals.

He hoped she didn't encounter Sushi either.

Trudging onward, deeper into the thickening woods, he called her name over and over.

"Jade!"

The call was swallowed up in the dense trees. He paused to listen, longing for the answering call. Only the awful silence of a dark winter's night replied.

He had to find her. Soon. He was a grown man and the cold and fatigue was wearing on him. How could a child hold out for long?

Fear and dread pulled at him, much stronger than the weariness.

If anything had happened to his baby, he couldn't go on. He would have no reason.

Another hour passed with no sign of the dark-haired angel. He found himself murmuring half-formed prayers.

"Please help me find her. Please protect her."

The weight on his chest grew until he thought he'd smother. Finally, when he could bear the stress no longer, he cried out, half in anger, half in hope-filled despair. "God, are You listening? Do You care?"

An owl hooted in the distance and, had the situation not been so serious, Jesse would have laughed. Leave it to Jesse Slater to pray to God and be answered by an owl.

But he didn't know what else to do. Lindsey believed in prayer. Clarence said God always answered, one way or the other. The way he figured it, no one was out here to hear him anyway or to know that Jesse had lost his reason along with his daughter. Praying would keep his mind from considering all the terrifying possibilities. And it sure couldn't hurt anything.

His prayers began in desperation.

"Lord, I know You're up there watching. I've always believed You were real, but I don't know You very well. Not like Lindsey and Clarence do. I have no right to ask favors, but maybe You'll do this one thing for Jade. Help me find her, Lord. Show me where she is."

A tree branch sliced across his face. He jerked back, fingered the skin and dismissed the scratch as inconsequential.

"Take care of her, God. Don't let her be scared. I know she is. I promised Erin I'd take care of our baby. Now look what I've done. I've lost her." A cry of grief pushed at his windpipe. "Don't let anything happen to her. I beg You not to take her, too."

The words of his prayer became jumbled, tumbling out from a heart filled with fear and seasoned with suffering.

"Was it me, Lord? Have I done something so bad that everyone I love gets taken away? Mama and Erin are gone. Don't take Jade. I'll do anything. Anything."

Somewhere—far too close for comfort—coyotes yipped and howled, raising the hair on Jesse's neck.

Pausing next to an outcropping of boulders, he shouted, "Jade! Jade!", until his voice broke.

As he collapsed exhausted onto the rocks, tears gathered behind his eyelids. He hadn't let himself cry when Erin died, fearing his grief would be too terrible for Jade to witness. Truth be told, he hadn't cried in a long time.

"Oh, God, I don't know what to do. She's out there and she's scared." He buried his cold, damp face in gloved hands. "Please help me."

Clarence claimed God was a friend who cared, who longed for friendship in return. Could that be true? All these years, he'd assumed he was last on God's Christmas list. Could he have been wrong all this time?

He began to pray in earnest then, pouring out the sorrow and agony of his past as if God didn't already know his life story. And yet the telling cleansed him, released him from the torment and anger he'd harbored so long, as though God Himself took on the load and carried his sorrows away.

He didn't know how long he sat there talking, but when he raised his face to the star-sprinkled heavens he was a new man—still terribly afraid for his child, but renewed in a way he couldn't begin to explain or understand.

All these years he'd thought God had abandoned him. But now he saw as clearly as he saw the Milky Way above—he'd been the one to pull away and forget the Lord. Now he understood what Lindsey had meant when she'd said that God would never leave or forsake us. God didn't. But man did.

At the reminder of Lindsey, regret pushed into his consciousness. Every time his own guilt started to eat at him, he lashed out at her, and he'd done it again tonight over the dog.

Maybe Jade had become frightened and run away from Sushi, but he couldn't blame Lindsey for that. She only meant good for Jade. She loved her.

And she loved him.

"Lord, I'm so unworthy. Of her. Of You. I hope she can forgive me." He raised his head and stared into the heavens. "I hope You will too."

A gentle warmth, startling in the cold, suffused him as if someone had draped an electric blanket over his shoulders.

With restored courage and a Friend to guide him, he pushed off the boulder and set out to find his daughter.

At the first gray promise of morning, Jesse turned back and headed out of the woods. All through the long night, he'd walked and searched and prayed. Twice he and Lindsey had crossed paths and then parted again to cover more ground. The wooded area expanded to the north and eventually became a state park. There were miles and miles to cover if Jade had gone in that direction. Now, he had little choice but to call in a search team.

Eyes scratchy and dry from cold and sleeplessness, he continued to strain at every shadow, hoping, praying. He was peering beneath a low-hanging cedar when a terrifying sound raised the hair on his neck.

Growling, snarling animal sounds—whether of dog or coyote or wolf, he couldn't tell—came from somewhere to his left. Breaking into a dead run, he headed toward the sound.

A gunshot ripped the morning quiet. Birds flapped up from the trees, filling the air with rushing wings and frightened calls.

Jesse's heart jump-started. Though beyond weary, the rush of adrenaline propelled him faster.

Barking and snarling became louder, and he recognized the sound—a dog. Sushi.

Fear mixed with anger whipped through him.

Breaking through the dense growth of trees, he glimpsed a purple coat. A small form, black hair spilled out all around, lay curled on the ground. Sushi, hair raised and teeth bared, stood over her.

Heart in his throat, Jesse cried out. "Jade!"

The dog spun toward the voice just as Lindsey arrived from the opposite direction.

"Daddy, Daddy!" Jade sat up, gripping Sushi's neck as though the dog was a lifeline.

Everything was happening too fast. Jesse couldn't comprehend anything except the sight of his little girl on the ground and the dog standing over her. Rushing forward, he fell to the earth and yanked Jade into his arms, away from the animal.

"Are you all right? Did the dog bite you? Did she hurt you?" Pushing her a little away, he frantically checked her for injuries. Her cheeks were red and her face dirty, but otherwise she appeared all right.

Lindsey's smoky voice, strained with exhaustion came toward them. She still carried the flashlight and her gun. "Sushi didn't hurt her, Jesse. She protected her."

Pressing his child close to him for warmth and safety, he looked up into Lindsey's red-rimmed eyes.

"What do you mean? She was standing over Jade's helpless body, ready to attack."

"No, Daddy, no." Jade pulled his face around to

gain his full attention. "Sushi tried to fight the bad dogs that came."

Jesse blinked in bewilderment. "Bad dogs?"

He looked at the German shepherd sitting a few feet away, and then toward the woods from whence Lindsey had come.

His mind began to clear and reason returned. Lindsey had fired the shots and followed something into those woods. "Coyotes?"

Carefully placing her rifle on the ground, Lindsey knelt in front of him. With a soft smile, she stroked Jade's tangled hair. "Coyotes don't usually approach humans, but she was small and still and probably looked vulnerable. I heard Sushi's warning growl and arrived in time to chase them off. Thank God."

A shiver ripped through Jesse. He squeezed his eyes closed against the unthinkable image of Jade and a pack of coyotes. "Yes. Thank God."

Lindsey noticed the words of praise. Her eyes questioned him, but she made no comment. As naturally as if he'd done it forever, he pulled Lindsey against his other side and held her there. His girls, one on each side, where he wanted them.

"And Sushi, too, Daddy," Jade insisted. "She stayed the night with me. She snuggled me up and made me he warm. I cried, but she licked my face."

Jesse's heart ached at the image of his daughter alone and afraid and crying. But he was happy too, and relieved beyond words.

"Where were you, sweetheart? How did you get lost?"

Jade pointed at the sky. Her knit gloves were dirty and loaded with bits of grass and twigs.

"I wanted the star."

Lindsey appeared as puzzled as he. "What star, Jade?"

"The falling star. For Daddy." She cupped a hand over her mouth and leaned toward Lindsey. In a conspiratorial whisper, she said, "For a present. So he would like Christmas again."

A lump filled Jesse's throat. Jade had ventured into the dark and frightening night alone to capture a shooting star for him. To make him happy.

He pressed his face into her hair, chest aching enough to burst. "Oh, baby. Daddy's so sorry."

She patted his ears. "It's okay, Daddy. I didn't find the star, and I got lost. But my guarding angel was with me, just like Lindsey said. Sushi and me went to sleep, and I wasn't scared anymore."

The German shepherd sat on her haunches, tail sweeping the brown earth, eyes shining as if she knew she'd done a good thing. With a final hug, Jade pushed up from Jesse's lap and went to embrace the big furry dog.

"Sushi is my friend."

Who would think a guardian angel had a fur coat and four legs?

His gaze locked with Lindsey's.

Or had another kind of angel protected his daughter?

"I owe you an apology, and this dog a T-bone steak," he told Lindsey.

She shook her head, tangled, windblown hair swinging around her tired face. He thought she looked beautiful. "No apologies or steaks are needed. We can thank God He used Sushi to protect Jade when we couldn't."

"I was wrong about the dog." Now was his chance to tell her the rest. "I've been wrong about a lot of things. But last night, when I was scared out of my mind, God and I had a long talk."

Hope sprang into her expression. "You did?"

They were cold and tired and needed to get back to the house, but some things couldn't wait to be told.

"You were right. God was here all the time, waiting for me to make the first move. I'm only sorry I waited so long."

"Oh, Jesse." Lindsey threw her arms around his neck and kissed his rough, unshaven cheek. Then, as if she regretted the spontaneous act, she drew back, blushing.

Her golden eyes were inches away and the look of love was there for any fool to see. Suddenly all his reservations faded away as easily as the daybreak had chased away the night.

He loved Lindsey Mitchell. He wondered why he'd fought it so long. She was everything good and beautiful he wanted in his life.

He waited, expecting to be engulfed with guilt because of Erin. This time the feeling never came. Loving Lindsey in no way negated the love he'd had for his wife, but Erin was gone, and she would have handed him his head for not letting her go sooner. She would have expected him to take care of their daughter and to get on with living.

And that's exactly what he intended to do.

"Come back here, woman." Elbow locked around her neck, he drew Lindsey close again. He hardly noticed the cold ground seeping through his clothes. "A kiss on the cheek won't cut it."

Her eyes widened, but she didn't pull away.

With a silent prayer of thanks, Jesse bent his head and kissed Lindsey's sweet mouth.

"What was that?" she asked when they parted, her voice even huskier after a night in the cold.

"Something amazing has happened. Something I thought was impossible. I have a lot of things to tell you later, when we're rested and warm, but there's one thing that can't wait." He cupped her cheek, unable to take his eyes off her, now that he recognized the truth. "I love you, Lindsey."

A multitude of emotions played over her face.

"Oh, Jesse, I'm going to cry."

He winced in mock horror. "Don't even think about it. At least, not until you say you love me too."

Eyes glistening with unshed tears, she stroked a hand over his jaw. "I do. With everything in me."

Jesse's heart filled to the bursting point. This woman had done so much for him. She'd made him a better man than he'd ever dreamed of being. She'd loved him in a way that healed the gaping wound he'd carried around inside for so long. And most of all, she'd led him back to the Lord.

The morning sun broke over the eastern horizon, orange as a pumpkin, and as bright as the new light shining in Jesse's soul.

The increasing temperature was welcome, but the morning air was still cold enough to be uncomfortable.

"Time to get you and the butterbean back to the house."

"Time to go to work," she argued, but didn't move from her place in his arms. "Customers won't wait, no matter how tired we are."

Customers. All night, he'd been so preoccupied with finding his daughter that he hadn't thought of the long day ahead.

"I'll take care of the farm today." He kissed her on the nose and then set her on her feet. "You and Jade will have a good breakfast and plenty of sleep."

"I'll argue with you later," she said. "Right now that breakfast sounds too tempting to pass up."

Jesse chuckled, shaking his head at this special woman. He'd have to lock her in the house to keep her away from the tree patch, no matter how much sleep she did or didn't get. As for himself, he felt as invigorated as if he'd slept for days.

Holding hands, they started toward Jade. The little lost angel jogged around in circles with Sushi, appearing unfazed by her eventful night.

"From the looks of her, Jade had a lot more sleep than either of us."

"Thanks to Sushi," Jesse admitted.

A soft smile curved Lindsey's mouth. The light in her eyes spoke volumes. "And her guardian angel."

The situation with the farm and his rightful ownership tried to press in, but Jesse shoved the thoughts away. Right now, he wanted to bask in all the good things that had come from this strange night. Today he was happy to love and be loved. He'd worry about his dilemma some other time.

Chapter Fourteen

"Hey, woman, get a move on." Eyes twinkling and step jaunty, Jesse burst through the front door of the farmhouse bringing the chill with him. "All work and no play—"

He stopped in his tracks when he spotted her.

"Whoa." A slow smile eased the perpetual sadness from his eyes. "If I'd known you'd look like that, I would have offered to take you Christmas shopping a long time ago."

Lindsey blushed, pleased but discomfited by the unaccustomed praise. "Slacks and a sweater aren't that impressive, Jesse."

He pumped his eyebrows. "Says who?"

Lindsey laughed, unable to resist this teasing, happy version of the man she loved. Since that anxiety-filled night of searching for the lost Jade, he'd been full of good humor and unbounded joy.

"I suppose after seeing me in pine-covered jeans and boots every day, anything is an improvement."

"What about me, Daddy? Am I pretty too?" Jade preened, showing off the red bow holding back her black satin hair.

"You are stunning." He swooped the child into his arms and blew onto her neck. Her giggle filled the room and brought Sushi in to investigate the commotion.

Jesse eased Jade to the floor and scratched the dog's ears. "Tom and his boy are all set to handle everything while we're gone. Any last-minute instructions you want to give them?"

Tom's teenage son had worked part-time for Lindsey last year and knew how the tree farm operated. She had no qualms about leaving the pair from her church in charge while she, Jesse and Jade spent a few hours in Mena. She looked forward to an afternoon of shopping, having dinner, and spending quality time with this pair that had won her heart.

"Tom and Jeff can handle it." She reached for his rough hand and squeezed, grateful and so full of love she could hardly see straight. "Thanks for thinking of this. I know how you feel about crowds and shopping."

He shrugged off the idea that he'd done anything special. "Everyone needs time off, even the invincible pioneer woman on Winding Stair Mountain."

She laughed. "I don't feel too invincible sometimes." Most of the time, to tell the truth.

She'd never admitted until now that she had insulated herself here on the mountain. Pastor Cliff had tried to talk to her once, and his gentle assessment had been correct. She'd used the tree farm as an excuse to distance herself from everyone but her church family, afraid of being hurt, afraid to trust.

Two nights ago, during their search for Jade, when Jesse had declared his love, her own fears had evaporated like morning mist. She'd seen Jesse's hard work around the farm, experienced his constant efforts to improve the place and to lighten her tasks. And she knew he was totally dedicated to his child. But there was something to the adage that adversity bonds.

Her gaze strayed to him, busily getting Jade into her coat and gloves. Jesse Slater's love had changed her. Something she'd never thought possible had happened. She trusted this good man with her life.

Most important of all, she trusted him with her heart.

A short time later in Mena, Jesse remained mildly surprised that he'd not only agreed to this trip, he'd suggested it. But Lindsey had that effect on him. He'd do anything in his power to see her smile. So here he was, in a crowded store where cashiers wore red Santa hats, Bing Crosby crooned "White Christmas" over the intercom, and he was almost enjoying himself.

Almost.

He would rather be on the farm or at a quiet little restaurant somewhere, but observing Lindsey's pleasure in such a simple outing made up for the discomfort on his part.

He let his gaze roam over the stacks of cologne

sets, gloves, wallets, candy and back massagers. From floor to ceiling the place reeked of Christmas.

With a wry shake of his head, he realized how far he'd come—from a Scrooge who hated Christmas to a man in love who wanted to please his woman. And he couldn't think of anything in the world good enough to give her.

"What do you think, Jesse?" Lindsey held some kind of computer software box in one hand. "Would a boy like this?"

From the looks of her basket, Lindsey was buying for every kid in her church. "Depends on the boy. I always wanted sports stuff."

He'd gotten that kind of thing too before his mother had become ill. Those last two years before she died, he'd received nothing. Les Finch wasn't much of a shopper. Reason enough for him to do better.

A disembodied voice interrupted the music to remind kids that Santa was available in the toy department for picture-taking.

Jade, who'd been examining every baby doll on the shelf, tugged at his hand and requested for the fourth time, "Let's go see Santa."

Jesse was about to refuse when Lindsey caught his eye. "That might be a good idea, Dad," she said. "You two go back there while I do a little bit of *special* shopping."

She put enough emphasis on the word special that Jesse got the idea. She wanted to shop for Jade.

A frisson of energy passed between them. Maybe

she wanted to shop for him too. His stomach lifted at the notion.

On the other hand, maybe the sensation was hunger pains. Dinner was beginning to sound good.

"Will you be ready to have dinner by then?"

Fingers curled around the handle of the shopping cart, she questioned pointedly, "Don't you have some shopping of your own to do?"

Jesse suppressed a shudder. Walking around in a huge department store, he could handle. But the pleasure in hassling through the jammed check-outs evaded him. He'd planned to buy Jade's gifts in Winding Stair. Run in the store, grab the doll, pay for it and run out. His way seemed much less trying.

"I don't suppose I could convince you to pick up a couple of things for me," he said hopefully.

Her cart was already littered with items. What would a few more matter? She knew what he wanted to buy Jade because they'd discussed it this morning over the phone.

A knowing twinkle lit her eyes. "Have we pushed you beyond the limits any male can endure?"

With a tilt of his head, he grinned. "Getting close."

Pushing up the sleeve of her blue sweater, Lindsey looked at her watch. "Okay. Tell you what. I'll gather up those last things and meet you back at the truck in thirty minutes. I'm starting to get antsy about leaving the farm for so long anyway."

He frowned. "Tom and Jeff will do fine."

"I know, but I don't want to impose on their

kindness forever." She took a box of candy canes from the shelf and placed them in the basket, never mentioning the fact that she was paying her friends good money to run the tree lot. "Besides, shopping does me in, too. I'm always anxious to get back home to my peaceful little farm."

He studied her face, noticing the softness that appeared whenever she talked of her home. Guilt tugged at him. He'd been doing a lot of thinking about his claim on that place.

Looking around to see if anyone was listening, he leaned toward her and whispered, "I love you."

With a parting wink at her blushing face, he and Jade jostled their way toward the back of the store.

He did love Lindsey. And she loved him. And he hoped the words just now hadn't been spoken out of guilt. The farm was an issue that could tear them apart and change her loving to loathing. He couldn't bear that, not now that he'd recaptured the joy sorely missing in his life for so long.

Over the last few days, he'd spent a lot of time praying for answers about the Christmas Tree Farm, but the continual nag of doubt and worry plagued him yet. He had a right to that farm. He must have said that to the Lord a hundred times. Then he'd remember what Clarence said about rights, and how sometimes there was a big difference between being right and doing right.

Hurting Lindsey was wrong, regardless of his true claim to the land. She trusted him—a huge leap of faith on her part. She put a lot of stock in loyalty and truth. If she discovered his original motive had been to repossess her land, would she reject him? Would her heart be broken at his deceit?

A lady elf, garbed in form-fitting tights and a short skirt greeted him with an interested smile as he and Jade joined the line waiting for Santa. Jesse barely noticed her. There was only one woman for him. And she wore flannel and denim and smelled as fresh as the pine trees.

In that moment, he knew the answer he'd been seeking. Loving Lindsey, in the way God intended man to love woman, meant doing what was best for her. *As Christ loved the church, so man should love his wife.* Jesse wasn't sure why he remembered the verse, but he was sure it came from the Bible. To the best of his ability, he wanted always to love Lindsey that way.

The farm belonged to her. She was the heart and soul of that place. He'd wondered what to give her for Christmas and now he knew. Even though she would never be aware of the secret gift, relinquishing his quest for the farm was the best present he could give. From this moment forward, the farm was hers. And he would no longer seek revenge for the wrongs done to him.

As if the shutters were opened and sunlight flooded in, Jesse saw the truth clearly. Jade had not been his motive. His rightful claim had not been his motive. He had wanted someone to suffer as much as he had—and that was wrong.

He would never again harass the pathetic old lawyer, Stuart Hardwick, to confess. And most of all, he would never hurt Lindsey by telling her of his original reasons for coming to the farm. She didn't ever need to know that the Christmas Tree Farm legally belonged to him.

He would find another way to provide well for Jade—and for Lindsey, if she'd have him. He had skills. He could work for any electric outfit in the area.

The final weight of his past lifted off his shoulders. Lindsey was his heart. Doing right *did* feel much better than being right.

Lindsey was in the house, wrapping all the gifts she and Jesse had purchased the day before. In exchange for her gift-wrapping favors, Jesse had agreed to man the tree lot. With only two days left until Christmas, business at the farm had begun to slack off. Only a few procrastinators waited this late to purchase a tree.

The grind and whine of a pickup coming up the drive rose above the television where Jimmy Stewart serenaded Donna Reed in "It's a Wonderful Life."

"Must be another of those procrastinators," she said to Sushi. The dog perked one ear, then rose and trotted to the door, whining.

"Need out, girl?" Lindsey put aside the silvery roll of foil paper and followed the dog.

The sheriff's SUV was parked in her drive, and Sheriff Kemp came across the yard.

Lindsey opened the door as he stomped up onto the porch. "Hi, Sheriff. Forget to buy your Christmas tree?"

Ben Kemp had been county sheriff for as long as Lindsey could remember, but he was still tall and strong and fit with barely a hint of paunch beneath his wide silver belt buckle. His trademark gray Stetson and cowboy boots made him even taller. In the pleasant December sunshine, he shifted from one boot to the next, looking decidedly uncomfortable.

Worrying a toothpick to one corner of his mouth, he said, "Wish that was the situation, Lindsey, but I'm afraid I have bad news."

Pulse leaping in sudden fear, Lindsey gripped the doorpost. "My folks? Kim? Has something happened?"

"No, no." He took off his cowboy hat and studied the inside. "Mind if I come in for a minute? Got something here I need to show you."

He pulled a file folder from inside his zip-up jacket.

"Of course not. Please." She stepped back to let him in, relieved that her family was all right but troubled about the purpose of his visit. Sheriff Kemp was too busy to make unnecessary calls.

While the lawman made himself at home on the edge of her couch, Lindsey turned down the TV.

"Would you like some coffee, Sheriff?"

"Nothing, thanks." He placed the Stetson on the couch beside him. "A real odd situation has arisen, Lindsey."

She tilted her head. "That concerns me?"

"In a way. It's about this farm."

Now she was really puzzled. A butterfly fluttered up into her chest. "My farm?"

"Well, you see now, there's the trouble." Opening the manila file folder, he removed a sheet of paper and handed it to her. "When your granddaddy bought this place—in good faith, I'm sure—something was sorely amiss."

Lindsey read the paper and then looked up. "This is the deed to my farm."

"Yep. Now take a look at that signature." He took another paper from the folder. "And then have a look at this one."

She did as he asked, but what she read made no sense. Another butterfly joined the first.

"I don't understand."

Sheriff Kemp rubbed at his forehead, clearly disturbed with the news his job forced him to share. "Here's the upshot, Lindsey. This eighty acres belonged to a woman name of Madelyn Finch. She inherited it from her grandparents. When she died, her husband, Les Finch, hired a lawyer name of Hardwick to help him gain ownership of the place. I remember Hardwick. He was dirty to the core but so smart he always got away with his shenanigans."

Lindsey's pulse accelerated. The butterflies were in full flight by now. "Are you telling me that Mr. Finch illegally sold this farm to my grandfather?"

"I'm afraid so. The woman's will was clear. The

farm was to go to her son. Somehow Hardwick and Finch forged the boy's name on the sale papers."

Dropping into the nearest chair, Lindsey covered her mouth with her hand to keep from crying out. A dozen questions crowded her mind. "They cheated a child out of his home?"

Suddenly the truth hit her. That child, whoever he was, owned the tree farm—her tree farm.

"The boy must be grown by now. Does he know about this? Is that why you're here? He's filed a claim to regain possession?"

"Yes, ma'am. He's the one stirred things up after all this time. Seems Stuart Hardwick got himself a conscience after Jesse went to visit him. Hardwick brought all this information to my office this morning. Now, I don't know all the ins and outs. I figure the courts will have to look this over and hear some testimony from Hardwick and Jesse, but the evidence looks pretty clear to me."

"Jesse?" Her hands began to tremble. What did Jesse have to do with this? "Why do you keep saying Jesse?"

Sheriff Kemp blew out a gusty sigh. "Your hired man should have told you this himself, Lindsey. He's Madelyn Finch's son, the rightful owner of this land."

Blood thundered in her temples. She, who'd never fainted in her life, thought she might keel over on the coffee table and scatter gift wrap and ribbon everywhere.

She remembered, then, the times he'd taken off

work to attend to personal business and the times someone had told her they'd seen Jesse at the court-house. He'd been searching for proof that he, not she, owned this place.

Her voice, when she managed to speak, sounded small and faraway. "So that's the real reason Jesse came here."

She ached with the realization that his profession of love had been a lie.

"'Fraid so. Not that you can blame a man for trying to reclaim what was stolen from him. Especially since he has a little girl to care for. But he should have told you."

"Yes. He should have told me."

Her face felt hot enough to combust. Her whole body shook. Jesse had lied to her. She'd trusted him. Loved him.

Jesse had even gone as far as pretending to love her. There was always the chance he wouldn't find proof, but by marrying her, he could still take over the farm. Jesse had romanced her in order to regain the land any way he could.

Her heart shattered like a fragile Christmas ornament. Once more she'd been fooled by a hand-some face.

Jimmy Stewart flickered across the silent television screen. He was sitting at a bar, tears in his eyes as he prayed in desperation.

Understanding perfectly, she stared bleakly at the screen, lost and broken.

"Could I get you something, Lindsey?" Sheriff Kemp's kind voice broke into her tumultuous thoughts. His weathered face studied her with concern.

Pulling the reins on her emotions, she shook her head. "I'll be okay, but I need to be alone right now, if you don't mind."

"Understandable. Do you want to tell Jesse about this, or should I?"

Her pulse stumbled.

Jesse, no doubt, would be ecstatic.

"He'll have to come by my office," the sheriff went on. "He'll need to sign papers and such to get the ball rolling."

Lindsey gripped the edge of her chair, trying not to break down in front of the sheriff. She licked her lips, her mouth gone suddenly dry. "You tell him, please. He's down in the lot."

She'd trusted him. Oh, dear Lord, why had she trusted him?

"Maybe you should call a lawyer. There might be some way to fight this thing."

"I'll do that." Suddenly, she needed him gone. She needed to pray. And most of all, she needed Jesse to stay away from her until she could get her emotions under control. "Please, go talk to Jesse before he comes to the house." She despised the quaver in her voice. "I don't want to see him right now."

The poor sheriff was worried about her losing her farm. He didn't understand that she was losing that and a great deal more.

* * *

Jesse was halfway to the house when the sheriff came out onto the porch. His curiosity had been piqued from the moment the SUV pulled into the yard. But after the sheriff had stayed inside the house so long, Jesse got a bad feeling in the pit of his stomach. Something was up.

Jesse broke into a lope. If Lindsey needed him…

"What's up?" he asked as soon as he reached the policeman. His heart pounded oddly, not only from the jog, but from some inner voice of warning.

Expression serious, Sheriff Kemp handed him a file folder. "Stuart Hardwick came to see me this morning and confessed his part in swindling you out of your inheritance."

Jesse's head swung toward the house. "Lindsey."

"I told her."

"Oh, no." He had to get to her, make her understand. Spinning away, he started that direction. The sheriff's big hand stopped him.

"Leave her be, Jesse. She doesn't want to see you right now. Give her some time alone."

"But I have to explain."

"Explain what? That you came here under false pretenses, looking for information that would take this farm from her and return it to you? That you've been dishonest with her from the start?"

Jesse relented. Remorse pinned his boots to the ground. The sheriff was right. He hadn't lied to her directly, but his silence had been as dishonest as his reasons for taking this job. Lindsey had trusted him with everything, and all the while, he'd gone right on with his devious plans.

No wonder she didn't want to see him now—or possibly ever. How could he expect her to forgive him for worming his way into her heart under such deceitful circumstances? She had been hurt before, betrayed by a man she loved. And now he had hurt her again. He didn't deserve a woman like Lindsey Mitchell.

Sadness shuddered through him.

His arms fell limply to his sides. "I don't know what to do."

Misunderstanding, the sheriff took the file folder from him and said, "Come by the office later today or tomorrow, and we'll get the ball rolling with the legal system."

With an aura of resigned disapproval, the man departed, leaving Jesse standing in the yard of his rightful home. The afternoon air was cool, but sweat covered his body.

He stared around at the quiet little farm that he'd coveted since he was fourteen. All his adult life he'd longed for this moment.

And now, instead of the exultant victory he'd expected, Jesse suffered a heartbreak so profound he nearly went to his knees.

Lindsey was hurting. She needed comfort. But as much as he longed to go to her, he resisted. Lindsey didn't want him. She'd told the sheriff as much. Going to her now, after what he'd done, would only compound the hurt. Nothing he could say would change the truth. Regardless of his good intentions, of his decision not to pursue ownership, he had betrayed her trust.

After one long last look toward the house and the woman who held his heart, he headed for his truck and the trailer park. He didn't know where he would go, but he'd done all the damage any one man should do in this quiet, loving little town.

At last he knew what to give Lindsey for Christmas. This farm wasn't enough, though he'd certainly leave that behind. What she deserved was a return to her peaceful life without him to bring her any more pain or humiliation.

Packing wouldn't take long. The Slaters traveled light. He'd have the truck loaded in time to pick Jade up from school.

The thought of his little girl gave him pause. She'd changed so much here on Winding Stair Mountain. She was happier, healthier and free from many of her fears, thanks mostly to Lindsey's love and care.

His poor baby. She'd be as heartbroken as he was.

But he had no choice now. Better to get out of Lindsey's life and leave her alone.

With a deep sigh of sadness, Jesse drove through the picturesque old town. The cheerful decorations mocked him.

Once more Christmas had brought him heartbreak, but this time, the fault was his own.

Chapter Fifteen

"You can fight this, Miss Mitchell."

Stan Wright, a forty-something lawyer with a soothing baritone voice and intelligent brown eyes, regarded her across his littered desk. Having called the offices of Wright and Banks as quickly as she'd regained her equilibrium, Lindsey was relieved when he'd offered to see her within the hour.

"I don't want to fight it, Mr. Wright." She drew in a deep, steadying breath, determined to do the hardest thing she'd ever had to do. "The farm belongs to Jesse Slater and his daughter. They were cheated out of it through no fault of their own."

She didn't admit that the decision wasn't her original choice. Her first instinct had been anger and hurt and bitter resentment. She'd wanted to rail at Jesse and send him away. She'd wanted to keep the land to pay him back for lying to her, for making her believe he loved her when, all the while, he was plotting to evict her.

But as soon as the first rush of emotion passed, she'd prayed. And as hard as the decision was, she'd seen that Jesse was as much a victim as she. The land was rightfully his, and she wouldn't rest until he'd legally regained ownership.

"I understand the circumstances. But you've lived there in good faith and made the land productive. Even if the courts decide in his favor, he could be forced to pay you for all the improvements you've made, for the tree stock, etc."

She held out a hand to stop him. "No, sir. I want you to do whatever paperwork is required for me to sign away any claim to the entire eighty acres. I want Jesse Slater to take possession."

Shaking his head, Mr. Wright leaned back in his executive chair and rubbed a hand across his chin, Brown eyes studied her thoughtfully. "I wish you would take more time to think about this."

"I've had all the time I needed." Standing, she shook his hand, and if hers trembled the slightest bit, the attorney didn't comment. "Call me as soon as you have the papers drawn up."

With a final word of thanks, she left his office and went to her truck. She had a great deal to do between now and the first of the year. A job. A place to live. Maybe she'd go to Colorado and stay with her sister, Kim, for a while.

But for all her bravado, the ache in her chest grew

to the exploding point. The Christmas Tree Farm was not only her home, it was her dream. Leaving would tear her in two. But more terrible than losing the farm, was the loss of Jesse and Jade and the sweet plans they'd begun to weave together.

"Why, Jesse?" she whispered to the windshield. But she knew why. He'd done what he'd had to do in order to retake the farm. And pretending to love her had been part of the plan.

Heading the Dakota through town, she let the tears come. As hard as talking to him would be, Jesse needed to know her decision. Harboring unforgiveness would destroy her relationship with Jesus. So she'd take the first, painful step and tell Jesse the farm was his—and that she bore him no ill.

And that was the truth. She wasn't angry. But oh, the hurt was far worse than anything she'd suffered before.

The palms of her hands were moist with sweat by the time her Dakota crunched over the narrow gravel lane leading into the mobile-home park. All the trailers looked sad and a little run-down, but strings of lights and green wreaths spread the joy of Christmas here as everywhere.

Lindsey wasn't feeling much joy at the moment. Swiping at her soggy face, she blew her nose and composed herself. The next few minutes would be hard, but she'd get through them.

As she neared his trailer, she spotted Jesse outside, and her pulse leaped. Foolish heart, she loved him even though he'd betrayed her so terribly.

Jean jacket unbuttoned in the cold air, he was loading boxes into the back of his Silverado. Her stomach twisted at the implication. Was he planning to push her out of the house today?

As she pulled in to his parking area and killed the motor, Jesse looked up. Expression serious, his silver eyes bored into her like laser beams.

Stilling the awful trembling in her knees, Lindsey breathed a prayer for help and climbed out of the cab.

She stood on one side of the pickup bed. Jesse waited on the other.

"Lindsey." A muscle worked in his cheek. She recognized the movement as stress and longed to smooth her fingers over the spot and reassure him. No doubt he thought she hated him. But she couldn't.

From what she understood of the situation, Jesse was the victim of two unscrupulous men who'd stolen his birthright and left him to fend for himself. Thinking of a teenage Jesse scared and alone filled her with sadness.

Resisting the need to touch him, to feel his arms around her once more, she said what she'd come to say.

She hitched her chin up, struggling for control. "I would never keep something that isn't rightfully mine, Jesse. You didn't have to pretend to love me in order to get the farm back."

Her voice cracked the slightest bit on the last words. She bit her lip to keep from breaking down again.

Deep furrows appeared in Jesse's forehead. "What are you talking about? I never pretended—" He stopped, his expression incredulous. "You thought—?" He stopped again, dropped the box he carried into the bed of the truck and started around to her side.

He strode toward her with the strangest look on his face. Lindsey wasn't sure whether to run or stand her ground. Her heart clattered against her rib cage.

Never a coward, she stood her ground.

Lindsey's words lit a spark of hope inside Jesse. The crazy woman thought he didn't love her?

Stalking around the truck, he jabbed a finger at the air. "Let's get one thing straight, Miss Mitchell. I didn't *pretend* to love you. I do love you. I didn't want to, never intended to, but you were too amazing to resist. When Erin died, I thought my capacity to love died with her, but you, with your sweet, caring, decent ways proved me wrong."

A curtain in the next trailer twitched, letting Jesse know his voice had carried and he'd attracted an audience. Across the road, in the other row of trailers, a woman came out on her porch and pretended to adjust the wreath on her front door. All the while, she cast surreptitious peeks toward Jesse and Lindsey. He heard the squeak and swish of windows being raised.

Jesse didn't care if the whole world listened in. All that mattered was the mystified, suffering expression in Lindsey's red-rimmed eyes. She'd been crying—because of him.

He reached for her hand, aching to touch her, but afraid at the same time. When she didn't yank away, he celebrated a small victory. At least, they could part on speaking terms.

"The one constant in all this mess is right here." He placed her hand over his heart. "My love for you is real and true. It has nothing to do with the farm."

She blinked, shaking her head in denial. Her tawny mane tossed around her shoulders and Jesse itched to smooth it, to comfort her somehow.

"I don't understand. I thought you purposely moved here to reclaim the land."

"I did."

She shrank away, forcing him to release her. How he longed to change the past, to take back his devious intentions. But it was too late for that. He'd hurt her too much to expect forgiveness.

Arms falling helplessly to his sides, Jesse knew defeat. He stared up into the tree growing behind the trailer. His insides felt as bare and empty as the naked, reaching limbs of the sycamore.

"Someday, sweet Lindsey, I hope you will try to forgive me." His gaze found her beloved face and soaked in every feature, storing the memory. "But whether you do or not, I will always be grateful for our time together. I'll leave Winding Stair a better man for having known you."

Tears gathered in her eyes, and Jesse despised himself for causing them. "The farm is yours, Jesse. I'm the one who will be leaving. I only ask that you wait until after the holidays so I'll have time to make some arrangements."

The idea of Lindsey moving away from the home she loved cut through him like a chain saw. He stepped toward her again, desperately wanting to hold her, but the distrust in her expression stopped him. He shoved his hands in his jacket pockets instead.

"You're not going anywhere. I'm packed and ready. I'll inform the sheriff of my decision to renounce any claim to your land. As soon as I go by the school and get Jade, we'll be on our way."

Lindsey stared at him in disbelief. "After everything that's happened, you're leaving? You're giving up a home that's rightfully yours?"

"The place means nothing to me without you there."

Tears shoved at the back of his eyelids. If he didn't escape soon, he'd shame himself more than he already had. Spinning on his boot heel, he grabbed for the truck door and bounded inside. He cranked the engine, slammed the gear shift into Reverse and started to back out. One last glance at Lindsey's face stopped him.

Without understanding his new propensity for rejection, he rolled down the window and said, "Remember this much. I loved you. I still do."

Her sorrow turned to bewilderment. After a pregnant pause while time seemed to stand still and the nosy neighbors appeared to hold their collective breath, a trembling smile broke through her tears. In her flannel and denim, she looked radiant.

"Jesse," she said. "Oh, Jesse."

In the next minute, Lindsey yanked open the passenger door and bounded into the seat next to him.

He watched her, hoping, praying and utterly ter-rified to believe. "What are you doing?"

"I'm going with you," she said, alternately laughing and wiping tears. "To get Jade."

"You are?" Please say yes. Please say yes.

"And then we are all three going home, to *our* farm, where we belong." She gave him another of those tremulous smiles. "We have Christmas presents to wrap."

Understanding, pure and lovely, dawned. Jesse slammed the truck out of gear and did what he'd been yearning to do since her arrival. He pulled her into his arms. This time, she came willingly.

"I'm sorry, sweetheart. So sorry." Showering her face with kisses, he muttered apologies and profes-sions of love. "I should have told you from the be-ginning, but I didn't know you. I didn't know I'd love you so much. I was wrong, so wrong."

"I'm sorry, too." She took his face between her palms, her golden eyes boring into him with a love so strong he felt humbled. "For all that happened to you as a boy. For my unwitting part in forcing you to take such drastic measures."

With a laugh of joy, Jesse hugged her to his happy heart. God had forgiven him and now Lindsey had too.

After years of searching, he had completely and finally come home. To his faith, to his farm, and to the woman who healed him in a thousand ways.

He was the luckiest man alive.

Epilogue

Lindsey was sure she would never be happier than she was this Christmas morning. She sat on the edge of an ottoman next to the Christmas tree, surveying her world like a queen.

The farmhouse smelled toasty warm with pumpkin bread and spiced cider and the promise of baked ham for dinner. Presents littered the living-room floor, some already unwrapped and exclaimed over while others still waited for their treasures to be discovered. And though these pleased her, the real joy came from the two people beneath her Christmas tree—Jesse and Jade—the loves of her life.

They'd arrived early, almost as soon as Lindsey was dressed in her Christmas best—an outfit she'd purchased especially for today—a silky emerald blouse, long black skirt, and matching dress boots. From Jesse's expression and brow-pumping compliments, she concluded she'd chosen well. She even felt pretty this morning.

"You open one now, Lindsey." Jade pushed a package at her.

Lindsey shook her head. She needed no other presents than the ones she'd already received. After considerable discussion during which each had tried to give the other everything, she and Jesse had agreed to share ownership of the farm. More importantly, she could spend this special Christmas Day with the man and child she'd come to love so deeply.

The Virginia pine in the living room had long since given up its stately status. Laden with ornaments and tinsel, popcorn strings and lights, homemade angels and clay-dough cookies, Lindsey's Christmas tree was loaded to the breaking point—thanks to Jade's daily additions. She thought it was the gaudiest, most beautiful tree ever.

"I want to see you open all of yours first." She lifted the camera from her lap and aimed.

Dressed in dark red velvet, her black hair pulled away from her face with a matching bow, the little girl was exquisite. With typical six-year-old exuberance, she hugged a stuffed dog to her white lace collar.

"This is my Sushi. I love her."

The real Sushi, watching from her spot next to the furnace, lifted her head and woofed once.

"She loves you too," Jesse said, his beloved mouth kicking up at the corners.

Snapping the ribbons from a box with one quick jerk, he opened a gift from Lindsey.

She held her breath as he lifted the sweater from the tissue.

"Wow." He held the rich blue garment beneath his chin. "Now I'll look decent enough to accompany you beautiful ladies to church this morning."

Lindsey snapped a picture, happiness bubbling inside her. Jesse was as eager as she to spend this holy day together in God's house.

"Do you like it?" She thought the blue looked stunning with his mysterious silver eyes.

"Love it." He leaned across the pile of discarded wrapping paper and grabbed her hand, charming her with a wink. "But I love you more."

Heart somersaulting in delight, she tapped him lightly on the head. "You'd better."

With a gentle tug, he pulled her off the ottoman onto her knees in front of him. "No problem there. But I do have another problem."

The sea-breeze scent of his cologne was almost as heady as the teasing, tender glint in his eyes. "What is it?"

"Some stubborn woman I know won't open her presents."

She'd been too busy relishing Jade's reaction to everything. "Christmas isn't about presents to me, Jesse. It's about loving and giving, the way God gave us Jesus."

"I couldn't agree more. And that's what I'm trying to do here."

Jade lay aside the gift she'd been about to unwrap and scooted toward the two adults. "Now, Daddy? Now?"

Her jittery behavior and dancing eyes told Lindsey something was up.

"Now, Jade. I don't think I can stand the suspense."

"Me either, me either, me either." Jade bounced like a rubber ball.

Lindsey laughed. "What are the two of you up to?"

Jesse left her long enough to go to his jacket and return with a small, gold-wrapped box. "This."

Her heart stuttered, stopped and then went crazy inside her chest. Mouth dry as August sand, she took the gift.

"Go on. Open it. It won't bite." Jesse tried to joke, but his eyes were serious and the muscle below those eyes quivered. Jade appeared excited enough to explode.

With trembling fingers, Lindsey removed the wrapping to find, as she'd suspected, a black velvet ring box.

"Oh, Jesse." Such a silly thing to say, but her mind was frozen.

Gently, he took the box from her fingers and flipped it open.

"Come on, Jade," he said. "Let's do this right."

He went down on one knee in front of her, and to

Lindsey's great delight, Jade did the same. The sweetness of the picture overwhelmed her.

Jesse cleared his throat. "We've rehearsed this, so bear with us."

When he took her hand in his, she felt him tremble, and loved him all the more. "Lindsey Mitchell, I love you."

"I love you, Lindsey," Jade echoed.

The lump in Lindsey's throat thickened.

"I love you too," she whispered.

"We don't have much, but we can give you the most important things we own."

Jade touched her own chest. "Our hearts."

Tears welled in Lindsey's eyes. "You have mine too."

"Then, will you make our family complete and marry us? Will you be my wife?" Jesse slid the dainty solitaire onto her finger.

"And will you be my other mommy?"

"Yes. Oh yes." Lindsey could contain her joy no longer. She tumbled forward, grabbing both her loves into a giant hug.

First, she kissed Jade's cheek. "I promise to be the best mom I can."

And then while Jade giggled, Jesse took his turn, sealing the proposal with a kiss that promised a lifetime of love and honesty.

When at last they parted and sat smiling into one another's eyes, Jesse said, "Glad that's over. I didn't sleep a wink last night."

"Did you actually think I'd refuse?"

"I was afraid if I went to sleep, I'd wake up and discover you were a dream." His words melted her. "You are a dream. And I want to get married as soon as possible. Like tomorrow."

"Tomorrow?" Lindsey burst out in surprised laughter. In truth, she wanted the same thing. "Sorry, Mister Slater, but I've always dreamed of a Christmas wedding, and since it's too late for that this year, we'll have to wait until next Christmas."

"No way," Jessed howled.

"No way," Jade echoed, carefully sorting gifts into neat little piles.

Jesse thrust out a palm. "Hold it. I feel an idea coming on." An ornery twinkle lit the silvery eyes that had once been so wary and sad. "Not every place in the world celebrates Christmas on December twenty-fifth. Right?"

"Right." Lindsey agreed, unsure where he was heading. Not that she cared. She'd follow Jesse anywhere.

Suddenly, he clapped his hands together in victory. "Problem solved. According to a very famous song, there are really twelve days of Christmas. So there you have it. Christmas begins today and won't end until we're married twelve days from now." He squinted hopefully. "Okay?"

Happiness danced through Lindsey's veins. She'd only been teasing about waiting until next Christmas. She wanted to be Jesse's wife now.

"We'll talk to Pastor Cliff today and if he agrees, we'll be married among the trees on the twelfth day of Christmas. Just don't bring me any partridges or maids a-milking."

With a whoop of joy, Jesse grabbed her and twirled her around in a circle. "This is the best Christmas of my life."

"Mine too."

He stilled and grew serious. "No kidding?"

"All my adult life, I've wanted my home filled with love and laughter. With a husband and children. This year, God has granted me those gifts."

"Do you think the people at church will be surprised? About our engagement, I mean."

"I don't know," she admitted. "But I'm eager to find out. Let's go early and tell everyone as they come in."

Jesse surveyed the disarrayed living room. "What about this mess and the unwrapped gifts?"

She slipped into the long wool coat she'd laid out earlier along with her purse and Bible. "They'll wait."

Jesse disappeared and came back wearing his new sweater. He was so handsome, he took her breath away. With a wide grin, he shrugged into his jacket and then helped Jade into hers.

Watching her two loves, Lindsey rejoiced. God was good. And on this glorious Christmas morning, He had blessed her exceedingly abundantly above all she could ever have thought or asked.

Jesse had come to Winding Stair with wrongful intent, but God had turned the bad to good. Only the

Lord could have foreseen that the two of them, both with claims to the Christmas Tree Farm, needed each other to make their life circles complete. Only God could have made everything turn out so beautifully.

"Thank You, Jesus," she said, her cup overflowing.

"Amen to that." Jesse held out a hand and she took it. Jade clasped the other.

Then, together as a family, the trio headed out into the bright sunny morning, eager to celebrate the birth of their Savior and to announce their best Christmas present ever.

* * * * *

Dear Reader,

Ah, the memories Christmas evokes in me. I can almost hear my son's voice coming through the darkness at 5:00 a.m. as he stands at my bedroom door asking if it's time to open the presents. I think of the smells, too. Of cedar boughs and baked turkey. Of orange slices and cinnamon cookies. And the beautiful sights. Colored lights and silver tinsel. My little girl dressed in red velvet with bows in her hair. Christmas is truly a time of wonder and joy. A time to celebrate all that's good and right. Most of all, it's a time for memories of past Christmases. For Jesse Slater, bad memories outweighed the good ones. If that's the case with you, I hope you'll do what Jesse did. Let the unsurpassed love of God restore and heal you this holiday season.

Wishing you an especially joyous Christmas,

Linda Goodnight

A VERY SPECIAL DELIVERY

There is now therefore no condemnation
to them that are in Christ Jesus.
—*Romans* 8:1

In memory of
(Bubby) Joseph Kayne Matthews

Chapter One

A wintry mix of freezing rain, sleet and snow peppered the roof and rattled the windows of the old farmhouse. Icy tentacles of cold snaked beneath the door to rush across the hardwood floors and over the gray cat sleeping on the colorful oval rug. Molly McCreight shivered, laid aside her book, and rose from her cozy spot in front of the blazing fireplace. The cat stirred, too, gazing up with curious green eyes.

"Ah, be still, Samson. I'm just going to poke something against that door. If Bart Crimshaw had fixed it last summer like he was supposed to…" She let the words and thoughts drift away. Bart, the beast, hadn't ever done anything he was supposed to do. He'd disappeared like all the others as soon as he realized she wasn't kidding when she said she would never be interested in having children.

"But we don't care, do we, Samson? We're doing fine, just fine, without any of them."

The cat's ears flicked, though he stayed beside the glowing fire. She wasn't doing just fine and even Samson knew it. She mourned for the loss of her once-close relationships with her mother and her sister, Chloe, and most of all, she mourned for baby Zack.

Since she'd taken the job at the Winding Stair Senior Citizen Center things had been a little better, but the estrangement from her family still lay like a rock in the pit of her stomach.

As she mumbled to the bored-looking cat, Molly took a towel from the bathroom, rolled the thick terry-cloth like a jelly roll and stuffed it under the front door.

"Listen to that wind." Hunching her shoulders, she rubbed her upper arms as if to ward off the outside chill. "It's a miracle we still have electricity."

Above the incessant howl of winter came a low hum.

"What in the world?" Molly pulled the heavy antique-rose drape away from the window and peered out. Though the time was not yet six o'clock, outside was as dark as sin. "Surely, that's not a vehicle way out here in this storm?"

Thick layers of ice already coated the windows, the porch and the front of the house. More of the icy pellets and rain fell in such abundance she was hard-pressed to make out the faint glow of lights in the distance. The hum of a motor increased, coming closer. Since her farmhouse sat a ways off the main gravel road, Molly knew the visitor was headed in her direction.

When the freezing rain had begun early that morning, she had done the sensible thing and prepared for the certain storm ahead. She'd filled the wood box and piled enough extra wood on the porch to keep her going for days even though the propane tank was full. She'd run water into buckets though the water had never frozen in the two years she'd lived on the remote farm in Oklahoma's Kiamichi Mountains. And she'd made a pot of vegetable beef stew to die for just because the rich aroma of stewed tomatoes and beef filtering through the house made her feel warmer.

"Looks like a truck of some sort," she muttered, frowning through the narrow window in the front door. She flipped on the porch light and strained her eyes against the darkness camped beyond the yard.

"It *is* a truck, Samson. A delivery truck." Her frown deepened. "Now, what kind of idiot…?"

The headlights disappeared as if they'd been sucked inside the dying motor. A smaller light signaled the opening of the van door. With a muffled thud, that light was extinguished also.

Molly made out the hurrying form of a man, not overly tall, but not short either, picking his way over the crusty ice toward her front porch. Bundled against the frigid weather, he looked thick and heavy but moved with speed and agility, his arms crossed in front of him in a posture Molly found odd for running.

He was carrying something. At times, she ordered a lot of things, but come on.

"No package could be that important."

When the man's feet thudded against the wooden porch, Molly yanked the door open, gasping at the sudden blast of frigid air. Shadowed beneath the glowing yellow light with sleet and bits of snow swirling around him, the man peered down at her from under a brown bill cap. He was a uniformed delivery man, all right. She recognized the familiar dark brown truck that sailed up and down the country roads delivering packages. The man himself looked vaguely familiar, but he wasn't her usual delivery man.

"Ma'am, I was wondering if you could—"

She didn't give him a chance to finish. The cold air was filling up her cozy little house, and she wasn't about to stand on ceremony in this kind of weather. He couldn't be a criminal. Even an ax murderer had better sense than to be out in this weather. Only a working stiff would be so dedicated.

"Get in here before you freeze." With one hand she shoved the storm door wide and with the other she grasped his thick, quilted sleeve and pulled. That's when she realized what he was carrying against his chest. Not a package. A bundle. A soft, quilted bundle decorated with yellow ducks and pink rabbits. She yanked her hand away and stared long and hard as the delivery man stomped into the house, sprinkling ice pellets all over the floor. He ushered in the unmistakable scent of cold air on a warm body.

Molly shut the door and kicked the towel against it, all the while staring in disbelief at the bundle in the delivery man's arms.

The man went straight for the fireplace and stood close, his back to her. Molly followed him, keeping her eyes on the bundle. Maybe it wasn't what she thought it was.

"The roads are so bad, I was afraid I wouldn't make it back to town. Don't need to tell you what would happen if I got stranded and ran out of gas in this weather."

"No."

There would be enough horror stories in the days to come of motorists or other hapless folks who'd gotten caught out in this. The occasional Oklahoma ice storms were notorious for paralyzing entire sections of the state. Sometimes weeks would pass before the roads were cleared, power back on, and life returned to normal. Aunt Patsy, the farm's true owner, had spent her share of days stranded up here while waiting for the ice to melt or the road grader to arrive in this remote portion of the county.

"I'm sorry to intrude on you this way." A pair of sincere blue eyes—worried eyes—peered at her. Normally she would have considered such eyes, rimmed as they were in black spiky lashes, especially attractive. And the rest of his face—clean-shaven, lean and honest—was only made more ruggedly attractive by a narrow scar that sliced one eyebrow and disappeared upward into a neat crew cut. She found the scar intriguing—and appealing.

The bundle in his arms was an entirely different matter.

"You're the closest house for miles," he said, as though that gave him the right to remind her of what she could never forget.

Most times she loved the solitude of living miles from nowhere, driving in to her job and then hurrying home to her little farm. In town she could always feel the stares, the eyes of suspicion, and hear the not-so-subtle whispers. No matter that the tragedy happened two years ago, a small town never forgot—or forgave—such a terrible transgression. How could they when she couldn't even forgive herself?

"You got a telephone?"

Her gaze flickered up to his and quickly back to the bundle. Yellow ducks and pink rabbits. Foreboding crept up her spine, colder than the outside temperatures. "Phone's been out since noon."

"Figures. My communication system is down, too, and cell phones are impossible up here in the hills."

Molly knew that. No one in these mountains even considered buying a cell phone.

Tormented by thoughts of the bundle, she turned her back to the fire and tried not to think too much. *Please, Lord, please. Let that be a doll. Or a puppy.*

The bundle stirred; a soft cooing issued from the quilt. Molly's pulse rate jumped a notch. That was no puppy.

"Ma'am…" the delivery man began.

"Molly," she interrupted, stepping back, terrified of what he was about to say. "I'm Molly McCreight."

"Pleased to meet you, ma'am, and I'm Ethan Hunter." He thrust the bundle toward her. "Do you know anything about babies?"

Her heart stopped beating for a full three seconds. She couldn't breath. There really was a baby inside that mass of quilts and blankets.

In all his thirty-three years, Ethan had never seen a female react this way to a baby. The red-haired woman turned deathly pale, her brown eyes widened in panic as she backed slowly toward the crackling fireplace behind her. Usually, little Laney was a regular chick magnet, drawing unwanted female attention even when he stopped at the supermarket for a carton of milk or a bag of diapers. But tonight when he actually desired that little bit of magic, the woman in question looked as if she'd rather jump into the fireplace than touch his baby daughter.

"I know this is unusual, ma'am."

"Molly," the woman whispered through white lips, her gaze never leaving Laney's blankets.

"Molly," he tried again. "I'm sorry to intrude on you this way, but I have a delivery that must be made tonight."

Her eyes widened in panic. "Here?"

"No, ma'am. To Mr. Chester Stubbs."

She looked up, interested, concerned, though her

blanched face never regained its former peaches-and-cream color. "I know Chester. He lives about as far back into the mountains as you can get and still be on this planet."

"Exactly. And the roads up in there are little more than winding trails." Every inch of the way from town, over slick and ice-packed roads, he'd prayed, believing with all his might that he was meant to deliver this gamma. For the last half hour he'd prayed to find some safe place to leave Laney. When he'd seen the glow of this farmhouse, the only place for miles, he'd been certain this was the Lord's answer. But now, given Molly McCreight's reluctance, he wasn't so sure.

"Can't the delivery wait until this ice storm thaws?"

"No, ma'am. It's gamma, and gamma can't wait."

Her startled eyes flicked from Laney to him. "What in the world is gamma?"

"A high-powered cancer treatment. Once a patient begins treatment, his infusion must be delivered on time. Gamma's shelf life is only eight hours. More than two hours has already passed since I picked up the gamma from the lab. In six hours Mr. Stubbs will die unless I can get up that mountain."

His declaration sounded overly dramatic to Molly, but she knew Chester was battling cancer. Chester and Mamie Stubbs were one of the nicest couples around, and if Chester needed that treatment, she wanted him to have it. The older couple had been kind to her, showing her what real Christian love and compassion was all about when her own family had turned its back.

"Then you have no choice. Go."

Ethan's shoulders relaxed as he began to unwrap the bundle in his arms.

Fear and a sudden premonition shot up Molly's spine. "What are you doing?"

"Your house is warm. Laney won't need all this cover in here. I'll just lay her in that big chair over there and she'll sleep most of the time I'm gone."

Panic raised the level of her voice. "You're not leaving her here?"

Baffled blue eyes blinked at her. "I thought we just agreed to that."

Molly rasped her tongue over lips that had suddenly gone as dry as baby powder. "I never agreed to any such thing."

"But I can't take her with me. What if I don't make it? What if the truck runs into a ditch?"

Knees trembling, Molly retreated to the other side of the room, placing a fat old easy chair between herself and the baby. She gripped the back, digging her fingers into the thick upholstery—holding on for dear life.

"Why did you bring her out in this weather in the first place?"

"I'm afraid I didn't have a choice in the matter. The daycare closed early because of the storm, and I had no place else to take her."

"Where's your wife?"

The man's face froze as surely as if he'd stayed out on her porch all night. Blue eyes frosted over. He pulled the sleeping bundle a little closer to his chest. "I don't have a wife."

He had a baby but not a wife. Now there was an interesting story she was certain, but not one she cared to explore. Men, especially a man with a motherless baby, were at the bottom of her social calendar.

Molly had only been hysterical once in her entire life—the last time she'd held a baby—and she didn't care to repeat the experience.

"I'm sorry, Mr…Ethan, babies and I don't get along very well. Someone else will have to deliver that medicine to Mr. Stubbs."

Impatience flickered across his face. The rugged-looking scar blanched. "There is no one else."

Molly knew he was telling the truth and that she was being unreasonable. He'd traveled this far in that truck, but the chances of him getting up that mountain were slim. The chances of anyone else making it this far were practically zero.

"Wait a minute." A sudden thought struck her. "If this gamma stuff is some sort of chemotherapy, who's going to do the infusion? Don't you need a nurse or a doctor for that?"

"Normally, but the home health nurse can't get there."

"What good will the medication be without someone to administer it?"

"I can do the infusion. That's why the company

sent me. Otherwise, Laney and I would be safely home for the night."

Molly squinted in consideration. A baby but no wife. A delivery man with medical expertise who was willing to risk his life to make a nearly impossible delivery. Ethan Hunter was as full of secrets as she was.

"Are you a doctor masquerading as a UPS driver?"

She wished she hadn't asked. The handsome lips narrowed to a thin line. The sculpted jaw clenched, blanching the beguiling scar snow-white.

"Look, Molly, a man's life depends on me, and the clock is ticking here. All I'm asking you to do is babysit for a couple of hours. You obviously aren't going out anywhere, and I'll pay you well. Why should that be such a big deal?"

If only he knew, he wouldn't let her within breathing distance of his daughter. But that was a secret she couldn't share with a stranger.

Suddenly too hot despite the frigid temperatures, Molly moved from the fireplace to the window. The ice pellets pecked incessantly at the glass pane like angry birds. In the glow of the yard light, ice glistened on everything in sight. Trees bent low and power lines bowed with the heavy encrustation of ice. In only a matter of time the lines would snap and the power would go.

What could she do? What choice did she have? Chester's life depended on this gamma stuff, and as much as she wanted to argue the point, taking a baby out in this weather was unconscionable. Regardless of her family's accusations, she'd never intentionally cause harm to anyone, especially a child.

She sighed, wishing she'd stayed in town with Aunt Patsy last night when the first warnings had come about the ice storm.

No, that was selfish. She didn't wish that. She wished she wasn't such a coward.

Ethan Hunter certainly wasn't. This man with the baby was willing to put his own life at risk to help an old man he didn't even know. And he was willing to put his child's life in her less-than-capable hands to do it.

Lord, what a mess. Please help me know what to do.

She dropped into the overstuffed chair and rubbed at shoulder muscles gone as tight as cheap shoes.

"Ethan, you don't even know me. How can you be sure I'll take proper care of your daughter?"

He studied her for a long, serious moment then smiled. Molly's breath caught in her throat. Goodness, gracious and mercy! Ethan Hunter was devastatingly handsome when he smiled.

"The eyes are the windows to the soul. That's what my mama taught me."

"Oh, so my eyes tell you that I'm good with children?"

He came toward her, hunkering down in front of the chair, the baby still in his arms. "They tell me you're a good person. A little sad, maybe, and real scared of something, but a gentle, caring woman who'll look after Laney with everything in you."

Disturbed by his all-too-accurate assessment,

Molly lowered her gaze to the baby, her stomach churning in trepidation. Chester's life hung on her decision. Spending even an hour alone with a baby would be pure torture, but she had no choice. She had to do this. She only hoped the baby's life wasn't in jeopardy, too.

Chapter Two

Molly stood at the window watching as the delivery truck struggled down the driveway, this time leaving her alone with a diaper bag and a small baby. The hazy fog of ice crystals blocked the van from view in no time and the howling wind covered the hum of the disappearing motor. He was gone. And she was alone for the first time in two years with someone else's baby.

She hadn't had a panic attack in the last six months, had believed she was finally past the painful valley of mourning, but she was near the point of panic now. The terror that closed off the windpipe and rattled the pulse wasn't far from taking over. Drawing in a deep breath, she rested her cheek against the frozen windowpane and quoted the scripture Aunt Patsy had made her personalize and memorize. *God has not given me the spirit of fear.*

Even though she still struggled to believe that God was with her, helping her, the scripture somehow calmed her terror. It hadn't at first, but over the months of constant repetition and Aunt Patsy's gentle counsel, she'd slowly gained control over the attacks.

A soft mewling sound issued from behind her. Whirling, hand at her tight throat, Molly hurried to the couch. True to his word, Ethan had moved the chair against the sofa and organized the cushions so that the baby wouldn't fall, but he'd been wrong about her staying asleep. Wide awake, blue eyes gazing up at Molly, the child gnawed at a tiny pink fist.

"God has not given me the spirit of fear," she mumbled as she pulled a straight-backed chair next to the couch to be near the baby. Maybe if she watched the child every second nothing terrible would happen.

The baby kicked and gooed, squirmed and sucked at her fist, but she didn't go back to sleep. Molly sat rigidly, afraid to move, afraid even to blink. After fifteen minutes her neck muscles ached and she needed to go to the bathroom, a dilemma that meant leaving the baby alone—unthinkable—or picking her up— terrifying. The last baby she'd touched had been dead.

Her scalp prickled from the memory. Baby Zack, his little body still warm, limp and lifeless against her chest as she ran screaming, screaming into the front yard of her sister's house. Neighbors had come running, she didn't know where from, though it was late summer when folks still enjoyed puttering in their gardens and cooking outside. One man carried a garden hoe to frighten away an attacker. But there was no attacker. And all the concerned neighbors in Winding Stair, Oklahoma, couldn't help baby Zack.

The panic started to crawl up Molly's spine once more. Her grip on the chair would surely leave the imprint of her fingers in the wood. She had to hold on. She could not suffer a panic attack while this child was in her care.

No telephone to call for help. No Aunt Patsy to talk her through. This time she'd have to rely on God alone.

A glance at the anniversary clock resting on the fireplace mantel told her that Ethan had been gone all of thirty minutes. At this rate she'd be crazy before he returned.

She refocused her attention on the baby. With a jolt, she saw that Laney's eyes were now closed. Was she asleep or—? The awful thought forced her to do what she dreaded most. Fingers trembling, she reached out, slowly, slowly, and laid a hand on the flannel-clad chest.

A shudder of relief rippled through her at the gentle rise and fall of the sleeping baby's ribcage. Some nameless emotion stirred in Molly's chest at the soft feel of an infant. Even the smell of her, that wonderful baby mixture of milk and lotion, made Molly's chest ache with longing.

Until Zack's death she'd always dreamed of getting married and having a big family. Lots of kids. That's what she'd told everyone. But now that would never happen. Her sister Chloe's healthy, perfect six-month-old son had died while in her care. She must have done something wrong. Or maybe she hadn't watched him closely enough. That's what her sister had said the last time Molly had tried to ask forgiveness.

As much as she'd wanted children, she could never take such a chance again. Chloe was right. Babies just weren't safe with her.

Rubbing gentle circles on the chest of the one now in her care, Molly felt an undeniable sense of loss.

"You sure are a pretty thing," she whispered.

Dark eyelashes curled against rose-over-ivory cheeks, and her round face was topped by a cap of fine, dark hair. Molly couldn't help but wonder about the mother. What had happened to her? And why had Ethan's face gone all tense when Molly had asked about her?

Healthy and well cared for, the baby looked to be about three or four months old, younger than Zack, but not by much. Her pink sleepers, emblazoned with the words Daddy's Girl were clean and neat. Whatever Ethan Hunter's situation with Laney's mother, he loved his little girl.

Samson rose from his spot near the fireplace, stretched his long gray feline body then padded across the room. Before Molly saw what he was about, the cat leaped onto the couch and tiptoed quietly toward the sleeping child.

"Samson, no. Get down."

The cat, as usual, ignored her. He sniffed curiously

at Laney's mouth, an act that must have tickled, for the baby's face scrunched up and she turned her head. Suddenly Laney remembered the old wives' tale that a cat could steal a baby's breath.

With more force than she intended, she grabbed Samson and sailed him onto the floor. The shocked animal stared at her in resentment, flicked his tail and stalked to his rug by the crackling fireplace.

Feeling worse than ever, Molly returned to her post beside the sleeping child. Cautiously, she placed her hand on the little chest once again and felt the movements that assured her the baby was breathing. If she had to sit this way all night long, she would. But oh, how she prayed that Ethan Hunter would soon return and take this responsibility off her shoulders.

Nearing midnight, eyes burning from staring into the frozen night, Ethan started back down the mountain. He hadn't reached the Stubbs's remote cabin until nearly nine o'clock, and the grateful couple had fortified him with coffee and brownies while the gamma infused into Chester's blood system.

During those hours with his patient the storm outside had worsened. The world around him was white and crystallized, a fairy tale turned into a nightmare. Chester and Mamie Stubbs had invited him to spend the night, but he'd refused. Laney was waiting. And from Molly's reaction to his child, she was waiting, too—waiting for him to return and take the baby off her hands.

A mighty gust whipped across an open pasture and the van rocked precariously.

Ethan couldn't remember ever driving—or flying—in an ice storm of this caliber. Since leaving the Stubbs's farm he'd stopped over and over again to break ice off his windshield wipers. The delivery van wasn't made to handle these conditions, and even chains on the tires wouldn't have helped on what was now a solid sheet of ice.

Shoulders hunched over the wheel, he stared hard into the night. His headlights reached only a few feet out into the blinding shower of white pellets. He could hardly tell where the road ended and the ditch began. Visibility was next to nothing. During his years as a paramedic helicopter pilot for a medical service he'd grown accustomed to flying by instruments when necessary. Too bad ground transport didn't offer the same technology.

Inch by inch, the van ground slowly forward. Like a shower of tiny rocks, ice tapped relentlessly against the outside. At this rate, he'd be hours getting back to Molly's place. In the past he would have thrown caution to the wind and taken the necessary risks, but no more. Speeding up was a deadly game, and he had a baby waiting for him.

Since the moment Twila had told him she was pregnant, Laney had become his sole focus in life. Though he'd felt safe in doing so, he disliked leaving her with Molly McCreight, a woman who obviously didn't embrace the idea of caring for an infant. His jaw tensed, remembering Laney's mother. What was the matter with women these days? Weren't females naturally supposed to enjoy babies?

He sighed heavily and squinted into the darkness. Maybe not. Maybe his was an old-fashioned dream. Just because his mother was a nurturer whose life had revolved around her kids, didn't mean modern women felt the same. Mom was from a different era when home and family mattered.

He'd had no choice but to leave Laney at the warm, safe farm. Even though she didn't want Laney there, Ethan knew in his heart Molly McCreight would take good care of her. He didn't know how he knew, but he knew. His baby was in good hands.

Ice-coated wipers scraped across the windshield, doing little good, even with the defrosters blasting constant heat. Time to stop again and clear them off. The window, too, was coated in ever-thickening sleet. Easing to a crunching halt, he put the truck in Park, and took the can of de-icer and the ice scraper from the seat beside him. As he leaped from the truck the ice pellets hit him with the force of a sandblaster, driving into his cheeks and neck. He shuddered once, hunched his shoulders against the cold before setting to work.

The world around him was a foreign place. Fence lines had disappeared and electric poles leaned threateningly. Before long there would be few landmarks to guide him. He'd have to be very careful.

"Just me and You, Lord," he said, and the wind slammed ice against his teeth.

In the few short months since he'd become a Christian he'd said those words plenty of times. And now, as every time, he'd felt that calm assurance that he was not alone. No matter what happened, God would be here with him.

Windshield cleared for the moment, he slammed back into the warm truck and dropped the gear into Low. The wheels spun but the van didn't move. Accelerating slightly, Ethan felt the tires start to slide sideways. He fought against the skid, used every bit of his considerable expertise to bring the vehicle under control, but the ice was too much. In seconds, one side of the van tilted sideways into a ditch he hadn't even known was there.

With a sinking sensation in the pit of his stomach, Ethan got out to survey the situation.

The van was hopelessly stuck. The Stubbs' place was at least four miles back. He'd never be able to walk that far in this weather. But he couldn't stay here either. No one would be along this road for days, maybe weeks.

He had little choice but to walk to Molly McCreight's farmhouse, even though he wasn't sure how far that was. With a heavy sigh of dread, he bundled himself as much as possible for the trek, took the flashlight from beneath his seat and stepped out into the wretched storm. He gasped as a sharp north wind slammed into him. Tears stung his eyes.

Less than ten minutes later ice encrusted his eyelashes and obscured his vision. He scraped at them, but his gloves, too, were covered with a fine layer of ice. Several times he slipped and nearly lost his footing, but he trudged on, keeping his focus on getting back to the baby he loved more than life itself. Thinking of Laney had given him the strength to do a lot of difficult things in the past year, and he thanked God every day for the gift of his daughter.

Molly McCreight's pinched face came to mind. He'd liked her the minute she'd pulled him into her house, welcoming him without even asking his business. And he'd liked her house. The neat country hominess—if that was a word—and the tantalizing fragrance of food cooking had reminded him of his parents' home.

He'd thought she was cute, too, with those brown-gold eyes and a sprinkle of freckles across her small nose. But from her reaction to his daughter, Molly was no different than Twila Thompson.

Still, there was something about her that appealed to him. And thinking of Molly and Laney safe and warm in the old farmhouse helped him keep moving.

Bending his neck against the north wind, Ethan shone the flashlight around him. No lights. No houses. Nothing. The flashlight danced wildly. For the first time, he noticed he was shivering and wondered when that had begun. His feet moved more slowly now, too. Even filtered through a muffler, the air hurt his lungs, burning so badly he could hardly stand to draw another breath. The scar over his eye throbbed painfully.

He'd never been this cold before. With every step, sparks, like frozen electricity, shot through his feet. Ethan considered this a good sign. They weren't frostbitten—yet.

He had no idea how far he'd walked, but he did know one thing for certain. Hypothermia was setting in. If he didn't find shelter soon, he'd freeze to death.

The idea sent a surge of adrenaline into his bloodstream. Nothing could happen to him. Baby Laney depended upon him. He was all the parent she had.

"Just me and You, Lord," he muttered through stiff, numb lips.

Snow and ice swirled around him, punishing him with every step, but the warm presence of God strengthened him.

He'd gone less than fifty more feet when he spotted the feeble glow of yellow against the raging white night. Had he not been so cold and miserable, he'd have shouted for joy.

He turned toward the light, trudging, struggling against the bitter wind and within minutes stumbled onto the now-familiar wooden porch.

Without bothering to knock, he shoved open the door. And fell face first into Molly McCreight's arms.

Molly wasn't sure whether to scream in fright or praise God that Ethan Hunter was still breathing. He weighed a ton compared to her, and most of that weight was now shifted to her shoulders. She half dragged, half walked him to a big blue easy chair. Shudders racked his body. His skin was red and windburned. The ice frozen on his eyelashes tore at her heart.

Where was his van? Had he had an accident? Had he made it to Chester's place?

"Ethan." He was by far the most nearly-frozen human being she'd ever seen, but she saw no sign of other injuries. "Are you all right? What happened?"

Stiff lips replied, "Heat exhaustion."

Molly held back a smile. Interesting man to joke under such dire conditions.

"I'll get something hot for you to drink. Stay right here."

Then she laughed at her own silliness. The man could barely move. After a quick glance at the baby, Molly hurried into the kitchen and shoved a cup of instant cocoa into the microwave. While the drink heated, she turned on the flame beneath the pot of beef stew. Ethan would need some hearty, hot food, too. Then she could find out what had happened.

At the beep, beep of the microwave, Molly grabbed the thick brown mug and rushed back to the stranger in her living room. His head lay back and his eyes were closed, but he opened them the minute she reappeared.

She offered him the steaming, rich-scented cocoa.

With a shake of his head, he spoke through chattering teeth. "Too shaky. I'll spill it."

Perplexed, Molly thought for a moment. He absolutely had to get warm—and fast. Ethan would be sick if she didn't get him warmed up soon. If he fell ill in her house so far from town, she'd be left to care for him and his infant daughter. And for her peace of mind, she wanted him and his baby out of here as soon as possible.

What he needed was a good hot bath to chase off the chill, but the idea of offering such a personal thing to a stranger was out of the question. The next best alternative was an electric blanket—and she did have that.

"Will you be okay for a minute?"

"Sure." His ice-encrusted eyelids fell shut. His red-blue lips barely moved.

"I'll get some blankets, but first let's move you closer to the fire."

Grabbing his ice-coated arm, she pulled as he heaved upward. They stumbled to the chair she'd pulled as close as possible to the blaze. As Ethan collapsed once more, he muttered, "Laney?"

What a great dad. Even half-frozen, he still worried about his baby. "She's asleep."

Molly gazed down at him for a second, curious to know more about a man strong enough to risk himself for someone else but tender enough to care for a tiny baby girl.

He was definitely different than most men she knew.

"I'll be right back," she said.

In winter the back of the big, rambling house was closed off to preserve fuel. A trip into the frigid space was always made in haste, so in minutes, she was back in the living room, loaded with blankets.

Ethan remained inert, but his chest rose and fell

in exhaustion. The ice attached to his hair and clothes had begun to thaw. Small puddles formed around his feet. Damp spots appeared on his jacket and hat. His leather gloves dripped onto his pant legs.

"You need to get out of that jacket and hat," Molly said, reaching for the stocking cap. It came away, leaving behind a rumpled mess of brown hair.

Ethan roused enough to struggle with his gloves.

"Your fingers are numb. Let me." Without considering the familiarity of such an action, Molly pulled the stiff, wet gloves from his hands, fretting over the reddened, icy fingers as she reached for the zipper on his jacket.

At her touch, Ethan's hand stayed hers. "I got it."

Suddenly embarrassed and more than a little self-conscious, Molly whirled toward the pile of blankets. Behind her, she heard the rustle of his jacket as she plugged in the electric blanket.

"Sorry about the mess."

"Don't be silly." Molly draped the blanket around his shoulders, adding two others for insulation and an old quilt around his legs. "We'll have you warmed up in no time."

"Appreciate it." His head fell back against the old stuffed chair that had been her late uncle Ray's favorite reading spot.

Gradually, Ethan's shudders subsided and he grew still. Except for the crackle of burning logs and the constant onslaught of sleet pecking at the windows, the room was unnervingly quiet.

She wanted to turn on the television, check the weather, but worried the noise might disturb the baby.

A jolt of fear, as powerful as an electrical shock, ripped through her.

The baby.

She had been so preoccupied with the near-frozen Ethan that she'd momentarily forgotten Laney. Was she all right?

Knees going weak, throat dry as talcum powder, Molly was afraid to look at the makeshift baby bed.

Her breath grew short and her heart rate accelerated as the beginnings of a panic attack threatened.

Ethan was in no shape to take care of himself, much less a baby. How could she be so stupid, so incompetent to forget that a baby was in her care after what had happened to Zack?

"God has not given me the spirit of fear." Approaching the couch, mind flashing photos of a dead child, she clasped a hand against her throat, panting.

A pair of midnight-blue eyes blinked up at her from amidst the yellow-and-blue bunny blankets.

Molly, limp with relief, melted to the floor beside the sofa. Laying her forehead against the cushions, she thanked God that little Laney had suffered no ill effects from her neglect.

She was still there, attention glued to the baby, when Ethan began to stir. He thrust off all but one blanket and stood up.

"Man, do I feel better."

As Molly looked up, her heart leaped wildly. He

looked better, too. The UPS driver, scar and all, was a hunk!

"You aren't shaking anymore."

"No, but you are." He frowned down at where she knelt beside the couch. "And you're pale. Are you okay?"

Molly pushed up from her spot on the oval rug and ran sweaty palms down the sides of her sweatpants. "Fine. How about that cup of cocoa now?"

Anything to avoid the subject of why she was so afraid of a tiny baby.

"Sounds good." Weariness emanated from him. If she'd known him better and the situation had not been so serious, Molly would have teased him about the hot-pink blanket draped around his broad shoulders—an incongruous sight if ever there was one.

"How about a bowl of beef stew with that cocoa?"

"Did anyone ever tell you you're a nice lady?"

"I take it you haven't had supper?"

"Coffee and brownies, but they're long gone."

"Did you get all the way up to Chester's?"

He nodded his head. "Yes, thank God."

"It couldn't have been easy."

"No, but my part was a lot easier than Chester's. He's one tough character."

Still, Molly couldn't help but admire Ethan's determination to help another person under such dire circumstances.

The clock had been ticking and Chester's life had

depended upon Ethan—and the Lord—to get the medication there on time.

Molly hustled into the kitchen, returning in a matter of minutes with the hot meal.

Ethan settled on the end of the couch next to Laney and told Molly about the trip up the mountain, the hours with Chester, and finally about the truck sliding into a ditch.

"Don't know how I made it in that light-bodied van." He shook his head and corrected himself. "Yes, I do. The Lord." He dug into the steaming bowl of soup. "Hot stew sure hits the spot."

Somehow she'd known Ethan was a Christian, though she'd learned the hard way that not all Christians were as self-sacrificing.

But Ethan was a man who took responsibility seriously and didn't give up easily. She liked that about him.

She liked the way he ate, too, like her dad and uncles, wholeheartedly as though he might never eat again. His appreciation of a simple bowl of stew made her smile.

From what little she'd seen, and from the way he cared for his child, Molly thought she could find a lot of things to like about Ethan Hunter.

He took a bite of cornbread, chewed and swallowed. "I hate to ask this of you, but I don't have a way back to town tonight. You wouldn't happen to have a bunkhouse or a barn I could sleep in, would you? Just for tonight, I mean. If my van was here, I could sleep in that, but..." He lifted one shoulder in a shrug.

"There's a barn, but you would freeze out there."

Practical to the bone, impropriety didn't concern Molly, but it would upset Aunt Patsy. She shifted uncomfortably, fretting. Letting a man freeze to death would be a lot worse than letting him spend the night. "I have an extra room in back. There's no heat, but…"

She let her voice trail off, uncertain how to handle the situation.

"No. It wouldn't be right for me to impose on you that way. If you'll keep Laney inside, I'll take the barn."

Molly jumped. Her windpipe tightened.

"No. That's not a good idea." Her heart thundered in her chest as she searched for a solution. No way could she spend an entire night alone with Laney.

Ethan studied her curiously. "I'm sorry she's so much trouble."

"It's not that—" How did she explain without admitting the ugly truth—that she was a danger to his child. She couldn't, so instead she searched for a viable solution.

"My uncle Robert keeps his fishing camper here during the winter months. It's self-contained and has a small propane heater. It stays cozy and snug once it's warmed up. I'm sure he wouldn't mind if you used it."

Ethan seemed relieved. He placed his bowl on the coffee table. "That will work great. I don't know how I'll ever thank you for this, Molly."

He was the hero, risking life and limb to help a sick man. She was a coward who wouldn't have done anything at all had he not forced her. She suddenly felt ashamed.

He drew in a breath and leaned forward, forearms on his thighs, palms pressed together. "So if you have that camper key, I'll go check it out, light the stove and such. Will you watch Laney while I go?"

No! As soon as the thought came, shame followed. If Ethan had nearly frozen to death to help someone else, surely she could find the courage to stay in a warm house with his baby for a few more minutes. She swallowed back the knot of anxiety. She could. She had to.

Pushing out of her chair, Molly went to the bedroom. When she returned with the camper keys clenched in one hand, Ethan was changing Laney's diaper.

She stopped dead in her tracks and watched. Something about a big, masculine man maneuvering a diaper around the chubby, thrashing legs created an endearing scene.

Ethan looked up and grinned, and Molly's heart fluttered oddly.

"She leaks like a sprinkler system." Deftly, he smoothed the plastic tabs into place before slipping the tiny legs into the pajamas.

"You're good at that."

"Practice." He lifted the infant in his big hands and laid her against a wide, blanket-covered shoulder, patting the tiny back with a tenderness that stirred Molly. One of his hands covered Laney's entire back.

"She's beautiful." Molly swallowed a lump and wished for what could never be.

"Yeah."

To break the spell of man and baby, Molly stuck out her hand, displaying the keys. "The camper is behind the detached garage. The propane bottle is still hooked up so all you have to do is light the stove. You can take these blankets with you."

"Perfect." He took the keys and rose, bringing Laney up with him. "Do you mind feeding her?"

Before Molly knew what was about to happen, Ethan placed the baby in her arms. The soft, warm body cuddled into her and made sucking noises against the little fist.

Two years. Two long years since she'd held a baby in her arms.

Molly thought she would collapse on the spot.

Chapter Three

Ethan found the camper accommodations more than acceptable and was thankful he hadn't been forced to sleep in a frigid barn—though he would have slept there rather than spend the night in Molly's house. After what he'd gone through with Laney's mother, he would never again put himself in a compromising situation. He didn't figure the Lord would approve of him putting Molly in such a questionable spot either.

Shining the flashlight around inside the camper, he found the propane stove and lit it. Molly had said the camper was equipped with electrical outlets, but it was too cold and too late to find the breaker box and make the connections. He opted for the camping lantern he found hanging from a peg inside the narrow closet next to the stove. Leaving it lit, he used the blankets to make up the bunk and, satisfied, started back to the house to ask another favor.

Stomping over the ice-packed ground to keep his footing, he came around the side of the house and onto the porch. Through the window, he could see Molly sitting by the fireplace, holding Laney. Firelight played through her barely red hair and cast a halo around her. Her face was pale, sending her spattering of freckles into relief. And though her eyes drooped with fatigue, she kept them trained on the now-sleeping baby.

Giving a soft knock of warning, he turned the knob, found the door unlocked, and stepped in.

Molly looked up, her relieved expression all out of proportion to his short absence. Did she dislike kids that much?

"You shouldn't leave your door unlocked." He wiped his feet on the rug and watched with dismay as ice fell from his clothes to the polished wood floor and quickly formed more puddles.

Molly stood and came toward him, moving with careful ease so as not wake Laney. "Who do you think would be out in this storm?"

"Me."

"Yeah, well, you're not dangerous."

"How do you know?"

Her soft laugh raised the hairs on his arms. "Because you're so tired you're about to fall over."

As Ethan took his daughter, Molly stretched and rubbed her arms as if they ached. Warmth crept into him that had nothing at all to do with the pleasant fire and comfortable house. "You didn't have to hold her all that time. Once she's eaten, she sleeps like the dead."

Molly's skin faded to white. Her eyes grew round. "She's fine. I promise. Nothing happened to her."

"I can see that," he said gently. What was that all about? He thought Molly's behavior was odd but blamed it on fatigue. "I seem to be melting all over your living room again."

"I can clean the floor in the morning." She yawned and shook her head. Her shoulders drooped with weariness. "Is the camper going to work out okay?"

"I'm so tired it looks like the Waldorf to me."

In preparation for the trek out to the camper, Ethan wrapped Laney in a pile of soft blankets. With a whimper, she squirmed and made sucking motions with her mouth.

Both adults stilled, waited for her to settle again, before Ethan continued. "I guess I'll say goodnight then. And thanks for all you've done."

He had considered asking Molly to keep the baby in the house for the night, but her nervousness around his daughter had changed his mind.

Molly McCreight had done enough.

"If you need anything before morning, just come on in. I'll leave the back door unlocked."

Even under the extraordinary circumstances, he was moved and heartened by the trusting gesture. Molly McCreight was a fascinating woman, and somehow he'd find a way to repay her kindness.

Exhausted as she was, Molly thought she'd fall asleep the minute her head hit the pillow. Instead, she lay awake for hours, listening to sleet rake the window panes and thinking about Ethan Hunter. Tomorrow, somehow, someway, she had to get him away from her house. Not that she didn't like him. That was the trouble. She not only liked him, she admired a man who would go to such extremes to help someone in need.

But Ethan had a baby and spending those hours tonight with her had taken an incredible toll. Hunger for a child coupled with the fear of losing her clawed at Molly's tenuous control.

A gust of wind rattled the house, howling. Molly sat up. Was that Laney crying? Would Ethan, tired as he was, hear her if she choked? Would he know if she needed him during the long, cold night?

She shook her head, rueful. She must be crazy to think she could hear Laney. Though the camper was near the house, it was too far and the storm too fierce for her to hear anything.

Fear was a tormenting bedfellow.

Samson stirred from his usual spot at the end of the bed and tramped up to stare at her with yellow, curious eyes as if to say, "Will you let me get some rest here?"

She lifted the cover, inviting him under as a peace offering. "Go on. I'll be still, I promise."

As the cat curled, warm and soft, next to her feet, Molly hoped she could keep that promise.

Forcing herself to lie down again, Molly pulled the pillow around her ears and began to pray, blocking out every obsessive thought.

* * *

When she opened her eyes again daylight streamed through the window, glistening painfully bright on the crystal kingdom outside. She heard someone moving around in her house, and the memory of last night came flooding back.

Quickly dressing, she shoved her feet into fuzzy slippers and her hair into a rubber band before hurrying into the kitchen. There she found Ethan warming a baby bottle in her microwave.

Wearing a smile that lit his eyes and accented the interesting scar over his eyebrow, Ethan turned to her. "I hope we didn't disturb you."

Stretching, she asked, "What time is it? I thought we'd all sleep half the day."

"A little after nine." With a wry grin he nodded at the baby cradled in one elbow. "She shows me no mercy. We've been up since six."

"Six!" She recoiled in mock horror. "That's obscene."

He laughed. "I try to tell her that, but she's a female. Has a mind of her own." Balancing the bottle with his chin, he said, "I hope you don't mind that I came inside. I didn't want to disturb you, but Laney insisted on breakfast."

"I told you last night to come in if you needed anything."

He nudged his chin toward the coffeemaker. "I made coffee. Care for a cup?"

With a mock groan, she said, "Ethan, you are my hero."

She'd made the joke without thinking, but she was right. He was a hero. "You sit down and take care of Laney, I'll get my own coffee. And once I'm fully conscious I'll make breakfast."

Settling onto one of Aunt Patsy's old chrome-backed chairs with decided grace considering he held a baby with one hand and a bottle in the other, Ethan said, "You don't need to do that. The coffee is enough."

She leaned against the butcher-block counter and poured a cup of the fragrant brew. With the first sip, she sighed with pleasure and said, "People have to eat."

Serious blue eyes captured hers. "How much do I owe you for all this? The food, the babysitting, the hotel room."

"Don't insult me with money. People help people. This was the right thing to do." Placing her mug on the counter with a thud, she opened the refrigerator and removed eggs and milk. The sooner he was fed, the sooner he'd be gone. "Will pancakes do?"

"Pancakes sound awesome." He lifted the baby onto one shoulder and patted her back.

Milk in one hand, eggs in the other, Molly stared at the sweet picture of father and daughter. Ethan stopped patting, and Molly realized he was watching her, curiosity in his gaze.

She whirled back to the counter, dumped flour and

sugar into a bowl, cracked two eggs, and stirred in enough milk to make a nice batter. All the while, she felt Ethan's eyes boring into her back.

"Have you checked the weather outside yet?" she asked when she could bear the silence no longer.

"The sleet has stopped and the wind isn't as stiff, but snow started falling right after I got up. Snow will be treacherous on top of this layer of ice."

"I haven't seen a storm this bad in several years."

She set the cast-iron skillet on the stove and in minutes, the sizzle and scent of hot pancakes filled the kitchen.

"I ran into a storm like this a few years ago when I was still flying. Grounded us for nearly twenty-four hours."

Molly turned, surprised and intrigued. "You're a pilot?"

"Was. I piloted medi-flight helicopters out of Tulsa."

She paused, spatula in the air, and frowned in thought. "Are those the medical helicopters that carry emergency patients to big hospitals?"

He tipped his head in agreement. "You know your helicopters."

"Hey, I watch reality TV, too," she teased. "You guys are amazing. Did you like it?"

An odd expression came and went on Ethan's handsome face, but he teased in return. "Reality TV? Or flying?"

It was impossible not to like Ethan Hunter. "Flying, silly."

"Flying's the best. I love it."

"Now I see why the company sent you to deliver Chester's medication." Turning to flip the pancakes, she spoke over one shoulder. "If you love flying so much, why did you stop?"

He hitched his chin toward the baby asleep on his shoulder. "Laney. The hours were too erratic for a single dad."

Though she wanted to know, Molly didn't think this was a good time to ask about Laney's mother. From his reaction last night the subject was taboo.

She set a plate of steaming pancakes on the table in front of him and turned back to the stove. "Do you think you'll ever go back to flying?"

"I don't know. Laney comes first now. After the Lord, of course."

He got up, carried the baby into the living room to the makeshift bed on the couch and returned to his pancakes. Molly refilled his coffee cup. Then the hot skillet hissed and sizzled as she poured in more batter.

"Do you live in this area?" She hadn't seen him around, but she didn't socialize as much as she once had.

A forkfull of syrupy pancake paused in front of his mouth. "I moved into Winding Stair about a month ago. UPS offered a transfer and a raise if I'd drive the area out of Mena. So I came down here from Tulsa and checked out the housing, the churches and the child care in a couple of the towns around."

"And Winding Stair filled the bill for all three?" That surprised her, given the housing shortage in the area. Scooping her pancakes onto a plate, she came to sit across the table from him.

"Winding Stair Chapel felt like home the first time I walked into a service. The people there are so friendly. They helped me find a small apartment and introduced me to the lady who owns the daycare."

A stab of longing sliced through Molly.

Winding Stair Chapel. Her church. Or it had been before Zack's death.

She gulped a buttery bite of pancake, felt the lump stick in her throat, and washed it down with coffee.

As much as she liked Ethan Hunter, she couldn't wait for him to leave. His presence—and that of his daughter—stirred up too many painful memories. Once he was gone, she'd never have to think about him or see him again, and that was best for all of them.

A baby's scream ripped through the house. Molly jumped so hard, she dropped her fork and knocked over the syrup.

"Hey, are you okay?" Ethan righted the syrup and laid a hand over hers. "You're shaking."

Ethan's hand felt much better than she wanted it to. Reluctantly, she drew away. "She startled me."

"Cry of the banshee. That's what I call it when she wails like that. The first time I heard her, she scared me silly, but that particular cry usually means she's wet."

While Ethan took care of his daughter, Molly

cleared the table and filled the sink with hot water. He must think she was crazy the way she behaved around an innocent baby, but there was no way she'd tell him about Zack.

She was down to washing the skillet when, without warning, the lights flickered once, twice and then went out.

"Oh, no." Although she'd been expecting to lose power, she was still dismayed. She could manage without lights, and the old house had propane heat, but the well pump was electric.

Ethan reappeared in the kitchen, holding Laney. "That's not good."

"Not good at all. No power, no water."

"It would be better if you didn't stay out here." He shifted Laney to his shoulder, holding her there with one hand. "Is there someone in town you can stay with?"

"My aunt tried to get me to stay with her yesterday."

"Great. After driving up that mountain last night, I think I could manage Mount Everest. If you're agreeable, I'll drive the three of us into town in your car. The company can send for the van when the roads clear."

"Sounds like a good plan. My car is in the detached garage next to the camper if you want to warm it up." The trip on flat ground would prove much easier than the one he'd made last night. "But there will be four of us."

At his raised eyebrow, she said, "My cat." If she

was holding the cat carrier, she wouldn't have to hold the baby.

"Right. Gather up the cat and whatever else you need while I go out and start the engine."

Ethan placed his daughter on the couch again, shoved his feet into his boots, shrugged into his coat, and disappeared out the back door.

Molly's tension eased as she went into the bedroom to pack. Soon she'd be in Aunt Patsy's cozy apartment at the Senior Citizens' Housing Project, sipping raspberry tea and reliving the last twelve hours. The stress of having an infant in her house would be over. Ethan and his tiny reminder of her greatest pain would be gone.

Bag packed and zipped, she carried the suitcase to the back door just as Ethan stomped through it. Cold emanated from him. He did not look happy.

Shivering against the sudden draft of frigid air, Molly reached behind him to push the door closed. "Is something wrong?"

Blowing out a frustrated breath, he pulled the stocking cap from his head. "Bad news. The power line over the garage snapped."

"No wonder the power is gone. That line feeds the breaker box to the entire house."

"Worse than that." He unzipped his coat as if he planned to remove it. "The garage and everything in it is electrified—a death trap until that line is repaired."

"Oh, no." Apprehension crept up her spine. He had to leave. He had to take that baby out of her house.

"Sorry." His mouth turned grim as he said the words Molly dreaded. "But none of us is going anywhere today—or maybe for a lot longer."

Chapter Four

"I could try walking into town," Ethan said. Given the expression on Molly's face he thought maybe he should at least try.

"Don't be silly. You nearly froze last night. We're safe and snug here so we'll make do until things begin to thaw out in a day or two," An attractive little frown pinched her eyebrows together. "Water will be our primary problem, but there's plenty of that frozen in the yard."

The tightness in his shoulders relaxed. He appreciated her practical attitude even if she wasn't thrilled to have him as a house guest. "Got more buckets? I can start chipping ice."

"The big stock pots are in the storage room. They'll have to do."

"I'll get them. Which way?"

"Back through here." She motioned through the kitchen and down a hallway. "But I can do it."

"That's okay. I might as well learn the lay of the land if I'm going to be here for a while."

Following her directions, he went through the door at the end of the hall only to see more rooms beyond. The old house seemed to ramble on forever. No wonder she didn't heat this section.

He opened the first room, spotted an old table loaded with boxes and assumed he'd found the storage area. He went inside to hunt for the pots.

He found something else instead. Familiar packages. UPS boxes. Most from children's stores. All of them recent additions to the room. All filled with kids' stuff.

"What is all this?" he murmured, gazing around at the surprising contents.

A stack of new sweatshirts and jeans and several pairs of tennis shoes had been transferred from their original packages into a larger box addressed to Hillside Children's Home. Another box appeared to be a work in progress, containing only a handful of toys. Catalogs lay strewn about, open to the kids' pages with certain items circled in red pen.

Either Molly belonged to some sort of charitable group that collected clothes and toys for needy children or she spent a lot of time and money doing the job on her own.

Either option seemed strange to him, considering her reaction to Laney.

What was the truth about Molly and kids?

More curious than ever about his hostess, he left

the room to complete his original errand, returning to the kitchen with two stainless steel pots in hand and a lot of unanswered questions in his head.

He found Molly still in the kitchen, except now she stood on a chair rummaging in the upper cabinets.

Holding up the pots, he said, "Found them."

She looked down at him and smiled. "I know I have some candles up here somewhere. Oh, here we go." She handed him a tall pillar. "I was thinking. What about Laney? Do you have everything you need for her?"

"Enough formula and diapers to last a day or two—maybe more." No point worrying about that yet.

She stuck her head back inside the cabinet, muffling her voice. "Then we'll just pray we can get out of here before she runs out."

"God won't let us down. He brought us this far."

Molly closed the cabinet door and turned, frowning. "Are you saying God had something to do with you getting stranded here?"

She started down from her perch and Ethan reached to offer a hand. Her cool skin felt almost as soft as Laney's.

"All I know is that I was meant to deliver that gamma last night."

She took the candles from him. "Because God told you to?"

He shifted uncomfortably. Some of his friends and family rolled their eyes when he tried to explain that still, small voice that spoke from somewhere deep inside him. Would she?

"Not in audible words, no. But somehow, on the inside of me—" he tapped his chest "—I heard Him."

Molly's tea-colored eyes grew thoughtful. "That's true. Sometimes you just know."

Relieved that she understood, Ethan smiled. "Exactly."

Lots of people thought he'd gone goofy since accepting Christ. And sometimes the criticism, the veiled sarcasm, hurt. He'd gone goofy all right, but in a way that filled him with a peace and reassurance he'd searched for all his adult life.

"What about Chester?" she peered inside a lower cabinet, came out with box of matches which she set on the counter. "If you were supposed to give his chemo and you're stuck here, how he is going to get his next dose?"

"By some miracle the Stubbses still had phone service. I contacted my company. They'll make arrangements for a chopper to take him to the hospital for treatments until the roads clear."

He didn't want to think about what might happen if the storm cranked up again. He'd done all he could. The rest was in God's hands.

"I'm glad. The Stubbses are good people." She glanced out the window above the sink. Two parallel lines between her pale brown eyebrows deepened. "What about the broken power line? Are we safe with all those volts bouncing around?"

"As long as we stay away from the garage." Years of flying low and watching out for electrical lines had taught him to be wary, but Ethan was still amazed that he had heard the sizzling electricity in time. What if he had touched that garage door? He shuddered to think what might have happened. Not just to him, but to Molly.

Which brought him back to her earlier question.

Was being stranded here, on this particular farm, with this particular woman, a part of some divine plan?

Snow fell for the rest of the day, but the sleet and wind seemed, mercifully, to have passed. Regardless of the discomfort of having a stranger—and a baby—in her house, Molly thought the day progressed reasonably well. In truth, Ethan Hunter was easy to be around and his masculine presence was a comfort. The fact that he spoke openly about his faith reassured her in ways she didn't understand or question.

The baby was another matter altogether, but with Ethan present, Laney was in no danger. And Molly would somehow handle the constant fear of a humiliating panic attack.

Together she and Ethan devised a simple plan for making the fuel and food last. Then, while she organized the meals and melted water, Ethan had brought in ice and firewood. He had also checked the sagging, ice-laden power lines around the house and fretted over the huge trees bowing over the porch roof. Most importantly he had not expected her to take care of Laney just because she was a woman.

She was particularly grateful for that, though each time he ventured outdoors, she counted the minutes until his return.

After putting the last of the supper dishes away, she wiped her hands on a towel. Heating dishwater on the gas stove gave her a new appreciation of pioneer women.

From the living room she heard Laney's baby voice and Ethan's manly one. He was giving his daughter a sponge bath in front of the fireplace. Hoping for one of those herself later, Molly filled another kettle and placed it on the burner before going into the living room.

The diapered baby lay on a quilt, tiny legs and arms bicycling for all she was worth. Her round face was alive with interest as Ethan, on his knees beside her, carried on a one-sided conversation.

"Are you Daddy's angel girl?" he asked, leaning over her.

Baby Laney cooed in response and slammed one little fist against the side of his face.

Ethan laughed and nuzzled the rounded belly, an action that sent Laney's arms and legs into fast motion.

Suddenly, he scooped the child into his big hands and lifted her overhead, waggling her gently from side to side. Laney's toothless mouth spread wide and a delighted gurgle filled the dimly lit living room.

Molly felt a catch beneath her ribs at the pleasure father and daughter found in one another. There was something beautiful and pure in that kind of love.

Tears pricked at her eyelids. A deep, tearing need took her breath, and she turned back toward the kitchen.

Outside, snow still fell in spits and spurts, skinny flakes that were as much ice as snow. Darkness descended, though the time was not yet six o'clock. Anything that had dared to thaw would soon refreeze.

With no electricity for reading and no TV, the evening with Ethan and his daughter would be a long one. He was a great guy, an attractive man, but he was also a father. Wouldn't he be horrified to know she had been investigated by the police for a baby's death?

The familiar wrench of sadness twisted in her chest.

She stood at the kitchen sink and stared out at the descending night, wishing for what could not be. According to Aunt Patsy she had to stop dwelling on the unchangeable. For a while she had begun to think she had—until the UPS man arrived with his unexpected delivery to remind her of all she'd lost and all she wanted but could never have.

A part of her wondered why the Lord had allowed her nephew's tragic death. And why He had allowed her Christian sister to turn against her.

Shivering, she rubbed her arms and tried to put aside the morbid thoughts. Some questions were unanswerable.

When she returned to the living room, Laney was dressed in red footed pajamas, her face shiny and pink from the bath, and her dark hair neatly smoothed. Cradled in Ethan's arms, eyes wide and earnest, she eagerly sucked down her supper.

A kerosene lantern which Ethan had carried in from the camper sat on the coffee table and cast a shadowy, golden glow over the man and child. Coupled with the fireplace, it shed an adequate, if dim light.

Molly settled into the easy chair opposite Ethan's, curling her legs beneath her.

"You're a good dad." It was true. She'd rarely seen a man so attuned to his child.

"I'm trying." He slid the empty bottle from the baby's mouth and lifted her against his shoulder for burping. "I made a lot of stupid mistakes before Laney came along. I don't want her to suffer for them."

Molly wondered if Laney's mother was one of those mistakes.

"Everybody has regrets." Recalling the way her mother and sister had turned their backs on her, sadness lay like a rock in her stomach. "Some you never get over."

Gaze steady, he patted Laney's back. "You talking from personal experience?"

She rose and moved to the fireplace, her back to Ethan. Why had she said anything at all? Sure, she was on edge with a baby underfoot, but Aunt Patsy was the only person she ever talked to about Chloe and the loss of baby Zack.

A log burned in two, snapped and fell, sending a shower of sparks upward like a Roman candle.

"Molly." Ethan's voice was quiet. "Would you like Laney and me to head out to the camper so you can have some peace and quiet?"

No more questions. No prying. Just consideration. How could she be inhospitable to such a man?

This whole situation must be as miserable for Ethan as for her. Stuck here in a stranger's home with an infant to care for, low on formula, no power, and completely out of his comfort zone. And yet, he was cheerful about the entire mess.

Shame spread through her. Neither Ethan nor Laney were to blame for her personal agony. If she were the Christian she claimed to be, she would be thinking of them instead of herself.

"I don't want you to go." Then she blushed at how that sounded. "I mean, I'd enjoy your company if you'd like to stay longer."

He spread his hands wide, lips tilting as he looked around the room. "No TV. No stereo. No computer. We might have to carry on a conversation."

Molly caught the twinkle in his eye and played along. "Could be scary."

"You could tell me about yourself."

She tensed, then realized she could talk without revealing too much. "I'm not very fascinating."

"Let me be the judge of that. Tell me about your job, what you like to do, that sort of thing."

She curled her legs under her again and sat down. "It's a rare man that enjoys conversation."

He laughed. "As I said. No TV."

"You go first."

"Cheater." But he did, telling her about his mother and dad in Tulsa, a married brother in the service in

North Carolina, his job and his love of flying. She noticed one glaring omission. He did not mention Laney's mother.

And in turn, she told him of her short-lived college days, about her crafting hobbies and her job at the senior citizens' center.

"What about your family?" he asked when she'd told him all she was willing to share.

Molly tensed. "I don't see them much."

The answer was abrupt, bringing a tension into the cozy room that hovered for several beats like a winged creature. Then, as if he knew he'd touched a nerve, Ethan shifted gears. "Tell me about your other hobby. Or is that also a taboo topic?"

"My other hobby? I don't know what you mean."

"I saw the boxes in the back room."

Molly's hand stilled on the rough upholstery. So he'd discovered her penance. She swallowed hard before answering in an intentionally light voice. "Oh, that. I have a soft spot for kids who don't have much."

"That says a lot about you."

Molly didn't want him thinking she was some unselfish saint. She wasn't. Giving to needy kids eased the awful ache inside her.

"No big deal. A little money out of each paycheck. I hardly miss it." She popped up from the chair, eager to change the subject. He was indeed, treading on dangerous ground. "Would you like some popcorn?"

Ethan's blue eyes turned violet in the lamplight. He studied her for a fraction of a second as if he was not fooled by her ploy. Finally, when Molly had grown uncomfortable from the silence, he said, "Is it humanly possible to make popcorn without a microwave?"

Relieved, she grinned. "That remains to be seen."

Ethan laid the wiggling baby on a quilt and stood. "You make popcorn. I'll set out those dominoes you found this afternoon."

"Deal."

By the time the popcorn's buttery scent filled the house, Ethan had rearranged the living room so that two chairs bracketed the coffee table in front of the fireplace. The yellow light from a kerosene lamp tossed shadows onto the walls and ceiling.

Outside the wind howled and the occasional crusted tree limb scraped the windows and siding, but the old farmhouse remained cozy and warm. Molly placed the heaping bowl of popcorn at one end of the rectangular table, and curled into her chair. Samson jumped onto her lap.

"Dumb cat," she said affectionately, resting one hand on his head. "How am I supposed to play dominoes with you in the way?"

"The same way I'll play and hold Laney." Ethan leaned around the baby as he reached for the popcorn. "Very carefully."

The child was propped in his lap, her back resting against his chest. One of his muscular arms wrapped around her middle. Her beautiful dark blue eyes were wide open, staring at Samson in fascination.

"Her radar's trained on my cat."

"I don't think she's ever seen one before." He shoved the popcorn into his mouth, then slid seven dominoes to his side of the table.

Molly did the same, standing the game pieces in two rows for examination. She lifted an eyebrow in his direction. "What? No pets? That's child abuse."

"I never said we didn't have a pet. Just no cat." He thumped a double-five on the table. "Ten points."

Molly made an *X* on the score sheet under his name, then glanced up at him. A little leap of… something stirred in her blood. "Don't tell me there's a poor dog trapped in your apartment with no food and no way to get out if he needs to."

"Nope. No dog."

"I'll take ten myself." She slid a blank-five onto the wooden tabletop and wrote her score on the yellow pad of paper. "What kind of pet do you have then? A boa constrictor?"

An amused smile lit his face and sent the beguiling scar into relief. "What would you say if I said yes?"

She could tell he was teasing. It had been a long time since she'd joked and bantered with a man, and it felt good. "I'd tell you never to invite me to your house."

"Which would be a terrible shame considering that I owe you a return invitation."

"Sorry, I don't do snakes." She heaved an exaggerated sigh and said dramatically, "I guess this is the beginning and the end of our friendship."

Releasing a gusty sigh of his own, he let his shoulders sag in mock resignation. "Okay, you win. I'll get rid of the boa as long as you don't take exception to the shark in the bathtub."

Molly couldn't hold back a giggle. "Ethan, you're crazy."

"That's what Laney tells me all the time." He kissed the top of the baby's head. "Isn't that right, sugar plum? Daddy likes snakes, sharks and goldfish. Dangerous stuff."

"Goldfish?" Molly placed her hands over the cat's ears. "Don't let Samson hear you say that. Fish is his favorite meal."

"That's what the snake and the shark said, too. Poor Goldie."

When Molly tilted back in her chair and laughed, Ethan's eyes danced. Molly's heart lurched in response. Her house guest was not only resourceful and heroic, he was funny and kind and incredibly nice-looking. And his devotion to his daughter was enough to make any unattached woman sit up and take notice.

Bad enough that she had to worry about Laney, but now she couldn't get Ethan out of her mind either. She liked him. And she didn't want to.

It would be better for all of them if the roads were melted in the morning, and Ethan and his baby were out of her life for good.

They weren't.

The next morning the world had refrozen and looked like a crystal kingdom in a fairy tale. All of outdoors wore a thick coat of ice that glistened in the morning sun, every bit as beautiful as diamonds. No matter how inconvenient the ice was, Molly found the sight breathtaking.

Laney lay on a quilt in the living room making baby noises while Ethan resumed his ice-chipping job. With all the work he'd undertaken, Molly couldn't expect him to carry Laney out in the cold with him. But every few minutes she felt compelled to race the ten feet from the kitchen to the quilt to make sure the child was all right.

She was exhausted, too. She had lain awake half the night worrying about Ethan and Laney out in the old fishing camper. Worrying that they might get cold. Worrying about the unstable electric lines sagging above them. And praying for the temperatures to warm and the roads to clear so they could leave. But the only thing that seemed to be thawing was the food in her freezer. So this morning she was loading meat into baskets to set outside in the winter wonderland.

"Look what I found." Ethan stomped in through the back door, grinning from ear to ear, a portable radio in hand. The intriguing scar lifted over his eyebrow.

Since breakfast he'd been as busy as a politician at election time, doing the odd jobs that no one else ever got around to. He'd repaired the front door, replaced a broken tile in the bathroom, and rummaged around in the barn until he found a tube of caulking to use on the windows. He claimed he was doing all these things in repayment for her hospitality.

Molly laughed ruefully about that one. She wasn't being hospitable by choice.

She piled another package of frozen hamburger into a clothes basket. "Where'd you find that?"

"In one of the camper cabinets." He set it on the dinette table and fiddled with the knobs. Static and a high-pitched *wee-ooh-wee* filled the kitchen.

At the unexpected noise, Laney squealed. Molly jumped and nearly dropped the heavy basket.

Ethan gave her a funny look and said, "She's okay. Cry of the banshee. Remember?"

Molly's throat tightened. She rubbed at it, forcing her windpipe to remain open. "Check on her."

She was behaving like an idiot, but she couldn't help it.

"Okay," he said quietly, and left the radio long enough to retrieve his daughter.

Molly followed him to the doorway, battling the creeping anxiety. Intellectually, she knew Laney was fine. Emotionally, she had to be certain.

Lord, would she ever stop feeling afraid?

As Ethan bent to pick up Laney, memories of the last two days flickered through his head. When Molly had avoided holding his daughter he'd chalked it up to another woman without a mother's instinct. But that didn't jive with her dedication to the homeless and underprivileged children nor with the woman he'd come to know and like.

Now, understanding clicked into place. In his

years as a paramedic he had seen that state of near panic dozens of times. Molly didn't dislike Laney. She was afraid of her. Though he couldn't imagine why anyone would fear an infant, the knowledge made him feel better. It also made him more curious than ever. What had happened to make a grown woman so anxious around an infant?

Whatever it was, he wanted to fix it.

Molly was a good woman with a caring heart. She'd proven that a dozen times since he'd barged into her home and started asking favors. During the long conversations and crazy domino game of last night, he'd come to a startling realization.

Somehow he had to reconcile his baby with Molly. Because he wanted to know her better—a lot better.

The idea shocked him no end. He'd thought he was finished with women forever.

Chapter Five

"You can't go up on that roof. It's too slick and dangerous." Molly's breath puffed white in the frigid morning, and sprigs of shiny red hair peeked from beneath her hooded parka.

"Got to." Ethan rested on his haunches next to the house where he had scraped away enough ice to set up the ladder. "That tree is wrecking your roof. You'll have a leak the size of Lake Erie."

Ever since the storm, he had worried about the many trees surrounding the big old farmhouse. Their strength was sorely taxed by the heavy layer of ice and all were bent into unnatural positions. Last night one had finally given way and collapsed onto the roof.

He and Molly had been engrossed in a serious game of Scrabble when the thundering crash had occurred. He had jumped, awakening Laney, who sent up a startled howl. Molly had screamed and tossed a handful of potato chips sky high. This had insulted the lap cat who yowled and stalked out of the room.

They had ended up laughing until tears blurred their vision and they were breathless. During that moment, he'd stared into Molly's gentle face and found himself wanting to please her, to make her laugh more, and most of all, to chase away the anxiety emanating from her.

Now the small redhead stood in the yard, head tilted back to survey the storm damage. He couldn't help but notice how pretty her pale skin looked in the morning sunlight.

"Do you really think the roof will leak?" Her small teeth gnawed at a peach-colored bottom lip.

"No doubt about it." He secured the ladder and started up. "You could steady this for me, if you don't mind."

Molly hurried to do his bidding and Ethan felt a rush of pleasure. She was a trooper, ready to help, willing to do her part. She not only didn't complain about their situation, she found ways to make it seem like an adventure: board games, lively discussions about religion and politics, creative meals by candle- and lamplight.

A man could get attached to a woman like that. After his mistakes with Twila, he was loath to get involved with any woman ever again, but Molly muddled his thinking.

And muddled thinking always led a man astray.

He squeezed his eyes shut for a moment. He had

plenty to do today, and fretting over his past wasn't getting any of it done.

To still the disquieting thoughts, Ethan started up the ladder, his boots clanging against the metal rungs.

Once on the gabled roof, he realized the tree was too large to move in one piece. He would have to saw it apart.

Slip-sliding to the edge, he called down to Molly. "I need that chain saw. Can you hand it up?"

She hefted the tool, then paused and glanced toward the front door. "You think Laney is still asleep?"

"Positive. She naps for a couple of hours at a stretch." He could see his response didn't satisfy, and he continued to puzzle over why a woman who refused to hold his baby worried so much about her. "Why?"

Molly made a twitching motion with one shoulder. "No reason."

She'd had plenty of chances to tell him what troubled her, but every time she'd backed away. Funny how that irked him.

"I can take it from here," he said, reaching for the saw.

Hanging on to the ladder with one hand, she passed the saw up and then surprised him by ascending the remaining rungs. "I want to see what the world looks like from up here."

Being a pilot, Ethan loved the view from above the earth. Nice to know Molly wasn't put off by heights. The fleeting thought drifted through his head that he might offer to take her up in a plane sometime.

Feet wide to maintain balance, he set the saw aside and offered his gloved hand. "Ice is devastating, but beautiful, too. You can see for miles from here."

The safest place on the roof was where the chimney met the long, sloping porch roof. The constant heat had melted a good portion of the ice and the roof was a gentle incline. Situated there, Molly would be relatively safe.

"I have pretty good footing. Let me steady you."

With easy grace Molly made the transition from ladder to overhang and settled into a corner of the eave. "Wow. You were right. This *is* awesome."

Pleased with her wide-eyed response, he hunkered down beside her and pointed. "Look in that big oak. See the woodpecker?"

Molly followed the line of his arm, face brightening. "He's huge."

"The largest of the species. A pileated woodpecker."

"Like Woody?" Her breath puffed small clouds into the frosty morning.

Ethan grinned at her teasing tone. "Hear him?"

The woodpecker's rat-a-tat-tat echoed through the still morning.

"The birds are everywhere today." Her gaze scanned the sparkling ice-coated trees. "See those bright red cardinals? They look so pretty against the white-and-silver ice. And over there, jays and chicka-dees and a nuthatch."

Ethan didn't bother to look. He was much more interested in watching her face than in watching the birds. Cheeks rosy from the cold and honey-colored eyes alight with interest charmed him. He resisted a totally unacceptable urge to smooth a finger over her soft-looking skin.

"They're probably hungry. The ice is covering up their food source."

Molly turned her head, caught him looking and blushed. He liked the way she did that, just as he liked the smattering of golden freckles across her nose.

"I normally keep seed out for them." She quickly shifted her eyes back to the wildlife. "But I suppose it's covered up, too. We'll have to put out more."

In an effort to turn his attention away from Molly's sparkling eyes and wind-kissed cheeks, Ethan searched the vast horizon below them. Birds flitted about, singing as though the frigid temperatures and frozen landscape wouldn't bring the demise of at least some of their kind.

And then something else caught his eye.

Index finger across his lips, he whispered, "Sit very still and look directly below us, near the edge of the front yard."

A white-tailed deer materialized, a spot of tan suede against the crystal forest.

"Oh!" Molly breathed, gloved hands bracketing her mouth. "A deer."

In seconds a fawn clambered into sight, his slick hooves troublesome on the icy ground. When his front legs went in separate directions, Molly slanted a smile toward Ethan.

Like co-conspirators they sat in hushed silence and watched the deer paw at the ground, digging for dinner.

Ethan had work to do but was reluctant to break the beautiful spell the wildlife—and time with Molly McCreight—created. Who knew sitting on the roof in the frigid morning sun could be so entertaining?

After a bit the doe stopped digging and ambled away. Her fawn followed along, white tail twitching.

"Food is scarce for them, too," Ethan said softly.

"I wish we had some corn. It makes me sad to see them hungry."

That was twice now that she'd said *we* as naturally as if the two of them had been working together forever. The idea felt better than it should have considering his less-than-perfect track record with women.

Even though he'd made those mistakes before he'd turned his life over to Jesus, the consequences remained. And he'd promised to concentrate on raising Laney and to leave the ladies alone.

He just hoped he could keep that promise. Spending time with Molly could become dangerously habit-forming. And until the roads cleared, he had little choice in the matter.

"I'd better get busy," he said more abruptly than he'd intended. "That tree won't saw itself."

"Let me help." She placed a hand on his shoulder and started to rise. Halfway up, her footing gave way on the frosted slope, and she slipped sideways.

Everything happened so fast but to Ethan the whole world stopped. Adrenaline shot into his bloodstream. Without considering the risk to himself, he grabbed for her, caught her around the waist with one hand, and yanked her back, all the while grappling for something to hold on to with his other.

Molly slammed into his chest, and his boots slid out from under him. Together they skidded over the frozen shingles unchecked for several feet.

Fear lifted the hair on his neck as he faced the inevitable. They were going to plummet to the ground below.

Molly wanted to scream but there was no time. She and Ethan picked up speed. Chilled wind pushed at her cheeks. Scenery blurred. Fear of the inevitable fall clogged her throat.

Convinced they would tumble over the edge, she squeezed her eyes tight and gave an inward cry. "Help us."

They came to an abrupt, jarring stop. Other than the sound of their frightened panting, all was silent. Even the birds had hushed.

Molly opened her eyes. They were inches from the edge, but Ethan gripped a vent pipe with one hand and held her with the other. Instead of amazement that she had narrowly escaped serious injury, Molly could only marvel at how strong Ethan must be.

For several frightened seconds they rested on the roof, cold seeping through their jeans, while their ragged breathing slowed to normal.

"That was close," Molly whispered. Her pulse

thundered against her temples; she was as unsettled by Ethan's nearness as by the near-accident.

Still clinging to the pipe for support, Ethan sat upright and drew her up beside him. He steadied them both until their position was secure. Molly wondered why he didn't release her.

"I shouldn't have let you come up here," he said. "You could have been hurt."

His naturally tan face was intense and pale and dangerously close.

"I came up under my own power, Ethan."

"But—" he started to argue. Molly placed a gloved hand on his cheek.

"Ethan, it's my roof. You were trying to help me. And thanks to you, neither of us is hurt." She knew she should move away from him, but she didn't want to. She hadn't felt safe in a long time, and Ethan's secure embrace was a haven of comfort and security.

Her hood had come off in the slide and her hair fell across her mouth. As tenderly as he touched Laney, Ethan brushed the lock back from her face.

Something more disturbing than a fall stirred inside Molly. Tenderness was such an alluring quality in a man. Hadn't she admired that characteristic over and over again in his care of Laney? And now he was treating her with the same tenderness.

"I'm glad you're okay." His troubled blue eyes studied her as if he wanted to memorize her face. His warm voice dropped to a murmur. "Very glad."

In that instant Molly thought he might kiss her. As

scary as that was, and as long as it had been since she had entertained such a thought, she wanted him to.

He swallowed and tilted his head. From the frozen north a slight wind pushed away the warmth of his breath, bringing with it a new sound. Not a cracking, groaning tree. Not a bird. But a baby's cry.

Molly jerked away and was in danger of going into another slide. Ethan clutched her shoulders. "Easy."

"Laney," she said, almost desperately. Her pulse trembled in her throat. She pressed a hand there to stop the impending anxiety. "We shouldn't have left her."

Ethan cocked his head to one side and listened. "She's awake. Better go see."

As though he hadn't just leaped over her carefully built wall, Ethan moved away to tend his baby.

And as quickly as that, the sweet mood dissipated like the call of the chickadee on the north wind.

During their moments of shared fright, Molly had all but forgotten the insurmountable barrier between them. Now all the reasons for her to stay far away from Ethan Hunter came rushing back in the cry of a tiny baby.

By midmorning of the fifth day, the temperatures hovered around freezing and Molly embraced a ray of hope along with this morning's ray of sunshine that the deep freeze would soon end.

To her relief, after the near-accident and the more disquieting near-kiss, she and her delivery man had returned to friendly banter and cooperative living.

Ethan had to be tired of the tiny, cramped camper, but he never complained. Still, he and Laney were normally in the kitchen for the baby's early bottle by the time Molly awakened each morning. Coffee, boiled the old-fashioned way in a pot from the camper, filled the kitchen with a rich scent.

This particular morning they were arguing.

"According to the radio anything that thaws will refreeze tonight," Ethan said, bouncing Laney on one knee. "So if I'm to have any hope of digging out the van, I need to get moving."

"Even if you succeed, the roads are still treacherous." Molly shoved her hair back, looping it over one ear. Considering she had had no dryer or curlers for nearly a week, she must look a fright.

"I have to try. Laney's running short on formula."

"What if you can't get the van out?" she asked.

"I'll walk to town."

"And leave us ladies out here alone?"

She tried to tease, but the quiver in her voice gave her away.

Ethan's jaw tightened. "I can't carry a baby six miles in this cold."

"I know." Self-loathing dripped inside her as cold and sharp as the icicles hanging outside the kitchen window. Why couldn't she just get over herself? "We'll be fine." She hoped. "But if you have to walk, how will you get back out here? To get us, I mean."

"I'll worry about that after I get to town. My truck is small and might not make it, but Pastor Cliff has a four-wheel drive." He arched his eyebrows, teasing. "In a pinch, I can commandeer a snow plow."

They both smiled at his silliness.

He was so incredibly brave and she was such a coward.

"Well, you're right. We can't hold out much longer. And you have to be as sick as I am of washing dish towels by hand every day."

Laney had long since used her last diaper and Molly had appropriated soft dish towels and safety pins as replacements. Ethan called her pioneer woman, but the task of melting and boiling ice, washing the towels and hanging them to dry in front of the fireplace had grown tiresome in a hurry.

Elbows on the tabletop, she sipped at her coffee, savoring the strong, hearty brew. Thanks to the supplies she'd bought when the storm was first predicted neither she nor Ethan had wanted for food. But now the most fragile member of their party was running short of formula.

"It's still so cold out there, Ethan."

"Yeah. But I'll be fine as long as I know you girls are safe and snug here." He rubbed at the scar over his eye, a reminder of how stark and white it had looked that first night when he'd almost frozen. She didn't want that to happen again. "Before I take off, I'll bring in another stack of firewood."

Molly pushed aside her empty plate, took one last sip of coffee and stood. "I'll do it. I think there may be another lamp in the cellar. I want to bring that up."

The candles and kerosene were running precariously low and if by some chance she was forced to be alone with Laney after dark, she needed light more than ever.

Before Ethan could insist on going in her place, she threw on a coat and gloves and hurried outside.

Chin tucked into the fleece-lined parka, Molly scooted through the teeth-aching weather to Aunt Patsy's storm cellar. At least here, on the south side of the house, the wind was blocked.

Ice crusts sealed the heavy cellar door. After several minutes of stomping and pounding, they gave way and Molly entered the dim shelter.

At the top of the steps, she shoved aside an old spider web with the elbow of her jacket and hoped a black widow wasn't waiting to seek revenge for the destruction of her home. Inside the cellar proper, she felt along the wall until her eyes adjusted to the darkness.

Winter or summer the old concrete storm shelter smelled the same—like a mixture of gym socks and pickle juice. She wrinkled her nose against the smell.

"There you are." On a shelf lining the far wall sat a green-globed hurricane lamp along with a collection of empty fruit jars, a blue speckled canner, and a pair of dry and withered gardening gloves. An ax and a shovel stood in one corner next to the folding camp chairs and a moldy tent.

She knew people who hated the inside of a storm shelter, but she'd never been one of them. She didn't love the close underground confines, but she wasn't afraid either. There was only one thing that truly frightened Molly McCreight. One irrational fear that controlled her life. And she'd give anything to have a phobia for cellars or crawly creatures, instead of tiny, beautiful babies.

She lifted the lamp down, gave it a gentle shake, and heard with satisfaction the slosh of much-needed kerosene. This was enough to keep her and Laney illuminated until Ethan returned.

As she started to leave Molly realized that Ethan would need the shovel. She took it from the corner and started back up the narrow, sloping stairs.

She was four steps up when the shovel caught on the door's tie-down chain and tipped sideways, knocking the lantern globe askew. Hands full, Molly tried to catch the teetering globe with her shoulder, lost her balance, and stumbled on the falling shovel.

The shovel clattered, the globe shattered and the base of the lamp flew out of her hands. Molly thrust both arms in front her…and crashed down onto the concrete steps and broken glass.

Molly lay prostrate for several stunned seconds. Her hands, knees and shins smarted from contact with the concrete. Her head spun and her stomach churned from the strong odor of lantern fuel spilled all around her. The kerosene's wetness seeped through her sweat pants.

Anxious for fresh air, she pushed off the steps and rushed out of the cellar.

"So much for stocking up on kerosene," she

muttered and started back to the house, her errand a failure.

A throbbing pain in her leg was the first warning that more than her pride was wounded. The bright red blood dripping from her lower leg onto the white ground was the second.

She looked behind her, saw the trail and knew she was in trouble. Between the reek of fuel and the sight of her own blood, she grew woozy.

If only she had a towel or something to staunch the flow.

Once on the porch, she stopped to have a look. A gaping slash cut through her sweats and ran from the side of her calf to above her knee. Several other smaller tears in the pants oozed blood as well.

This was not good. Not good at all.

She pressed her gloved hand against the tide.

Music filtered from inside the house.

"Ethan!" she called, hoping he could hear over the radio.

Immediately, the door opened behind her.

"Need some help with that wood…?" His voice trailed off when she twisted toward him.

"Molly!"

She tried to smile and failed miserably. All the nerve endings running from her calf to her brain had come to vivid life. "I cut my leg."

He dropped down beside her. "Let me see."

"You'll get all bloody."

He grunted an impatient, completely male dismissal and pushed her hands aside. She stared in surprise at her blood-soaked gloves while Ethan ripped the torn sweats up to the knee in order to assess the damage.

"Put your hands right here," he said, guiding her to press hard on the wound. "Looks like you've hit a bleeder."

"No kidding," she murmured, stunned at how the blood kept coming.

"We need to get you inside where I can have a better look."

With no further warning, he scooped her up as if she weighed no more than Laney, kicked the door open, and carried her into the kitchen where he lowered her into a straight-backed chair.

From a drawer, Ethan pulled a handful of towels and fell to his knees before her.

Her clothes stank of kerosene and her head reeled from the smell.

"I stink," she said, embarrassed both by the smell and the attention.

As if she were a troublesome child, he shot her a silencing glance and then went to work. His expert fingers probed and pushed at the torn flesh.

"This needs sutures," he muttered, his mouth a grim, flat line. "A lot of them."

"Got any on you?" Molly joked, gazing down at the top of his head where she noted, with unusual interest, the way his brown hair grew in a crooked whorl at the crown. The idea that he'd battled a powerful cowlick as a boy made her smile. He'd probably looked adorable.

Busy securing a pressure bandage over the wound, Ethan didn't answer her silly question.

When he finished, Molly tried to stand but was quickly pressed back into the chair. "Stay still. I have the bleeding under control for now, but moving around will exacerbate it."

"My floor—"

He reached for her wrist, felt her pulse. "I'll clean it up."

She favored him with what she considered a coquettish smile. "You're pretty handy, you know that, Mr. Delivery Man?"

A pair of serious blue eyes assessed her. "You're not getting shocky on me, are you?"

Good question. Maybe she was. "My head hurts and I feel a little woozy. I think it's the kerosene on my clothes."

He stepped back. "Better change. Just go very easy on that leg. I'd like the bleeding to be completely stopped before I leave."

"Leave?" She had to focus to remember. Where was it he was going?

He rubbed at the scar, brow wrinkling in concern. "To dig out the van. Remember? The sooner I do that, the quicker we can get you to a doctor."

Oh, yeah. She'd forgotten. Maybe she *was* a little shocky.

Holding to the cabinets, she made her way toward

the hall connecting the kitchen with the back of the house. The fat bandage of towels and masking tape made the cut throb more. Wavy lines, whether from fumes or dizziness, appeared before her eyes.

At the doorway, she paused, turning to find Ethan, hands on his thighs, watching her every move.

"I'm sorry," she said.

"For what?"

"Because I'm so much trouble."

His familiar grin replaced the worried frown. "I'll say you are. First, you try to knock me off the roof, and now you go out and cut yourself just so you can force me out into the cold. I'm starting to wonder if you're trying to get rid of me."

Well, he was certainly right about that.

But he was also completely wrong.

Chapter Six

Tired as he was, Ethan's energy resurged as he eased the van over the frozen earth and right up to Molly's front porch. He'd done it. Armed with a shovel and two bags of kitty litter, courtesy of Molly's cat, he'd dug and pushed and levered until the truck spun its way up out of the ditch. Even in the bitter breeze, he'd grown warm from exertion. Thankfully, the ice had done the same, melting enough from the heat of the tires to set the van free.

All the time he'd worked he had also prayed, thinking of Molly and the vicious laceration she'd sustained. Although he'd tried to downplay the seriousness so she wouldn't worry, the wound needed to be seen by a doctor today. It was deep, down to the fascia, and he'd been afraid to probe too deeply for stray glass and the severed blood vessels. Without equipment, there was little he could do about either.

In her condition, he hadn't wanted to burden her with Laney, but again he'd had little choice. His baby needed formula and Molly needed a doctor. Providing both was his responsibility.

He hoped they'd done all right.

Rapping softly on the front door as a warning, he let himself inside the farmhouse and breathed in the welcome warmth. He liked this house and everything in it, including the owner. Seeing her hurt bothered him a lot.

Right away he spotted his girls in the big blue easy chair. Neither stirred, and with a tired grin, he saw that they both slept.

He paused, recognizing the danger in thinking of Molly as his in any way. Since that day on the roof when he'd fought back the urge to kiss her, he had been forced to recognize a growing affection for his hostess. With his past, he had no right to think of her at all, but he couldn't help it. She occupied his thoughts constantly.

Perhaps it was the situation, being iced in together as though they were the only living beings around. He owed her so much. Maybe his feelings were nothing except gratitude. Since thinking that was the safer road, he took it.

Stepping around in front of the chair, he gazed down at the sleeping pair. Even though her eyes were closed, Molly cradled his daughter securely against her, protectively, almost lovingly.

They looked for all the world like mother and child.

Sadness pinched at him. Thanks to his and Twila's

foolish mistakes, Laney would never know this kind of nurturing from a mother. He would be the one to rock and sing to her and to comfort her when the bumps of life came along. He hoped he was enough.

His heart ached with love for the little girl who had changed his life. He would do anything to make up to her for all she wouldn't have.

His gaze drifted to Molly and the bandaged leg. She'd kept the foot up as he'd instructed, but upon closer inspection he saw signs that, while the bleeding had slowed, it had not ceased. All the more reason to stop ruminating and get her into town.

"Molly," he said softly.

Her body jerked and her eyes flew open. She sat bolt upright, Laney gripped against her body.

"Oh, no! I fell asleep."

Her lip quivered and her hands shook in what Ethan thought was a gross overreaction. He took the now-squirming baby from her trembling arms.

"Is she all right?" Molly's voice was frantic.

"Hey, calm down. She's fine." Laney cradled against his shoulder, he crouched down beside the chair. "You're the one with the injury."

"Oh, Ethan." She dropped her face into her hands. "Anything could have had happened. I can't believe I fell asleep."

"Nothing happened, Molly. She's okay." He patted her back as he would have Laney, offering comfort for some terror he didn't understand. "I'm sorry she's so much trouble."

"She's not. She's wonderful. It's just that…" She bit down hard on her bottom lip.

"It's what? Talk to me, Molly. Tell me what's wrong."

"I'm not…good with babies."

He frowned, baffled. She was great with Laney. "What makes you think that?"

"I just do. That's all."

In other words, she didn't want to tell him. And the notion bugged him. How could he fix what he didn't understand?

With a sigh, he levered up and went to pack Laney's diaper bag.

Someday he hoped Molly would trust him enough to tell the truth—whatever that might be.

"Ethan, relax. They'll be in here as soon as they can."

Molly, who sat on the end of an exam table in Winding Stair Hospital's emergency room, didn't know whether to be embarrassed, amused or touched. Ethan paced back and forth between the doorway of the ER and her side. At regular intervals, he disappeared down the hall to the reception desk to make a general nuisance of himself. Meanwhile, Laney slept like a rock in her carrier.

"I don't know what's keeping the doc." Ethan paused before a diagram of the ear, hands shoved deep in the pockets of his jacket. "Maybe I should go check."

Before Molly could argue that he'd already done

that a dozen times, he wheeled on his heel and stalked out the door. She stifled a laugh. No one ever fussed over her.

He'd no more than left when a nurse entered. Molly knew most people in Winding Stair, but this woman was unfamiliar. "That husband of yours is sure worried about you."

Husband? Is that what they thought? "He's not my husband."

"Well, if he's your boyfriend, you better grab on to him. Fellas with those looks and that sweet, concerned nature don't come along every day."

"We're just friends." She hoped they were that, given the time they'd spent together.

The nurse rolled her eyes and reached for a blood pressure cuff to wrap around Molly's upper arm. "Believe that if you will, but I don't think your guy feels that way." She pumped the machine and while waiting for the reading asked, "Running any temp with this?"

"It only happened this morning."

The nurse made a notation on a clipboard and poked a digital thermometer in Molly's ear. "What did you do? Fall on the ice?"

"Something like that." She told the story.

"We've seen tons of ice-related injuries since this storm hit. Broken wrists, hips, you name it. When was your last tetanus shot?"

"Forever. I never get hurt."

"We'll have to take care of that."

Ethan came strolling back in, looking pleased. "Doc's on his way."

"Good. Now, maybe you'll sit down and relax."

He offered an unrepentant grin, wheeled the doctor's exam stool away from the wall and perched on it. "Believe I will."

After her ridiculous reaction to falling asleep with Laney in her lap, she had expected Ethan to dump her at the hospital door and run. Instead, he had hovered as if her well-being was the most important thing in the world. He'd even badgered the nurses into bringing her a cup of coffee because he thought she was cold.

"You sure you don't want me to call your family?" He tilted forward, his strong fingers curled over the edge of the brown vinyl seat.

She shook her head, careful not to splash the warm coffee. "Aunt Patsy is too old to get out on this ice. A fall would be disastrous."

"Isn't there anyone else?"

"Uncle Robert lives in Oklahoma City. The rest wouldn't care."

The chair rollers clattered against pristine tile as he drew closer. "Sure they would. Families always care. Let me give them a call."

Her chest ached at the reminder of how lonely she'd been for family since Zack's death. But neither Mom nor Chloe would come. Mom wanted to keep the peace and Chloe—well, her sister hated her.

It occurred to her then that Ethan must be longing to take his baby and go home, a perfectly natural desire after five days of confinement with a stranger. But out of kindness and an overblown sense of responsibility, he didn't want to leave her alone.

"You don't have to wait with me any longer, Ethan. I know you have other things to do."

"Molly." He took the foam cup from her hand, set it aside, and then wrapped her fingers in his. With the most patient expression, he said, "I've made my phone calls. My job and friends know where I am now, and this won't take that much longer. After all you've done for Laney and me wild horses couldn't tear us away from here. I only asked because I thought you might want a family member instead of a virtual stranger."

To Molly, Ethan was no longer a stranger. Not even close. The admission sent a troublesome warning to her brain.

Just then the door swooshed open and a doctor entered, white lab coat flapping out at the sides. Another nurse, clad in green surgical scrubs, followed. Molly recognized her as the doctor's long-time assistant and smiled a greeting.

Ethan squeezed Molly's hand, then pushed off the stool to greet the newcomers. "Dr. Jamison."

"Ethan, good to see you. How's the class going?"

"Good. I'm learning a lot."

"Let me know if I can help."

"Thanks. I appreciate it. The people here in Winding Stair have been really good to me."

"The way I hear it, it's the other way around."

Molly wondered what the doctor meant by the remark, but before she could ask, he ended the pleasantries and turned his attention her way. "So, what have you done to yourself, Miss Molly?"

Dr. Jamison was the last of a dying breed, a family doctor who knew most of his patients personally. He was not only her physician, he was the McCreight family's doctor, and thus he knew the whole ugly story of Zack's death.

She held her breath, praying he wouldn't say anything in front of Ethan.

The graying doctor pushed up his glasses and bent to examine her injury. "Quite a bandage you have here."

The tension eased out of her. "That's Ethan's doing. He's a paramedic."

Dr. Jamison raised his eyes toward her companion, curious. "I remember someone telling me that. The lab, I think. Didn't you take the gamma up to Chester Stubbs?"

Nothing much happened in Winding Stair without the whole town knowing.

"Yeah, that was me. Did the chopper make it out there?"

"No trouble at all. They flew the Stubbses to Tulsa to ride this thing out. Now, what can you tell me about Molly's accident?"

"She has some loose bleeders," Ethan answered. "I couldn't ascertain their origin, so in lieu of proper supplies, we did the best we could to put pressure on it. The laceration's deep and at least ten centimeters from knee to calf." He spewed out a technical description of the cut, all the while hovering over the table, watching as Dr. Jamison removed the kitchen-towel bandage.

"Hmm. I see what you mean." The wound began to ooze immediately. "We'll have to probe a bit, check for glass or other debris while we seal off those seeping vessels."

Ethan moved up to Molly's side. His face was kind, sympathetic, almost tender.

"It's easier if you don't look."

"You think I'm a coward?" she teased.

But Ethan took the question seriously. "I think you're as brave as they come."

He eased a pillow beneath her head and helped her lean back. All the while, her insides jumped and quivered. Ethan thought she, the biggest coward on the planet, a woman who suffered from anxiety attacks, was brave?

He didn't know her at all.

As the liquid fire of the deadening agent entered Molly's already insulted flesh, Ethan took her hand. "Squeeze if you need to. This stings a little."

She hissed though her teeth, trying hard not to give in to the pain. He'd called her brave. And even though she knew it wasn't true, she didn't want Ethan to know.

"The worst will be over in a minute," Ethan encouraged. "And afterwards, we'll see if the van can ice skate over to the Rib Crib for dinner. What do you say?"

She concentrated on his words in an effort to blot out the burning anesthetic. "What about Laney's formula?"

"We'll stop by the store first, grab some supplies." He frowned as if in deep thought. "On second thought, let's grab some steaks and take them over to my place. I'll make us dinner."

"I don't know," she hedged. Saying goodbye was already going to be harder than she wanted it to be.

"What?" He asked in mock offense, eyes crinkling in humor. "You don't think I can grill steaks? Why, I'll have you know, Miss Molly McCreight, people come from miles around, from other states, even from outer space to sample my steaks."

She laughed. "Are you trying to feed me or distract me?"

"Both. Is it working?"

"Yeah," she said. "And you're really sweet for making the effort."

He winked down at her, the long scar wrinkling with the movement. "That's me. A sweet guy."

And she realized it was true. Ethan Hunter was a very nice man, kind and brave and thoughtful. He was everything a girl could want.

Nearly an hour later, Ethan carefully pulled the van out of the hospital parking lot. Laney kicked and cooed from her carrier in back, and Molly's cat mewed impatiently from his cage on the floorboard.

Though Ethan was tired to the bone, the idea of

an impromptu steak dinner with Molly energized him. He didn't know why. They'd had every meal together for days, but for some reason, he wanted to be the host, to spend time with her on his turf.

"So," he asked, careful to keep his attention on the slick streets. "You still up for my fabulous cooking?"

"Ethan," she started and then paused to stare out the windshield. Pale, her mouth drooped in exhaustion.

With a sinking feeling Ethan realized he was about to be turned down. To spare them both, he said, "You're worn out. You need to rest."

She touched his sleeve. "Thanks for understanding."

"No problem." But he realized her refusal was a problem. He didn't want to leave her with someone else. Who would look after that wound? Who would make sure she didn't get an infection? "Maybe another time."

She didn't answer and his stomach sank deeper. He liked her. Thought she liked him. Had he been wrong about that?

"Doc Jamison did a nice job on that cut." To everyone's relief, no permanent damage appeared to be done and, if all went well, the cut would heal in a week or two.

"He's a good doctor."

"A good man, too. He teaches the singles' class at church."

"Yeah, I know," she said in a funny, faraway voice.

"You do?"

"I used to attend that class."

"No kidding? I've never seen you there. Why did you stop going?"

She shrugged and he could tell the story, whatever it was, bothered her. "My family attends the Chapel."

Now he was more curious than ever. She wouldn't let him contact her family, and she didn't attend church because they were there. "What's wrong with that?"

"Nothing. I'm glad they go, but my sister and I have some—" she gnawed at her lip, expression stark as she searched for the right word "—unresolved issues. So it's better if I stay away."

He didn't like the sound of that. If not for his parents, he'd have gone nuts during the last year and a half. And though he'd messed up Laney's opportunity to have a strong nuclear family, he was thankful for the extended family that would sustain her. Family was everything.

"Want to talk about it?"

"No." Molly turned her face away and leaned down to tap at the cat carrier on the floor.

He wondered if her family problems had anything to do with her anxiety around Laney? Someday he'd find out. "If you'll tell me your aunt's address, I'll drop you off before I go to the store."

"On Cedar Street in the senior citizens' housing complex."

"I know some folks there. Which one is your aunt?"

"Patsy Bartlett in apartment six."

The name and address were as familiar to him as

his own. Patsy Bartlett was one of the many people
in this warm and wonderful town who had taken a
single father under their wings.

"I know her. She's a great lady. More outspoken
than anybody I've ever met."

"That's my great-aunt Patsy. If you don't want
the truth, don't ask her."

"Well, how about that? You and Miss Patsy are
related."

The fact that Ethan knew her aunt Patsy didn't
surprise Molly in the least. Her father's aunt still
attended Winding Stair Chapel and had a way of
collecting friends from every age bracket and walk
of life. Naturally, she would draw Ethan and Laney
into her fold.

Though the idea didn't surprise her, it did bother
her. In such a short time, she'd gotten to know Ethan
Hunter better than she knew most people after
months of acquaintance. But their friendship needed
to end here, today. With Aunt Patsy in the picture,
staying away from Ethan and his daughter might be
harder than she'd thought.

Staring out the windshield at the piles of dirty snow
and ice pushed to either side of the street, she shifted
in the seat, moving her bandaged leg with care.

Ethan glanced her way. "Are you hurting?"

His concern sent that now-familiar warmth
drifting through her. She wished she wasn't so sus
ceptible to him. "No. The leg's still numb."

"That won't last much longer."

"I know," she said. But a throbbing leg didn't worry her. The unsteady condition of her emotions did.

Ethan's questions about her family stirred up a much worse kind of pain. And to make matters worse, she yearned to talk to him, to let his cool reason and strong shoulders help her carry the awful load of guilt.

But Laney's happy babble from the back reminded Molly that confiding in Ethan was impossible. Totally impossible.

With heavy heart, she turned her attention back to the restless cat.

In moments, Ethan pulled the van alongside the curb in front of apartment six.

The front door swung open and Aunt Patsy's jolly, apple-cheeked face appeared in the doorway. Molly's mood lightened. Aunt Patsy was a tonic to anyone's wounds, be they physical or emotional. She strained forward in the seat, but from her spot on the opposite side of the van Patsy didn't notice her.

"Ethan Hunter, where have you been?" Aunt Patsy scolded, but the smile on her face said she wasn't the least bit angry. "I've been worried about you."

Ethan gave Molly a wink and shoved the door open with his shoulder.

"I brought you a present," he called as he hopped out and went around to the passenger side.

"Don't think another of your presents is going to get you off the hook this time, young man. Where's that baby?"

"Right here, Miss Patsy. I'll bring her up first."

Opening the storm door a crack, the old lady peered toward the van. "Who's that you got with you?"

"The surprise." Gingerly, he made his way to the apartment and turned the jabbering Laney over to Miss Patsy. "Be right back."

Patsy disappeared inside the apartment and returned to the door empty-handed.

Molly suppressed a giggle at Ethan's game. She couldn't cross the frozen yard on her own, so she sat still and waited for his help.

Sliding a little on the frozen grass, Ethan laughed as he returned to the van. Molly pushed the door open.

"Easy now," he said as he looped an arm around her waist and assisted her to the ground.

With little feeling in one leg, her balance was off and she slid a bit.

"I've got you," he said, blue eyes shining down at her in a way that made her wish it was so.

"Thanks," was all she could manage as they navigated the slick surface.

The minute they rounded the front of the brown van, Miss Patsy recognized her, saw the bandage, and set up a fuss.

"Oh, my darling girl is hurt. What's happened?" She shoved the storm door wide. "Get in this house right now."

"I'm okay, Auntie. Don't fret." Assisted by Ethan's strong arm, Molly hobbled through the door to the small mauve couch and eased down. "Ethan took me to the ER and I'm all patched up now."

"Ethan did?" Patsy bustled around the sofa, pushing pillows behind Molly. "Don't suppose that should surprise me any, the way he looks after folks around here."

Hadn't Dr. Jamison said something similar? As she settled back onto the couch, she looked up at Ethan, curious.

He gave an answering shrug. "Miss Patsy and the other ladies are the ones who do the looking after. I'd starve to death if they didn't feed me once in a while."

Molly could see he was downplaying her aunt's compliment. She gingerly slid both hands under her knee and lifted her wounded leg onto a pillow.

"Nonsense," Patsy said. "A meal now and again is nothing compared with all the handyman jobs he does around here. Last week he fixed my leaky faucet and cleaned out Margie's chimney so she'd quit fretting about the house burning. It's always something around these apartments, and Ethan's Johnny-on-the-spot if we need him. We old people can't do everything we once could."

Molly's esteem for the delivery man, already high, went up another disturbing notch.

"Aunt Patsy, you'll never be old."

"Tell that to my knees." To prove the point, she shuffled to an ancient recliner, grasped the arms, and sat. "My hinges are plum worn out."

"The knees may give you trouble, Miss Patsy, but you've got enough heart to go on forever," Ethan said.

Patsy chuckled and shook her head toward Molly. "See how he goes on? Got all us old hens clucking over him and his chick." She stretched her arms out. "Give me that baby."

Ethan lifted the kicking Laney from her carrier and placed her in the older woman's arms. "We ran out of plastic diapers. She might get you wet."

"Wouldn't be the first time. That one there," she indicated Molly, "did the same when she was a tyke."

"Aunt Patsy!" Molly lifted up, mortified.

"Oh, sorry. Some things shouldn't be told." But the sparkle in her aunt's eye said she wasn't sorry at all. She held Laney to her ample bosom and patted the diapered behind while rocking back and forth. "I've had you on my mind—and on God's mind, too—ever since this weather started. Worst ice storm I've seen in years. I knew something wasn't right out at the farm. No phone. No way of getting out there. And no word from anybody. What happened?"

Between the two of them, Molly and Ethan told the story while Patsy rocked and patted, rocked and patted. Molly envied how natural her aunt was with the child. She had been like that once.

"I don't like to think," Ethan concluded, "what might have happened if Molly hadn't taken us in that night."

Patsy waved the notion away. "I wouldn't expect her to do any less. That's the way she was raised. Take care of your neighbors."

"I would have been in a fix without Ethan, too, Auntie. The electric line across the garage probably would have killed me if Ethan hadn't been there to notice the danger."

Patsy stopped rocking. "I should have known the Lord would work everything out. And sure enough, he put you two together to look after one another." She resumed rocking. "What a blessing."

For Aunt Patsy, life was that simple. Either something was the Lord's will or it wasn't. Molly wished her faith was as strong and trusting. Instead she constantly wrestled with the "whys" and "what ifs" of life.

Ethan stood and took the now-sleeping baby from Patsy's fleshy arms, placing the infant in her carrier. "Much as I enjoy you ladies' company, Laney and I have to make a grocery run."

Disappointment stirred in Molly, but she refused to acknowledge the emotion, naming it relief instead. He needed to go, she told herself. To take his precious child as far away from her as possible.

Patsy pushed out of her recliner and bent to kiss Laney's forehead before snugging the blankets around her. "You bring that baby back over here anytime she needs a good huggin'."

"Only if you promise to call if you need anything."

"You got a deal." She patted his arm and moved toward the small kitchenette where the scent of stewing chicken filled the air. "Gotta check on my dinner. You sure you won't stay?"

"Wish I could." He started for the door, then stopped and turned to Molly. The look in his eyes did funny things to her insides. "I can go to the pharmacy and get your prescription filled if you'd like."

She shook her head. "No need. Gary delivers."

For the first time since she'd met him, he seemed uncomfortable. An uneasy feeling crept over her. Why didn't he just go?

"Look, Molly, I—" He hesitated. "I really appreciate all you've done for me and Laney."

"We've been over all that, Ethan. The relationship was symbiotic."

His lips twitched. "Symbiotic or not, I'd like to take you to dinner as repayment."

A knot formed in her stomach. "No repayment necessary."

His gaze traveled to the kitchenette where Patsy banged pot lids, then came back to rest on Molly's face.

"I'd like to see you again," he said, voice quiet.

A lump formed in Molly's throat. She didn't want him to want to see her. The temptation was great, but the danger was even greater.

"I don't think so, Ethan." She spoke as gently as she could but knew the words would sting. They'd shared much. Seeing each other again would be the normal, ordinary thing to do. But regardless of how much she wanted to know him better, nothing in her life was normal anymore.

A spot on her calf began to ache. She leaned up,

rubbing at it to avoid Ethan's earnest gaze. "You're nice to ask, but I can't. I…" Her voice trailed off.

She couldn't tell him the truth—that she was afraid to see him again. Afraid of having a panic attack. Afraid of what might happen to Laney.

Afraid of her feelings.

Except for Aunt Patsy's clatter—a clatter that seemed louder than usual—the apartment grew quiet. She picked at the white tape with a fingernail.

Finally, Ethan broke the silence. "Well, it's been an adventure," he said. "Believe it or not, I enjoyed myself."

"Me, too," she admitted. And she had—most of the time.

Looking up, she caught the puzzled hurt in his blue eyes and hated herself for putting it there. His expression spoke volumes. If she liked him, if she'd enjoyed their time, why wouldn't she see him again?

Because she couldn't risk him ever finding out.

Ethan was barely out of sight when Aunt Patsy shuffled in from the kitchen, dish towel in hand and said, "Why did you turn him down like that, child? He's a nice young man."

"Don't start, Auntie. You know where I stand on the subject. Ethan has a baby. And that's the end of it as far as I'm concerned."

Patsy perched on the edge of the sofa. "Honey, I love you and I've watched you suffer for two years over this. But you have to let go. Give it to God."

Molly squeezed her eyelids together. "I wish I could."

"You can. What happened to our little Zack was a tragedy. You and your sister have to get over it and move on with your lives."

Get over it. If only it was that easy. But the horror was seared into her memory like a brand, too deep to heal.

Irrational. Phobic. Obsessive. Molly knew all the terms, for what little good that did.

"You think I'm neurotic, too."

"I do no such thing," Aunt Patsy breathed, indignant. "You've lived through something awful. Anyone not affected by that is made of ice. But, honey, you can't keep living in fear this way. Fear is the opposite of faith."

Distressed, Molly sank deeper into the couch. She didn't want to be afraid. She didn't want to be alone. But avoiding danger was the only way to keep the panic at bay.

Aunt Patsy didn't understand. She hadn't been the one to find Zack's limp and lifeless body in his crib. She hadn't been suspected by the police and accused by her own family.

"Are you turning against me, too?"

"Never. The way Chloe treated you is terrible and I've told her and your mother so a hundred times. If your daddy was still alive, he'd put a stop to that nonsense. But I'm not thinking of them. I'm thinking of you. You need a life. For two years I've watched you spin your wheels, going nowhere. You're stuck on that terrible day, hiding out with us old people, hiding on the farm, hiding from life."

"I'm not hiding." Not in the way Patsy meant. Her presence upset her sister. And as the person responsible for Chloe's heartache staying out of sight was the least she could do. And staying away from people, kids in particular, was a matter of preserving her sanity. The fear of a panic attack hung over her every time she ventured out into the community.

"Ethan Hunter is a good man. Some smart woman is going to snatch him up."

"He deserves a good woman." Her heart pinched when she said it. "And Laney deserves to be loved by a woman who can keep her safe."

"Oh, sugar pie," Patsy said wearily, shaking her head. "You're only a danger to your own happiness, never to a baby."

Molly wished that was true. "I'm tired, Aunt Patsy."

"I know you are. In more ways than one." She patted Molly's arm. "I'll let you rest 'til dinner, but just you mark my words. Ethan Hunter is special and he likes you. If he's the man I think he is, he'll be back."

"Won't do any good."

Molly burrowed into the pillow and closed her eyes again. Ethan's handsome face was there to haunt her. She pushed him away. A baby was dead because of her, and regardless of how much she liked Ethan, she couldn't bear to live through that again.

Chapter Seven

W ithin the next couple of days, the capricious Oklahoma temperature shot up to a balmy forty-seven degrees and ice melted with the speed of the sunlight beaming down upon it. Chunks fell with thuds from branches and eaves.

"Are you sure you want to go back to the farm so soon?" Aunt Patsy asked.

Molly could hardly wait. Every moment in town made her uneasy.

"The Center's going to reopen tomorrow. I need a day at home to get things back in shape before returning to work."

That much was true. But the whole truth rested in the worry that her sister or mother would drop by to check on Aunt Patsy. They had both already called several times. Once Molly had answered. Her sister's frosty tone, ordering her to, "Put Aunt Patsy on the phone," was enough to bring the terrifying tightness into Molly's throat.

One wrong word, one suspicious stare could instigate a panic attack. She had moved to the farm in the first place to avoid the townsfolk's stares and whispers and the inevitable encounters with her sister. The old house was her haven.

To make matters worse, Ethan had called every day to check on her injury. And she'd struggled long and hard to ignore his not-so-subtle hints that he and Laney drop by for a visit. The need to see him again was strong and troubling.

She pulled her coat closed and then hugged her aunt's shoulders. "Thanks for asking Pastor Cliff to drive me out."

"He was glad to do it. He misses you. We all do."

"I'll call you when I get there. Don't worry."

Taking care not to fall on any of the many remaining patches of ice, she headed out the door and climbed into the waiting pickup truck. She hadn't seen her pastor in several months, not since the last time he and his wife had come to the farm, trying to set up a counseling session between Molly and Chloe. They meant well, but she had already tried everything to repair the rift, only to have her sister scream accusations in her face. She understood that. Accepted it. Nothing could fix the wrong she'd done to Chloe. And the panic attack she'd suffered that day had sealed her decision for good.

"How ya doin', Molly?" The young preacher was

a blond giant the size of a wrestler but with a gentle nature that was as disarming as it was surprising.

"Good. Yourself and Karen?"

"Great." Beefy hands on the steering wheel, the minister headed the truck down the slushy street. "Karen's already gearing up for the spring bazaar."

"So soon?"

"Not much else to do until this weather settles. You know how she loves making knickknacks." His sky-blue eyes slanted in her direction. "You ought to get involved again, Molly. You're good at that sort of thing, too."

Painfully bright sun reflected off the melting ice. Molly squinted at it, heaviness centering in her chest.

Yes, she was good at crafts and "knickknacks" and loved the creation process so much that she and Chloe had once planned to open a shop together. She also missed the social contact. But Chloe was a mainstay for the women's group, her prize-winning quilts and crocheted items in much demand.

"My sister would have a fit."

Cliff slowed and turned off the main road. The truck geared down, working harder on the now-muddy country roads.

"Maybe if you were around every Sunday, Chloe would be forced to adjust, and both of you could get past this stand-off."

"I doubt it." Chloe had made her feelings very clear. Molly was a reminder of all she had lost, the person whose very existence had caused her grief. If Chloe never saw Molly again, it would be too soon.

"Did you know she's been getting counseling?" Pastor Cliff asked. "She and James both."

Other than the tidbits her aunt shared, Molly knew little about her sister these days. "I'm glad. I hope it helps. She's suffered enough."

"They're considering going to a support group that meets down in Mena. A group of people who've each lost a child."

"That's good." Her chest began to hurt. She rubbed the base of her tightening throat, sorry she'd broached the topic in the first place. "Could we talk about something else?"

Pastor Cliff gave her one of his compassionate looks. "Still having the attacks?"

"Not in a while." But she'd come far too close recently to want to take a chance.

"Ethan Hunter said the two of you rode out the storm together."

Molly groaned inwardly. Another difficult subject.

"He stayed in Uncle Robert's camper, the one he takes to Broken Bow Lake every summer." She didn't want any rumors getting started. She had enough of those to deal with. "He's a good guy."

"I think you made an impression on him, too." A grin split his wide face. "He came by the house yesterday afternoon."

Molly wanted to know how Ethan looked, how he

was, and what he'd said about her, but didn't ask. Some things were better left alone.

"He told me about the cut on your leg."

"Clumsy me." She patted the sweat pants covering the area. "But it's almost healed now."

"Lucky thing you had a paramedic on hand."

"Aunt Patsy says Ethan's presence was part of God's plan. Do you believe that, Pastor Cliff?"

More than once she'd wondered what she would have done if Ethan had not been there to help her.

"I never argue with Miss Patsy. She is a wise woman."

Molly couldn't deny that, but she still struggled to understand God's hand in all that had happened, not only Ethan's presence during the ice storm, but baby Zack's death. A plan that included such a tragedy didn't make much sense to her.

They rode along in silence for a while, jostling and straining over the patchy ice and red mud until the farm came into sight. The broken tree limb, looking naked and forlorn, lay in the front yard where she and Ethan had left it. Other limbs had given way and lay scattered about. The yard remained frozen with only patches of dead grass visible beneath the shiny ice.

"I really appreciate the ride, Cliff," Molly said as they pulled into her driveway and parked.

"Don't you want to check the house before I leave, make sure everything's in working order?"

She hopped out, eager to be home, to reclaim the relative peace she'd fought so hard for.

"That's okay. The electric company repaired the broken line. If I need anything I'll have my Jeep."

Cliff hesitated. "You sure?"

"Positive. Tell Karen hello for me."

"Come to church Sunday and tell her yourself."

Molly grinned and slammed the door. Pastor Cliff would never give up. It was both an endearing and an exasperating quality.

The truck spun away, mud and water splattering the fenders. Molly waved, then walked carefully across the yard and into the house, eager to get busy. Most of her refrigerated goods would have to be discarded, and laundry was piled high in the basket, so after removing her coat, she set to work.

Deciding to get the laundry started first and save the more time-consuming clean-ups for later, she went into the utility room and sorted through the stack of clothes. A tiny pink terry-cloth sleeper peeked from beneath the pile.

Lifting out the baby pajamas, she got a funny catch beneath her ribcage. The memory of Laney's warm, sweet scent and soft baby skin rolled through her.

She placed the item in a stack of delicates. Laney needed this, and keeping it would be wrong. She'd have to return it.

Some perverse part of her leaped at the idea.

After filling the washer, she pulled the on knob—and heard a deep, airy gurgling.

Great. Just what she didn't need. With the power

off for such a long time, the water pump must have lost its prime.

But as she started out the back door to check, another sound took preeminence. Not gurgling, but humming. The humming of an overworked well pump. One look at the yard told her why. Water stood in small lakes and flowed from beneath the house. Not the gentle trickle of melting ice, but a flood that could only mean one thing:

The water pipes had burst.

With a sinking heart, she rushed to the main valve and shut off the water.

Five phone calls later, she leaned her head against the back of the couch and groaned.

Pipes were burst all over the county. No one was available for weeks.

Dread weighed her down as she accepted the inevitable.

"Well, Samson," she said to the cat who'd trailed her all over the house, curious about her fidgetings. "Looks like you and I are heading back to town."

She'd survived an ice storm. She only hoped she could survive the aftermath.

"Don't you worry, Mrs. Gonzales." Molly squeezed the old woman's cold fingertips. "I'll get someone over to your place to relight the furnace right away. You stay here, have a nice lunch and enjoy yourself until I do."

One of Molly's favorite things about working in

the seniors' center was the relief on a client's face when she solved a problem for them.

Since the ice storm there had been plenty of problems to solve. The center had been inundated with calls. In addition to their regular Meals-on-Wheels and other programs, everything from the need for a ride to the doctor to folks out of food and medicine had kept Molly and other staff members hopping. Many of the seniors were only now beginning to brave the cold weather to return to the center for lunch and socialization. Mrs. Gonzales was one of them.

Molly escorted the bird-like lady from her small office to the main recreational and dining area. She liked this large common room, finding it cozy and welcoming despite the size, due in large part to the warm colors and decorations on the walls. At one end, a sectional surrounded a fake fireplace. At the other, a quilting frame awaited the expert fingers of the Quilting Club. Small game tables lined the walls and longer dining tables centered the room.

Molly and Mrs. Gonzales made their way to a table where two other women chatted over hot coffee. One of them, Iris Flowers clunked down her cup and said, "Molly. Just the girl I wanted to see. How in the world did you know Maud Jennings needed groceries?"

"Intuition, I suppose. I called her and she didn't sound right, so I ran by her house on the way to work."

Phoning clients who hadn't made an appearance at the center was something Molly did on her own, but she believed making that contact, especially with those who lived alone, was important and necessary.

Iris, who wore wild floral prints befitting her name, pursed crimson lips in irritation. "The proud old thing never told a soul she was in trouble."

"Some folks are like that. Don't want to impose, but I was glad to help out." And she was.

The seniors accepted her, never whispered behind her back or made snide remarks. And in return, she gave them her all, sometimes working long after the center closed. She didn't mind. Usually she had nothing but a cat to go home to.

"You're more and more like your Aunt Patsy everyday," Mrs. Gonzales added. "Isn't she, Iris?"

The other two women nodded and beamed looks of approval her way.

Molly hoped the compliment was true. She couldn't imagine a better person to emulate than her great-aunt.

"Thank you, ladies. Now if you'll excuse me, I need to find someone to go out and light Mrs. Gonzales's furnace so the place will be cozy when she gets home."

"Why don't you get that cute UPS man to do it?" Iris said. "He's right handy at such things."

The old ladies giggled like teenagers and Molly laughed with them, though hers was more forced. All the seniors seemed to know that she and Ethan had ridden out the storm together and teased her about him on a regular basis.

"I imagine he's in Mena today making deliveries."

"And then again," Iris said pointedly, giving her glasses a shove. "Maybe he's not."

The ladies giggled as Molly followed the direction of Iris's gaze.

Her heart tumbled to her toenails.

Ethan, carrying a load of packages, pushed through the glass double doors and came toward her.

When he spotted her gaping at him as though she'd never seen such a good-looking sight, he smiled. Her heart tumbled a little farther.

"Close your mouth, Molly," Iris whispered.

Though her mouth wasn't really open, Molly knew she had to get a grip. She took a deep breath and returned his smile.

"Hi," she said and was amazed to sound so natural.

"Hi, yourself." He stopped in front of her and gazed down with the strangest light in his eyes. She stood there like an idiot, mesmerized.

He looked rested and well. And really, really handsome in the brown uniform that set off his brown hair and blue eyes to perfection.

She'd missed him. Had he missed her?

"Yoo-hoo, Molly. Ethan," Iris trilled while two other ladies tittered. "Helloooo."

Ethan broke the magnetic stare long enough to nod in their direction. "Ladies. How y'all doin'?"

"Couldn't be better." The three women beamed. "Isn't that right, Molly?"

Molly decided to ignore their pointed attempts at matchmaking.

"Deliveries for us?" she asked.

"There are more in the van. Must have been a backlog while the roads were so bad."

He seemed in no hurry to move, but Molly knew she had to do something besides stare like a lovesick cow.

"I'll help you unload."

"Great." Ethan grinned as if she'd offered him the grand prize.

Iris's voice intruded, "Don't forget about Mrs. Gonzales's furnace."

"I won't," Molly said and started forward, eager to get away from the well-meaning women.

The delighted chatter of the trio followed them across the room and into Molly's little office. "Sorry about the ladies. They're all hopelessly infatuated with you."

Setting the boxes on the indicated table, he laughed. "Is that a fact?"

"Every one of them. You must stop emptying their mousetraps and unplugging their sinks."

"Can't. I'd starve to death without their cooking."

"You would not." She stuck a hand on one hip, realized she was flirting, and let it drop. "It's nice of you to help them out."

"Symbiotic relationships seem to be an important element in my life." His grin widened as he repeated the word she'd used in describing their time together. "What's wrong with Mrs. Gonzales's furnace?"

"Never mind. I'll handle it."

"Might as well tell me. I'm going to ask her if you don't."

No use fighting it. The man was a born rescuer. "The pilot went out last night."

His eyebrows rose in concern and the white scar rose, too. "She was in a cold house all night?"

"Unfortunately. And on her fixed income she can't afford to pay for something like that. So I told her I'd find someone to re-light it for her."

"Okay. Let's unload the rest of those boxes and head over there."

She liked the sound of that "let's" a little too much. "I can get someone else."

"No need. I can do it in a jiffy. Do you have her key?"

"It's under the flower pot on the front porch."

He thumped the heel of his hand against his forehead. "Doesn't she know that's the first place a thief will look?"

"Yes, but she thinks Freddy might come home while she's gone." Freddy was the son who'd taken off for parts unknown years before and never returned. Mrs. Gonzales refused to give up hope.

They walked out to the van and carried the rest of the boxes inside. Then while Molly logged in the deliveries on her computer, Ethan moved around the common area greeting the older adults. They all seemed to know him.

Her eyes kept straying from the monitor to watch his long, athletic strides. Once, he disappeared but a few minutes later, she had spotted him again.

Although they had talked on the telephone a few

times, she hadn't seen him since he'd brought her home from the ER. She'd forgotten how his presence could fill a room—or at least, she'd tried to forget.

Encountering him now created a problem. She was much happier to see him than she wanted to be.

She typed in the last bar code and swiveled away from the desk and the window that looked out on the common room. Maybe he'd be gone by the time she unpacked the boxes.

"Molly?" His handsome face peered around her office door. "Going with me?"

Her pulse did a happy dance. Not a good sign.

"I'd better stay here."

"I really need you to come along. This is my first trip to Mrs. Gonzales's. I wouldn't want the neighbors to think I was a burglar and call the police. Besides, I went all the way back to my apartment for my own truck so you could ride with me without making my company angry. You gotta go."

"Oh." She gnawed at her lip.

The pilot had to be lit and Ethan was willing. Only her selfishness stood in the way. Mrs. Gonzales needed this favor badly. With Laney safely at daycare, Molly was in no danger of a panic attack. And they wouldn't be gone long.

"Okay," she said at last. "Let me tell my boss."

"Tell her we'll be back after lunch."

Lunch. She usually ate with the seniors, but a meal with Ethan sounded really good.

What could it possibly hurt?

* * *

Thirty minutes later, Molly sat at a round table across from Ethan inside the Caboose, Winding Stair's most popular diner. The scent of apple pie hung in the air like potpourri, and townspeople she'd known all her life filled the long narrow dining room.

Tension knotted Molly's stomach as she gazed around. She hadn't been here in more than a year.

At the senior's center she felt safe. Here, she was open to the speculative stares and whispers of any and all. Maybe this lunch wasn't such a good idea after all.

"I thought that dog was going to eat my leg off," Ethan said with a laugh as he shook out his napkin.

Mrs. Gonzales's schnauzer had welcomed Molly with a wagging tale and friendly whines, but she'd taken exception when Ethan had begun to dismantle the floor furnace.

"Daisy doesn't bite. She was looking for treats."

"You calling my leg a doggie treat?"

Trying to hide her anxiety, Molly managed a smile. Ethan was good at making her forget. "Isn't that what mailmen are for? Dog treats?"

"See why I have a goldfish?"

"Don't forget the snake and the shark."

The waitress arrived, earrings swaying, order pad at the ready. She took one look at her customers and said, "Well, hello, Molly. Haven't seen you in here in a long time."

Though the woman's tone was friendly, Molly

stiffened. The dread expanded in her chest. "Hi, Debbie. How's the family?"

"Growing. One more kid and we'll have to buy a hotel."

At the mention of kids, Molly's pulse rate rocketed. Her insides trembled, but instead of the expected reference to Zack's death, Debbie pointed her pencil at Ethan and grinned. "Better watch out for this one. He's trouble."

"Is that right?"

"Positive. Just ask Tom. According to my husband, Ethan cheats at every sport known to man, even in the church fellowship hall."

Ethan's lips twitched.

Across the room someone hollered, "Hey, Debbie, I need some coffee."

"Be there in a sec, Willis." She hollered back, and then said to Ethan, "Better get moving. What are you two having today? The special is fried chicken."

"Sounds good. How about you, Molly?"

Molly agreed, though as nervous as she was, she doubted her ability to eat a bite.

Debbie took their order, flipped over their coffee cups and filled them, then whirled away, bantering with customers and refilling cups.

Ethan folded his arms on the tabletop and leaned toward her. "So how have you been? You're not limping anymore so I'm guessing the cut healed just fine."

"All gone except for a long red line. Doc Jamison says it will fade with time."

At the mention of a scar, Ethan's hand moved to the one dissecting his eyebrow. He smoothed his finger over and over the scar. As before, Molly was tempted to ask about the wound that had caused it, but Ethan didn't give her a chance.

"Any progress on the plumbing problem?"

Moving her gaze from the scar to his eyes, she shook her head. The local plumber was still backed up. "Not yet. How are you and Laney doing since the ice storm?"

Ethan's hand paused at his temple, expression tender. The corners of his eyes crinkled. "Laney's awesome."

"Growing, I imagine."

"Like a weed. She had a cold a couple of weeks ago, but that didn't slow her down."

"A cold?" Her voice rose. "Is she all right?"

Ethan's look questioned her. "A cold, Molly. Not the Black Plague. Mrs. Stone brought over some kind of concoction to rub on her chest."

Molly tried to relax, but the worry nagged her. Had Laney caught a cold while in her care? Had she caused the sickness by making Ethan and the baby spend five days in the old camper?

"I've used Mrs. Stone's home remedies," she finally said. "They're usually effective. Did it work?"

"Worked great. Even worked for me."

Molly paused from stirring sugar into her coffee.

As much as she worried about Laney, she worried more about Ethan. He put in long hours in addition to caring for Laney and doing oddjobs for those in need. And there was no one to care for him or Laney if he became ill.

"Were you sick, too?"

"Nah. But the smell of that stuff cleaned out my sinuses anyway."

Captivated by the pure fun in Ethan's blue eyes, Molly laughed. Ethan had that power—to make her relax, to help her forget her worries, to remind her that she was a woman.

Still holding her gaze with his, he rubbed a finger over the back of her hand and grew serious. "I've missed you."

She'd missed him, too, a troublesome truth.

Fortunately, she was saved from saying anything when a man paused at their table to chat with Ethan about a hunting lease.

In the background, plates clattered, voices rose and fell, and occasional laughter broke out around the long room.

Here were people she'd known all her life. Yet Ethan seemed more comfortable with them than she did. Natural, she supposed, given the cloud of suspicion she'd lived under for so long. Ethan had proven trustworthy. The jury was still out on her.

Throughout lunch, townspeople continued to stop at their table with greetings. Each time she tensed, but no one mentioned Zack. No one stared at her as if she'd done something terrible. By the end of the meal, she had relaxed and was actually enjoying herself.

And then her sister walked through the door.

Chapter Eight

Ethan watched a radical change come over his luncheon partner. One minute she was giggling at something silly he'd said and the next she turned as white as one of Laney's diapers.

"Molly? What's wrong?" He laid his fork aside and looked around the noisy diner. The only difference he noticed was a too-slim woman with short-cropped red hair standing in the entry. He recognized her from church, though theirs was only a passing acquaintance.

Apparently Molly knew her far better than he did.

He was no rocket scientist, but he wasn't stupid either. Though different in style and stature, the familial likeness was striking. Two redheads with the same almond eyes and high cheekbones could only mean one thing.

"Is that your sister?"

Molly nodded, hand at her throat. "Chloe."

Her tone, broken and anxious, touched him. So this was the sister with whom she had "issues."

Curiosity tempered by concern, he asked, "Should we leave?"

But it was too late. The woman spotted them, jerked as if she'd suffered an electric shock and began twisting the straps of a black shoulder bag round and round in her hands.

She stared in disbelief for several long, tense moments before striding toward their table. If she noticed Ethan's presence at all, she didn't acknowledge it. Her wounded gaze bore into Molly.

"What do you think you're doing?" The words hissed out of her mouth like noxious gas escaping a canister.

Molly seemed to shrivel. Hurt and longing hung over her like a darkness. "I'm sorry, Chloe. I didn't know you'd be here."

Ethan leaned back in his chair and gripped the table's edge, hardly able to take in the bizarre conversation. Since when did Molly, or anyone else for that matter, have to apologize for eating in a public restaurant?

Though he had no idea what was going on, he considered intervening. From the looks of Molly, she was about to collapse.

Before he could, Chloe, her skin as pale as Molly's, spoke again.

"I don't understand why you keep doing this." She stuck out a trembling hand. "See this? Do you realize how upset I get? Even tranquilizers don't help in situations like this."

"Tell me how to make things better, Chloe. What can I do?"

Molly's reply was gentle and so filled with sadness, Ethan could almost see her broken heart. Without another thought, he slid a hand across the table to touch her. Her fingers were as cold as the icicles they'd melted for water.

"My counselor says I have to find a way to resolve things with you if I'm ever to be happy again," Chloe said, her narrow chin tilting in a martyred pose. "But he doesn't understand. Every time I see you, I remember—" Her voice broke. Tears welled in eyes so like Molly's…and yet so different.

"I'm sorry." Molly's voice was barely a whisper. Her knuckles had gone white against her throat. "Please forgive me. Please, Chloe. Forgive me."

"Forgive?" The redhead's lower lip trembled with victimization. "How can I? All I ask is for you to leave me alone, and yet here you are."

Ethan was fast moving from bewildered to annoyed. If this woman didn't back off pretty quick, she'd have someone else to blame for her problems—him.

He caught Molly's gaze, lifted an eyebrow to ask if he should intervene. She gave her head a tiny shake and pushed aside her plate.

"We'll leave now."

She started to rise but Ethan stopped her with a hand on her arm. "No. Sit down and finish your chicken."

"Ethan, please." Huge golden eyes begged him. "Let's go."

If she said *please* one more time he would come unwound. She had no reason to beg him or anyone else. But her anguish disturbed him enough to let her win.

"All right. If you're certain that's what you want."

"It is. Please."

Ethan ground his teeth and barely refrained from cursing, a bad habit he'd thought was long gone.

"Let me take care of the check." Rising, he reached for his wallet and tossed a tip on the table. Reluctant to leave Molly alone, he locked eyes with the vindictive sister and stared hard, signaling as much of a warning as possible without upsetting Molly even more.

Chloe emitted an affronted hiss and hitched her narrow chin.

Ethan couldn't believe this woman. She seemed to believe she had a right to treat her sister with such cruelty.

Molly leaped up and grabbed her coat from the back of the chair. "I'll wait in the truck."

As she brushed past her trembling sister, Molly whispered, "I love you," and Ethan thought either his heart would break or his anger would explode.

He made his way to the cash register, aware of the whispers coming from the other tables, but too concerned about Molly to listen. After settling the bill, he hurried out to the truck.

Once inside, he started the vehicle to ward off the

chill and then turned sideways in the seat. "What was that all about?"

Molly still shook like a wet kitten. "Nothing. Just take me back to the center."

He clenched his jaw, fighting off the very real threat of his temper. "No way. This vehicle doesn't move until you talk to me."

He'd had all of her secrets he was willing to take. They'd been strangers before so he hadn't pried, but now he was a friend. And friends helped each other.

Her hand went to her throat again in that anxious action he'd witnessed far too often. "I can't talk about it, Ethan. You'll hate me."

Hate her? She was making less sense than her sister had. But whatever troubled her cut deep and lay like a boulder on her slender shoulders. Having him lash out, too, wasn't the way to help.

Without stopping to think about it, he reached out and pulled her into his arms. She needed comfort. He could give it.

As soon as her forehead touched his shoulder, she broke. All the resolute composure he'd observed during the confrontation with her sister gave way to tortured sobs.

As much as Ethan hated for a woman to cry, Molly needed this. Heavy-hearted, bewildered and worried, he stroked her silky hair and let her cry herself out.

There had been a time in his own life when he had needed someone this way. Thank God his parents had been there ready to catch him when he'd fallen. From the looks of things, Molly didn't have that safety net.

When the storm of tears passed she tried to pull away, but he held her fast against the damp shoulder of his coat. She required little resistance to keep her there, and he wondered how long it had been since Molly had had a shoulder to cry on.

Holding her was a simple thing to do. And, regardless of the circumstances, he liked having her in his arms. She smelled like the vanilla candles his mother liked so much. He liked them, too, more now than ever.

The foolish thought flitted through his head that he would buy one for his apartment and burn it whenever he wanted to think of Molly.

Disgruntled by such silliness, he shoved the idea away. Right now, something way more serious than Molly's sweet vanilla scent weighed on him.

He needed to know what terrible secret had torn her family apart. And was still tearing her apart.

Gradually, the tremors in her body subsided to occasional jerks and sniffs. When at last she lifted her head, he smoothed the hair back from her tear-streaked face.

"How can I help you fix this if you don't tell me?" His throat was thick with more emotion than he normally wanted to deal with. Molly had that strange effect on him.

Averting her face, she grappled in her coat pocket and came up with a tissue.

"Some things can't be fixed, Ethan." Her voice,

too, was wrought with emotion, only hers carried the added layer of sorrow.

"Not true. God can fix anything." Didn't he know from personal experience? "Maybe not in the way we expect, but He can make things right again."

"Chloe won't let Him. Won't even try."

"Why not?"

She lifted puffy, red eyes that tore at his heart and brought the anger surging up inside him again. Somebody needed their heads cracked for this. Two years ago, he'd happily have done the honors. If nothing else his walk with Christ had helped him see the futility in such behavior. It hadn't, unfortunately, taken away his natural inclination to take matters into his own hands.

"I hurt her, Ethan. I wronged her in the most terrible way."

"What did you do that could have been that bad?"

She fell silent for a moment while the hum of the heater filled the space between them with sound and warmth. He could see the war going on inside her. She didn't want to go there, and yet she couldn't escape the memory.

Shoulders hunched, she took a deep breath and exhaled slowly, shakily.

"After today, you're bound to hear about it from someone. It would probably be better if I tell you myself. You'll hear the truth this way."

He narrowed his eyes. The truth? Did the good people of Winding Stair tell lies about Molly? Regardless of the fact that he attended church with her troubled sister, he'd never heard a negative word about Molly.

A car pulled in beside them. A door slammed, and his peripheral vision caught the flash of a plaid jacket. Ethan kept his attention riveted on Molly. No matter how long she stalled, he would wait.

"Talk to me," he said in the same soothing, cajoling tone he'd once used to gather vital information from injured patients.

Molly stared out the fogging window and followed the plaid coat with bleak eyes.

Ethan clicked on the defroster.

As if the switch had also activated her tongue, Molly whispered, "Chloe believes I killed her baby."

The awful words echoed in the moist, heated air for a full minute. Stunned, Ethan fell back against the seat to absorb her meaning. His brain buzzed louder than the humming van motor. He couldn't take it in.

The Molly he knew wouldn't hurt a flea. She fed birds and fretted over strangers, she provided for countless needy kids, and she pampered the elderly. No way she'd ever hurt a child.

"I don't believe you," he said when he'd regained his voice.

"It's true. Anyway that's what Chloe and most of the people around here think."

She looked so small and alone, sitting huddled against the door with her terrible secret hanging heavy between them.

All of his protective instincts screamed to gather her close and block out the ugliness, to be the shield between Molly and the rest of the world. But it wasn't the world that tormented Molly. It was her own guilt and sorrow.

He reached out, tried to pull her back into his arms, but she resisted, scooting away to dig another tissue from the pocket of her beige coat. Red marks spotted her neck where her fingers had squeezed.

He eased back against the driver's door, allowing her the distance she seemed to need. As much as he longed to touch her, he resisted. The shots were hers to call. "What happened?"

A beat passed. Then two. Her breath whooshed out, adding more fog to the windshield.

"Chloe and James wanted an afternoon out, so I offered to babysit for Zack. He was six months old. I loved him so much." She fidgeted with the tissue, picking it apart in tiny pieces. "We played. I fed him and gave him a bath. He smelled so good." She closed her eyes as if remembering. "I can still smell him if I try."

Something inside Ethan twisted. He knew that sweet, special baby scent very well.

"He was fine when I put him in his crib. Sleeping so peacefully. I kissed his soft little cheek and went into the living room." She pressed her fists together in front of her face, shoulders hunched. "If only I hadn't watched that TV show. Maybe if I had looked in on him sooner."

His medical knowledge clicked into place. He knew of only one malady so unexpected and so devastating in perfectly healthy infants.

"SIDS?" he asked quietly. He'd gone out on a couple of those calls in his paramedic days. No call was more shattering.

"That's what the autopsy revealed." She shuddered. "An autopsy, Ethan. I can't bear to think about it."

Neither could he. He blocked the thought and moved into objective medic mode. If he let his emotions have free rein, he wouldn't be any help to her at all.

"SIDS happens, Molly. You didn't cause it."

"But don't you see? That doesn't matter. Fault or not, my sister's baby is dead. She lost the most precious thing in her life."

"But why punish you?"

"I was the adult in charge. I was the one she'd trusted to protect her baby."

What could he say? No amount of argument would change the hideous loss all of Molly's family had suffered. He couldn't begin to imagine how he would feel in the same situation. Laney was his everything. After all he'd been through to keep her, nothing could be worse than losing her.

But regardless of the tragedy, Chloe had no right to vent her anger and bitterness on Molly. Didn't the woman realize that Molly was grief-stricken, too?

"One thing for certain, Molly. Neither you nor your sister can heal until the rift between you is mended."

He'd had enough psych classes to know the negative impact of hanging onto guilt and unforgiveness.

"But being around me hurts her, and I don't want her to suffer anymore. She's been through too much already."

And so have you, he wanted to say, but knew the sentiment would be rejected. Instead he said, "Is it like this every time you see her?"

Pale red hair brushed her chin as she nodded. "I've only seen her a few times, mostly by accident. But every time she looks at me with those accusing eyes, and I feel so horribly ashamed, I leave. I do that to her, Ethan. Seeing me breaks my sister's heart."

As Ethan absorbed the heartrending information, some of the things that had puzzled him about Molly began to make sense.

"This is why you're so anxious around Laney, isn't it?"

"I don't want anything to happen to her."

As terrible as it was, understanding this made him feel better. The fear around Laney coupled with the boxes for children's charity had confused him. One minute he'd wondered if she was as self-focused as Twila and the next he hadn't known what to think. Now he knew. It wasn't that Molly didn't care. She cared too much.

His admiration—and sympathy—rose several notches.

"What can I do to help?"

"I don't know."

Neither did he, but he wasn't about to let this go without some serious thought and prayer. She might not have an answer, but Somebody did.

He touched her cheek. "Are you going to be all right?"

"Sure." She straightened her shoulders and sat back in the seat, giving a mirthless, self-conscious laugh. "Sorry. I don't usually cry all over someone nice enough to buy me lunch. You must think I'm an idiot."

That wasn't what he thought at all.

After scrubbing at her face one more time with the tissue, she fastened her seatbelt. "I'd better get back to work."

One hand on the gearshift, Ethan studied her. She looked exhausted. "Wouldn't you rather I take you to Miss Patsy's?"

With a shake of her head, she drew in a deep, quivering breath. "Not necessary. I'm okay. But thanks."

He put the truck in gear, waited while a passing car arched a spray of dirty water against the back window, and then backed out of the parking place. His thoughts swirled with Molly's predicament.

He considered himself a man of action, a fixer. If a faucet leaked, he repaired it. If a patient needed gamma, he delivered it. When Twila had rejected Laney, he'd taken over.

He'd find a way to help Molly, too.

As the truck splashed through melted puddles along the street's edge, more water sprayed onto the windshield. Ethan turned on the wipers, listened to the rhythmic *whoomp-whoomp* for the last few blocks of the trip back to the center as he considered all he'd learned today.

He parked at the curb in front of the long brick building. Leaving the motor running, he turned to Molly.

"Thank you for telling me."

She tried to smile. "Thank you for listening. And for not running away."

"Why would I do that?"

She shrugged and Ethan saw the hurt hanging on her like an oversized shirt. Her family had rejected her. She expected the same from everyone else.

Unbuckling her seatbelt, she reached for the door handle.

"Molly." He was reluctant to let her go. She needed more than a listening ear.

She paused and swiveled her head toward him, amber eyes questioning.

He cleared his throat. "I still owe you that home-cooked steak dinner."

Her face lit up for the briefest of moments, and he thought she would agree. Then as if by some pre-programmed signal all the life went out of her. "I can't, Ethan. Please understand."

Understand what?

"Why not?"

"I don't date."

His gut tightened. "Anybody? Or just me?"

She reached across the seat and touched his

sleeve. "Don't think that. You're the…nicest guy I've met in a long time."

His hopes rose. Now he was getting somewhere.

"Then why not come over tomorrow night and let me amaze you with my culinary skills?"

"I like you, Ethan. And if that was all that was involved—" She stopped herself, shook her head and started again. "I don't want to hurt your feelings."

Realization hit him like a fist in the gut.

The wipers thumped the edge of the windshield and vibrated, scraping at the glass gone dry. Ethan let them scrape.

"I get it now," he said, jaw tight enough to break a molar. "You don't date guys like me. A single man with a baby."

A man with baggage. A man with an unsavory past. A man whose illicit affair had produced a child.

"I don't date, Ethan. Not you. Not anybody. Not ever."

Nobody? A girl as pretty and sweet as Molly didn't date? Ever?

She whirled away and yanked at the door with both hands. Ethan resisted the urge to pull her back and make her explain. Something more than estrangement from her sister troubled Molly. Something that made her reluctant to be with people, and yet she cared deeply for others. Somehow he knew she wasn't telling him everything.

He reached across the seat and pushed the door open, holding it for her.

Without turning to look at him, Molly hopped out and hurried up the water-darkened sidewalk.

Ethan narrowed his eyes and studied the departing figure. The way her shoulders huddled into the neck of her coat. The way her fingers returned time and again to rub at her throat. Yes, something was very much still amiss. He was certain of that. He wasn't sure why it mattered so much to him, but it did.

And he was also certain that he would not back off until he knew what else troubled pretty Miss Molly McCreight.

Molly spent the weekend fretting over the calamitous lunch with Ethan. Come Monday, the incident still played in her head like a bad movie.

She'd had a good time until Chloe arrived, and then she'd come apart right before Ethan's eyes.

What must he think of her?

A better question might be. Why did she care? He knew the truth about her now. At least part of it. He wouldn't be back and that was the way it had to be.

She couldn't be interested in him, a man with a baby. The risk was too great for all of them.

With a weary sigh, she pulled a file from the metal cabinet. One of the center's regulars who had slipped on the ice and broken an arm was due home from the hospital. Molly wanted to be certain the appropriate services were in place to take care of him during his recuperation.

After a couple of phone calls, she replaced the file

and sat staring at her computer screen. A goldfish swam across the blue screensaver and turned her thoughts right back to Ethan.

He probably thought she was a neurotic ninny. Maybe she was. And that was just as well. She'd come close to suffering a panic attack in the diner and closer still when they had discussed baby Zack. She couldn't bear the thought of giving in to the humiliating weakness in front of anyone, especially Ethan.

The all-too-public scene with Chloe must have embarrassed him. So why had he invited her to dinner?

She worried her lip. Probably out of pity.

Not that it mattered. After her breakdown in his truck, she didn't expect ever to hear from him again. And that was as it should be. As it had to be.

At noon, the tantalizing scent of homemade chicken and dumplings drew Molly into the center's dining room. With the ice finally gone, people had returned in droves, eager for the hearty meals and fellowship the center provided. Voices rose and fell around her as she took a tray and found a place in the buffet line.

The long queue of familiar faces stretched almost to the doors, but Molly didn't mind the wait. It was good to see everyone out and about again.

"Hi," a rumbling masculine voice said in her ear.

Whipping around, she gasped. "Ethan, what are you doing here?"

And how can you look so wonderful in an ordinary delivery uniform?

"Came by to have lunch with you."

She hefted the red food tray in front of her like a shield. "I told you I don't date."

He pretended shock, but mischief crinkled the corners of his blue eyes. "Did I say anything about a date? I don't want a date. I want lunch."

Her pulse leaped and pounded like bongo drums gone mad. "Then go to the diner."

She didn't want to be rude, but his presence did strange things to her resolve.

"Can't. I already paid my money." He jerked a thumb toward the cashier. Seniors ate for free or for a nominal amount, but others paid full price.

She gave in, unable to be unkind to someone she liked so much. She put her tray back on the stack. "I have some things to do in the office. I'll eat later."

Ethan reclaimed the tray, handed it to her. He looked down at her, more serious now. "Come on, Molly, it's only lunch."

The heat of a blush traveled up her neck. How idiotic to assume Ethan still wanted to date someone like her. She took the tray from his strong fingers. He was right. It was only lunch. Everybody had to eat.

So they shared a table that day. And the next and the next until Molly found herself watching the doorway every day at noon. She didn't understand why she couldn't tell him to leave her alone. It was as though she had some perverse need to stay emotionally tied up in knots.

On the days he didn't come, she fought off disappointment with a stern reminder that they were not dating. They were only having lunch.

Some days she almost believed it.

Chapter Nine

"**H**ere, Molly. You finish painting the faces on the animals while I staple the greenery in place."

Aunt Patsy's cheeks glowed rosy red beneath the bright kitchen light as she took up a stapler and set to work with her usual robust energy.

Between the two of them, Molly and her aunt had turned the kitchen into a mini-craft factory in preparation for the church's bazaar, still a couple of months away. For Molly the return to something she loved to do felt good and right.

Dipping the artist's brush into a pot, she painstakingly painted black eyelashes onto a white bunny. "Think we'll have enough door wreaths to meet the demand?"

"Never do. But with your help this year, we should have a hundred." The stapler made clack-snap noises as Aunt Patsy arranged flowers along a preformed circle. "Ethan still coming by to have lunch at the center every day?"

"Not every day." Like today. She'd almost missed lunch waiting for him, which was ridiculous. She knew he often drove too far out of town to get back by noon.

Patsy gestured in the direction of the back door. "That lock's been sticking. Can't always get my key to work. I told Ethan about it at church, and he promised to fix it."

Molly paused, holding the brush above the small plastic rabbit. "When?"

"Tonight."

A little quiver of anticipation mixed with a healthy dose of anxiety raced around in her veins. Seeing Ethan at the center was one thing. Seeing him here was another altogether. "He'll bring Laney."

Patsy pointed the stapler at her. "Now don't get your tail in a twitch, young lady. That baby won't hurt you and you won't hurt her."

"But what if I—" She bit her lip. As much as she longed to see the baby, it was too dangerous.

"Have one of them attacks?" Her aunt set the stapler down with a thump. "Nonsense. You didn't have one all the time you were stuck out there on the farm together."

"But Ethan was there."

"Well, there you are. He'll be here tonight, too." Patsy glanced toward the digital clock on the cook-stove. "Any time now."

"Oh, Aunt Patsy." Just what she didn't need, a matchmaking aunt.

"Don't 'Aunt Patsy' me. Ethan is my friend, too. And this is still my house."

Molly knew full well her great-aunt wasn't trying to be cruel. She was trying, in her own no-nonsense manner, to help. What Patsy didn't understand was how much more humiliating a panic attack would be now that she knew, and liked, Ethan so much better.

"I'm being selfish. Forgive me." Molly circled the table to kiss her aunt's wrinkled cheek. "I'll behave."

She hoped she could. Patsy was right. Ethan would be here. Her heart, traitor that it was, leapt at the prospect.

Tenderness emanated from her aunt's gray eyes. She patted Molly's hair. "Everything will be fine. Now hurry up with those before he gets here."

Molly still had a dozen baby animal faces left to paint when Ethan arrived, ushering in the scent of outdoors and filling the house with his masculine presence.

Across the joint living-dining room, his blue eyes found her. "Hi, Molly. What's up?"

"Go on in there and see for yourself," Aunt Patsy said.

From beneath a blanket, Laney kicked and protested, eager to be uncovered. Between the two of them, Ethan and Patsy lifted her free. Her aunt held the chubby baby while Ethan shrugged out of his jacket.

Laney's bright blue eyes, so like her father's,

gazed around the apartment. In the nearly three months since Molly had last seen her, she had gained complete control of her brown-capped head and had grown tremendously. When she spotted Molly, her tiny mouth opened in a smile to reveal a pair of bottom teeth.

Molly's arms ached to hold the beautiful little girl, but her chest constricted in a warning that said she had better not chance such a crazy action.

She gripped the top of the kitchen chair. "She's grown so much."

Ethan grinned, tossing his jacket and the baby blankets onto the couch as he came across the living room and into the dining space. He carried Laney under one arm.

"Babies do that, I guess. I can't believe she's six months old already."

Six months. Molly pushed away the reminder of Zack's age and practiced breath control.

God has not given me the spirit of fear.

When she opened her eyes Ethan stood next to her, admiring the craft items spread out on the tabletop.

"Hey, you're good at this."

His praise was wonderful balm. She tried to concentrate on the bunnies instead of the baby. "It's a fun hobby."

"No. I mean, you're *really* good. Not just hobby-good." He shifted Laney's weight so that she perched on his narrow hipbone. "You could open a store."

"Chloe and I actually considered it before—" She

stopped, heart pinching. Setting up a shop with her sister had been a dream they'd both shared.

Sympathetic blue eyes studied her. "Just the same," he said gently. "You ought to give the idea some further thought. People love this kind of stuff."

Aunt Patsy, who had disappeared into the tiny kitchen, returned with a plate of peanut brittle. "We've got at least fifty more of them to make. You any good with a stapler?"

He grinned and snitched a piece of peanut brittle. "I thought I was here to fix a door."

Patsy gently tapped the back of his hand. "Work first. Eat later."

"Slave driver," he said around a bite of the crunchy candy.

"You had supper yet?"

"Nope. Lunch was a drive-by burger over in Mena. I was hoping you would feed me a good supper."

"Spoiled rotten. That's what you are." The twinkle in her eyes conveyed great affection for their guest. From Ethan's reaction, the feeling was mutual.

"It's all your fault. You keep luring me over here with promises of a work-for-food arrangement. Must have been that cardboard sign that did the trick."

Molly laughed along with her aunt. The idea of Ethan and a cardboard sign was too funny.

"I made a casserole," Patsy said. "Lasagna. Molly and I already ate but there's plenty left for you."

Molly snickered. "Imagine that. She made enough for an army."

"And I'm a grateful man." Grinning, he placed Laney in her aunt's outstretched arms. "Show me that door. I'm starving."

In minutes, he was on his knees at the back door, pounding away. Acutely aware that they were separated by only a few feet, Molly dabbed her brush in bright blue paint and created eyes for her bunnies—eyes that looked like Ethan's. She wanted to go in the kitchen, sit on the floor and talk to him in the way they did most days at lunch. They always had so much to discuss. But she didn't want Aunt Patsy getting any more of her ideas.

Spending time with Ethan at lunch in the company of several dozen senior citizens was far different than seeing him elsewhere. Especially when Laney was along.

But tonight, for some reason, seeing the baby didn't stress her as much as she'd feared. There was no tightness in her chest. Her throat was open and she breathed normally.

But that was to be expected, wasn't it? Ethan was here. Aunt Patsy was here. Nothing could happen to Laney with them present.

Aunt Patsy sat at the table bouncing the pink-clad infant on her knee and talking nonsense that had the baby babbling in return.

Molly glanced up and smiled at the charming scene.

"She's a dandy, isn't she?" Patsy asked, shaking a set of measuring spoons.

"Beautiful."

"And healthy as a horse. I never saw a child so perfect. I bet she's never sick, is she, Ethan?"

Screwdriver in hand, Ethan pivoted toward them. "Hardly ever. I've been really lucky in that respect."

"Some babies are sick a lot the first year. But not Laney. Happy and healthy, she is."

Focused on painting the finishing touches on a bow mouth, Molly recognized her aunt's endearing attempts to assuage her fears.

"Ethan's a great dad," she murmured, glancing up at the handsome man tinkering with the back-door lock.

"I heard that." He gave one more twist of the screwdriver, grasped the doorknob and gave it a shake. "There. Done. Safe and secure again."

Aunt Patsy rose, Laney in her arms. "Then you've earned your supper." She started around the table and then paused. Behind the wire-framed glasses she peered at her niece. "Want to hold this perfect little doll while I microwave that lasagna?"

The gentle, loving face of her aunt pleaded with her to try.

Molly longed to please the dear, wonderful woman who had been her mainstay. More than that, she yearned to cradle a baby in her arms again without fear.

The room seemed to hold its breath. She was aware that Ethan hovered in the kitchen doorway, watching. Laying aside her paintbrush, she said, "Let me wash my hands."

Moments later, heart thundering in her ears, she

stretched out her arms. Aunt Patsy smiled and handed over the squirming child.

Relishing the feel of the soft, plump little body, Molly carried Laney to the couch and sat down. Her throat was dry and her insides trembled the slightest bit, but she wasn't short of breath. She could do this.

"Hey, princess," she said. "You sure are beautiful."

Laney's chubby arms and legs paddled in response. Expression animated, she stuck her tiny pink tongue between her lips and blew a wet raspberry.

Molly giggled, a sense of freedom and hope swelling inside her like a cleansing wave.

For the first time in two years, she entertained the hope that the panic attacks were behind her, and that she was no longer a danger to children.

"It's getting late," Ethan said, but he made no move to get up. Laney slept face down across his knees. The peanut brittle plate on the coffee table held only crumbs. And Aunt Patsy had long since retired.

He and Molly both had to work tomorrow but Ethan was reluctant to leave. Tonight had been fun. It had also been progress for Molly.

At the sight of her chattering baby talk to his daughter, something had turned over in Ethan's chest. Some nameless emotion that felt so right and good that he wanted to laugh out loud. She hadn't held Laney long, but the fact that she'd held her at all was important, both to her and to him. She needed to know that he trusted her with his child. And he needed to know she cared.

The admission hit him square in the chest.

"I'm glad you came over."

Molly sat with her feet curled beneath her as he'd seen her do so many times at the farm.

"Me, too." The TV flickered, moving from one commercial to another. He had no idea what programs had come and gone in the past two hours. And he didn't care. Talking to Molly, listening to her laugh, sharing his day with her, was far more pleasurable than any television show.

He wasn't lonely. Didn't have time to be, but whenever Molly wasn't around, something seemed to be missing.

Uncomfortable with the notion, he gently lifted his sleeping child from his lap and placed her in the carrier. She stirred, making sucking motions with her mouth. Ethan smiled.

Molly came to stand beside him, smiling, too. "It's cute the way babies do that."

"She must dream about that bottle."

As if she'd heard and understood, Laney's bow mouth curved into a smile.

They stood there for a heartbeat, gazing down at the sleeping infant. "Aunt Patsy says when babies smile in their sleep, they're playing with angels."

Ethan turned his attention to Molly. The top of her head barely reached his shoulders. "Think that's true?"

The corners of her mouth tipped in a smile. "I don't know, but I like the sound of it."

"Me, too." He also liked the curve of her lips and the faint flush of color over her cheekbones. "What do you dream of, Molly?"

He didn't know where the question had come from, but there it was.

She looked surprised, then thoughtful for a millisecond. With a small laugh, she shook her head. "I don't know. Silliness mostly. Things that make no sense. What do you dream about?"

"You." There. He'd said it. And if she wanted to throw it back in his face, fine. He'd been rejected before and lived.

"Oh, Ethan." She laid a small hand on his shirt-front. "What a sweet thing to say, but—"

He stopped the inevitable with fingertips pressed to her soft mouth. "No buts, Molly. No buts." And then before he could think better of the action, he leaned down, replaced his hand with his mouth and kissed her.

In the next instant she was in his arms, and Ethan's world centered for the first time in a long time. When Molly's arms circled his neck and pulled him closer, something exploded in his chest. This was the moment they had been working toward since that first stormy night when he'd seen the terror and the goodness in her eyes.

After the bad time with Twila he'd set his mind not to take any more chances with women, to concentrate on being a good father and raising his child to the best of his ability.

And yet, here he was, falling for Molly. Falling hard. He didn't know if it was right. Didn't know if he should, considering his tainted history, but it was happening. He wondered if God would approve of a relationship between a decent girl like Molly and a messed-up man like him.

The question had him slowly pulling away from her sweet kiss.

She rested her cheek against his chest and Ethan was sure she could feel the pounding of his heart. He smoothed the flyaway hair and held her close for the longest time, wondering, worrying.

He didn't want to cause her more trouble than she had already suffered. A good Christian would be unselfish and walk away rather than risk hurting her. A good Christian would concentrate on being a single dad,

Cupping Molly's face, he stared down into a pair of clear, honest, hopeful brown eyes and faced the truth about himself.

He wasn't such a good Christian after all.

Chapter Ten

Wisps of cirrus clouds played peekaboo with the early April sun. A steady wind, blowing in from the south, brought warming temperatures, and Molly was glad to see the harsh winter give way to spring.

She and Ethan had braved the wind for an after-dinner walk in the small courtyard behind his apartment complex. Laney, bundled in a fleece outfit, a purple stocking hat on her head, rode along in her stroller. Big blue eyes, more alert and curious by the day, alternated between the colorful shapes hanging from her stroller and the activity in the courtyard.

Every time she was with Ethan this way, Molly promised herself not to see him again. But then he'd come by or call, and her foolish heart would take control and totally ignore her common sense.

Though still reluctant to call their time together

dates, Molly had to admit she felt more than friendship for her handsome delivery man.

"The jonquils are up," she said, rubbing her sweater-covered arms against the slight chill. "I always feel better when I see them. All that yellow, I guess, after the dreary browns of winter."

Ethan, handsome and athletic in a hooded sweatshirt and blue jeans, bent and snapped one off, presenting it to her. "A pretty flower for a pretty lady."

"Flatterer." But she smiled and took the sunny blossom, stroking the velvet smoothness against her cheek.

Since that night when she had held Laney without panic and Ethan had kissed her, Molly's frozen insides had begun to thaw as slowly and surely as the weather. Scary as that felt, it also felt good. Regardless of her sister's animosity and her own guilt, Aunt Patsy and Ethan were right. She needed to move forward.

Somehow she had to get past the fear of being alone with Laney. She adored the happy little baby. She had even grown brave enough to hold her and play with her and talk to her, though only with Ethan present.

She hadn't had a panic attack in a long time, hoped they were gone for good, but she was still afraid to take the chance. She never wanted Ethan to see how weak and lacking in self-control she really was. And yet she adored Laney, yearned for her as if she were the baby's mother.

The inner battle raged continually until she wondered what to do. Break it off? Keep going though they had no future? Or pray for a miracle to change her fear to faith?

"I talked to the plumber this afternoon," she said to escape her troubled thoughts. "He thinks he can get out to the farm by Thursday."

"That's good, I guess." Ethan's words came out a little doubtfully, hesitantly, as if he wasn't all that thrilled.

"I'll be glad to get home. Aunt Patsy must be tired of having me underfoot."

"You're good company for her." He reached for her hand, his warm, strong fingers wrapping around hers like a glove. "For me, too. I like having you here in town, close by." His mouth kicked up in a grin that made her heart go flip-flop. "To feed me when I'm starving."

She whopped him with the jonquil. "Did anyone ever tell you that you are a bum?"

He dodged, rubbed the spot where the flower had touched him and laughed. "All the time. But a single man's gotta eat."

He was teasing, she knew, because more than half the time he either cooked for her or ordered out. Take tonight. He'd charcoaled burgers for them on the outside grill while she'd whipped together a pan of fudgy brownies in his small efficiency kitchen.

They strolled on, comfortable together, circling the empty swimming pool, crunching over brown leaves that no one had bothered to rake the previous fall.

"Have you thought about Easter?" he asked.

"I've thought about it." He'd tried for weeks to get her to attend Chapel with him.

"You should come. We're doing a sunrise pageant. I'm Pontius Pilate."

"Type-casting?" She grinned. Nothing could be further from the truth.

"It was either Pilate or Judas, the betrayer. I thought I'd look better in a governor's robe than in a hangman's noose."

They both chuckled.

"Come on," he said. "You don't want to miss my acting debut, do you? Say you'll be there."

She wanted to. "I don't know if I'm that brave."

"Sure you are. You just don't want to upset your sister."

"That's true. Ruining her Easter would be pretty selfish of me."

"Ruining yours is pretty selfish of her."

She hadn't thought of it that way.

He paused to retuck a blanket around Laney's kicking legs. Crouched on his haunches in front of the stroller, he glanced up and smiled. Molly's stomach lifted as if she had dived off the high board. "Will you at least think about it?"

How could she refuse? She wanted to make him happy, to spend time with him. She also longed to be with her church family again. "Okay. I'll think about it."

His smile widened. "I feel a victory coming on."

She pointed the jonquil at him. "Don't be so sure of yourself, buster."

"Hey, I convinced you to fly in a plane with me."

"No danger of running into my sister up there," she joked. Ethan's skilled piloting had made the flight fun and safe. She'd seen her beloved Winding Stair Mountain from a whole new perspective. She'd also witnessed Ethan's love of flying and wondered how he'd ever left it.

"Think you'll ever go back to that line of work?"

He hitched one shoulder. "I don't know. Right now, Laney needs a parent more than I need to fly. Don't you, sugar?"

He smacked a kiss on Laney's chin. She rewarded him with a bubbling laugh.

His remark reminded Molly that Laney had another parent, a parent Ethan never mentioned. Since the first time she'd asked about the woman who had given birth to Ethan's daughter and had been rebuffed, Molly had avoided the subject.

"What about Laney's mother? Why didn't she help out so you could go on flying?"

For the space of several seconds Ethan didn't answer. He stared up into the sky he loved with an expression of immense sadness. When he looked at her again, his blue eyes had gone as distant as the wispy clouds.

"Laney's mother is dead."

"Oh, Ethan. How tragic." Stunned and filled with remorse for broaching the sensitive subject, Molly reached to touch him. "What happened?"

He stepped away, rounding to the back of the stroller.

"Does it matter? She's dead. And Laney only has me."

He started off toward the back door of the apartment, pushing the stroller ahead of him.

"Ethan, wait." Though he paused, he didn't turn around. Molly hurried to catch up. When she reached his side, she said, "I didn't mean to pry. Forgive me?"

He softened then and looped an arm around her neck. "Nothing to forgive. Twila is a bad subject. That's all."

A bad subject and one he didn't care to pursue. A subject so painful that he wouldn't share it with her, though she'd shared her deepest hurt with him.

The idea depressed her. She had a sinking feeling that she might be falling for a man who still loved a dead woman named Twila.

Ethan loved church dismissal, that time immediately following worship service when folks milled around the foyer visiting, too full of love and peace to leave.

This Sunday was no different. As he made his way toward the nursery to get Laney, he stopped over and over again to shake hands, to exchange pleasantries, and to share ideas for the upcoming Easter pageant.

He was sorry Molly still refused to come to church with him but he was sure she was weakening on the issue. She was already attending a small home Bible study with him. Any Sunday now, he expected her to jump in his truck, all dressed up and pretty as a sunrise.

Like a family, he thought. Molly and Laney and him, together. The more the idea took root, the better he liked it.

By the time he fetched Laney from the nursery and made his way back to the foyer, the crowd had begun to thin. A few stragglers chatted in small groups. A man in one group, Jesse Slater, called out to him.

"Ethan. Over here."

He liked Jesse Slater and his sweet wife, Lindsey, who ran the Christmas tree farm outside of town. They'd been one of the first couples to welcome him when he'd joined the church at Winding Stair.

Approaching the group, he said, "Hey, Jesse. Lindsey. What's up?"

The silver-eyed Jesse hooked an arm around his pregnant wife. "Lindsey's making a brunch at our house after service on Easter. Wanna come?"

He hesitated. Until Molly made up her mind, he didn't want to make other plans. "I appreciate the invitation. Can I get back to you with an answer after I talk to Molly?"

"Molly?" Lindsey's face lit up. "Do you think there's a chance she might come, too?"

"I'm working on her."

"I didn't know the two of you were dating." She turned to her husband. "Isn't that cool, Jesse? Don't you think they're perfect together?"

Jesse rolled his eyes, though his voice was warm with affection for his wife. "Sorry, Ethan. The woman's a hopeless romantic."

"Don't tease, Jesse," Lindsey said. "Molly's had a rough time. I think it's wonderful that she's starting to date again." She looked toward Ethan. "Tell her that I'd love to have her come to brunch. We'll catch up on old times and I'll try to talk her into making some Christmas crafts for my shop."

"I'll do that." He exchanged nods with Jesse. "Y'all take care."

Hoisting Laney, who grew heavier every day, he headed toward the exit.

Seemingly from out of nowhere, Molly's sister appeared at his side to pluck at his jacket sleeve. Since the confrontation in the diner, Ethan had kept his distance, not wanting to rub salt in the wound. This time he hadn't spotted her in time.

Dressed in black that accentuated her pallor and skinniness, she asked, "Did I hear you say you're still seeing my sister?"

Her tone was incredulous.

"Yes," he said as kindly as he could manage. "As often as she allows."

"If you care anything at all for your baby, you'll stay away from her. She's dangerous."

Given the grief she'd caused Molly, the old Ethan wanted to blast her with his temper. The new Ethan resisted. Anger would only exacerbate the problem.

Taking a deep breath, he prayed inwardly.

Lord, don't let me blow this. It might be my one shot at helping Molly.

"She told me about your son. I'm sorry."

"Really? She told you?" Bitterness dripped from her, stronger than acid. "And you still allow her near your child?"

A tall blond man whom Ethan recognized as Chloe's husband pushed through the crowd and grabbed his wife's arm. "Chloe, don't. Honey, please," he said gently. "Let's go."

She yanked away and stalked off, shoving the glass door open hard enough to attract the stares of other stragglers.

James turned to Ethan, hands spread in a gesture of helplessness. "I hope you won't hold that against her. She's gone through a lot."

"Molly told me. You haven't had it easy either." As a dad he could sympathize as readily with James as with Chloe.

"It's been a trial for the entire family, but Chloe hasn't even begun to heal. Zack's nursery is exactly like it was the day he died. She refuses to let me change a thing." He raked a hand through his thick hair. "She tortures herself with memories and pictures and by teaching the toddler class. I think if we were able to have another child…"

Ethan clapped a sympathetic hand on the man's shoulder. He wanted to say something. Wanted to have the answer to the man's heartache and felt helpless because he didn't. Only God could fix this.

"I wish I knew what to do," he said. "The situation is killing Molly, too. Except for her aunt, she's lost her whole family."

"I know. She loved Zack. Chloe knows it, too, but she needs someone to blame. Her mother doesn't help any. She's always doted on Chloe too much, even before Zack's death. Now she tiptoes around Chloe, babying her, and making everything worse instead of better. I can't get either of them to see reason. If her dad was still alive, he'd never have stood for any of this."

"Molly told me she was really close to her dad." Ethan stared out toward the parking lot where the bitter woman sat like a stone statue in the front seat of an SUV. "Losing him. And now this. I don't know how she handles it."

James gave him a strange look that Ethan couldn't interpret. "Like the rest of us, I guess. She's just surviving."

"There has to be a solution. Some way to get Molly and Chloe to resolve this stand-off. Neither is going to be happy until they do."

"Is my sister-in-law's happiness important to you?"

"It's starting to be," Ethan admitted.

For the first time a ghost of a smile touched the man's worried brown eyes. "Good. Two years of this is long enough. I love my wife, but I don't know how much more I can take before…"

James's voice trailed off as if he'd revealed too much.

Ethan shifted, bringing a drooping Laney to his shoulder. Something had to give.

"What if I can come up with a plan?" he asked, and then wondered what on earth he was talking about. "Something that will get the two of them at least on speaking terms?"

"Got a miracle in that baby's diaper bag?"

"No. I don't even have an idea yet. But something has to change."

"Well…" James stared blankly into space, the worry lines around his eyes pronounced. "The situation can't get any worse. I'm ready to try just about anything. If you can think of a way to breach this gap between Chloe and Molly, I'll help you."

"Good. It's a deal then. I'll pray about it. Think on it. And I'll let you know what I come up with."

A flicker of hope played over James's face as the two men shook hands. Then he stepped away and looked toward the parking lot with a weary sigh. "Better get her home. She'll cry all afternoon."

Thinking hard, Ethan watched him go. He'd thought his own troubles were heavy, but there was a man who made his situation look like a picnic. He wondered if Molly knew her sister had been unable to conceive another child? Probably not.

He hoisted Laney's diaper bag over his other shoulder and crossed the parking lot to his Nissan. Maybe it was time she did.

"Pizza delivery man," Ethan called as he slammed out of his truck in front of Molly's farmhouse. The place looked so different with the buds of spring pushing up through the cold ground and tipping the branches of trees recently broken and pruned by nature's ice.

Molly was on her knees in a flower bed, a trowel in one gloved hand. "What are you doing? I thought you were going to church."

"Don't you ever look at a clock? It's way past noon." He crossed the grass and handed her the pizza. "Take this inside while I get the baby."

She sniffed appreciatively. "Health food. What's the occasion?"

Grinning, he jogged back to the truck and carried Laney inside where Molly was busy setting out plates and soda pop. A stream of afternoon sun shone through the double windows and warmed the kitchen with a golden glow. The scent of pizza made his belly grumble.

"It feels good to be here again," he said. And it did. Funny, how this place had the feel of a family home, even though Molly lived here alone.

"I'm glad to be back here myself," Molly answered.

The fireplace lay dormant and all vestiges of the week without power were gone. Otherwise nothing had changed.

Two boxes, packed and ready for the UPS man, waited by the door.

"Business for me?" He perused the addresses, noted they were headed for an orphanage in Colombia. "How do you afford to do this so often?"

She opened a drawer, lifted two forks, saw him

shake his head and pushed them back inside. "I buy a little out of each paycheck. Bargain hunt."

"And do without things yourself?"

She lifted her shoulders. "A gift without sacrifice is not much of a gift."

He was glad she thought so. Because he was going to ask her for a gift. And it would definitely require sacrifice on her part.

Molly came around the table and removed a blanket from Laney's carrier, spread it on the floor, and held out her hands. "Hello, beautiful angel."

Laney practically leaped into Molly's arms. Joy, like a sunburst, went off inside Ethan as he watched the woman who had come to mean so much to him, kiss his child and settle her on the blanket with a colorful toy. It was a simple action, one that normally would draw no attention at all, but given Molly's anxiety around his child, Ethan was ecstatic to see this much progress.

"I can't believe she's already sitting up." As she pulled out a chair to sit down, Molly beamed at Laney. "Next thing you know, she'll be crawling everywhere."

"She's already trying to." Ethan joined her at the table. "And she gets furious because her bottom won't follow her arms."

With fond looks at the infant the two adults dug into the fragrant pizza.

"So," Molly said as she peeled a chunk of melted mozzarella off the wax paper. "I thought you were running errands this afternoon. Why are you here, plying me with hundreds of my favorite fat grams?"

"I missed you." That much was true. Being away from her all day was starting to be a problem. "Didn't you miss me, too?"

She propped her elbows on the table, pizza slice drooping from one hand. "Helllooo. I saw you last night. Remember? Buttered popcorn and Junior Mints at Mena's movie theater."

"Seems longer than that."

"Yeah." She grew serious for a second, studied her pizza as if the black olives were fly specks. Ethan wondered what was going on inside that complicated head of hers.

"I actually do have an ulterior motive for being here," he said, placing his half-eaten pizza on a plate. "Finish your food first."

She paused in midbite. "I don't like the sound of that."

"No, you won't like this conversation, but we have to have it. I talked to James today after church."

The pizza slice plopped onto her plate. One hand reached reflexively for her throat. "My brother-in-law?"

"Yes. He told me something that might help."

Her eyes grew as large as the flowered plate. "Help with what? Nothing can change the fact that my sister hates me, if that's what you mean."

"I don't think she does, Molly. I think she's angry at God and is afraid of admitting that so she blames you. Did you know she and James haven't been able to conceive another child?"

She closed her eyes, stricken. Her small body seemed to draw into itself. "Oh, that's awful."

"I didn't tell you to make you feel bad. I thought knowing would help you to understand that you aren't the cause of her unhappiness."

"Ethan, her son is dead and now she can't have another child. That makes me feel ten times worse. Not better."

"Look, Molly, you and Chloe have to resolve this issue. It's killing you both."

"I want to. More than anything. But she won't let me."

"Then take steps to change that. Start going to church again. Make her face you, and by doing so, face the problem."

"I can't." Molly's skin paled, and she pushed the pizza plate away. One hand stroked the column of her throat over and over again. "I wish I could, but I just can't."

Torn between exasperation and compassion, Ethan rounded the table and knelt beside her chair. He hated to see her upset. "Hey. It's okay. I understand."

"Do you?"

"Not completely," he answered honestly. "But in a way I do. You feel guilty. And responsible. I know something about that kind of thing myself."

Molly studied him for moment, and then her

voice grew gentle. "You're talking about Laney's mother, aren't you?"

His gut knotted. Would she think less of him if she knew the truth?

"Yeah, I am."

His failure with Twila was nothing compared to losing a child, but the two situations related in a way. They both changed the directions of lives and caused a great deal of heartache. He'd wrestled with his own culpability enough to understand how difficult it could be to forgive oneself. In truth, he was still working on it.

Laney's toy banged repeatedly against the floor while Ethan debated the wisdom of telling Molly about his past.

His partying days seemed like another life. Someone else's life. Reliving that time, even in memory, pained and shamed him. But maybe sharing his own struggle would help Molly through hers.

Finally, when the silence between them grew long, Molly brought her hand to rest lightly, comfortingly next to his temple and said, "You can tell me anything, Ethan. I've told you plenty of painful things."

But she had been innocent. He hadn't been.

He drew in a strengthening breath and exhaled in one rushing gust. "I didn't become a Christian until shortly before Laney was born." He grasped her hand and pressed it against his cheek. "That's not an excuse for bad behavior, but I want you to understand that Christ changed me."

"Nobody's life is perfect, Ethan. Even after we accept the Lord."

"True, but I wanted you to know that I've changed. I'm not the kind of man I was back then." He didn't know how much to tell, what to leave out, so finally, he said, "In my family if a guy gets a girl pregnant, he marries her."

To her credit, she didn't pull away, and he understood that she must have long ago guessed this much about Laney's birth. "Some people call that old-fashioned," she said.

"Do you?"

She gazed down at him with gentle eyes. "I call it honorable."

"Twila didn't."

"Did you love her?"

He stifled a smile. Leave it to Molly to go straight to the important stuff.

"I hope you won't think less of me for this, but I doubt if I ever did love her. I never want Laney to know that. She'll never know that. I want her to feel special and wanted every day of her life."

"She will." Molly glanced at the happily babbling baby. "She already does. But what about Twila? Did she love you?"

He shook his head and rose, pulling a chair around so that they sat knee to knee, facing one another.

"Not even close. She was furious when she found out she was pregnant. We had a huge fight." He rubbed at the scar over his eye, remembering the ugliness. "She screamed and cried, said she wasn't going to be saddled with a kid."

"Sad." They both looked at the beautiful child playing on the patchwork quilt. "She threw away the best thing that ever happened to her."

"Laney? Or me?"

Molly turned her head, met his eyes. The corner of her mouth tilted. "Both."

Liking the sound of that, Ethan allowed a smile but quickly sobered again. The subject was far too serious. "Twila didn't agree, and if I hadn't threatened her with every lawsuit known to man—some that don't even exist—Laney would never have been born."

"It must have been a very bad time."

"The worst. But good, too. Getting into that predicament, having to fight for nine long, frightening months to save my child, made me examine my own life. I didn't like what I discovered."

"So you turned to God?"

"Eventually. One of my paramedic co-workers was a Christian. He helped me a lot during those months. I noticed a peace in him that I didn't have. I wanted that. Needed it." He propped an elbow on the table and rubbed at his chin. "Boy, did I need it."

Molly took up a slice of pizza again, turned it around in her fingers and picked disinterestedly at an olive. "What happened to Twila?"

Her eyes flickered to his and then back to the pizza. He could tell she wasn't thinking about food.

"The day after Laney was born she signed over all

parental rights, told me I was the world's biggest loser, and went back to her life without me or my baby." He tapped a knuckle against his chin, readied himself for the wave of guilt that was sure to come. "She died in a car wreck five weeks later. Under the influence."

Molly's head snapped up. The pizza thudded to the tabletop. "Ethan!"

"Yeah. She'd been out with our old party gang. The same crowd I had been running with only a few months before."

"You weren't with her?"

"No." He frowned, surprised at the question. Hadn't he just told her that Twila had walked away from him and Laney without a backward glance? "Why would you think that?"

"The scar. A car accident. I just thought…"

He reached up, touched the long white line above his eye.

"No, not then." But he could understand why she would think a car accident had caused such a long, ugly scar. "This was her reaction when I went to her apartment with a court order."

"She cut you?" Molly's eyes grew wide with horror. "On purpose?"

He tried to make a joke of it, though the memory of a knife blade slashing within inches of his eye was anything but funny. "Never make a woman mad when she's slicing tomatoes."

Molly didn't see the humor. "That's hideous. How could she do such a thing?"

"Twila had a lot problems I didn't know anything about at the time. We hadn't dated all that long." Another fact that shamed him. He hadn't really known her as a person, only as a beautiful face and body. "She wasn't a terrible person. Just terribly…lost."

"You did the best you could, Ethan."

"Did I?"

"Under the circumstances, what else could you have done? You couldn't let her abort Laney."

"No. But I wonder if things would have been different if I had been a Christian then. Maybe I could have been a better influence. Maybe I could have helped her instead of making things worse." He sighed, lifting his shoulders in a gesture of helplessness. "But by the time I had started to turn my life around, she was six months along with Laney and would no longer speak to me except to cuss and scream that I was ruining her life."

He heard the regret in his voice and knew that Molly heard it, too. She took one of his hands in hers and rubbed a thumb across the calloused palm. Her need to comfort him brought a smile.

"You're good for me."

"How so?"

"I've been afraid to tell you all this. Afraid you'd think less of me."

Molly returned the smile as she linked her fingers with his. "Everybody has regrets, but you've taken a bad situation and worked hard to make it right."

"And that's what I'm asking you to do, Molly."

"I don't understand." Her face registered confusion.

"Come to the church league basketball game Tuesday night. Take a step toward reconciliation."

She pulled her hand away. "I can't. People at the church don't want me there."

"Sure they do."

She shook her head. "No. They think I did something terrible. They whisper and stare."

"You don't have a problem with the Bible study group. What's the difference?"

"Bible group is four other people. And my sister isn't there to remind everyone of what happened."

"According to Aunt Patsy you haven't been to the chapel since Zack died. Naturally, people were whispering then, but, Molly, no one is talking about you now except to say they miss you."

"Do they really say that?"

"Yeah. Lindsey Slater wants to invite you to Easter brunch. She told me so today."

Fear, longing, indecision all flickered over her face. "I don't know."

Why wouldn't she try? She wanted to. What made her back away every time the issue tried to come to a head?

"Tell you what." He stood and held out both hands to pull her up with him. "Go with me to the ball game. If you feel uncomfortable at all at any point, I'll bring you straight home. Immediately. Just say the word and we're out of there."

Her amber eyes clouded with indecision. She wanted to so badly, he was certain of it, but fear paralyzed her.

"Chloe hates sports. She won't be there," she said, more to herself than to him.

He grasped her chin and tilted her face upward, longing to wipe away the anxiety, to protect her against the demons that tormented her.

"Please. Try. If not for yourself, for me. I'll take care of you."

"Why are you so sweet to me?"

"Why?" He blinked at her, as bewildered by the question as he was by the obvious answer. "I think you know why."

In the next instant, he lowered his lips to hers and kissed her.

She sighed against his mouth, and he tightened his embrace, drawing her as close as he dared. She was fragile, pure and special, and he cherished that about her.

When the kiss ended, she looked at him with eyes now shining instead of troubled. "You cheat."

He leaned his forehead against hers and laughed softly. "Did it work?"

"Promise you'll bring me right home if anything happens?"

He studied the smooth curve of her cheek, the tiny smattering of golden freckles across her nose, and the full tilt of her lips, troublingly aware that he wanted more than a basketball game from Molly McCreight.

"Promise." His heart thudded with hope as he watched her struggle against self doubt and move toward trusting herself—and him.

"Okay," she whispered. "I'll try."

And the burst of pleasure Ethan experienced was far out of proportion to the victory. She hadn't agreed to meet with Chloe. She hadn't even agreed to go to an actual church service. But Molly was going with him to a church function, and nothing had felt that right in a long time.

Chapter Eleven

M̲olly's heart pounded so loudly, she could feel the rush of blood through her temples. All afternoon at the center, she'd thought of little except this moment.

Crunching over the graveled parking lot with Ethan at her side, she had to force her legs to keep moving toward the long metal building that housed the Winding Stair Chapel's Fellowship Hall.

"You're gonna be fine," Ethan said, one hand riding gently at the small of her back.

She sucked in a lungful of cool, clean mountain air and nodded, still amazed that he'd talked her into this. And even though she knew he was right, she was scared.

But Ethan knew about being scared. He'd been scared too. Scared during those long months when Twila wanted to abort his child. Scared of being a single father. Scared he wouldn't measure up. But he'd turned it all over to the Lord and kept putting one foot in front of the other.

Sharing his story with her couldn't have been easy either, but he'd done it to help her. And she could do this to please him.

Hand on the metal doorknob, he looked down at her and winked. "Piece of cake."

"I'm okay."

"It's not you I'm worried about. It's Tom Castor's team. They beat the pants off us last time. I don't want to be humiliated in front of my girl."

His girl? Was she his girl?

The title settled on her like a crown on a princess. Ethan's girl. Whether she was smart to develop a relationship with a single father or not, it was happening.

"Then you better play hard, mister. Tom has the killer instinct."

While Ethan kept her attention with his silly talk of the upcoming game, they entered the rec hall and moved into a group of people. Molly hardly noticed.

A teenage girl she didn't recognize pushed through the crowd. "Hi, Ethan."

Ethan, looking a little uncomfortable, shifted Laney's weight. "How ya doin', Cass?"

"Good. Want me to watch Laney while you play?" The girl held her arms out. The baby strained forward and Ethan let her go.

"She's a handful lately," Ethan said as the transfer was made from his arms to the girl's.

"That's okay. You know I don't mind." Cass's

bright smile was more for Ethan than for Laney. "I'm always available to you." She giggled and made calf eyes at Ethan. "As a sitter, I mean. I adore babies. Especially Laney."

Molly fought the urge to grab Laney away from the girl. What was Ethan thinking, allowing a teenager to watch Laney? What if something happened? And why was she so flirty with Ethan? She was just a kid.

"When you get tired of playing with her," Molly heard herself say. "I'll be in the stands. Bring her to me."

She couldn't believe she'd said that. Having someone other than herself look after Laney made perfect sense. But Molly had the possessive desire to keep Laney with her.

Cass shot her a quick, dismissive glance before returning her attention to Ethan. "I'll be cheering for you, Ethan. Have a great game."

"Thanks." Casually, Ethan looped an arm over Molly's shoulders and drew her against his side. "And, like Molly said, bring Laney to her if she gets fussy."

The teenager couldn't miss the implication and Molly felt foolishly vindicated.

"Sure. Whatever." The girl walked away, toting Laney on one hip.

"She has a crush on you." Not that I blame her, though. I am ridiculously jealous.

Ethan blew out a sigh. "Tell me about it."

"Is that why you let her take Laney?"

"She's a good sitter. I hired her a few times before

this crush thing started. I have enough of a reputation to live down without someone thinking I'd play around with a high-school kid."

Before they could say more, a voice called out. "Molly! Is that really you?"

Lindsey Slater came toward them. Molly tensed, afraid that the sound of her name ringing through the gym would cause a tidal wave of disapproving glances. Not everyone was as kind-hearted as the Christmas tree farmer.

"Lindsey, hi." She glanced around nervously, expecting the worst. Ethan's strong fingers massaged the back of her neck, a comforting reminder that he was there and ready to leave at a moment's notice. All the more reason to hang tough and get through this if she could. Having her here mattered to Ethan.

To her relief, the only faces looking in her direction were either smiling or mildly curious. No one stared with condemning disapproval. Not yet anyway.

"Ethan said you might come," Lindsey said. "I'm really glad. We could use another guard on our team."

"I haven't played ball in a long time, Lindsey. I'm here only as a spectator tonight."

"Then I hope you'll think about rejoining soon. We're raising money to build a school in Mexico, and I can't play anymore until after the baby comes."

Molly's gaze went immediately to Lindsey's tummy. Happiness for the other woman, accompanied by a twinge of envy, slid through her. "I didn't know you were having a baby."

Lindsey laughed and touched the small mound protruding from beneath the oversized T-shirt. "You'd know these things if you'd come around more often."

Molly fell silent, not knowing how to respond. Didn't Lindsey and the others understand why she had stayed away?

Ethan, bless him, felt her discomfiture and filled the gap. "She's here tonight to help us out in the stands. Tom's team has all the noisy fans."

Lindsey laughed, and the awkward moment passed. "Most of that racket comes from his kids."

"Must be why Tom calls his team the Wild Bunch," Ethan joked.

Tom Castor was a popular local fireman with a competitive nature and a houseful of kids. He and his wife, Debbie, who waited tables at the diner, were mainstays of the church and worked tirelessly for the community. Molly had helped them with a number of charitable undertakings.

By this time several other people, including Pastor Cliff and his wife, Karen, had joined the conversation. No longer the focus of attention, Molly relaxed as the talk took hold and ebbed and flowed around her. It felt good to listen to small talk and the teasing banter of people who knew and trusted one another. She had missed this kind of thing more than she had realized.

From all appearances, Ethan was well liked and accepted. Not that Molly had doubted, but seeing him laugh and tease with other members of the church reaffirmed the kind of man she knew him to be. And the fact that he was cautiously kind to the gushing teenage Cass was, if she'd needed it, further proof of his integrity.

After a bit, Pastor Cliff clapped his hands once and rubbed his palms together in a gesture of anticipation. "You folks ready to get this show on the road?"

"Ready for the blood bath," Tom called, pumping one arm in the air to the groans and chuckles of those around him.

"In that case, tonight's devotional is all the more important," Cliff answered good-naturedly. "Gather round, everyone. I have a couple of verses from Romans and Second Corinthians. Then we'll pray and get the game started."

When the crowd of a hundred or more people, both church regulars and community members who had come to support the good cause, had settled, Pastor Cliff read from the Bible and gave a brief talk about the relevance of the scripture to today's life.

Following prayer, he lifted a glowing face and a huge right arm and announced in oratorical style, "Let the games begin."

"Are you okay with this?" Ethan asked, before taking to the floor with his team. He stood a step below her, one sneakered foot raised to the bleacher. He looked awesome in loose sweat pants and a red basketball jersey emblazoned with the word Crossfire.

Trepidatious, but less anxious than before, Molly managed a smile. "I'll be fine."

He tilted his head toward the teenage Cass who sat

a couple of rows behind Molly. "Will you keep an eye on Laney for me?"

Molly's confidence rose a couple of notches. She didn't understand why, but Ethan trusted her with his most prized possession. And she'd do anything to keep that trust.

"Should I go up and get her?"

"Nah. I don't want to hurt Cass's feelings. She or one of the other teenagers usually watch Laney while I play, but I feel better knowing you're here. Laney loves you." He squeezed her hand, and Molly thought he wanted to say more.

"I love her, too," she answered. It was true. She had fallen in love with the baby girl whose brown hair and blue eyes were so like her daddy's. She hadn't wanted ever to love another child the way she'd loved Zack, but she did. Surprisingly, the admission brought joy instead of pain. The risk of loving was a good thing.

"Wish me luck."

She lifted her hand for a high five. "You'll need it against Tom's team."

Ethan groaned. "*Et tu, Brute?*"

They both grinned as he jogged onto the gym floor.

"Mind if we sit here with you?" Lindsey asked as she and her little girl, Jade, slid onto the wooden bench next to Molly.

She'd always liked Lindsey, though the Christmas tree farmer was a little older, more Chloe's age than her own. They had been in the same singles' class until Jesse Slater came to town.

"I'd be glad for the company," Molly answered truthfully, relieved not to be left entirely alone.

"Ethan said you might."

"He talked to you about me?"

Lindsey shrugged. "Just said you were a little uncomfortable, having been away for so long."

Molly gazed out on the court at her delivery man, heart filling at his obvious thoughtfulness. So Ethan had paved the way to make this awkward evening easier for her.

"Ethan's a nice guy," she answered simply.

"I didn't know until last Sunday that you two were dating."

Molly sighed. She'd tried to convince herself that what she and Ethan were doing was not dating, but everyone else called it that. Might as well stop fooling herself.

"Oh, here they go." Lindsey sat forward in rapt attention as two men took center court for the tip-off. "Look, Jade. There's Daddy."

The game commenced in a crazy mix of camaraderie and competition. The Wild Bunch's fans did the wave and stomped the wooden bleachers hard enough to vibrate the entire gym. As Molly had expected, Ethan was a good athlete with a deadly three-point shot that kept Crossfire in the game.

At the half, with the Wild Bunch leading by five points, Ethan came up into the stands. Wiping his face with a towel, he plopped down beside Molly. Sweat plastered his shirt to his skin.

"You doin' okay?" he asked.

"Fine." And she was. Though several people had come by to talk, no one had mentioned Zack or Chloe. "Your team is hanging in there."

"Closest we've ever played the Wild Bunch. You must be our lucky charm." He tossed the towel over one shoulder. "Would you like a Coke or something?"

"You look like you could use one."

"You got that right." He hitched his chin toward the spot where Cass, flanked by two other girls, held Laney on her lap. "Let's grab the baby and head to the concession stand."

Molly followed him up the steps. Laney saw them coming and began to bounce and chatter, stretching tiny hands toward Molly. Her chest expanded with love for Ethan's child.

"Hey, wait a minute. What's with this? You don't love Daddy anymore?" Ethan pretended hurt, but Molly could see he was pleased.

Snuggling the soft, warm body against her chest, Molly had to admit she was pleased, too. Carrying Laney, they headed to the lobby area.

Molly's plan to remain quiet and inconspicuous went out the window as they stopped over and over again to chat and laugh and joke about the crazy, unorthodox game. Ethan and his child were people magnets, and the community drew her back into the fold as if she'd never left.

Slowly, the awful weight of worry lifted from her shoulders. She had assumed the church sided with

Chloe and hated her, but no one here was judging or condemning her. Here, at least, she could experience the warmth and joy of being part of a family, even if it wasn't the one she hungered for.

The spring evening was dark and cool by the time the game ended and they made their way to Molly's place. Ethan's heart was full. Tonight had done some good, he was sure of it. After the initial ice had been broken, Molly had seemed to enjoy herself, and he'd not only been glad, he'd been proud. In the good-natured atmosphere of a ball game, she'd gone from tense and anxious to heartrendingly grateful for the warm acceptance of the church members. It wasn't the same as reconciliation with her sister, but the plan he'd formulated with James was off to a good start. One step at a time, he would gradually push Molly forward.

In the glow of the dash lights, he admired the side of her face as she leaned over the seat to appease a tired and cranky Laney. The curve of her swingy hair brushed her chin and danced around her pretty mouth.

He thought of the last time he'd kissed her, that day when he'd told her about Twila. He'd known then that Molly was important to him and to Laney.

He wasn't much. Probably had no business getting involved with a decent girl like her, but his heart told him this was right.

He turned into the gravel drive and pulled to a stop in front of her house. The porch light glowed yellow as it had that first night months ago when he'd stumbled into her house out of the freezing cold.

He hadn't realized then, but he did now. He'd been out in the cold emotionally at the time. He'd stopped trusting women, afraid they were all like Twila. But time with Molly, seeing her care for others, including him, had warmed his frozen, aching heart. Oh, she hadn't said she cared, but he was certain she did. He could feel it in everything she did. Even tonight, moving outside her comfort zone because he'd asked had proved that she cared.

Killing the motor, he turned in the seat. "I had a great time." He made a silly face. "Even if we did lose again."

She smiled. "Want to come inside for a while? Some hot chocolate might soothe your wounded pride."

"Better not." He hitched his chin toward the back seat. "The boss needs to hit the sack."

Molly laid a hand on his jacketed arm. Filled with an emotion too wonderful for words, she said, "Thank you for this, Ethan. As scared as I was to go to that game, I'm glad you talked me into it. For the first time in two years, I don't feel like people are saying bad things about me."

She realized now that the whispers and exclusion had mostly been in her mind, a part of her own guilt and self-punishment. She just hadn't been able to recognize the truth until now. If only the rift with Chloe was imaginary, everything would be great. But it wasn't. Tonight had helped, but her sister still hated her.

As if he read her thoughts, Ethan pulled her into his arms and said, "The situation with Chloe will improve. We have to keep praying, keep believing and keep being brave."

"I'm not all that brave."

"Sure you are. You were dynamite tonight. I was so proud of you."

"Really? I was proud of you, too." She'd felt more than pride. She'd felt special when his eyes had found hers during the game and they'd exchange smiles or she'd lift Laney's hand in a wave.

"See? We're great together. A regular team. You and me and Laney."

A team. She liked the sound of that.

"Molly," he started, then tipped his head back and stared at the truck's dark ceiling.

She touched his cheek, drew his face back down so that their eyes met in the faint light. "What?"

He smoothed her hair back, then bracketed her face with both hands. The look in his eyes sent adrenaline swirling into her bloodstream.

"Maybe it's too soon to say this. Maybe I should never say this at all, considering my checkered past." He closed in so that his face was inches from hers. When he spoke, the words were but a breath of warmth against her lips. "I love you, Molly."

Her heart lurched, banging against her rib cage.

"Oh, Ethan." She touched his beloved cheek with the tips of her fingers.

In the next heartbeat, his mouth closed over hers

in a kiss so full of sweet emotion that Molly wanted to cry. She loved him, too. Had loved him for a long time.

He was good for her in so many ways. Too good perhaps. And she wanted desperately to make him happy, to make up for the wrong Twila had done to him and Laney.

Laney.

The thought of the child stopped her cold.

How could Ethan even consider falling in love with someone like her? Wouldn't he always wonder in the back of his mind if Laney was safe? Wouldn't she?

When the kiss ended, his forehead tilted against hers. "I know I'm no prize, and I have baggage that some women wouldn't want to deal with—"

"Laney's not baggage. She's a treasure." The very reason why his declaration scared her so much.

He kissed the tip of her nose. "She's *my* treasure. I want her to be yours, too."

She already was, but for Laney's sake, Molly couldn't say so. All the "what ifs" had begun to roll around inside her head again. What if she had a panic attack? What if something happened to Laney while she was in Molly's care? Would Ethan still love her then?

Her hesitation wasn't lost on Ethan. He backed off a little and asked, "Are you afraid you can't love another woman's child? Is that what's bothering you?"

"No. Ethan, don't think that. Don't ever think that. I love that baby with all my heart." Almost as if she was the woman who had given birth to Laney.

"Then what is it? Is it me? Is it because of the things I did before?"

"None of that. You're a wonderful man. The problem isn't you. It's me." She swallowed the lump in her throat and admitted, "I'm afraid of failing you."

He gripped both of her hands in his. "Are you still worried that something will happen to Laney, and it will be your fault? Is that what this is all about?"

"Yes," she whispered, head down, embarrassed but relieved as well to admit the fear.

"Molly, sweetheart, no one can predict the future. But one thing I know. You would protect my baby girl with your life." He tapped her chin with a knuckle, lifting it. "Wouldn't you?"

"If I could."

"Then forget about everything else for a minute and answer me this. Do you care for me? I think you do, but I need you to say it."

"You know I do," she whispered. "Very much."

"Ah, Molly. You make me so happy." He kissed her again and, for a moment, her worries melted away in the warmth of his embrace.

"Remember the scripture Pastor Cliff read tonight?" he asked, eyes shining in the darkness.

Of course she remembered. She'd felt as though Cliff had picked that verse especially for her. "There is now no condemnation to those who are in Christ Jesus…Old things are passed away and all things are new."

Happiness bloomed inside Molly. Ethan was right.

She couldn't go back, but she could move forward. She'd taken the first step by renewing her church friendships, and, as a result some of her pain and guilt had disappeared. Best of all, she hadn't had a panic attack in months, a sign that they were gone for good.

Overjoyed and filled with love for this man who'd given her hope, she threw herself into his arms. When he laughed with joy, she laughed with him.

Maybe, just maybe, they could make this work.

Chapter Twelve

Rain threatened all night before the Easter sunrise service. About an hour before dawn, to the relief of several hundred people, the clouds cleared.

As they had each year for longer than anyone could remember, every church in town had come together in a cooperative effort to present the pageant. Ethan and all the other actors and musicians had practiced for weeks. The play, which had begun last night with the story of the crucifixion, would conclude this morning with the resurrection. Cars, people, lawn chairs and blankets speckled the darkened hillside outside Winding Stair where the dramatic retelling would occur.

Since the basketball game and Ethan's beautiful declaration of love, they had attended two church services together. Today was the third. Returning to her family's church was the scariest, most wonderful thing she'd done in ages, but if she and Ethan were to have any hope of a future together, getting her spiritual life on track had to come first.

When she had fretted about her sister's possible reaction to her return, Ethan, bless him, had talked to James on the telephone. Chloe had been told and the choice to attend church or not would be hers.

Sadly, her sister had chosen to stay away. The idea hurt, as Chloe's rejection always did, but Molly stiffened her resolve and attended anyway. She loved her sister and would try until her dying day to reconcile, but she refused to be a party to Chloe's bitterness any longer.

Molly scanned this morning's crowd for a glimpse of her sister or mother and came up empty. The gathering was large enough to hide in, though, so perhaps Chloe had ventured out. Molly hoped so. The beauty of a sunrise service was good for the soul.

"Your baby is darling," a woman murmured as Molly opened her lawn chair and settled into it with Laney on her lap.

"She's not my—" She started to explain and then changed her mind. Why bother? Laney belonged to her heart and that was what counted. "Thank you," she said instead.

Aunt Patsy, who had ridden to the service with Molly and Ethan, set her lawn chair on the opposite side. Holding on to the plastic arms for support, she eased down. Molly knew her great-aunt's knees bothered her something fierce, but she would never complain.

She leaned toward Molly and whispered, "Laney looks precious in that outfit you bought."

Molly had spent hours on the Internet searching for the perfect Easter dress for Ethan's baby. She'd finally found the pink-and-white confection complete with lacy bonnet, white tights and patent-leather shoes. The price had been shocking, but Ethan's reaction had been worth the cost and effort. He'd thanked her with so many kisses, she'd blushed.

A disembodied voice, sounding much like Pastor Cliff's, opened the service, and a holy hush settled over the crowd. In the gray dawn, Molly watched with rapt attention as a hill outside of Winding Stair, Oklahoma, was transformed into ancient Jerusalem. Against the lighted backdrop of three wooden crosses and a cave-like tomb, ministers gave readings, and a chorus of voices swelled in song.

At exactly the right moment, when the mother of Jesus approached the tomb weeping, sunlight broke over the horizon in beams so radiant that some folks later said that God Himself smiled on the day. The stone rolled away from the tomb and the choir began to sing "He Is Risen" with such power and passion that goose bumps prickled Molly's arms.

She pondered the symbolism of Jesus as the sacrificial Lamb who came that mankind might be reunited with a Holy God, of the new beginnings made possible by His life and death and resurrection, of all the fresh possibilities embodied in Easter.

She thought of her own new beginnings, too, and a wonderful peace enfolded her. As the light of the new day spread across the land and the service concluded in glorious song, Molly felt as though she, too, had come out of a dark place and into a marvelous light.

She hugged Laney to her chest and closed her eyes in gratitude.

As the quiet crowd slowly broke up, going separate ways to contemplate the holiness of Easter Sunday, Ethan, in his long governor's robes, joined her.

He hunkered down in front of her chair and took Laney into his arms. The baby's ruffles and lace made crinkling noises as he rubbed his nose against her neck.

"What did you think? Did it look all right from out here?" The eagerness in him was boyish and charming.

"Ethan, it was awesome. You were awesome. I've never been to such a beautiful pageant."

"Neither have I," he said, grinning. "But then, this is my first and only Easter pageant."

Aunt Patsy reached over and patted his arm. "Well, it won't be your last. You made a formidable Pontius Pilate."

"Why, thank you, Miss Patsy." He bowed his head in mock humility. Laney grabbed one ear and twisted. With a yelp, Ethan unwound the tiny fingers. "Are you girls as hungry as I am?"

Molly rose and folded her lawn chair, then took Laney from Ethan while he assisted Aunt Patsy. "Probably not, but coffee sounds good."

"The church has coffee and rolls waiting. That should hold us until ten."

Although they were not technically a couple, they had promised Lindsey and Jesse to eat brunch with the young couples' class at ten. Later in the afternoon, the church was hosting a giant Easter-egg hunt for all the kids. Aunt Patsy and her group of friends had spent hours stuffing plastic eggs for the event.

"It's going to be a busy day."

"But a good one."

"We've got to get some pictures of that baby in her finery," Aunt Patsy said as they walked toward the parking area. "She'll only have one first Easter."

Ethan stopped in his tracks and turned to face the hillside, now washed in bright sunlight. "I just thought of something. This is my first Easter, too. The first one that ever meant anything."

Molly understood his awe. Even though she had been a Christian for a long time, today felt like a renewal to her, too.

Smiling up at him, she hooked her arm through his. "Pretty cool, huh?"

"Yeah." His gaze shifted to Laney, lying across Molly's shoulder. "You want me to carry her?"

"No. We're fine." And they were, just as they had been for sometime now. She could hold Laney and love her without a racing pulse or the awful tightness in her chest and throat. She'd almost stopped worrying that something terrible would happen.

She hugged the bundle of ruffles and lace a little closer.

When they reached the parking area other members of the cast milled about. The rise and fall of voices mingled with engines cranking and doors slamming. A man in Roman centurion gear called out and Ethan drifted off to speak with him.

Molly unlocked the car and bent to fasten Laney in her car seat. When she straightened, Aunt Patsy stood on the opposite side of the vehicle in conversation with an older woman Molly recognized from their church.

"I don't really think that's any of your concern, Hazel," she heard Aunt Patsy say.

"It's not right, I tell you, Patsy. That boy has his nerve dating a decent girl like Molly. He never did marry that baby's mother, you know." She announced the fact in a low, gossipy tone as if she hoped it was news to her listener.

"I know." Aunt Patsy's rosy cheeks grew redder, a sign, Molly knew, that she was getting angry. "I know about a lot of other things, too, that you apparently have forgotten. Things like Christian charity and forgiveness."

"Oh forevermore, Patsy." Hazel drew herself up in a straight line. "I would think as her aunt, you would be more concerned about that niece of yours. She's had enough trouble without getting involved with a philanderer who goes around making illegitimate babies."

"It's Easter, Hazel. I suggest you think about what that means and let the Lord worry about Ethan and Molly." Aunt Patsy turned her back on the woman, opened the car door and got in, slamming it a little harder than necessary.

As Hazel stalked away, gait stiff and insulted, Molly noticed what she'd missed during the confrontation. Ethan. Standing at the back of the car, expression stricken.

Molly's stomach hurt and her knees trembled for him. She was angry at the woman but ached for Ethan.

"I'm so sorry," she said, going to him. "She shouldn't have said that."

His jaw flexed. "I'm okay. I've heard worse."

He had? "What she said was cruel and wrong. She hurt your feelings."

He jerked one shoulder. "I have thick skin."

Not all that thick. She could see he was disturbed. Words wounded, even when they were untrue and the recipient didn't deserve them.

"Come on," Ethan said with false joviality, tugging on her hand. "I'm starving."

Molly tiptoed up on her new spring shoes to kiss his cheek.

"I love you," she whispered against his freshly shaved skin. No matter what anyone else thought of him or of his former life, Ethan Hunter was a good man.

Ethan rubbed his cheek, his eyebrows arching high. Mischief replaced the hurt in his eyes. "Maybe being gossiped about is not so bad after all."

"And then again, maybe it is. But there isn't a thing you can do about it anyway."

"Except to win her over with my devastating charm."

Gesturing to his robes, Molly teased, "You're Pontius Pilate. You could have her executed."

"No," he said. "Banished. No Easter-egg hunt for her. No chocolate bunnies. No marshmallow eggs."

Molly pressed a hand to her heart in pretend horror. "Cruel and unusual punishment. You are a wicked ruler indeed."

They both laughed and climbed inside the car, letting the banter soften the sting of the woman's cruel comments. At least for now.

By six o'clock that evening, Molly had eaten more chocolate bunnies and marshmallow eggs than she could count. She had also, along with Ethan, participated in an adult egg hunt at the Slater Farm that had been more fun than she thought possible. Who would believe grown men would tackle one another in pursuit of a plastic, candy-filled egg?

Now, as she plopped down on the couch in Ethan's apartment and kicked off her shoes, she said, "Wasn't this a great day?"

She leaned back and ran both hands through her messy hair, tired but content.

Ethan stood in the adjoining kitchenette, staring into the refrigerator. When he looked up and smiled, Molly's heart did a happy dance.

"Aren't you glad you went?"

"Mmm. Very glad. What are you doing in there?"

"Making the queen a bottle. She'll wake up howling any minute."

"After the day she's had, being passed from person to person and played with by every kid in town, I thought she might sleep all night."

"She will after she eats." He added cereal to the bottle and gave it a shake. "There she goes."

Sure enough, a restless whimper turned to a loud howl. Ethan plunked the bottle onto the coffee table, trotted to the small nursery and returned with a squirming, squawling baby.

"Let me have her," Molly said, holding up her arms. "I'll feed her."

Something she'd never thought possible had happened. She wanted to hold and feed a baby. For once, the fear only flitted across her mind and disappeared.

Ethan's smile lit the living room. He tossed the burp towel over her shoulder, lowered Laney into her arms, and handed her the bottle. The baby's pudgy hands batted at her dinner, trying to pull it into her mouth.

"Hold on, Miss Greedy." Molly slid the nipple between the bow lips.

"There you go," she crooned. "There you go."

Ethan stood before them, smiling down. "You two look all cozy."

"We are." She kissed Laney's forehead. "Aren't we, sweetie pie?"

Laney's answer came in contented slurps and grunts.

"I'm gonna run out to the truck for a minute," Ethan said. "To get that CD Jesse loaned me. Be right back, okay?"

Molly tensed. It had been a while since she'd been alone with Laney, but she loved Ethan and if they were to have any future together, she had to take care of his baby—alone. The attacks were gone. She needed to act as though they were.

"Sure. Go ahead. I wanted to listen to it, too."

He bent forward to kiss her hair. The pleasant mingle of aftershave and chocolatey marshmallow made her smile.

As he slipped out into the darkness, Molly rocked back and forth and hummed a lullaby. Laney's blue eyes stared wide and intent.

Without warning, the tiny face mottled. Laney coughed, sputtering cereal-laced formula onto Molly's hands.

Molly jerked the bottle from the baby's mouth and sat her upright, patting her back. Laney coughed and struggled, pushing air out but never inhaling.

Molly's pulse clattered into her throat. Laney was choking. Strangling.

"Ethan," she screamed. "Ethan, help!"

She flipped the baby over and dangled her across her knees. With the heel of one hand, she applied a not-so-gentle rap to the center of Laney's back.

Laney coughed again and then began to cry. Loud, wailing cries rent the apartment.

Ethan's footsteps thundered from outside. The

door slammed open on its hinges. "What's wrong? What happened?"

He rushed to her side, jerking Laney upright.

"She choked. She choked." Molly's voice shook with fear.

Ethan made a quick examination of the baby. "She's okay now."

But Molly wasn't.

What if she hadn't been able to stop the choking? What if Laney had died? What if...

Her chest tightened and her hands began to tremble.

Oh, no. Oh, no, no, no. Not the panic. Not now. Not in front of Ethan.

The tingling crept into her fingers like millions of crawling ants. Fear, terrible and consuming, gripped her.

"Molly?" He frowned, concerned. "Laney's okay. Calm down."

She shook her head at him, humiliated, terrified. It was happening and Ethan would see. He would know her shame, her weakness.

She jumped up and rushed out of the room. She'd no more than reached the back bedroom when a tidal wave of panic closed in. Her heart thundered faster and faster. Sweat beaded her face, her hands and knees trembled as violently as an earthquake. Her throat closed tighter and tighter.

What if another baby had died in her care?

She stumbled toward the wall. Spots danced in front of her eyes.

"Molly?" Ethan came through the door, and she longed for the floor to open and swallow her up. He reached for her, his face full of concern. "What's wrong?"

She pushed him away. He was blocking the air, crowding her. "I can't breathe. I can't breathe."

She was going to die this time. She wanted to.

He grabbed her shoulders, squared her toward him. She fought at his hands. They smothered her, cut off her oxygen.

"Talk to me. What's happening?"

"I can't breathe. Go away. Take care of Laney."

"Laney is fine, I tell you. She's fine. Now calm down."

She fought away from him, turned her back and went to her knees, shaking too hard to stand. But lying down strangled her. She had to prop up, get air. Her heart hammered incessantly, wildly. She was smothering. Dying.

Suddenly, strong hands lifted her up and whirled her around, bracing her back against the wall. Ethan dropped to the floor beside her.

He grasped her chin in his hard fingers, forced her face up. "Has this happened before?"

She nodded. "Can't breathe."

"Panic attack," he said, making a paramedic's quick assessment. "Listen to me. Let me help."

She nodded again. What else could she do? He was here. He'd witnessed her shame.

"You're hyperventilating. Breathe into this bag."

From somewhere he produced a paper bag and cupped it around her mouth.

"Take a long, deep belly breath," he said, laying a hand over her abdomen.

Molly shook her head frantically, wanting to scream. How could she take a deep breath? She was strangling.

"Do it," he commanded in a voice that brooked no argument. "Look into my eyes and take one long deep breath. Now."

She locked eyes with him and did as he commanded. It wasn't easy, but she did it.

"Good girl. Do it again. Only this time, in your mind, count backwards starting at twenty. With every number think of someone you care about. Concentrate on that. Visualize that."

Twenty. She thought of Ethan.

Nineteen. Laney.

Oh, dear Lord, what if Laney had choked to death?

Her fingers tightened on the paper bag. She started to pant again.

Ethan tapped her knuckles. "Relax, Molly. Don't pant. Breathe, slow and easy. This is going to pass. You will get through this and be all right."

She nodded again, concentrated on the soothing encouragement in his voice.

"Count for me. What are you on?"

"Eighteen." *Aunt Patsy.*

"Good. Keep counting. Concentrate on good things, good places, good people. Count your blessings."

Seventeen. The smiles of children when they opened the boxes she sent.

Sixteen. The seniors who made her laugh and told her stories.

"You're doing fine, sweetheart. It's passing." Ethan stroked her shoulders in circular movements, soothing, calming. She took another deep, cleansing breath.

Thirteen. Daddy. Oh, how she missed that laugh.

By the time she'd counted backward to nine the tightness in her chest began to subside. Knees up, she dropped her head back against the cool plaster. There was a water spot on the ceiling of his apartment. She studied it, concentrated on it. Did Ethan know his roof had leaked at some point? Maybe during the ice storm?

Ethan's voice rumbled on, a low purr in her ear.

At three, the fear dissipated. Her pulse slowed. She laid the paper sack aside.

"You're not trembling anymore."

"I'm better now." She couldn't meet his eyes.

In the other room, Laney began to cry.

"Go." Molly pushed at him. "Take care of her. Hurry."

Ethan studied her face as if weighing which hysterical female needed him the most. "Stay put."

He left the room and Molly wished she had the strength to get up and leave. Before she could even try, Laney quieted and Ethan returned.

He hunkered down beside her. "How long has this been going on?"

Her chest started to hurt again. "Is Laney okay?"

"She's fine." His sweet face was stern. "Answer my question. How long?"

"Since Zack died. I thought I was well. I thought they were gone."

But they weren't. A few minutes alone with Laney had brought them back in full force. She would always be in danger around babies. She'd accepted that before Ethan came along. And now look what had happened the minute she'd let her guard down.

"Have you seen a doctor about it?"

She nodded, picking at a stray carpet thread. "Yes, but I don't like pills."

"What about therapy?"

"That, too. For a while."

The only thing that ever really helped was staying away from her sister and children, the triggers as her therapist called them. As long as she was at home on the farm or working in the center, she was fine. Every book she'd read and every doctor she'd seen had insisted avoidance was not the answer. But they were wrong. Hadn't this incident proved as much?

She pushed up off the floor and went into the kitchen for a drink of water. Her legs felt like cooked noodles.

Ethan followed, attentive and watchful. She appreciated his concern, but the sooner she got away from him the better off they'd both be.

Gripping the counter with one hand, she tipped her head back and let the cool water wash away any residual tightness in her throat. Too bad it couldn't wash away the attacks, but she was trapped in a vicious prison of fear that nothing could eliminate. Nothing except avoidance.

She drained the glass then set it in the sink. With the clink of glass against porcelain, she stared at the white tile backsplash and said, "I need to go home."

"Are you sure you're ready to be alone?"

"I have to get away from here, Ethan." She managed a glance at him. Then wished she hadn't.

He studied her, worried, uncertain and loving. Right now, she didn't want him to love her. She wanted him to let her go.

"Okay," he said, slowly, as if trying to gauge her mood. "If you want to go home, I'll drive you."

"No need," she said, a little too sharply, but why prolong the agony. "I can drive myself."

She'd driven her Jeep into town because it had more room than Ethan's truck, and now she was glad she had. Making her escape back to safety would be easier.

Gently, Ethan gripped her arms and turned her to face him. "I won't take no for an answer, Molly. I want to help. You're upset. I don't want you to be alone."

"I said I can drive myself, Ethan. I don't need you."

What a terrible lie that was, but it stopped him cold. He dropped his arms and stood inches away, his wounded expression a jab at her already tattered heart. He looked so confused, and she hated herself for letting their relationship come this far.

For a short, beautiful time she'd believed they could make it. She loved him. Never wanted to see him hurt.

All the more reason to get this over with. Tonight

had proven that a relationship between her and a man with a child would never work.

The sooner she got away from Ethan and Laney, the better for them all. She'd thought she was well. She'd thought her love for Ethan and Laney made all the difference. But love wasn't enough to heal what was wrong with her.

Gathering her purse, she started to the door. Ethan followed, worried. "I wish you'd stay a little longer or let me go with you. You're still pale as a ghost."

"I'm fine. Take care of your baby."

"Call me when you get home."

She shook her head. "I don't think so."

He reached for her, but she backed away. A tide of emotion already threatened to destroy her resolve. If he touched her, she'd fall apart.

"Goodbye, Ethan. I'm sorry."

Before he could stop her, she fumbled the door open and rushed out into the parking lot to her Jeep.

Hands shaking, she started the vehicle and shifted into gear.

It was over. She couldn't take any more chances. The brief and lovely dream with Ethan was over for good. Eyes dry and hot with unshed tears, she headed out of the parking lot and into the gaping emptiness of her future.

Chapter Thirteen

Ethan spent the next hour pacing the floor, praying, thinking and trying to understand what had happened with Molly.

Their day had been amazing. With every minute together, he fell more in love with her. She was silly and warm and kind. And she loved him. He was certain of that.

But something far more serious than a panic attack had occurred tonight. Something had happened inside that pretty head of hers that she wasn't sharing with him. Her goodbye sounded too permanent.

A sick churning started in the pit of his stomach.

He paced into the tiny nursery and gazed down at Laney, his heart filling with wonder at this gift from God. The spill of light from the hallway washed over her face, and her long eyelashes cast shadows on her cheekbones. She slept in that relaxed way of babies, knees tucked to her chest, bottom in the air.

Molly said she had choked, but by the time he'd come in, she was fine. Except for the formula and cereal on her face and bib, he couldn't tell anything unusual had occurred.

But whatever had happened had been enough to send Molly into a state of panic. The aftermath of cold aloofness had been every bit as scary to him as the panic attack.

A colorful mobile, a gift from Molly, circled over the crib. The music box of lullabies had long since wound down. Absently, he tapped a dangling monkey with one finger.

Molly's behavior disturbed him. Why hadn't she let him drive her home? Why had she left so abruptly?

Was she giving up on them?

Spinning around, he went to the living room and picked up the phone. He would never sleep until he knew she was all right anyway. Might as well get some answers.

She picked up on the second ring. Some of the tension left his shoulders.

"Molly. It's me. Ethan."

"I know."

"Are you all right?"

"Yes." Her answer was curt as though she didn't want to talk. He wasn't having that.

"Talk to me."

"I'm really tired."

"Me, too. It was a great day, huh?"

He tried to sound upbeat and casual. Maybe if he could get her talking about the day everything would normalize. "How about coming over tomorrow night? We'll rent a video."

"Ethan." Her voice sounded distant. "I'm not coming over anymore."

She was starting to scare him. "Because of a little anxiety attack?"

"I thought Laney was going to die. I thought I was going to cause another child's death."

His stomach started churning again.

"You were not responsible for her choking, Molly, any more than you were responsible for Zack's death. Don't you see that? Laney's choked on me before. And yeah, I'll admit, it's scary, but she gets over it." He walked to the window and pushed the drapes aside. "You have to do the same."

"I can't."

"Can't? Or won't?"

"If something happened to her in my care, I would lose my mind, Ethan. I can't live through that again." The tiny quiver in her voice got to him in a hurry. "Please. Just let me go."

His grip tightened on the receiver. She was upset and as a result, unreasonable. Surely, she wasn't saying what he thought she was.

"What do you mean, let you go? We can work this out."

"We can't. I can't. Don't you understand? You

have a child. I can never be alone with a baby again. Ever."

He'd thought Molly was different, but like Twila she didn't want his child.

He shoved the drapes farther apart and pressed his forehead against the cool glass windowpane. A sense of doom as dark as the street outside descended.

"Laney and I are a package deal. You knew that from the start."

"Yes, I did. And that's the way it should be. I'm sorry."

"But you love me." He ground his teeth in frustration.

She loved him but not his kid. He'd heard that before.

"I do love you. And I love Laney." She sucked in a deep breath, and he braced himself knowing instinctively that the worst was yet to come. "That's why we have to end this now before it's too late."

She loved him. She loved Laney. But she was willing to give them both up. And why? Because of fear? Because she was afraid Laney would die in her care?

He slammed a fist against the window facing. "This is crazy, Molly. It makes no sense."

"It does to me."

"Don't make a decision tonight while you're upset. Take some time. Pray about it."

"I already have. And look what happened."

She was starting to tick him off. "God didn't

cause that baby to choke, and He doesn't cause your panic attacks."

"Do you think you have the answer to everything? If God cared—" She stopped, ending with a sob.

Ethan reined in his emotions. Going off half-cocked could only cause more trouble. He had the scars to prove it.

With intentional gentleness, he said, "Blaming God won't solve anything."

"I'm not blaming God."

"Aren't you?"

"I don't know what you mean. You're the one not making sense now."

"You think God has let you down, first when Zack died and then when your family turned against you. Now you think he's done it again. But He didn't. He sent Laney and me along to make things better, not worse. You have to trust that everything will work out for the best."

Ethan wasn't sure where the ideas came from, but he knew he had hit the nail on the head. Somewhere in all the tragedy Molly had lost her trust in God's ultimate goodness.

Her end of the phone hummed with silence. Finally, she whispered, "I don't know what to believe anymore."

"Then let me tell you. Believe that I love you. Believe that God loves you. And together the three of us can work through any problems we encounter. Nothing's too big for God. I'm living proof of that."

"I can't take the chance again, Ethan." Her voice was small and lonely. "Look what happened."

"Avoiding the problem is not rational. And it won't fix things."

"It's the only way I know how to cope."

He was starting to get desperate here. Really desperate.

"That's not coping. That's hiding. Existing in a tiny realm of perceived safety, terrified of seeing a baby or your sister or anything that might trigger an attack."

He couldn't believe this was happening. Not again. Another woman tossing him aside like yesterday's hamburger wrapper. Only this time he loved that woman and she loved him. And she loved Laney, too, so much that she feared harming her.

His palms grew damp against the telephone. "Don't do this, Molly." He wasn't too proud to beg. "Don't throw away something beautiful and right."

"It's over, Ethan. I'm sorry." Sobs broke free. "So sorry."

And the line went dead in his ear.

Ethan sat in the darkened living room for hours staring at the wall and watching the occasional sweep of car lights beam in from the parking lot. The refrigerator kicked on. The ice maker dumped. Once, Laney whimpered in her sleep.

He wanted to do the same. Whimper like a kicked dog, then go to sleep and pray that tonight was all a bad dream.

No matter how he examined the situation with Molly, he came away without an answer. He rubbed a hand over his chest. It hurt.

After the ordeal with Twila he'd vowed to be smarter about women.

He gave a huff of self-reproach. There was his answer plain as day.

As cruel as she'd been, the woman in the parking lot after the sunrise service had been right. A man with his tainted past had no business falling in love with a nice girl like Molly.

If he'd listened to his common sense, none of this would have happened.

He drew in a deep breath and let it out slowly. All the common sense in the world wouldn't change one thing. He loved Molly. Being with her energized him and gave him hope for a better future. She was the other half of his heart. Giving her up without a fight was out of the question.

But was it unfair to pursue her? Was God trying to tell him that he was wrong for Molly?

Taking his Bible, he flipped it open, thumbed through the pages looking for comfort or guidance. Nothing caught his eye. He closed it again, laced his fingers and leaned forward, head down, hands dangling between his knees.

"I am one messed-up dude, Lord," he said. "I sure could use some help."

Inexplicably, the words *Joy comes in the morning,* filtered through his head. He frowned in thought. Was that in the Bible? Had he heard it somewhere?

He didn't know about joy, but for certain daylight would come in the morning and with it a ten-hour day of driving.

He stood and stretched his back.

"Just me and You, Lord," he murmured. "Just me and You all over again." And then because he could do nothing else, he went to bed.

Morning came and went, but Ethan didn't feel a bit of joy. He'd awakened with a headache and a knot in his belly that he hadn't been able to shake. When his lunch went sour on him, he'd pulled into a quick-stop for antacids and chewed a handful of the chalky tablets, washing them down with bottled water.

Molly was on his mind all day, and he'd vacillated between anger, pity and prayer.

He drove by her workplace, saw her Jeep in the lot, and thought of going inside. He could confront her, make her listen to reason. He loved her. He could make her happy.

But the voice in his head stopped him. Maybe he couldn't make any woman happy. Hadn't he failed miserably with Twila?

By late afternoon, he wheeled his van down the streets of Winding Stair ahead of schedule. He'd made good time today regardless of his heavy-hearted mood.

As if on automatic pilot, he turned down Cedar

Street toward Miss Patsy's apartment. A check of his watch said he could stop for a minute. He wasn't sure what he would say.

She came to the door, wearing her rosy-cheeked smile and a jogging suit with dirty knees. In one hand she carried a large wooden bird house.

"Just the man I was wishing for," she said as he slammed out of the truck and started up the incline.

His spirits lifted. Molly's aunt had that effect on just about everybody. "What are you up to, Miss Patsy?"

"Oh, I was out here puttering around in these flower beds when I saw those red wasps trying to take over my martin house. Thought I'd better clean it out. Now I can't get it back up on the post."

Ethan took the tiny apartment house from her. "How did you get it down?"

She waved him off. "Don't ask. Molly would wring my neck if she knew."

"I probably would too," he answered with a grin A stepladder leaned against the side of the house, the obvious culprit. He took it and started up.

Patsy stood beneath him, head tilted back. "Yesterday was sure a wonderful Easter, wasn't it?"

With his shins balanced against the top of the ladder, Ethan set the birdhouse onto the pole and fastened it down.

How could he answer her question? Yesterday had been great. And it had been terrible.

He gave the pole a shake and, satisfied that the house was stable, descended the ladder.

"Molly had a panic attack last night," he said without preliminaries.

The older lady's face twisted with dismay. "I guess she'd never told you about them?"

"No. I had known something was wrong as far back as the night of the ice storm, but she never said a word."

"She hasn't had one in a long time."

"That's what she told me." He rubbed the dust from his hands.

"Is she all right this morning?"

"I don't know."

"Why not? Didn't you give her a call?"

He looked up at the birdhouse, down at the greening grass, and then into Miss Patsy's wise eyes. Here was a mentor he'd always been able to talk to, even about her own niece.

"She broke things off. Said she couldn't take the chance."

Behind her wire-framed glasses, Patsy frowned. "Of what?"

He lifted the ladder and carried it to the front porch. Patsy walked alongside him.

"That's what I asked. And her answer was all confused. She's afraid she'll hurt Laney. She's afraid the panic attacks will start again." He didn't understand well enough to explain.

"That's a bunch of nonsense."

He leaned the ladder against the alcove next to Miss Patsy's gardening tools, waiting for the metallic clatter to subside before he spoke again.

"I know it. You know it. But Molly doesn't."

"She's walked a hard, lonely road in the last two years, but since you came along she's been happier, better. Just look at how you've gotten her out of that house and back involved with the church and with people. Don't give up on her, Ethan. Give her a little more time."

Ethan wished it was that simple. Patience he could do. Time he could do. He leaned against the porch post, pondering the question that had haunted him all night. Even if those things would bring her around, did he have a right to be with her?

An old faded green metal chair sat at one end of the porch. With a scrape of metal against concrete, Patsy twisted it toward him and sat down.

"You love her, don't you?" she persisted.

"Yeah. I do." He ran a hand through his hair. He'd even been thinking about marriage. Now there was a concept.

"And she loves you," Patsy said in that matter-of-fact manner of the aged. "Fact is, she's crazy about you and that baby. I can tell by the way she looks at you when you aren't paying attention. So what are you going to do about it?"

He gnawed the inside of his cheek and thought about the question. He knew what he wanted to do. He wanted to tell Molly that nothing she could do, short of denying she loved him, would drive him away. He could wait forever if he had to.

His answer wasn't as optimistic. "Nothing."

"Nothing? Boy, what are you talking about? You don't know how long I've been waiting and praying for the right man to come along and sweep that niece of mine off her feet."

"That's the problem, Miss Patsy. I'm not the right man for Molly."

"What makes you think such a silly thing?"

He hitched one shoulder. "Molly's a nice girl. She's never done a bad thing in her life."

"Oh, I see. Hazel Rodgers and her self-righteous comment about your past." Lips pursed, Patsy shook her head. "That woman is so busy hunting for the speck in someone else's eye she can't see the two-by-four in her own."

"I'm not Mr. Clean."

"Well, I never liked a man with an earring anyway," she said and then laughed and flapped her hand. "I'm just going on with you, Ethan. But you listen to this old woman and you listen good."

White tennis shoes squared, she leaned forward and pointed out at the brown van.

"See those mirrors on your truck? God doesn't have those. Some people do, but God don't. He never looks back at what you've done, only forward to the good you're doing now. There's no Reverse in God's kingdom."

Ethan allowed a smile. Miss Patsy had a way of laying out the gospel unlike any he'd ever heard.

"Are you saying that God doesn't hold my mistake against me? That He isn't trying to tell me I'm not good enough for Molly?"

"That's exactly what I'm saying. Oh, some people will criticize no matter what you do, but you have to give it to God. Move on. Put the past to rest once and for all."

"But part of my past will always be with me."

"The Lord has a purpose in all things, even mistakes or tragedies. Now, I'm not saying He causes them, but I do know that He takes anything that happens in our lives and works something good from it. Just look at you and Laney. Isn't she worth the trouble? Aren't you glad she's in your life, no matter how she got there?"

The light inside Ethan came on as bright as if the sun rose in his chest. When he'd turned his life over to the Lord, the nightmare with Twila had culminated in a beautiful thing—his daughter. Then, from the ashes of his unrestrained lifestyle, a new and better man had risen.

"I've been as bad as Molly about hanging on to guilt, haven't I?"

"Most likely. But if we trust Him, the Lord will take us from where we are to where He plans for us to be. And it's always better than anything we can imagine."

Patsy was right. Even the time in his life that began as a mistake had become his greatest blessing—Laney.

"I think Molly's struggling with that, too, Miss Patsy. Because of all that's happened she's lost confidence that God has her best interest at heart."

Hadn't he almost done the same?

"Well, mark my words. The Lord has a plan. You and me have just got to be smart enough not to get in His way."

"I can't make her want me and Laney."

"No, you can't." She pushed up out of the chair and came to him. "But I'm asking you as a friend, Ethan. Don't give up yet. Give her some space and some time. And keep on praying."

"What if she never comes around?"

"What if she does?"

He laughed, surprised at the simple logic. "How did you get so smart?"

She patted his arm. "Life's a good teacher. I've learned a few things through my own blunders."

"Not you," he said, gently teasing.

She swatted his arm. "Get going, you big lug. People want their stuff delivered on time."

He pulled her to him for a quick kiss on the cheek. "Thanks, Miss Patsy."

Face flushed with pleasure, she flapped her hands. "Go on now. And bring that baby by sometime soon."

Ethan executed a smart salute. "Yes, ma'am."

As he jogged to his truck, Miss Patsy's cleansing words circled inside his head and took root. God never looks back. And he shouldn't either. He was doing his best to walk in God's will, and he had to believe Molly was a part of that.

Time would tell if Molly could overcome her fears, and learn to trust.

And if there was one thing Ethan had, it was time.

Chapter Fourteen

Molly spotted Ethan and Laney the moment she arrived at the church picnic. Her traitorous heart leaped to see how handsome Ethan looked in a plaid shirt hanging open over a white T-shirt and a pair of ordinary jeans. His wide white smile flashed at something Pastor Cliff said when he placed Laney in the outstretched arms of the pastor's wife.

Molly's arms ached to be the ones holding Laney. And she wanted to talk to Ethan so badly her throat hurt.

Not for the first time, she questioned the wisdom of attending this annual event. For a week after the break-up with Ethan she'd confined herself to home and work. Then Aunt Patsy had gotten hold of her. This time she hadn't been gentle. Worse still, Aunt Patsy had cried, and Molly couldn't stand to see her beloved aunt upset. Not if she could do something to prevent it. So she'd gone back to church again.

Chloe hadn't been happy, but Molly had kept her distance and soldiered on. If she'd learned anything, it was that she needed her church family and she needed God. Ethan said she'd stopped trusting God, but he was wrong. She trusted God. It was herself she didn't trust.

Strangely, glimpsing Ethan across the churchyard or in the foyer had proven harder than dealing with Chloe's silent stares. Sometimes he said hello, his blue eyes full of hurt. Those days she'd go home and cry.

She'd known he would be here today and thought she was prepared to see him. Now she wasn't so sure she could get through an afternoon with Ethan so close—and yet so far away. Keeping her commitment to let him go was the hardest thing she'd done in a long time. And she had done some difficult things.

The day after Easter he'd sent flowers. Yellow tulips. She'd cried that day, too. His phone calls, every day for a while, had dwindled away to none at all now. Perhaps he'd given up on her. Maybe he'd even found someone else.

Molly ran nervous palms down the side of her jeans and considered getting back into the Jeep.

"Don't even think about it."

Molly swiveled around to find Lindsey Slater coming across the dirt road, her pregnancy noticeable beneath a big T-shirt advertising her Christmas-tree farm.

"Come on. We need some help getting all the food organized. Church folks do love to eat."

A horde of people surrounded the concrete tables beneath a huge pavilion complete with outdoor grill. Pastor Cliff manned the grill, his booming laugh as pleasant as the scent of burgers. Ice chests filled with pop and water would be put to good use throughout the afternoon.

Two men were setting up a volleyball net while some of the older folks pitched horseshoes and the kids chased each other in circles, yelling at the top of their lungs.

The lake, about a hundred yards away, was still too cold for swimming, but the late-spring day was warm and sunny enough for a potluck picnic.

"I brought cake," she said, reaching into the back seat to withdraw a rectangular pan.

"What kind?"

"Turtle cake."

Lindsey's tawny eyes went dreamy. "With caramel and nuts?"

"That's the one."

"Now I know you're staying even if I have to tie you up."

Molly managed a smile, some of her nerves settling.

Falling in step beside Lindsey, she walked up the grassy knoll to the pavilion.

Aunt Patsy bustled around near the food table, poking spoons into casseroles and salads. When she saw Molly, her face lit up.

"There's my girl." She rushed forward, wrapped Molly in a motherly hug and whispered, "Thank you, darling."

And Molly remembered all over again why she'd come. And why she would stay.

Along with Lindsey and Aunt Patsy she plunged into work, readying the potluck spread for the Seventh Cavalry, as Aunt Patsy called the gathered crowd.

She was slicing a pecan pie and listening to Clare Thompson chatter about the upcoming bazaar when Aunt Patsy leaned toward her. "Chloe's here."

As she followed her aunt's gaze, a cold knot formed in her stomach.

Her sister stepped out of a church van and began unloading toddlers.

"You said she wasn't coming."

"That's what James told me yesterday."

Molly laid the pie knife aside. "Maybe I should leave."

"You will not." Aunt Patsy grabbed her upper arm. "Chloe knew you would be here, and she chose to come anyway. She saw you last weekend at church and this is no different."

Maybe Aunt Patsy was right. She and Chloe had managed to be in the same church building together without causing an explosion. Granted, they'd ignored each other and stayed on opposite sides of the building. Maybe they could do the same today.

Squaring her shoulders, she picked up the knife again and resumed cutting.

"Good girl."

Molly watched from beneath her lashes as her sister came up the rise. Long involved in the church's bus outreach to kids, Chloe was followed by members of her Sunday School class whose parents didn't attend.

Molly marveled that Chloe, who grieved so violently for her son, preferred to teach the little ones. Where Molly panicked around kids, her sister seemed to draw comfort.

Chloe, accompanied by her husband, clucked around the children like a mother hen. When her eyes found Molly, she stared long and hard, then hitched her chin in the air and herded the kids toward the sand pile.

Foolishly disappointed, Molly watched the thin woman move away from her. When would she stop hoping and longing that Chloe would forgive her? That they could once again share the special bond of sisterhood?

She turned aside, only to find Ethan watching her over a can of pop. Great. From one heartache to the other in zero point two seconds. Luckily, Deb Castor came up just then looking for volleyball recruits.

"Come on, Molly. We need another warm body on our team." Earrings swinging, Deb tugged Molly toward the net set up in back of the pavilion. "Tom's team is blitzing us, as usual."

Though husband and wife, Deb and Tom got a kick out of competing against each other.

Glad for the tension reliever, Molly trotted to the back court. Good-natured insults volleyed across the net long before the first serve. She relaxed and tossed a few back, feeling good to be in the midst of old acquaintances.

Hands on her knees, she waited while the other players got into position.

Suddenly, her arms tingled with awareness. She instinctively knew who stood next to her.

"Hi," Ethan said quietly when she glanced over at him.

"Hi." His eyes were incredibly blue today, as blue as the spring sky.

Heart in her throat, she had so much to say. She wanted to know how he was. What he'd been doing. How Laney was. She wanted to apologize for the sadness she detected in those gorgeous blue eyes of his, and to tell him what a difference he'd made in her life.

But, of course, she couldn't.

Tom's team served and the ball came at her, falling with a thud onto the sand.

"Sorry," she called, trotting to collect the ball and send it back to the other side.

If she was going to play this game, she didn't dare look at Ethan again.

She concentrated, and the next time the ball came her way, she leaped into action with a decent forearm pass. Ethan darted beneath her, slammed the ball up and over the net for a side out.

Without thinking about it they turned and slapped congratulatory high fives. As soon as they touched, Molly regretted the action. Touching him, looking at him, was killer.

Deb moved up to serve and everyone rotated. Ethan stepped to the net, leaving Molly in the back.

He looked great from her view. So good she missed the next ball that came in her direction. And the next.

"Time to eat." Pastor Cliff's voice boomed the news. Molly almost fainted with relief. Another five minutes of drooling over Ethan and she would be tempted to do something stupid.

Back beneath the pavilion, she slid in line behind Lindsey and took a paper plate. Pastor Cliff gave a short prayer and then the crowd surged forward like sharks after blood. Shoulders jostled, voices buzzed. A teenager put ice down Molly's back, and she yelped and danced, all to the delight of her tormentors.

She loved being here. She hated being here. Crazy, mixed-up woman that she was.

"I'll get you for that," she said, glaring in mock anger at the clutch of teenage boys who tried hard to appear innocent.

"You have admirers," a rich, purring voice said in her ear.

Her pulse leaped, warning her long before she looked that the speaker was Ethan. Even his after-shave, woodsy and dark, told on him.

"Teenagers like to pester. It has nothing to do with admiration."

His plate piled high with enough food to last Molly a week, he gestured toward an empty table under a shade tree.

"Sit with me. Tell me what you've been up to."

I'd love to.

"I don't think that's a good idea."

"It's only a hamburger."

She couldn't stop the smile. "That sounds a lot like, 'It's not a date.'"

His blue eyes danced at the memory. He took her paper plate from her hand. "Get us a soda. Then come and sit. If at any point this feels like a date you can get up and run."

She hesitated. Had she come hoping this would happen? Was she that big a fool?

"Where's Laney?"

"With Karen." Both hands full, he hitched his chin toward the pastor's wife. "Want to get her?"

Molly let the suggestion slide. Yes, she desperately wanted to hold Laney, to smell her baby smell and kiss her soft skin. But that was a risk she couldn't take.

Just as spending more time with Ethan was a risk she couldn't take.

She reached for her plate, took it from him. "We'd better not, Ethan. I'm sorry."

Before she could change her mind she walked away, feeling his eyes on her back. Searching the tables for someone comfortable to sit with, she saw Lindsey and her family.

"Mind if I join you?" she asked.

Lindsey scooted to one side. "We'd love to have you."

Truth be told, her appetite had gone with Ethan, but she threw a leg over the concrete bench and sat. Lindsey's step-daughter, Jade, beamed her good will. "My mommy's having a baby."

Jesse laughed. "Eat your burger, Butterbean, before I do." He pretended to reach for the sandwich. Jade squealed and jerked it away in a full body swing.

"You two kids stop fussing," Lindsey said, laughing with them.

Jesse slid an arm around her waist and hugged her close. "Yes, ma'am. We'll be good."

He winked at Jade, and Molly envied the love flowing through the little family.

She picked at her food, found it flavorless. Around the crowded table, the conversation flowed, but she felt no compunction to participate other than to smile or nod. Try as she might, she couldn't stop thinking about Ethan.

From where she sat, she could see the side of his face. Some girl she didn't know sat across from him. A bit of jealousy curled in her stomach, so she doused it with root beer and potato chips.

He leaned back and laughed. Molly watched, mesmerized. On his lap, Laney waved her chubby arms, grabbing at everything within her reach. Ethan efficiently thwarted her attempts to steal his potato chips, handed her a toy instead and kissed the top of her head.

Molly remembered the strength of those hands and the warmth of his mouth on hers.

"Why don't you go over there and sit with them?"

She jerked to awareness, embarrassed that Lindsey had caught her staring at Ethan like a sick dog.

"Not a good idea."

"Why not?" Lindsey asked. "I thought you two were a couple."

"Were. That's over."

"And that's too bad. He's a terrific guy."

Molly didn't need anyone to tell her how terrific he was. Pieces of her heart broke loose every time she thought of what might have been.

She bit into a forkful of potato salad, barely tasting the tangy mustard. The food was good but she'd lost her appetite, even for turtle cake.

Ethan liked her turtle cake. She wondered if he'd gotten a slice.

There he was again, in her head. She furtively slanted her eyes in his direction, trying not to draw attention.

As if he heard her thoughts, Ethan turned and captured her gaze with his.

She had to stop this nonsense. Now.

She stood abruptly, garnering curious glances from her table mates. "I think I'll take a walk."

Dumping her half-empty plate in the trash, she

started toward the lake a hundred yards downhill from the pavilion. Trash littered the beachfront, an acceptable excuse for getting away from the crowd and Ethan's tempting presence. She found an empty sack and started picking up cans and bottles and paper along the water's edge.

The cloudy green water lapped against the shore in gentle waves. She inhaled, taking in the freshness of the air and the slightly fishy scent of the lake.

She hadn't been out here in a long time. Once she and her dad had fished for bass in this lake, and as kids she and Chloe had learned to swim here.

Gazing out across the wide expanse of Winding Stair Lake, she remembered. Good memories that no amount of heartache could erase.

A wave swelled and white-capped, pretty as a painting.

Something orange, a buoy perhaps, caught her attention.

She frowned and strained her eyes. No. Not a buoy. Something that ballooned up over the wave top and flapped with the motion.

A chill of fear skittered down her spine.

A shirt. An orange shirt. A very small orange shirt.

Surely, it wasn't attached to a person.

She squinted against the glare, her hand going to her mouth. "Oh, Lord. No."

A child's head bobbed up and down. The orange object was the bulge of his air-filled T-shirt holding him, barely, above the water.

Molly whirled toward the pavilion where Ethan walked toward a Dumpster, plate in hand.

"Ethan," she screamed. "There's a child in the water!"

Ethan whirled toward her voice. He dropped the plate and took off in a gallop. But he was more than a hundred yards away. The child didn't have that much time.

She looked back toward the lake. Only the orange shirt bobbed on the surface. The child's head had disappeared beneath the waves.

Like a bad dream, time froze. A child was going to die and Molly was the only one close enough to do anything.

Her heart accelerated into panic mode. Her throat constricted.

Another child was going to die. And it would be her fault—again.

Chapter Fifteen

"No!" she screamed and broke toward the lake, shedding her shoes and over-shirt as she ran.

She hit the water in a dead run. The icy cold sucked her breath away. Her pulse rattled wildly, threatening.

She would not, could not let the fear take over. A child's life was at stake.

With a silent prayer for help, she plunged beneath the murky water. Her body rebelled against the cold. Her calves tightened at the unexpected temperature drop.

Molly ignored everything but the need to get to the child.

She fought through the incoming current, training her eyes on that distant spot. Then the orange shirt disappeared. Molly dove beneath the surface, eyes wide and stinging as she frantically searched.

All the while, she prayed. "Show me where he is. Help me get to him in time. Help me. Help me."

An eternity seemed to pass while she thrashed beneath the waves. Her cold limbs grew heavy from exertion. Her chest felt as though it would explode.

Suddenly she glimpsed orange and, with one final burst of energy, lurched toward it.

Grabbing the loose shirt, she yanked the child's head above the water.

Molly's heart, already thundering from effort, nearly shattered.

He was nothing but a baby. A toddler, perhaps three years old. His eyes were closed. And his lips were blue.

"You're okay, baby," she said. But looking into his small, waxy white face she feared he was already dead.

Wrapping an arm around him, she lifted his limp body above the surface and, with every ounce of energy she could muster, raced toward shore. All the while, she remembered the last lifeless body she'd held.

Don't let another one die on me, Lord, she prayed silently. *Not another one. He can't die. He won't die.*

The words became an internal chant as she stroked hard and fast toward the crowd gathered along the bank. Long before her feet touched bottom, Ethan, grim-faced and determined, came wading toward her. He shoved the water aside with power and impatience—as if he controlled the very waves.

Exhausted, she drew on the last of her strength to thrust the child across the short distance that separated her from Ethan.

Ethan yanked the toddler into his arms and ran back toward land, whipping the water aside with his powerful strides.

Molly followed, relieved that Ethan was there to help. He'd know what to do. Numb and cold and terrified, she watched as his broad back bent over the boy and puffed a breath into the tiny nose and mouth.

Let him live. Let him live. She wasn't sure if she thought the words or spoke them.

When she stumbled ashore someone draped a tablecloth over her shoulders. She realized then that her body shook wildly. Water dripped from her hair into her eyes and mouth.

But she didn't care. All that mattered was the boy.

She pushed through the ring of onlookers to where Ethan was performing CPR. She prayed. And begged.

Other than whispered prayers, a hush hung over the circle. The time seemed an eternity.

From somewhere nearby came a woman's keening cry. Molly wished she would stop. Wailing meant they had given up. And they couldn't give up. Not yet. Not ever.

Another eternity passed while Ethan pressed the narrow chest and breathed into a nose and mouth so small that the rescuer's lips easily eclipsed them.

Shoulders tight as stretched leather, teeth chattering, Molly commanded, "Breathe, baby, breathe."

As if her words were what he waited for, the toddler coughed. Ethan quickly turned him on his side and a gush of water spewed forth.

Then the most beautiful sound in the world filled the clearing. The little one began to cry. In seconds, he was calling for his mama.

Molly went limp, weeping with relief into her chilled palms.

"We got to him in time. He should be okay," she heard Ethan say. "But you need to take him to the ER. Have him checked over to be sure."

It was then that Molly saw her sister standing white-faced and horrified. Tears streaming from her eyes, she stood riveted to the scene.

"I only turned my back to get Tracy a drink," Chloe said. "How did Corey get into the water so fast? How did…"

The keening noise issued from her lips, and Molly realized it was Chloe she'd heard before.

Her stricken gaze fell on Molly. "I nearly caused a child's death. If you hadn't seen him— If you hadn't gone after him…"

Hysterical sobs broke loose and racked her thin body.

Regardless of what had gone on before, Molly couldn't ignore her sister's cries. No one understood the feeling of despair and remorse and horror any better than she did.

Gently, she touched her sister's quaking shoulder.

"No, sis, don't. Don't blame yourself. Sometimes bad things just happen."

Miraculously, as she comforted her sister, Molly, too, was comforted. The truth of her words soaked into the deepest part of her mind and blossomed there. *Sometimes bad things just happen.*

A shudder rippled through Chloe. She lifted her teary face. "How can you be nice to me after the way I've treated you?"

"Easy." Letting the tablecloth fall, Molly held out her arms. "I love you, sis."

Chloe stumbled forward and fell against the much-shorter Molly. Her words, punctuated with sobs, were the redemption Molly had long prayed for.

"I'm sorry. So sorry for blaming you." Molly realized she spoke of Zack. "It wasn't your fault. I always knew that. Will you forgive me?"

Though she was tired to the core, Molly couldn't remember when she'd felt such joy or release. She rubbed Chloe's bony shoulder in comforting circles.

"There is nothing to forgive. All I want is to have my sister back again."

Chloe pulled away and managed a damp and tremulous smile. "I've missed you so much."

Most of the other people had wandered off, following the accident victim, murmuring in low, shocked tones. Chloe's husband appeared at her side.

His own complexion, usually ruddy, was pale. "You girls all right?"

Her eyes were red, her face streaked with tears, but Chloe's smile bloomed for real. "More than all right. Everything is going to work out now, James. I promise."

"Thank God." He closed his eyes briefly. When he

opened them, Molly recognized her own hurt, confusion, and finally relief in him. James had suffered, too. Everyone suffered from unresolved bitterness.

"Yes," Ethan said, moving up to stand beside Molly. "Thank God."

James's smile was gentle and loving as he slipped an arm around his wife. "Come on, honey. We could all use some rest. But first we need to round up these little tots and get them home."

"I want to go to the hospital to make sure Corey's all right." Chloe's tear-filled eyes followed a car streaking away with Corey inside.

"Then let's get going."

With a final hug and a promise to call tomorrow, Chloe and James started up the rise toward the dispersing crowd.

Molly's emotions were a jumble as she watched her sister walk away. Fear, relief, joy and, most of all, hope swirled around inside her. As awful as it had been, the near-tragedy had given her hope that she and Chloe could be sisters again.

Shivering with reaction and cold, Molly bent to retrieve the tablecloth. As her shaking fingers touched the vinyl, Ethan swooped it up. He placed the soft flannel backing around her shoulders, along with his strong arm.

"You were amazing." He gazed down at her with an expression that almost made her forget how scared she'd been.

"So were you."

"No. I mean you were more than amazing. You saved that little boy from a certain drowning. You didn't panic, Molly. You took control and did what had to be done to save his life."

The truth washed over her. She'd been scared, but she hadn't panicked. She had faced a crisis with a child, and she had not crumbled into hysteria. She had not lost control.

Both she and the little boy were fine.

For the first time in two years, her thoughts became crystal-clear as the truth awakened within her. She turned her face into the warmth and protection that was Ethan's chest. "I have been such an idiot."

He said nothing, only rubbed his hands up and down her shivering arms. And then, as if he understood, he heaved a great sigh and enfolded her.

Burrowing close, Molly absorbed his wonderful warmth, the scent of his skin, the essence of him. "I've been scared for so long that I had forgotten how to live. Only an idiot would hold on to crippling fear and let go of you and Laney."

His grip tightened.

"Are you saying what I hope you're saying?" he asked, his voice a deep purr of hope against her ear.

"I need you in my life, Ethan. You and Laney. Will you forgive me?"

"Forgive you? All I ever wanted was to make you see yourself as I see you. A woman of compassion and love. Brave and strong." He rocked her back and forth. "The past is the past. Let it stay there."

The past is the past. Yes, she could accept that now.

Tilting her head back, she contemplated his wonderful face. She was incredibly blessed to be loved by him. Why hadn't she seen that before?

She raised a fingertip to tenderly trace the long scar over his eyebrow. "I love you, Ethan Hunter."

"Scars and all?" he asked.

"Scars and all."

The doubt lingering in his expression faded away. He rocked her back and forth and said, "I think you've seen the end of the panic attacks, don't you?"

"Maybe. But even if I haven't, I won't let them interfere with us again. I'll get through them and keep going. Someday they'll only be a bad memory."

A sigh of relief shuddered through him. She'd hurt him, and yet he was here, ready to give her another chance.

"We'll get through them together," he murmured, placing a kiss on her wet hair. "Marry us, Molly. Me and Laney."

Her heart slammed into her ribcage. Her breath came in short puffs, but this time only happiness came along for the ride.

It wasn't the kind of proposal she'd dreamed of, but somehow it was perfect. "Okay."

Ethan tilted her away from him a little and stared into her eyes. "Did you just agree to be my wife? And Laney's mom?"

"Yes, I did."

With a whoop of joy, Ethan lifted her high into the

air, twirling her round and round. In the distance, their friends turned startled faces in their direction.

Molly didn't mind. Cold and wet and absolutely ecstatic, she laughed down at this man who'd helped her escape from her frozen prison and step into the warm sunlight that was life and love.

Slowly Ethan lowered her to the sand, pulled her close, and warmed her shivering lips with his.

From the rise a hundred yards away, Molly heard the sound of applause.

Epilogue

A winter storm watch had been issued by the National Weather Service for the entire quadrant of southeastern Oklahoma. As yet, nothing fell in Winding Stair and the temperatures hovered above the freezing mark. None of this mattered one whit to Ethan. Like the postman, no amount of rain, sleet or snow could keep him from his appointed rounds. Not today. No way.

Heart thump-thumping like the blades of a chopper, he stood in front of the Winding Stair Chapel's sanctuary wearing his Sunday best and waiting for a glimpse of his bride.

With his brother beside him as best man and his parents beaming approval from the second pew on the left, he experienced an overwhelming sense of gratitude for all that had transpired over the course of a year.

On the advice of family and pastor he and Molly

had waited most of a year to take their vows. Time to know one another better, months of counseling and spiritual growth, months to confirm what they already knew: God had blessed them each with exactly the right helpmate.

He heard titters, saw the smiles of indulgent amusement, and followed the guests' turned heads to see his baby girl, now over a year old, barreling toward him. Mouth wide open, her blue eyes danced with the thrill of spotting her daddy.

Ethan grinned. Since she'd learned to walk, Laney had one gear and it was stuck on run. An awkward, fall-down-at-any-moment run.

Dressed like an angel in some kind of white fluffy material Molly had chosen, she wore tiny gossamer wings and a head wreath of flowers and streaming purple ribbons.

She arrived in front of him with her arms stretched upward. He swooped her into his arms, planted a kiss on her nose, and hoped she continued to behave. But whether she did or not made no difference, really. Molly had insisted Laney be part of the ceremony. After all, when he'd proposed he asked her to marry both of them. And so she would.

His chest filled with happiness. Until Molly came along, other than raising his child, he'd had no plans, no dreams for his future. He'd been stuck in a rut as surely as he'd been stuck in the ice on the night they met.

Now, they had plans and dreams together. They

would build a house, a big one with plenty of rooms. Someday they'd have more kids.

With his blessing, Molly and her sister had opened their dream craft store. And Molly had stolen his heart even more by insisting on caring for Laney while she worked. As a result, the bond was so strong between woman and child that he'd suffered a twinge of jealousy the first time Laney cried for Molly instead of him.

And because of Molly's encouragement, he would be a full-time pilot again come spring. Truly he was a blessed man.

The music changed just then, and with a lurch, he recognized the chords announcing the bride's entrance. She took his breath, did his Molly. Simple and elegant, she looked like a snow queen floating toward him.

Laney strained toward the beautiful apparition, babbling wildly. Ethan considered doing the same.

Molly had watched as her daughter-to-be raced toward Ethan and leaped into his arms. Her own excitement level on overdrive, she wanted to follow suit.

Instead, she took her time, gliding down the aisle, giving tiny waves and big smiles to all the friends and family gathered in the chapel. She stopped at the third pew to hug Aunt Patsy and at the second to kiss her mom.

Chloe, her matron of honor, waited beside the pastor, playing one-handed patty-cake with Lancy.

So many things had changed for the better. Her

faith was stronger. She had her family back. Fear no longer ruled her life.

All because of Ethan.

She glided into place and turned toward him, unable to keep her eyes off the man who would finally become her husband today. Movie-star handsome in his rented tux, he winked at her, his smile wide and white and jubilant as he handed Laney into Chloe's waiting arms.

The soloist began to sing, "Make My Heart Your Home," their promise to each other.

Molly leaned her head toward Ethan and whispered, "We may spend our honeymoon iced in."

"Sounds good to me," he murmured against her ear. "I know this perfect little farm outside of town. We could pop some popcorn. Play a little Scrabble. Snuggle in front of the fireplace."

Suppressing a giggle, she whispered back, "Sounds good to me, too."

And it did. It truly did. How fitting to return as husband and wife to the place where God had shaken their worlds and led them to each other. The place where both of them had begun to thaw.

The music ended and Pastor Cliff began to speak. Molly heard nothing except the singing in her heart.

Yes, the painful past seemed light years ago.

Ethan turned in her direction and smiled.

Lost in the blue eyes of her beloved, Molly placed her hand in his outstretched one and let the future begin.

* * * * *

Dear Reader,

The idea for this book first came to me out of the blue several years ago. At the time I had never met anyone who had lost a child to SIDS.

Then a terrible thing happened. I had written the first chapter and was fiddling with the rest of the plot when my niece's seemingly healthy baby boy died in his sleep, a tiny victim to Sudden Infant Death Syndrome. The pain for the entire family was so excruciating that I felt it inappropriate to finish the story at that time.

I put it away only to come back to it recently. Although fictional, I hope I've adequately and respectfully conveyed the terrible feeling of shock and loss and grief that families suffer during such a time.

Most importantly, I hope it conveys the comfort and healing that only God can give after such a tragedy.

Please let me know if you enjoy Molly's and Ethan's story. You can reach me c/o Steeple Hill, 233 Broadway, Suite 1001, New York, NY 10279, or through my Web site, www.lindagoodnight.com.

With blessings,

Linda Goodnight

LARGER-PRINT BOOKS!

**GET 2 FREE
LARGER-PRINT NOVELS
PLUS 2 FREE
MYSTERY GIFTS**

Larger-print novels are now available...

YES! Please send me 2 FREE LARGER-PRINT Love Inspired® novels and my 2 FREE mystery gifts (gifts are worth about $10). After receiving them, if I don't wish to receive any more books, I can return the shipping statement marked "cancel". If I don't cancel, I will receive 4 brand-new novels every month and be billed just $4.49 per book in the U.S. or $4.99 per book in Canada. That's a savings of over 30% off the cover price. It's quite a bargain! Shipping and handling is just 50¢ per book.* I understand that accepting the 2 free books and gifts places me under no obligation to buy anything. I can always return a shipment and cancel at any time. Even if I never buy another book, the two free books and gifts are mine to keep forever.

121 IDN EYLZ 321 IDN EYME

Name	(PLEASE PRINT)

Address	Apt. #

City	State/Prov.	Zip/Postal Code

Signature (if under 18, a parent or guardian must sign)

Mail to Steeple Hill Reader Service:
IN U.S.A.: P.O. Box 1867, Buffalo, NY 14240-1867
IN CANADA: P.O. Box 609, Fort Erie, Ontario L2A 5X3

**Are you a current subscriber of Love Inspired books
and want to receive the larger-print edition?
Call 1-800-873-8635 or visit www.morefreebooks.com.**

* Terms and prices subject to change without notice. Prices do not include applicable taxes. Sales tax applicable in N.Y. Canadian residents will be charged applicable provincial taxes and GST. Offer not valid in Quebec. This offer is limited to one order per household. All orders subject to approval. Credit or debit balances in a customer's account(s) may be offset by any other outstanding balance owed by or to the customer. Please allow 4 to 6 weeks for delivery. Offer available while quantities last.

Your Privacy: Steeple Hill Books is committed to protecting your privacy. Our Privacy Policy is available online at www.SteepleHill.com or upon request from the Reader Service. From time to time we make our lists of customers available to reputable third parties who may have a product or service of interest to you. If you would prefer we not share your name and address, please check here. ☐

LILP09

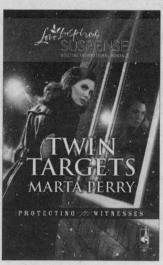

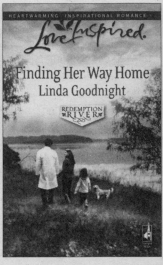